MATT JENSEN,
THE LAST MOUNTAIN MAN
DIE WITH
THE OUTLAWS

D0206811

MATT JENSEN,
THE LAST MOUNTAIN MAN

DIE WITH
THE OUTLAWS

WILLIAM W.
JOHNSTONE

AND J. A. JOHNSTONE

PINNACLE BOOKS
Kensington Publishing Corp.

www.kensingtonbooks.com

PINNACLE BOOKS are published by

Kensington Publishing Corp.
119 West 40th Street
New York, NY 10018

PUBLISHER'S NOTE
Following the death of William W. Johnstone, the Johnstone family is working with a carefully selected writer to organize and complete Mr. Johnstone's outlines and many unfinished manuscripts to create additional novels in all of his series like The Last Gunfighter, Mountain Man, and Eagles, among others. This novel was inspired by Mr. Johnstone's superb storytelling.

All Kensington titles, imprints, and distributed lines are available at special quantity discounts for bulk purchases for sales promotions, premiums, fundraising, educational, or institutional use. Special book excerpts or customized printings can also be created to fit specific needs. For details, write or phone the office of the Kensington sales manager: Kensington Publishing Corp., 119 West 40th Street, New York, NY 10018, attn: Sales Department; phone 1-800-221-2647.

PINNACLE BOOKS, the Pinnacle logo, and the WWJ steer head logo are Reg. U.S. Pat. & TM Off.

ISBN-13: 978-0-7860-3579-3
ISBN-10: 0-7860-3579-9

First printing: May 2020

10 9 8 7 6 5 4 3 2 1

Printed in the United States of America

Electronic edition:

ISBN-13: 978-0-7860-3580-9 (e-book)
ISBN-10: 0-7860-3580-3 (e-book)

Chapter One

When Matt Jensen rode into town, he stopped in front of the Morning Star Saloon, then pushed through the batwing doors to step inside. Saloons had become a part of his heritage. There was a sameness to them that he had grown comfortable with over the years—the long bar, the wide plank floors, the mirror behind the bar, the suspended lanterns, and the ubiquitous iron stove sitting in a box of sand. He was a wanderer, and though his friends often asked when he was going to settle down, his response was always the same. "I'll settle down when I'm six feet under."

Matt considered himself a free spirit, and even his horse's name, Spirit, reflected that attitude. Much of his travel was without specific destination or purpose, but so frequently was Glenwood Springs a destination that he maintained a semipermanent room in the Glenwood Springs Hotel.

"Haven't seen you for a while," the bartender said

as Matt stepped up to the bar. "Where've you been keepin' yourself?"

"Oh, here and there. Anywhere they'll let me stay for a few days before they ask me to move on."

"I envy people like you. No place to call home, no one to tie you down."

"Yeah, that's me, no one to tie me down," Matt said in a voice that the discerning would recognize as somewhat half-hearted.

"So, here for a beer, are you?"

"No, I just came in here to check my mail," Matt replied.

"What?"

Matt laughed. "A beer would be good."

"Check your mail," Max said, laughing with Matt. "That's a good one. I'll have to remember that one."

"How's Doc doing?" Matt asked.

"You're asking about Holliday?" the bartender asked as he set the beer before Matt.

"Yes. Does he still come in here a lot?"

"Not as much as he used to. He's pretty wasted by now, just skin and bones. Sort of wobbles when he walks. Big Nose Kate is here though, and she looks after him."

"Is he at the hotel or the sanitarium?"

"Hotel mostly, either his room or the lobby."

"I think I'll go see him, maybe bring him in here for a drink if I can talk him into it."

"Are you kidding?" the bartender asked. "He'll come in a military minute. That is, if Kate will let him come."

"What do you mean, if she'll let him come?"

"She watches over him like a mother hen guarding her chicks."

"Good for her. Well, I'll just have to charm her into letting him join me."

"You're going to charm Big Nose Kate? Ha! You would have better luck charming a rock."

Matt stepped into the hotel a few minutes later and secured his room. Looking around, he saw Doc Holliday and Big Nose Kate in the lobby sitting together on a leather sofa near the fireplace. And though it wasn't cold enough to require a fire, one was burning.

As Max had indicated, John Henry Holliday was a mere shadow of his former self. Matt had met him in his prime, though even then, Doc had been suffering from consumption and had had frequent coughing spells. He had also been clear-eyed, sharp-witted, and confident. He was a loyal, and when needed, deadly friend to Wyatt Earp.

Big Nose Kate, Mary Katherine Haroney, was by Doc Holliday's side. Despite the sobriquet of "Big Nose," she was actually quite an attractive woman. Matt had asked once why they called her Big Nose and was told that it wasn't because of the size of the proboscis, but because she had a tendency to stick it into other people's business.

"Hello, Doc," Matt said as he approached the two.

"Matt!" Doc Holliday greeted enthusiastically. He started to get up.

"There's no need for you to be getting up," Kate said with just a hint of a Hungarian accent.

"Hello, Kate. It's good to see you here."

"And if Doc is here, where else would I be?"

"Why, here, of course. Doc, I was just over to

the White Star Saloon and noticed something was missing. It took me a moment to figure it out. Then I realized that it was *you*, sitting at your special table playing cards. How about going back with me so you and I can play a little poker?"

"Oh, I don't know," Doc said. "I'm not as good as I used to be."

Matt chuckled. "Yeah, that's what I'm counting on. I thought if we could play a few hands I might be able to get some of the money back I've lost to you over the years."

Doc laughed out loud. "Sonny, all I said was that I'm not as good as I used to be. But I can still beat you. Let's go." He began the struggle to rise, and Matt quickly came to his assistance.

"You don't mind, do you, Kate?"

"Keep a good eye on him, will you, Matt?"

"I will," he promised.

Doc was able to walk on his own, but his frailty meant that the walk from the Glenwood Springs Hotel was quite slow. When they stepped into the saloon a few minutes later, he was greeted warmly by all as two of the bar girls approached.

"We'll get him seated," one of the girls said as she took one arm, and the second bar girl took the other.

"Your table, Doc?" one asked.

"Yes, thank you."

After they were seated, one brought a whiskey for Doc and a beer for Matt. Shortly after that, two more men came to the table and a game of poker ensued.

They had been playing for about half an hour when Matt saw a man come into the saloon. He stood just inside the swinging batwing doors, surveying the saloon until his perusing came to a stop at the table where Matt, Doc, and the two others were playing poker. The man pulled his pistol from the holster and held it down by his side.

Matt had no idea who this man was, but it was pretty obvious that he was on the prowl. For him? It could be. He had made a lot of friends over the years, but he had also made a lot of enemies.

"There you are!" the man said. He didn't shout the words, but they were easily heard. Curiosity had halted the conversations when he'd first come into the saloon. With his raised pistol, the curiosity had changed to apprehension.

"An old enemy, Matt?" one of the players asked.

"No, gentleman. I'm afraid that one is after me," Doc said.

"Stand up, Holliday! Stand up and face me like a man!"

"I'm not armed, Hartman. In case you haven't noticed by my emaciated appearance, I am in the advanced stages of consumption, so you can just put your gun back in its holster. If you are all that set on seeing me die, all you have to do is hang around for a short while, and I'll do it for you. Your personal participation in the process won't be needed."

"Yeah? Well, I want to participate," Hartman said.

"All right. Well, go ahead and shoot me. I've no way of stopping you." Doc's voice was calm and measured.

"I wonder if I could intervene for a moment?" Matt's voice was calm and conversational just like Doc's.

"Mister, you 'n them other two that's sittin' at the table there had better get up and get out of the way.

I come in here with one thing in mind, 'n that was to kill the man that kilt my brother. 'N I aim to do it."

The two others at the table heeded Hartman's advice and moved out of the way.

Matt stood, but remained in place. "Speaking as John Henry's friend, and on behalf of several others who I know are also his friends, I'm going to ask . . . no, I'm going to *tell* you to put aside any grievance you may have with Doc, and let nature take its course. Let him die in peace."

"Mister, I'm standin' here with a gun in my hand and you're tryin' to tell me what to do? Suppose I tell you I'm goin' to kill him anyway?"

"You'll have to come through me first."

"All right, if that's what it takes. Doc, I'm going to ask you to get out of the way for a moment," Hartman said. "I intend to kill you, but I don't want it to be an accident. When I kill you, it's goin' to be purposeful."

"Oh, I'm not worried about it, Hartman. I'm in no danger here. If you really are dumb enough to engage my friend here, you won't even get a shot off."

"What is he, some sort of fool? I already have my gun in my hand," Hartman said as if explaining something to a child.

"Yes, well, go ahead and do what you feel you must do," Matt said.

Hartman lifted his thumb up from the handle of his pistol, preparatory to pulling back the hammer, but his thumb never reached the hammer. Matt drew and fired. His bullet crashed into Hartman's forehead, then burst out through the back of his head taking with it a little spray of pink. Hartman was dead before he ever realized that he was in danger.

"My God. I've never seen anything like that!" said one of the other card players.

A buzz of excited chatter came from all the others in the saloon, and several gathered around Hartman's body.

"Gentlemen," Doc Holliday said, "can we please get back to the game? I plan to teach this young whippersnapper here a lesson he won't soon forget."

Chapter Two

The man who dismounted and walked over to examine the fence was in his midforties, about five-feet-nine with sloping shoulders and a slight, but not pronounced, belly rise. He had steel-gray eyes below heavy brows, a narrow nose, and a pronounced chin dimple. This was Hugh Conway, owner of the Spur and Latigo, a horse ranch.

Seeing the loose end, he picked up the piece of barbed wire and examined it closely. This strand, as were the five other strands he'd found, had been cut, leaving behind an empty pasture that, yesterday, had held thirty horses. The horses would have brought one hundred thirty dollars apiece at the market. That meant a loss of nearly four thousand dollars, money that the Spur and Latigo Ranch could ill afford to lose.

Hugh shook his head in disgust and despair, then rode back to the house, where he was met by a some-what larger than average man in denim trousers, a red and black plaid shirt, and a hat that may have been white at one time but was so stained that the actual color was nearly indistinguishable. This was Ed

Sanders, Hugh's foreman. At the moment, though, he was a foreman without anyone to supervise. Economics had forced Hugh to let all of his hands go. Sanders had agreed to take a cut in pay "until things got better."

"Did you see any of the horses?" he asked as he took the reins to Hugh's horse.

"No. Every horse we put out there was gone. All thirty of them."

Sanders shook his head. "We shouldn'ta separated 'em from the others, most especial when we don't have no men to keep an eye on 'm."

"It's my fault," Hugh admitted. "I'll be honest with you, Ed. I don't know why it is that you're staying on. You're doing the work of three men, and I had to cut your pay in half."

"Once you get your horses sold, you'll be back on your feet again," Sanders said.

"That's assuming I will have enough horses left to sell. We've lost more than fifty in the last three months. And when I say *lost*, I don't mean they just wandered off."

"No, sir, they didn't. They was stoled is what they was," Sanders said. "'N there ain't no doubt in my mind but what them Regulators is the ones that's doin' all the stealin'. They may call themselves deputies, but what they actually is, is horse thieves. 'N they're stealin' cattle, too, if you ask me. I was talkin' to Harley Mack Loomis the other day, 'n he said that they been missin' cattle over at the Rockin' P."

Hugh nodded. "Yes, Mr. Pollard shared that information with me." Darrel Pollard was the owner of the Rocking P Ranch.

"Mr. Conway, you go on in 'n get yourself some

dinner. I know Miz Conway has been some worried about you. I'll get your horse put away."

"Thanks, Ed."

When Hugh stepped into the house, he was met by the enticing aroma of fried chicken.

"You're just in time," Lisa Conway said. "I'll have supper on the table in a minute."

Lisa was only one inch shorter than Hugh, slender but with hips and breasts that the long gingham dress she wore did little to hide. Her hair was auburn, and her eyes were almost green. She had long lashes, high cheekbones, and a narrow nose. She was, in short, an exceptionally pretty woman, and because Hugh was some fifteen years older, those who didn't know them sometimes mistook Lisa for Hugh's daughter.

"Were the horses gone?" she asked as she put a pan of freshly baked biscuits on the table.

"Yes."

"I thought they probably were, but Mr. Sanders didn't want to tell me. He didn't want to worry me, I guess."

"The problem is, we have no one to keep an eye on the herd. I can't afford to hire anyone right now, and Ed and I can't do it by ourselves. To make matters worse, the mortgage payment is coming due soon and we don't have enough money to pay it. If I can get the bank to give us an extension until we can get the horses to market, we'll be all right. You said you wanted to do some shopping tomorrow, didn't you?"

"Yes."

"All right. We'll go into town tomorrow. You take care of your shopping, and I'll see Mr. Foley at the bank. I'm sure we have enough equity in the herd for him to grant the extension."

"Do I understand you correctly that you want to buy the mortgage the bank holds on the Spur and Latigo Ranch?" Bob Foley asked.

"Yes," Garrett Kennedy said. He and Sean O'Neil, partners on the Straight Arrow Ranch, sat across from the bank president.

"You do understand that in order to do that, you will have to pay the principal and all interest due. You will also have to honor the bank's obligation to the owner. In other words, if Mr. Conway makes the payment on time, he will retain ownership and all rights."

"There's a payment due now, isn't there?" Kennedy asked.

"Not for another month, then it'll be six more months before the next payment is due."

"We understand," O'Neil said. "If Conway is able to make his payment, we will have the satisfaction of knowing that we have helped a neighbor. If he isn't able to make the payment, this will be a good business investment for us."

"Yes, as it was for the other three properties you have done this for, and subsequently taken possession of, I believe, when the notes could not be met."

"Why would that be your worry?" O'Neil asked. "The bank didn't lose any money."

Foley sighed and drummed his fingers on the desk. "I am inclined not to do this, but the board of directors has strongly suggested that I accept your offer."

"The board knows that it is a way of protecting the bank's loan," Kennedy said.

"You would know, since the two of you make up two-fifths of the membership. I suspect you brought a little pressure on the other three."

"I wouldn't call it pressure," O'Neil said. "I would call it good business sense."

"Very well. Pay the principal, plus interest, and the mortgage is yours."

"Bob, we would like to hire you to manage this investment for us," Kennedy said.

"Manage it?"

"Yes. We will pay you a management fee. That way, Conway need never know that we, and not the bank, hold the paper on his ranch."

"How much of a management fee are you willing to pay?" Foley asked.

"Fifteen percent."

"Fifteen percent?" Foley replied in surprise. "Why man, interest on the loan itself is only six percent."

Kennedy smiled. "Then you are getting a good deal, aren't you?"

As Foley considered the money he would make from the arrangement, any concern over the ethics of the deal faded, and he returned Kennedy's smile. "Gentlemen, I accept your proposal."

The next day Hugh Conway was standing outside the mercantile leaning against the post that supported the awning and smoking a cigarette while he waited for Lisa to finish with her shopping. They had come into town by buckboard earlier, not only to get some necessary shopping done, but also for

Hugh to visit with Robert Foley, president of the Bank of Rongis.

Like many of his neighbors, Hugh had little regard for railroads or banks. Railroads had made long drives unnecessary, but they charged too much, whereas banks had a tendency to foreclose too quickly without regard to whatever difficulty the rancher was going through, be it weather or rustlers.

Hugh took a deep puff of his cigarette, then squinted through the exhaled blue cloud of smoke as he thought about the meeting that he had just concluded with Foley.

"I'm sorry, Mr. Conway, but I'm going to have to turn you down," Foley told him. "I'm afraid my board would consider the extension of your loan too risky."

"Where is the risk?" Hugh asked. "I have more equity in the ranch than the amount of the loan. And once I get the horses to market I'll have more than enough money, not only to make the loan payment, but to completely retire the mortgage."

"I'm sorry," Foley said. "Your note is due one month from now, and we will expect prompt payment."

It had not escaped Hugh's attention that Foley had addressed him as *Mr. Conway* rather than Hugh. At one time it had been *Hugh* and *Bob*, because the two men moved in the same social circles. But now that Hugh was facing some financial difficulty, it was Mr. Conway and Mr. Foley.

Being turned down for the loan was disappointing, but not devastating. A horse broker in Cheyenne was paying $130 per head. Hugh had a few over two hundred head remaining. The difficult part of that operation would be in getting the horses to market. To do that he would have to drive the herd one hundred miles through a pass in the Sweetwater Mountains and across the Red Desert to get to Bitter Creek.

At Bitter Creek it would cost him ten dollars a head to ship the horses to Cheyenne. But even after shipping costs, he would have enough money to completely retire the mortgage, as well as operating expenses to get him through until he could build up his herd again.

The question was, could he and Ed Sanders get the horses delivered without help? The long drive and number of horses would be quite a challenge for only two men to handle.

Kennedy and O'Neil had offered him fifty dollars a head. That would be enough to make the payment, but not enough to retire the debt. And he wouldn't have enough operating funds left to rebuild his herd. It was not an offer he took seriously.

"Hello, Mrs. Conway," said a young woman, also a customer in the mercantile.

"Hello, Colleen," Lisa replied. "Will I be seeing you at the Rongis Betterment Social next week?"

"I would like to attend, but I'm not sure I would be welcome."

"Oh, don't be ridiculous, Colleen. Nobody holds against you that your father is . . . let us just say an aggressive businessman. You surely have nothing to do with any of that."

"No ma'am, I don't, but my last name is O'Neil.

And I'm branded by that name as surely as are all the cows on the Straight Arrow ranch."

"Here are your purchases, Mrs. Conway," Ernest Dunnigan, owner of the mercantile, said. "I'll have Tommy carry them out for you."

"Thank you, Mr. Dunnigan. Colleen," she said to the other customer, "do try and come to the social next week."

"I'll try," Colleen replied. "And thank you for the personal invitation."

"You can put them in the back of the buckboard," Lisa said, her voice interrupting Hugh's thoughts.

He turned to see that Lisa was emerging from the store and giving the directions to young Tommy Matthews.

"Yes, ma'am."

"What did Bob Foley say?" Lisa asked as she settled on the seat beside her husband.

"He said no."

Lisa put her hand on Hugh's arm. "Oh, Hugh."

"Don't worry about it, my dear." He snapped the reins to get the team started. "All we have to do is get our horses to Bitter Creek. From there it'll be an easy thing to ship them on to Cheyenne."

"But can you and Mr. Sanders drive the horses there by yourselves? And do we have enough money to pay the rail freight?"

"We'll figure out a way," Hugh replied.

"By the way, I saw Colleen O'Neil in the store. Such a sweet girl. I feel so sorry for her."

"What's there to feel sorry about? Her father is one

of the two wealthiest men in the entire county. He's a dyed-in-the-wool son of a bitch, but he is wealthy."

"Now, Hugh, we can't hold Colleen accountable for the sins of her father."

"No, I guess not."

That night as Lisa lay in bed with her husband sleeping beside her, she thought of their situation. Perhaps they should just sell out to Kennedy and O'Neil. She had once suggested to Hugh that they might consider selling out and moving away, but Hugh had been adamantly against it.

"We wouldn't even get half of what the ranch is worth," he'd said. "We wouldn't get as much as we can get from the horses once we get them to market."

"Yes, but can we get them to market?"

"We will, somehow," Hugh had assured her.

But Lisa wasn't so sure.

Never, while she was growing up, did she think she would wind up on a horse ranch. But being married to Hugh Conway was every bit as unlikely as being a rancher. Sometimes she asked herself if she really loved him.

Lisa had tremendous respect for Hugh, for his intelligence as well as his character. Was their relationship the kind of fair young maiden/knight in shining armor partnership of the romance stories? No. But was there really such a thing?

He was honest, he treated everyone fairly, and from the very beginning of their relationship, he had been nothing but kind and considerate of her. She reached over to lay her hand on his.

Yes, she decided. She did love him. And she was going to do something to help, but she would have to do it without consulting him. Above all else, Hugh was a man of great personal pride. And he would disapprove of what she had in mind.

She was going to do it, anyway. She would write the letter tomorrow.

Chapter Three

The Conways' closest neighbors, Jim Andrews and Mary Ella Wilson, had houses separated by about one hundred yards, but that was for appearances only. Hugh and Lisa knew that they actually lived together and were business partners in the Circle Dot Ranch. It was small, with a herd of no more than five hundred head of cattle.

Lisa had invited the two of them over for dinner.

Jim was a tall, slender man with close-cut hair and a well-trimmed moustache. He was a man with a rather storied past. Born in Baltimore, he moved easily into the life of a sailor and was an able-bodied seaman for three years sailing to England, France, Italy, and once rounding the horn to sail to China.

He left ship in Galveston and became a drive contractor bringing up a large herd from Texas to the railhead at Abilene. Getting paid out in Abilene, he decided to come north and homestead some land, settling on his claim in the Sweetwater Valley.

Mary Ella Wilson was a particularly pretty woman who openly, some would say *brazenly*, augmented her looks with makeup. Mary Ella had been a school-teacher in Hays City, Kansas, where her husband Garland worked in a bank. When her husband was caught embezzling money from the depositors, he was tried, convicted, and sent to the state prison in Lansing to serve a penalty of twenty years. Even though Mary Ella had known absolutely nothing about her husband's scheme, she was fired from her teaching job for fear of being a negative influence on the children.

Mary Ella left Hays City, but the stigma of her firing came with her so that it was impossible for her to get another job in teaching. As an act of survival, Mara Ella fell into "the life" and became a prostitute. Her looks and easy way with men soon made her one of the most popular of all the girls. As a result, she began making more money in one week than she had made in a month of teaching. Her initial reluctance to enter the profession was replaced with enthusiasm.

Jim and Mary Ella had met shortly after he arrived in Sweetwater Valley. At the time she was working as a bar girl in the Pair O' Dice Saloon. After several paid visits, Jim asked Mary Ella if she would consider coming off the line and marrying him.

She couldn't marry him, because she was already married, and her husband, a prisoner, refused to give her a divorce. Nevertheless, Mary Ella did agree to live with Jim, even investing the money she had saved into the ranch so that they were truly business partners.

Although most of the "decent" ladies of Rongis snubbed Mary Ella as being beneath them, Lisa liked her. Mary Ella was well educated, had a good sense of humor, and was quick to offer help when it was needed. As far as Lisa was concerned, Mary Ella was a good neighbor. And of course, Jim was always welcome as well.

"There's nothing fair about this maverick law," Jim said as he spread butter on a slice of freshly baked bread.

The law Jim was talking about had been passed a year earlier by the Wyoming legislature. Cattlemen who owned large ranches were growing concerned about the increasing number of small ranchers coming into the region and homesteading land that had once been free pasture range for the big herds. In an attempt to limit, or even end, the reach of the small ranchers, the large-ranch owners used their influence to get the law passed. The maverick law made it illegal to brand any cattle, regardless of age, found roaming the open range without a mother and without a brand.

Jim continued. "There isn't a cattleman in the country who hasn't rounded up mavericks to add to their herds. I'm talkin' about Kennedy 'n O'Neil, too . . . especially Kennedy 'n O'Neil."

"There's only one reason for that law," Hugh agreed, "And that is to run as many of the smaller ranchers out of business as they can."

"You were smart to get into horses instead of cattle," Jim said. "You don't have to worry any about any maverick law because there are no maverick horses."

"That's true. But what I do have to worry about is rustling. I've been hurt by horse thieves."

"Horse thieves? But aren't the Regulators supposed

to be protectin' us all from rustlers?" Jim's words were dripping with sarcasm.

"They are supposed to, yes. But the operative words here are *supposed to*."

Purgatory Pass, Wyoming Territory

Tyrone DuPont had chosen Purgatory Pass in the Rattlesnake Mountains as the headquarters for the Regulators. Here, the Sweetwater River had carved a narrow cleft in the Sweetwater Rocks that was about 370 feet deep and 1,500 feet long. The cleft was 30 feet wide at the base but nearly 300 feet at its top. He had built a couple of adobe cabins far enough from the nearest settlement to give the Regulators the freedom from observation they required for their various operations.

DuPont stood a little over six feet tall, and was straight as a tent pole. He was originally from St. Louis, where had been a policeman, and after that and he had spent some time as a riverboat gambler. He left the river after he killed a man who was the husband of the woman with whom he had been caught in bed. He was fearless by nature, coolheaded in the face of imminent danger, and quick and deadly with the Colt .44 he carried.

He had less than three years of formal education, but he was a very smart man and was schooled in life's experiences. Having had the experience of once being a policeman, DuPont was the one who came up with the idea of assembling a group of quasi lawmen.

He had approached Kennedy and O'Neil with the idea.

"Let me get this straight," O'Neil had said after

DuPont told him what he had in mind. "You want to form a group of lawmen, and you want us to pay you?"

"All I need is just a little money to get started. Once I get organized we'll not only make enough money to support ourselves, we'll make enough to cut you in as well. In addition, you will have a private police force at your disposal."

"Exactly how would we benefit from a private police force?" Kennedy asked.

"I've been keeping an eye on you two. Straight Arrow is a big ranch, and every time one of the smaller ranchers in the valley gives up the idea of ranching, Straight Arrow gets even bigger. If some of the other ranchers find it hard going—say they start losing livestock—they may decide to quit. Once they quit, you'll be able to take over their ranch and add it to the Straight Arrow. If my men and I happen to find some livestock that's not bein' looked over real good, we'd be willing to sell it to you real cheap."

Kennedy had nodded. "I think we might be able to do some business together."

The Rongis Betterment Social was held in the ballroom of the Rongis Hotel. Several of the women had baked pies and cakes, and Pastor E. D. Owen, president of the Betterment Society, had given a short talk on their current project, the improvement of the bridge that spanned the Sweetwater River. He thanked Miss Colleen O'Neil for her contribution of five hundred dollars.

"If that woman thinks she can buy respectability, she has another think coming," Emma Rittenhouse said.

"Oh, Emma, don't hold her father against her," Lisa said. "Do you know her? She is actually a very sweet girl."

Emma shook her head. "I'm sorry, but I just want to have nothing to do with Kennedy, O'Neil, or his daughter."

Later, Lisa saw Colleen standing near the pastries table. She was alone, her isolation self-imposed because she was aware of the unfriendly attitude of most of the other women.

"Oh, here you are," Lisa said. "Let me thank you again for your generous donation."

"It was actually my father's donation," Colleen said.

"But it was your influence," Lisa said.

"Are you sure you want to be seen talking to me? Some might hold it against you for talking with an O'Neil."

"Colleen, you are much more than a name," Lisa said. "You are your own person, and I happen to like the person that you are."

Colleen smiled at Lisa. "I wish everyone else was like you."

"Choose your partners for the Virginny Reel!" someone shouted.

"Miss O'Neil?" A young man approached Colleen hesitantly. "Would you dance with me?"

"Cooter Gregory," Colleen said with a smile. "Tell me, did Papa send his foreman to keep an eye on me?"

Cooter returned the smile. "You're easy to keep an eye on."

"All right. If you're going to be my watchdog anyway, we may as well dance." Colleen's response was playful, not one of irritation.

Sugarloaf Ranch, Colorado

The horseshoe made a loud clang as it hit the stop, then it spun around and flew off.

"Ha!" Cal said. "You can't beat me, Pearlie. I've put a haint on that stob."

"You've done what?"

"I've put me a haint on that stob and it will only let the horseshoes stay on there that I want to stay on there."

"It's your turn, Matt," Pearlie said.

Matt Jensen had taken advantage of the closeness of Glenwood Springs to ride up to Sugarloaf Ranch. He had been there for nearly a week, visiting with Smoke and Sally Jensen, as well as Smoke's top two hands, Pearlie Fontaine and Cal Wood.

Matt held the horseshoe out in front of him as he sighted on the target. Then he tossed the horseshoe, which made a perfect ringer.

"Well now, what happened to your haint, Cal? Did it run away?"

"I didn't have a haint against Matt. Just against you, Pearlie," Cal said.

"Here comes Smoke," Pearlie said, seeing him coming from the main house.

"Gentlemen, I'm sorry to interrupt your game, but Sally has dinner on the table and I would hate to see it get—"

Even before Smoke could finish his sentence, Cal started toward the house at a quick walk.

"Has anyone ever had to call that boy twice to a meal?" Matt asked.

"Not since I've known him," Pearlie said. "And that's been a while."

Dinner was a baked ham with scalloped potatoes, sautéed green beans with bacon, and rolls.

"I don't expect you get many meals like this in all your travels, do you?" Smoke asked Matt.

"Sure I do. When I come here in my travels."

The others laughed.

"How are you finding Glenwood Springs?" Sally asked.

"Just the way it was when I left it," Matt replied.

"Have you had a chance to visit with Doc yet?" Smoke asked.

"Yes, he's looking really bad, Smoke. I don't imagine he has much time left." Matt smiled. "But we got to play a little poker and I almost held my own with him."

"Really? Well if you can stay with him in a poker game, he must really be off his feed," Smoke said.

"Is Kate still with him?" Sally asked.

"Looking after him the way a mama wolf looks after her cub."

"Bless her heart. She's a good woman for doing that," Sally said.

"Yes, she is."

"How long are you going to hang around Glenwood Springs this time?" Smoke asked.

"I don't have any particular length of time in mind. I thought I might like to just relax a little."

"Matt, for as long as I've known you, you've never relaxed for more than a few days. There has always been something over the next ridge that you just had to see."

Chugwater, Wyoming Territory

Meagan Parker picked up her mail at the post office, then smiled when she saw the neat penmanship of her sister, Lisa. Meagan had other mail as well, most of it related to the dress emporium she owned and ran, but she opened the letter from her sister with eager hands.

The smile left her face as she read the letter, because it was not the breezy, informative letter she expected.

Dear Meagan,

Forgive me for coming to you with this, but our situation is getting desperate and I don't know where else I can go. We have run into some difficulty, and while I know that Hugh would be capable of making a living for us anywhere, he has invested himself heart and soul into making a go of it with the ranch. Now, though, there is a distinct possibility that we may lose the ranch.

I will start by telling you that we have a little over two hundred horses, and at the anticipated income of one hundred dollars per horse, you can see that our potential is quite lucrative. However, we have been suffering a terrible degradation of our herd, due to an influx of rustlers and horse thieves.

We have a mortgage payment of fifteen hundred dollars due within the month that we can easily pay off if we successfully deliver our horses to market, but I don't know if we can get our horses delivered. Hugh has had to let go all of our men but one, and while it will be difficult enough for the two of them to handle the herd by themselves, it would be even more

*difficult if they have to defend it against any
potential rustlers.*

*I know that you are very good friends with Duff
MacCallister, and I know that there have been times
when he has come to the aid of the underdog. Now
would be such a time if he would be predisposed to do*

> *Your loving sister,*
> *Lisa*

"I can't," Duff said. "'Tis sorry I am, lass, but I just
cannae get away from the ranch now. I would be
more than glad to help your sister if I could."

"I know," Meagan said. "But Lisa asked, and I had
to try."

Inexplicably, Duff smiled. "But I know who can
help."

"Who?"

"Matt Jensen."

"Yes, he could," Meagan replied with a wide, animated grin. Then the enthusiasm waned. "But how
would we get word to him? You know how Matt wan-
ders around so."

"Aye, but 'tis happened that I got a letter from him
yesterday. He is in Glenwood Springs at the moment
and says the he plans to stay there long enough to get
mail. He asked that I send him a letter. I'll be sending
the lad a letter, but it'll nae be the kind of letter he is
expecting."

"Duff, do you think he'll come?"

"Aye, for 'tis a good friend, he is."

Chapter Four

Smoke had been accurate in his remark that there was always something just over the next ridge for Matt to see. He was a lone wolf whose adventures had led him to wearing a deputy's badge in Abilene, riding shotgun for a stagecoach out of Lordsburg, scouting for the army in the McDowell Mountains of Arizona, and panning for gold in Idaho. He had rescued a governor's niece in Colorado, saved a ranch in Idaho, defended an editor in the Dakota Territory, and taken a herd of Angus through a blizzard in Kansas.

He could move from place to place quite easily because he traveled light. A bowie knife, a .44 double-action Colt, a Winchester .44-40 rifle, a rain slicker, an overcoat, two blankets, two spare shirts, socks, two extra pairs of trousers, and extra underwear was all he carried.

"Mr. Jensen, I have mail for you," the desk clerk said when Matt came in that evening after being out for most of the day.

"Thank you, Mr. Deckert."

Matt took the letter to his room to read.

Matt,

Thank you for your letter. It is good to know where a body can find you when there is need to do so. I wonder if I could prevail upon you to come to Chugwater to pay a visit. It would be most appreciated.

> *Your friend,*
> *Duff*

The letter caught Matt's attention, not for what it said, but for what it left unsaid. It was short and cryptic, unlike the long, informative letters Duff MacCallister usually sent. Matt read between the lines, even though there were only four lines to read between.

Duff had asked him to come to Chugwater to pay him a visit, and that is exactly what he was going to do.

The next day Matt took the train from Glenwood Springs to Cheyenne. Arriving late that afternoon, he offloaded Spirit from the attached stock car then made arrangements for both to spend the night.

The next day, which was only two days after receiving the letter from Duff, Matt rode into Chugwater, a town he hadn't visited in several months. Dismounting in front of Fiddler's Green Saloon, he looped the reins around the hitching rail and stepped inside. He smiled when he saw Biff Johnson, owner of the saloon.

"Matt Jensen!" the old 7th Cavalry sergeant major said by way of greeting. "Why, I haven't seen you in a month of Sundays! Come over here and drink a beer to get the travel dust out of your mouth. On me," he added as he drew the beer. "What brings you to Chugwater?"

"As you know, there are some folks I keep up with all the time, no matter where I am. A couple of days ago I got a letter from Duff asking me to come up," Matt said. "He didn't give me any specifics, but I got the feeling that it was more than a casual request."

"Yes, Meagan Parker," Biff replied.

"Has something happened to Meagan?" Matt asked anxiously. She had been Duff's lady friend for some time.

"No, no, she's fine, but, well, I think I'd better let Duff tell you himself. You'll be riding out to Sky Meadow, won't you?"

"Yes, of course."

Biff reached under the bar and pulled out a package. "Give this to Duff, would you? It's a drone-reed that he ordered for his bagpipes. I picked it up at the post office for him."

"I'll be glad to." Matt smiled. "This way I won't arrive empty-handed."

Duff MacCallister's ranch, Sky Meadow, spread out across several thousand acres of prime rangeland, lying between the Little Bear and Big Bear creeks.

Elmer Gleason was a ranch partner and foreman of Sky Meadow. The position of Wang Chow, a Chinese master of martial arts, was somewhat less defined, though his loyalty to Duff was unquestioned and was cemented by the fact that Duff had once saved him from a lynching. Wang's crime was that he was a Chinese man riding with a white woman.

When Matt rode up to the buildings that made up the main compound of the ranch, he saw Elmer and Wang standing outside the machine shop watching one of the ranch hands as he repaired a torn stirrup. Both were offering instructions.

"Make stitch go over," Wang said.

"No, now don't go listening to anything this heathen tells you," Elmer protested. "What does a Chinaman know about repairing a saddle anyway? That stitch should go under."

"Over or under?" the ranch hand asked.

"I told you, under," Elmer said. "Come on, Dale, you've been around here long enough to know that that heathen don't have no idea what he's talkin' about most of the time."

Matt chuckled at the banter. He knew that Elmer and Wang were actually very close friends.

"Hello, Matt," Elmer greeted effusively. "Duff said you'd probably be paying us a visit sometime soon."

"Yes, I got a letter from him asking me if I would come up. I have a feeling it's more than just a visit, though. Do you have any idea what it's about?"

"Well, I got me an idea, yeah, but I think Duff should be the one to talk to you about it," Elmer replied.

"Yes, I'm sure you're right.

"It works better over," Dale said after completing the procedure.

"Yeah, just like I said," Elmer insisted.

Matt chuckled as he headed up to the main house, where Duff came down from the porch to meet him.

"Matt, sure 'n I knew ye would be for comin' to be offering yer help to an old friend."

"Of course, I'm glad to help," Matt replied. "Help with what?"

"Would ye be for comin' to town with me, lad? 'Tis Meagan that needs the help, 'n I'll be for letting her tell you the reason for it."

An hour later Matt, Duff, and Meagan were having lunch in the City Café in Chugwater. So far the conversation had been a general catching each other up on the latest news items.

After a few more exchanges of news and pleasantries, Duff got down to the reason he had sent for Matt. "It actually has to do with Meagan's sister. I would be for taking care of it myself, but 'tis nae possible for me to away from the ranch right now."

"Take care of what?" Matt asked.

"Since it does involve Meagan's sister, I'll let herself tell ye."

"Matt, I can't thank you enough for coming," Meagan began. "And if you decide this isn't something you want to get involved in, I'll understand. Believe me, I'll understand. I know this will be asking a lot from you."

"Meagan, they say a rolling stone gathers no moss. You could modify that and say that a wandering man gathers no friends, or very few anyway, and I consider you and Duff to be among those very few. So whatever it is you want me to do, if it is within my power to do it, then I will."

"'N was I not for tellin' ye that Matt would be willin' to do as ye ask?" Duff said. "Sure 'n he is the salt of the earth, Matt is."

Smiling at Matt, Meagan reached across the table and lay her hand on Matt's.

At that moment he felt a bit envious of his friend

for having someone like her, not only because she was an exceptionally pretty woman, but also because she was someone who was important to Duff.

Matt had no female friend who was important to him.

"My sister Lisa and her husband, Hugh Conway, own the Spur and Latigo Ranch, which is a horse ranch just outside of Rongis. The town is about a hundred miles northwest of here on the Sweetwater River," Meagan said. "They've had some bad years and at one time were well on the verge of losing their ranch." The frown on Meagan's face was replaced with a smile. "But the last two years have been very good for them and now they have enough horses that they'll be able to pay off the mortgage and own the land free and clear. That is, once they get them to market.

"The problem is, they've been losing so many horses to rustlers that when the time comes, they may not have enough left to sell. And even if they do have enough to sell, they'll still have to get them down to the railhead at Bitter Creek. That would be a one-hundred-mile drive, and Lisa says that Hugh has but one man working for him.

"So what I'm asking you is—"

Matt held up his hand to stop her in midsentence. "You don't even have to ask, Meagan. Of course I'll go to Rongis and make certain that your sister and her husband get their horses to the market in time."

"Close your eyes, Duff," Meagan said.

"Close my eyes?"

"Yes, close your eyes. I'm about to give your friend a kiss, and I don't want you to be jealous."

"Sure now 'n if ye be for kissin' the lad, 'tis thinking I am that it'll scare him away."

"Yeah? Let's just find out," Matt said with a little laugh as Meagan came around to kiss him chastely on the cheek.

"And now, Duff, m'lad, if I'll nae be scaring ye away, I'll be for kissing ye as well," Meagan said with a little laugh, perfectly mimicking Duff's brogue as she kissed him, as well.

Chapter Five

"Philpot, what is it you're doin' standin' there at the bar with Ramona?" Angus Shardeen spoke the words in a cold, determined voice that got the attention of everyone in the Wild Hog Saloon.

"What does it look like I'm a-doin'? I bought her a drink, 'n me 'n her is talkin'," Harmon Philpot replied. He was one of several small ranchers who over the past few years had homesteaded a section of land on which he was running about one hundred head of cattle.

"Yeah, well I want 'er to have a drink with me, so you get away from 'er."

"You ain't got no right to tell me who I can 'n who I can't talk to," Philpot replied.

Shardeen's smile was evil and mocking. "Oh yeah, I do." He tapped his hand against the butt of the pistol that hung at his side. "This here gives me the right."

"You can't just come in here 'n buffalo a man for no reason."

"I got a reason. I told you, you're standin' there

drinkin' with Ramona, 'n I don't like that. You got a gun. Now use it."

"What?" Philpot said, suddenly realizing this could go further than just bluff and bluster. "What are you talking about?"

"I said go for your gun." Again the evil smile. "I'll even let you draw first."

"No, no, I ain't goin' to use my gun," the belligerence in Philpot's voice was replaced by fear. "Now leave me alone."

Shardeen shook his head. "Uh-uh. I can't do that. It's like I said, you was with Ramona. What kind of man would I be if I didn't defend my woman?"

"Shardeen, what are you talkin' about? I ain't your woman!" Ramona literally shouted the words, her voice on the verge of hysteria. "I'm anybody's woman who can pay me. You know that!"

"Yeah, that's fine, just as long as it's anybody but Philpot," Shardeen said menacingly.

"All right, all right. I ain't with him no more!" Ramona said, moving quickly away from Philpot.

Looking at Shardeen and licking his lips nervously, Philpot said, "There ain't no need for this to go any further. I'll find another woman to have a drink with."

"Sure, honey, I'll drink with you," one of the other bar girls said quickly, hoping thereby to ease the tension.

"Too late. He's done got my dander up. Draw your gun," Shardeen ordered.

"No, I ain't goin' to, 'n there ain't nothin' you can do that'll make me do it."

"You think not?" In a lightning-fast move, Shardeen drew his gun and pulled the trigger.

Ramona screamed, her scream mirrored by a couple of the other girls. There was a universal gasp from those in the saloon, as everyone thought that Shardeen had just killed the small rancher. But when the gun smoke drifted away, Philpot was still standing, holding his hand to the side of his head with blood spilling through his fingers. Shardeen's well-placed bullet had clipped off about a quarter-inch of the rancher's earlobe.

"Draw your gun," Shardeen ordered again.

"No."

A second shot and Philpot's right earlobe, like his left, turned into a ragged, bloody piece of flesh.

"Look at that, will you? Ol' Shardeen's cuttin' Philpot up pretty good, ain't he!" The speaker was Asa Carter, who had come into the saloon with Shardeen.

"Shardeen, please stop!" Ramona shouted. "Why are you doing this?"

Shardeen looked at Ramona, and though he said nothing to her, his stare was enough to cause her blood to run cold.

"Why don't you let 'im be now, Shardeen?" the bartender asked. "You've purt nigh taught him a real good lesson, I'd say."

Shardeen pointed his pistol at the bartender. "You stay out of it."

The bartender stuck his hands in the air. "I ain't goin' to say nothin' no more."

Shardeen turned his attention back to Philpot standing at the bar with both bloody hands covering his ears.

"I ain't a-goin' to tell you no more. Draw your gun!"

"No! Please, stop now!" Philpot begged.

"You willin' to tell me in front of ever'body in here that you're sorry you was with my woman, 'n you won't be with her no more?"

"Yes, yes, I'm sorry!" Philpot said, shouting the words.

"That ain't quite enough," Shardeen said. "You ain't goin' to bother her no more."

"I ain't goin' to bother her no more," Philpot responded in a quiet, weak voice.

Shardeen shook his head. "Uh-uh, that ain't enough. You got to say it out loud. You ain't goin' to be botherin' Ramona no more."

"I ain't goin' to bother Ramona no more." As Shardeen had ordered, Philpot's words could be heard throughout the saloon.

"That's more like it," Shardeen said as he put his pistol back in the holster.

"Shardeen, why are you doin' this? I'm tellin' you, he ain't been botherin' me," Ramona said. "Me 'n you ain't never been nothin' special, 'n he's only doin' what all the men who come in here do."

Shardeen turned toward Ramona. "Don't you understand? That don't matter none. I told 'im not to, 'n that's all that really matters."

While Shardeen was talking to Ramona, Philpot watched through fear-crazed, hate-filled eyes. Then, the most perceptive among the saloon patrons saw a gradual shift in the young rancher's demeanor. The wild hysteria left his eyes and they became flat and void, as if he had accepted the fact that he was already a dead man. He had one emotion left, and one emotion only—absolute blind rage. Taking advantage of what he thought was Shardeen's distraction, Philpot made a mad grab for the gun, managing to pull it from his holster and bring it up to bear.

Shardeen turned back toward the man he had been tormenting and watched, allowing a slow smile to play across his face.

"What are you going to do now, you ornery cuss?" Philpot called out in a triumphant yell.

Shardeen made no move until Philpot actually had the gun cocked. Not until that time did Shardeen pull his own gun in a draw that was incredibly fast. He pulled the trigger, and his bullet caught Philpot in the neck. Surprised by the suddenness of it, Philpot dropped his gun, unfired, and clutched his throat. He fell back against the bar, then slid down, dead before he reached the floor.

"Damn! I'll bet there ain't nobody that's ever seen shootin' like that!" Carter called out in a triumphant yell.

Shardeen, who was an ugly little man, looked around the saloon, the broad smile on his face showing his yellowed, crooked teeth. Everyone studied their glass or bottle, avoiding Shardeen's eyes.

"Is there anybody in here a-plannin' on sayin' how this was anything other than a fair fight?" Shardeen challenged.

"I'm a witness," Asa Carter said. "I seen ever'thin', 'n I'm sayin' it was a fair fight, just like Shardeen is a-sayin'. Anybody in here plannin' on disputin' my testimony?"

Carter and Shardeen looked around, studying the others in the Wild Hog. Saloon.

"Fancy, what you got to say about it?" Carter asked.

Fancy was an attractive young black girl, dressed as provocatively as any of the other bar girls. "I ain't got nothin' a-tall to say about it, honey," she replied, consciously keeping her voice as devoid of all expression as she could.

The sound of the gunshots had brought two or three outsiders into the saloon, including Sheriff Clark. He saw Philpot on the floor, but in the sitting position leaning back against the bar. His eyes were open and sightless, his hand clenched tightly around the unfired pistol.

Sheriff Clark looked over at Shardeen. "You did this, I reckon?"

"Look in his hand, Sheriff," Carter said. "It was self-defense, pure 'n simple. Why, if Shardeen hadn't shot him, he woulda shot Shardeen."

"You 'n Shardeen both bein' Regulators 'n all, I wouldn't expect you to say nothin' different," Sheriff Clark said.

Nobody else volunteered any information.

Sheriff Davey Clark looked again at the dead man. "That's Harmon Philpot. He's a small rancher, ain't he? I don't expect Kennedy or O'Neil is goin' to be all upset about a small rancher gettin' hisself kilt."

"He warn't a real rancher," Shardeen said. "He was a cattle rustler is what he was. Hell, more 'n half his herd was mavericks he rounded up, mavericks that belonged to the Straight Arrow."

"So what if they are? Until the maverick law was passed, any unbranded cow or calf found wandering around on the free range belonged to anyone who rounded them up. So any of his cattle that were mavericks before the law was passed belong to him."

"You mean *belonged*, don't you, Sheriff?" Carter said

with a mirthless laugh. "They don't nothin' belong to him now, seein' as the lowdown scum is dead."

Sheriff Clark looked directly at the bartender, who had been quiet from the moment the sheriff entered the saloon.

"Buster, do you agree with Carter? Is it what he was sayin'? Was it self-defense?"

Buster Kendig looked at the others in the bar but, as before, none of them would return his gaze. No one seemed willing to make a comment.

"Yeah," he mumbled. "It was self-defense."

Sheriff Clark stared at Shardeen for a moment, then he turned and left the saloon.

Shardeen called out, "Hey, Buster, what was Philpot drinkin'?"

The bartender pointed. "That's what's left of his beer."

Shardeen stepped over to it, lifted the mug, and finished the beer. Then, with a sigh of satisfaction, he set the empty mug down on the bar, ran the back of his hand across his mouth, then left.

Straight Arrow Ranch

"Are you sure that was the best way to handle Philpot?" O'Neil asked DuPont.

"What do you mean? You wanted his ranch, didn't you? Now you can take over his ranch."

"Yes, but to have been killed in such a way, witnessed by so many people."

"This way there ain't no question 'bout what happened 'cause all the witnesses who seen it say it was in self-defense. And Shardeen made it out to be that he was mad at Philpot for bein' with his woman. There won't nobody be thinkin' it had anythin' to do with his ranch 'n cows, which is all yours now, ain't it?"

O'Neil smiled. "He hasn't paid taxes on his property. We'll pay the taxes, and his section will be absorbed by the Straight Arrow. Give Mr. Shardeen our appreciation."

"He'll be expectin' a little more than appreciation," DuPont said.

"Yes, two hundred dollars I believe was the agreed-upon sum. If you and he will come to the ranch office this afternoon, we'll have the funds available for you."

"We'll be there," DuPont promised.

Chapter Six

Matt Jensen arrived in Bitter Creek by train then made the hundred-mile ride to Rongis in two days.

Typical of towns that had sprung up all over the West in the last fifty years, it had one main street that was crossed at least four times during its length. The main street was anchored at each end with a church, Our Lady of the Mountains Catholic Church at the south end and Church of Salvation, a non-denominational protestant church, at the north end. The street was lined with business establishments— two general stores, a drugstore, a leather goods shop, two cafés, a gunsmith, feed store, a bank, a livery, the Rongis Hotel, a newspaper, sheriff's office and jail, a post office, a land office, a freight office, a stage-coach depot, a blacksmith shop, and two saloons.

The boardwalks on either side of the street were busy with pedestrians, and the street had traffic from small buckboards to large freight wagons.

Of the two saloons, the Pair O' Dice looked the most inviting. The two-day ride had built a thirst for more than tepid canteen water, so Matt dismounted, pushed through the batwing doors, and stepped inside.

Though it was still midafternoon, the saloon was already crowded and noisy with the sounds of idle men and painted women having fun. Near the piano three men and a couple of women filled the air with their idea of a song, the lyrics a bit more ribald than the composer intended.

Matt stepped up to the bar.

"Yes, sir, what can I do for you?" the bartender asked. He was wearing a stained apron and carrying a towel he used to alternately wipe off the bar and wipe out the glasses.

"What's your whiskey?" Matt asked.

"Got some Old Overholt. Cost you two dollars the bottle, or ten cents the drink."

"I'll take a glass of whiskey and a beer chaser," Matt said, slapping the necessary silver on the bar.

The bartender poured a shot of whiskey, then drew a mug of beer and put both before him. "You just passin' through?"

Matt chuckled. "You get a lot of people passing through Rongis, do you? If you do, where are they on their way to?"

The bartender laughed. "Well now, there you have me, mister. No sir, we don't get a lot of folks passin' through town on account of, like you just said, they ain't really got no place to go to that makes you have to come this way."

"I have to say, it does look like a pretty lively little town, though, especially being as remote as it is," Matt said.

"You don't have no idea how lively it is. Why we just had us a killin' here, yesterday."

"Here, in the saloon?"

"Well, no sir, not 'n this saloon, but across the

street 'n just down a ways it was. It happened in the Wild Hog, which is the other saloon in town. Ain't as nice as this one is," he added, taking the opportunity for self-promotion.

Matt lifted his whiskey and held it out in a toast. "Well, when I rode into town, this is the saloon I picked."

"Shardeen, it was," the bartender said.

"I beg your pardon?"

"Angus Shardeen. He's the one that done the killin'. You ever heard of 'im?"

"Yes," Matt said. "I've heard of 'im."

"I figured maybe you have, him havin' hisself quite a reputation 'n all."

"If you got somethin' stickin' in your craw, cowboy, I think maybe you'd better just spit it out," someone said in a cold, challenging voice.

The loud voice interrupted all other conversation, and like everyone else in the saloon, Matt turned his attention toward the disturbance. The one who had issued the challenge was a hard-eyed man with a hawklike nose. He was wearing a pistol, the black, silver-studded holster low and kicked out for a fast draw.

The man he was yelling at was obviously a working cowboy with worn jeans and a frayed shirt. He wasn't armed.

"I ain't got nothin' stickin' there on account of I already said it," the cowboy said. "'N if you didn't hear it, I'll say it again. What I said was, you 'n that feller standin' beside you that's wearin' a ten-dollar Stetson on a ten-cent head, act as if you're a-chasin' rustlers. But all you're actual doin' is tryin' to run the little ranchers outta business. It wouldn't surprise me none if Shardeen didn't kill Philpot yesterday on account of 'cause he was a small rancher.

"And the rustlin' is goin' on all along, like the horses that's been stoled from the Spur and Latigo Ranch. I wouldn't be none surprised if it warn't you a-doin' it, 'n if it ain't you, it'll be some other no-account Regulator."

"Are you callin' us *no-accounts*?" the loudmouthed one said.

The cowboy's smile was disdainful. "Well, maybe you ain't as dumb as you look, seein' as you figured out what I was sayin' after all."

"You ain't goin' to let 'im get away with callin' us no-accounts, are you, Toone?" said the man in the Stetson.

"Who is that cowboy?" Matt asked the bartender quietly.

"The cowboy is a feller named Sanders."

"He mentioned the Spur and Latigo. He works for Hugh Conway, does he?"

"Yes, he's the foreman there. Conway's a good man. Do you know 'im?"

"Not really, but he is the brother-in-law of a friend of mine. Who's the loudmouth?"

"His name is Toone, Walter Toone. He's a real hardcase. The one standin' there beside 'im, eggin' 'im on, is Moe Greene. Both of 'em rides for Tyrone DuPont 'n his Regulators, which is the same outfit that Shardeen rides for."

"Regulators?"

"Yeah, they's a bunch of 'em claim to be a posse of volunteers to keep the rustlers away from the Sweet-water Valley."

"Yeah, only they don't really keep the rustlers

away," Sanders said, having overheard the bartender's remark. "Seein' as how it's more 'n likely they're the ones doin' the rustlin'."

"Tell me, Sanders. You wouldn't be callin' us horse thiefs, would you?" Toone's tone was as belligerent as before, and his question recaptured Matt's attention.

"Nah, I'm sure you ain't doin' no horse stealin'. It's more 'n likely that them horses is just followin' you around on account of 'cause you smell so good," Sanders said, and a few of the others in the saloon laughed nervously.

"You think you're funny, do you? Well let's just see how funny you really are. Me 'n you is about to have us a fight."

A broad grin spread across Sanders's face. "A fight? Yeah. Yeah, there's two of you and only one of me, but I'd say that makes the odds about even. Come on. I think I'm goin' to enjoy this." Sanders made his hands into fists then held them out in front of his face, moving his right hand in tiny circles. "Come on. I'm goin' to put the lights out for both of you."

"Uh uh," Toone said. "That ain't the kind of fight I'm talkin' about. I plan to make this permanent."

"You mean a gunfight? No, I ain't goin' to get into no gunfight with the likes of you," Sanders said. "Anyway, there's two of you 'n only one of me."

"Oh, don't let that bother you," Toone said. "Greene, here, won't have nothin' to do with it. It'll just be me 'n you. Right, Greene?

"Yeah," Greene said, smiling evilly. "Yeah, this is just between you 'n Sanders. All I'm goin' to do is just watch."

Toone let his arm hang down alongside his pistol, and he looked at the cowboy through cold, ruthless eyes. "Just to show you how nice I am, I'm goin' to let you draw first."

"How am I goin' to draw, you ignorant fool?" Sanders asked. "Hell, I ain't even packin', which you could see if you'd just take a look."

Matt couldn't help but have a sense of respect for Sanders for speaking to Toone in such a way even though Toone was armed and Sanders wasn't.

He doubled up his fists again. "But if you'd like to come over here and take your beatin' like a man, I'd be glad to oblige you. 'N there ain't no need for you to be a-feared o' me, I mean, bein' as there's two of you like I said. Come on 'n take your medicine."

"You ain't listenin' to me, are you, cowboy? I tole you that I plan to make this here fight permanent. Now, draw your gun, like I told you to," Toone repeated in a cold, flat voice.

The others in the saloon knew that the cowboy had carried things too far. Knowing there was about to be gunplay, they began, quietly but deliberately, to get out of the way of any flying lead.

It wasn't until that moment, seeing the others move out of the way, that Sanders began to worry that he might actually be losing control of the situation. He lowered his fists and then stared at Toone incredulously. "Are you blind, Toone? I told you I ain't armed. Ain't you even noticed that I'm not wearin' a gun? If you're figurin' on forcin' me into a gunfight, you can just figure again, 'cause I ain't a-goin' to do it."

"If you ain't goin' to fight, then you can just apologize to me 'n my friend, then get out of here. Get out of this saloon, out of this town, and out of this valley."

"No, I ain't a-goin' to apologize for tellin' the truth," Sanders said.

"Sanders, you walk through that door right now, or I'll shoot you where you stand, whether you got a gun or not," Toone said.

"Mr. Sanders," Matt said, speaking for the first time, "I wonder if you would mind if I came down there to have a few words with you. Mr. Bartender, set up another drink for my friend there."

"Mister, I don't know who you are, but if you got any sense, you'll butt out of this," Toone said in as sinister a voice as he could muster.

"Now why should I do that? I've just arrived in town and I'm anxious to make new friends, so I thought I might start with Mr. Sanders."

"Don't you see what's goin' on here? If you're a-standin' next to him when the shootin' starts, you're liable to wind up gettin' yourself kilt," Toone said in a low, growling voice. "'N to tell the truth, the way you've butted in like you've done, it don't really make me no never mind whether you get kilt or not."

"Oh, I think I'll be all right," Matt said. "I think—" He interrupted himself in midcomment and pointed to Moe Greene, whose hand had started to move toward his holster. "Friend, if you move your hand one inch closer toward that gun I'll kill you and this loudmouth both."

"You'll what?" Toone asked incredulously. "Who the hell are you, anyway?"

"The name is Jensen. Matt Jensen. And I've come out here looking for a job with Hugh Conway. Since that means Mr. Sanders and I will be working together, I thought it might be a good idea for me to get acquainted with him."

"Jensen? Matt Jensen?" one of the saloon patrons said. "Damn, I've heard of him."

"How do I know you're Matt Jensen?" Toone asked. "You could just be some drifter decidin' to run a bluff by usin' his name."

"You know what? You could be right," Matt agreed. "I might just be running a bluff."

Toone forced a smile. "Then I've got me an idea, mister. Why don't I just call your bluff?"

"I suppose you could call it if you wanted to. But then, you would never find out whether I was bluffing or not."

"What do you mean, I would never find out? Why won't I?"

"Oh, because you will be dead," Matt said as if explaining something to a child. "You and—" He glanced over toward Greene. "What is it my new friend called you? A ten-gallon Stetson on a ten-cent head?" Matt chuckled. "That's a good one. Anyway, as I was saying, you'll both be dead."

"Even if you are Matt Jensen like you say you are, I don't think you're good enough to take both of us," Toone continued.

"You might be right. It could be that I'll just get one of you, but I'm not going to tell you which one I'll kill first. I'll just let the two of you think about that," Matt said with an easy smile.

"What are you buttin' into this for anyway? This here is just between Sanders 'n me."

"You mean because he called you a horse thief?"

Toone didn't reply.

"Well now, you see, that's why I want to talk with him for a few minutes. Apparently someone is stealing horses from the Spur and Latigo Ranch, and that's why I've come here to offer my help. If you and Greene are the ones doing the rustling, then why not settle it right here, right now? Go ahead, draw your pistols and let's get this over with. It may be that killing you two might just take care of everything."

Toone began nervously licking his lips.

"I . . . I ain't a-goin' to draw agin you," Greene said. "This here's between you and Toone."

"Oh, I'm sorry if I wasn't clear enough. Let me explain it to you," Matt said. "You see, even if just one of you draws, I'll kill both of you anyway."

"Y-You'll what?" Greene's voice was so choked with fear that he was barely able to speak. "Toone, h-he says he's goin' to kill us both."

"Yes, I will if either one of you draw. But it doesn't have to be that way. Nobody needs to be killed. You want a fight, and Mr. Sanders here has shown a willingness to oblige you. To tell the truth, I'd like to see a good fight. Mr. Sanders, do you really want to take them both on?"

Sanders smiled. "Yeah. Yeah, I would like that a lot."

"All right. I'll just arrange it for you. Toone, Greene, both of you drop your gun belts."

"What? You're crazy! I'm not going to drop my gun belt!" Toone declared. In what he thought might be an act of defiance, he reached for a glass that sat on the bar.

Matt made a lightning draw and shot, the bullet shattering the glass when Toone's hand was less than one inch away. With a little cry of alarm, Toone drew his hand away.

"Like I said, drop your holsters," Matt repeated.

With shaking hands, first Toone, then Greene un-buckled their gun belts and let them fall to the floor.

"All right. There are two of you against one," Matt said. "Let's see how you do against my new friend."

Toone and Greene looked at each other. Then, with a nod and a yell, they rushed toward Sanders. Toone got there first, and Sanders took him down with a crushing right cross. He set up Greene with a left jab, then took him down with a right.

Though neither man had been knocked out, both remained cowering on the floor.

"Mr. Sanders, would you bring their pistols to me, please?" Matt asked.

The big cowboy, keeping an eye on the two men with whom he had just scuffled, pulled the pistols from the holsters, then took them over to Matt.

Matt emptied both guns of their bullets, then laid them on the bar. "You can have them back when you leave."

"Let's go, Toone," Greene said.

"You had better listen to your friend, Mr. Toone," Matt said. "He's giving you good advice."

"This ain't over, Sanders," Toone said, pointing at the cowboy. "This here feller, whoever he is, ain't goin' to be around forever. 'N one of these days it'll just be me 'n you."

"What makes you think you'll be alive long enough to ever encounter Mr. Sanders again?" Matt asked.

Toone took several deep breaths. Then retrieving his empty pistol from the bar, he started toward the door with Greene trailing close behind.

After the two were gone, the bartender slid Matt's money back across the bar to him. "Mister, here's your money back. My name is Cheatum, Lonnie Cheatum. I not only tend bar here, I own the place. And watchin' that was well worth the price of the drinks for you and Sanders."

"Hear! Hear!" said one of the other patrons, and the quiet was broken by excited and boisterous conversation.

"Mr. Sanders, I wonder if you would be so kind as to take me out to the ranch and introduce me to Mr. Conway."

"You mean you've come here to help him 'n you don't even know him?"

"I've never met the man," Matt replied.

Chapter Seven

Straight Arrow Ranch

"Papa, is it all right if Cooter takes me into town?" Colleen asked.

"What? Yes, go ahead. I don't care," O'Neil said.

"Would you like me to pick something up for you while I'm in town?"

"No, I'm fine," O'Neil said distractedly. "Go ahead."

"See, I told you Papa wouldn't mind," Colleen said as she climbed into the surrey to sit beside Cooter Gregory.

"He might not like it if he knew we was goin' out to eat together instead o' me just takin' you into town for you to do some shoppin' 'n such."

Colleen reached over to take Cooter's hand. "You're like everyone else out here. You can't seem to separate me from my father."

Cooter chuckled. "Believe me, I know the difference between you and Mr. O'Neil."

* * *

Back at the ranch, O'Neil and Kennedy were discussing business.

"We'll be able to pick up Philpot's ranch by paying taxes, and we hold the mortgages to four other ranches. Thanks to the difficulty these small ranchers are facing as a result of the Regulators, I'm sure that all four will soon default on their loans. By next year, we'll own this whole valley from the Rattlesnake Mountains to the Wind River Range, and from Granite Ridge to Seminoe Pass." Sean O'Neil was illustrating his comment by pointing to the map that had been tacked to the wall.

"Of the four ranches that we have paper on, Conway's Spur and Latigo is the best," Kennedy said. "But the Circle Dot is also a good ranch. It's a shame we don't hold the mortgage on the Circle Dot. They have good water access and rangeland, to say nothing of the five hundred head of cattle. That would be a fine acquisition for us."

"Yes," O'Neil said. "Don't worry. We'll get it. DuPont says he has an idea."

"What is the idea?"

"I don't know. I didn't ask."

"Sean, about the Regulators," Kennedy said.

"What about them?"

"Do you ever worry about them?"

"I'll admit I worry about them some, but once we have absolute control, we'll no longer have any need for the Regulators and we'll find some way to cut our ties."

"It may not be so easy to get rid of them then,"

Kennedy said. "Especially as long as they have someone like Angus Shardeen to enforce their will."

"Maybe when the time comes, we can find someone who could handle that problem for us."

Purgatory Pass

Tyrone DuPont sat on a bench on the front porch of his cabin at the hideout. The bench was made from half a log sitting on short legs that had been cut to fit. He had just paid Shardeen the two-hundred-dollar bonus for killing Philpot.

DuPont had seen a lot of criminal types during his time as a policeman and since leaving the police to ride the outlaw trail. But never, in any of his experiences, had he met anyone like Shardeen, who actually enjoyed killing. Kennedy and O'Neil might be the most powerful ranchers in the valley but DuPont, with his Regulators, was the most feared. And that fear, DuPont knew, was maintained by the presence of Angus Shardeen.

Having escaped from prison in New Mexico the night before he was to be hanged, Angus Shardeen was DuPont's most valuable asset. He was a small man, just over five feet three inches tall, but in a world ruled by guns, Shardeen was a giant. He was not the kind of man to put notches on the handle of his pistol, but if he had been, he would barely have room for all of them.

Shardeen was a fast draw and he was a good shot, but what made him so dangerous was less a testament to his skill than it was to his psychopathic willingness to kill without compunction. And that willingness to kill was what generated the fear in others, a fear that provided the Regulators, and by extension, DuPont, with an effective balance of power.

That balance of power might be at risk. DuPont had been told of the confrontation between Moe Greene and Walter Toone and a man who'd identified himself as Matt Jensen. Was the person Greene and Toone encountered in the Pair O' Dice Saloon really Matt Jensen?

DuPont had never met, nor even seen, the man, but he had heard of him. According to what Greene and Toone had said, Jensen had come to the Sweetwater Valley to work for Hugh Conway.

Toone stepped up on the porch and sat beside DuPont. "If Jensen's here to work for Conway, he ain't goin' to be herdin', or breakin' no horses for 'im," Toone said. "More 'n likely he's here to sell his gun."

"I'm having a hard time believin' that, Toone, 'n I'll tell you why. I know for a fact that Conway is so far in debt that he has nobody left still workin' for 'im but Sanders. So if he's down to only one man, it just don't seem to figure to me that he would have enough money to pay a man like Matt Jensen to come work for 'im."

"That's what this Jensen feller said he was here for," Toone said.

"I guess we'll have to wait and see whether it's really Matt Jensen or not, 'n if it is, if he's really goin' to start workin' for Conway. Though I just don't understand how that could be."

Spur and Latigo Ranch

On the ride out to Conway's ranch, Matt learned that Sanders's first name was Ed. The Spur and

Latigo Ranch was well kept and made a very good first impression. A carriageway covered with white rocks cut through the middle of a well-maintained lawn, which was surrounded by a split log fence. On the grounds were several buildings, including a barn, the machine shed, the bunkhouse, and the main house.

The main house was a two-story white clapboard house with a gray shingled hip roof and two dormer windows. The pillared porch stretched all the way across the front of the house, then wrapped around to the left side. A couple of swings on the porch hung from the ceiling at right angles to each other to afford a congenial conversation area for the occupants.

Even as Matt and Ed were dismounting, a man and woman stepped out of the house, made curious by the stranger who had arrived with Ed.

Matt didn't even have to ask who the woman was. She bore such a striking resemblance to Meagan Parker that he knew it must be Meagan's sister, Lisa.

"Mr. Conway, this here feller is Matt Jensen," Sanders said. "He, uh, well sir, a little while ago, he helped me out in town. You know them two gunsels that's a-ridin' with Tyrone DuPont 'n his Regulators, Toone 'n Greene?"

"Yes, of course I know them. Despicable characters, both of them."

"Yes, sir, that's what they are, all right. 'N they was about to throw down on me, despite me not even wearin' no gun or nothin'. But Mr. Jensen here, he braced both of 'em."

"One man braced those two?" Conway asked.

"Yes, sir, that's what he done all right." Sanders laughed. "No shootin' come of it, though, on account of what happened is that both of 'em went a-slunkin' out o' the Pair O' Dice like whupped dogs with their tails between their legs."

"Actually it would be more correct to say that they *were* whipped dogs," Matt added with a little chuckle, "seeing as, once they were disarmed, Mr. Sanders here took them on and whipped both of them."

"Good for you, Ed, good for you," Hugh said. "Mister . . . Jensen is it? You have my appreciation for coming to Ed's aid."

"I would like to come to *your* aid as well," Matt said.

"Oh, I uh, very much appreciate your offer"—Conway shook his head—"but I'm afraid I can't afford to take on anyone right now." He pointed toward the bunkhouse. "Truth to tell, except for Ed, here, the bunkhouse is empty because I can't afford to keep any hands."

"You don't need to worry about paying me anything until we get your horses to market," Matt said. "Then if you want to pay me something, I'll leave whatever you might want to pay me up to you."

"Who are you?" Conway asked again, the question more curious than challenging. "And what do you know about me having to get my horses to market?"

"I have a letter for you from Miss Meagan Parker. I think it will explain everything."

"You have a letter from my sister?" Lisa asked in surprise.

"Yes, ma'am," Matt said, removing the letter from his shirt pocket. He handed it over to Conway.

"How is it that you know Meagan Parker?" Conway asked.

"Like I said, it's all explained in this letter," Matt replied.

Dear Hugh,

I would like, by way of this letter, to introduce you to Matt Jensen. Mr. Jensen is a very good friend of Duff MacCallister, and as you have met Duff, you know that he is most discerning as to who he allows into his circle of friends.

And yes, this is THE Matt Jensen, and I emphasize THE because Matt is of such a reputation that I'm sure you have heard of him. Believe me when I tell you that his reputation is well earned, not only for his unique skills in dealing with difficult people, but also because he is an exceptionally good person and a man who is quick to come to the aid of those who might be in need.

Lisa has told me of the plague of horse stealing that you have had to endure. She expressed some concern as to whether you would be able to get your horses to market. If getting your horses to market will alleviate your current situation, I can guarantee you that Matt Jensen will be able to help you do just that.

> *Your sister-in-law*
> *Meagan Parker*

Hugh Conway read the letter, then passed it over to Lisa. "You wrote to Meagan?"

"Yes, I did. I hope you aren't upset with me, Hugh,

but I wanted to do something, anything, that would help us."

"I don't know what to say." Hugh frowned.

"You might say yes, you'll accept Mr. Jensen's help, and thank you to my sister for sending him to us," Lisa said with a pensive smile.

"All right. Yes, I will accept Mr. Jensen's help, and I am thankful, though it might all come to naught," Hugh said. "You know I wasn't able to get that loan extension from the bank. Lisa, I'm probably going to have to sell fifty or more horses just to get enough money to make the mortgage payment, and I can't get even one third of their value if I sell them here. There will hardly be enough horses left to take to market, and we'll have to pay freight on them. We'll be lucky to come out even. Then where will we be? We'll be fighting horse thieves for another year just so that we can break even next year."

"Hugh, we have to try," Lisa insisted.

Hugh looked at the letter again, then he looked up. "My sister-in-law says that you are *the* Matt Jensen. I'm not sure what she means by that."

Matt smiled. "To tell you the truth, I'm not sure what she means by it, either."

"I can tell you what it means, Mr. Conway." Ed made a motion with his hand toward Matt. "This here's a famous man which most ever'body that's lived out here for any time has heard of. I reckon on account of you ain't lived out here all that long is why you ain't never heard of 'im."

"I suppose so," Hugh replied. "Mr. Jensen, I am indeed honored to have your assistance. But you must understand that even if I take you on to help, there is still the problem of raising enough money to satisfy an upcoming mortgage payment in order to give us time to get the horses to market in the first place."

"Mr. Conway, that letter isn't the only thing Miss Parker sent," Matt said. From his saddlebag, he took another envelope. "She asked me to give you this."

Hugh, with a questioning expression on his face, took the envelope, opened it, then pulled out a thick wad of bills. "My God! What is this?"

"Twenty-five hundred dollars," Matt said. "It's a loan from Miss Parker."

"Oh, Hugh!" Lisa said.

Hugh looked at Matt with a wide smile. "Mr. Jensen, there is no doubt but that you could have taken that money and gone your own way with nobody ever the wiser. As far as I'm concerned, the very fact that you brought it here is all the testament to your honesty that I need."

"You're hired!" Lisa said with a happy laugh.

"Mr. Conway?" Matt asked.

"You heard what my wife said, Mr. Jensen. You're hired."

"Please, if I am to work with you, won't you call me Matt?"

"Matt it is," Hugh said. "Matt, why don't you have supper with us tonight?"

"Yes, please do. And you can tell me all about how my sister is doing," Lisa added.

Chapter Eight

During supper that evening, Lisa questioned Matt extensively about Meagan.

"What she's really trying to ask you is," Hugh said with a smile as he took a bite of the apple pie, "what is going on between Meagan and Duff MacCallister?"

"Yes," Lisa said, validating Hugh's comment. "What kind of man is Mr. MacCallister?"

"He's a big man," Matt said. "Somewhat taller than I am. He's a Scot and talks with a heavy brogue, but he's an honest man and you couldn't ask for any better friend or, for that matter, any worse enemy."

"You're not answering my question. What I really want to know is, will he and my sister ever get married?"

Matt chuckled. "You do get to the crux of things, don't you? My guess is that someday, they probably will. But for now I don't think Meagan wants to give up her dress shop, and Duff's ranch, Sky Meadow, is too far away from Chugwater to live on the ranch and come into town to run the shop every day. But if you asked me, I would say that yes, someday they will be married."

Lisa flashed a warm smile toward Matt and, quite unexpectedly, he felt a sudden attraction to her, something that he knew should be quickly suppressed. He also thought that he saw, just for an instant, a similar reaction from Lisa, but it passed so quickly that he couldn't be sure.

"I'm glad he isn't just stringing her along," Lisa said.

"Hugh, on the ride out here, Ed was telling me about Tyrone DuPont and the Regulators. Tell me what you know about them." Matt's change of the subject was as much to get his mind off Lisa as it was for information.

Hugh shook his head slowly, not as if refusing to respond to Matt's request, but rather to express his feelings for the man in question. "DuPont claims to have been a policeman once. I don't know if that's true or not. I do know that he was once a riverboat gambler. A while back he approached the Ranchers' Association with the proposal that he could provide us with a private police force. There had been some horse thieving and cattle rustling, and the Ranchers' Association took him up on it. I was the only one who voted against taking him on, and I was right. Instead of stopping it, it has gotten worse."

"And the Ranchers' Association has done nothing about it?"

"A few of us have tried, but Kennedy and O'Neil want to keep them on, so the Regulators are still an official police force for the association."

"What about the law?"

"Garrett Kennedy and Sean O'Neil *are* the law, at least, for all intents and purposes. They own the

Straight Arrow Ranch, which is the biggest ranch in the Sweetwater Valley, and they contribute enough money to elect the town and county officials they want. They control the sheriff and the judge, and that gives the Regulators a façade of legality. Sheriff Clark has given Tyrone DuPont the title of first deputy, and every other member of the Regulators is a deputy."

"Ed seemed to suggest that DuPont and his Regulators might be the ones who are actually doing the stealing."

"It's more than just a suggestion. I'm certain they are. And the most contemptible thing about it is their accusation that it is the smaller ranchers who are doing the rustling. They are enforcing a damnable law that makes rustlers out of anyone who rounds up a stray calf now and then. Just within the last six months two ranchers and their families have been forced to leave the valley."

"What about Kennedy and O'Neil? Aren't they aware of what's going on?"

"Who do you think wound up with the two abandoned ranches?"

"Kennedy and O'Neil," Matt said. It wasn't a question. It was an answer.

"Yes, as no doubt I'm sure they will wind up with Harmon Philpot's place. I'll be honest with you, Matt, I'm not really sure what the situation is with them," Hugh said.

"Colleen isn't like that," Lisa said quickly.

"Colleen?"

"Colleen is O'Neil's daughter," Hugh explained. "She's twenty-two years old, and she has been out here less than a year, arriving shortly after her mother died. And, like Lisa says, she's not like the rest of them."

"Why doesn't she leave them?"

"Well, O'Neil is her father, and I don't think she's quite ready to totally abandon him yet," Lisa said. "But she is basically a very good person, and I think that one day she'll get the courage to do what is right."

"You say the smaller ranchers are losing cattle to the rustlers. What about Kennedy and O'Neil? Are they losing cattle as well?" Matt asked Hugh.

"They don't seem to be losing any, but as to whether or not they are actually directly benefiting from the rustling, well, I'm not prepared to make that charge."

"What do you mean by *directly benefiting*?"

"As I said, when the smaller ranchers give up and leave, somehow their property seems to be absorbed by the Straight Arrow Ranch."

"The first thing I need to do is find out as much about Kennedy and O'Neil, and about DuPont and his Regulators, as I can," Matt said.

"You might start with Art Walhausen," Hugh suggested.

"Who is Art Walhausen?"

"He is the owner and publisher of the *Red Desert Gazette*."

Matt continued his questioning. "Can he be trusted?"

"He has never done anything to make me think he can't be. And he has written a couple of editorials challenging the need for a private police force."

"And it cost him," Lisa added

"Cost him, how?"

"A bunch of thugs broke into his newspaper office one night," Hugh explained. "They broke his window and scattered his type around. He had to suspend publication for two weeks until he got everything put back together."

"Do you think it was Regulators?"

"They denied it of course, but I know damn well they were the ones who did it. Who else would have a reason?"

"What about Kennedy and O'Neil? What did they say about it?"

"Oh, they insisted that they had nothing to do with it. They even replaced his window and paid for the damages."

"But you don't believe them," Matt stated.

"I have no reason not to believe them." Hugh paused for a moment before he continued. "But I don't believe them," he added with a wry smile.

Art Walhausen was shorter than average, bald headed, and had gray eyes that seemed almost too large for his face. That illusion was even more pronounced because they were magnified by the glasses he wore.

He couldn't remember when he didn't want to be a newspaperman. As a boy he had "published" a newspaper for his neighbors on Water Street in Boston, Massachusetts. Of course, he had no printing press at the time, so he had laboriously printed by hand twenty copies of the "paper" that he'd called the *Water Street News*, then he hand delivered them to every house on both sides of the block. He had subsequently worked on such newspapers as the *Boston Evening Transcript, Harpers Weekly*, and the *St. Louis Republican*. The *Red Desert Gazette* was the first paper he had ever owned.

Walhausen was working on the copy for an ad for Dunnigan's General Store when the tinkling bell on the front door told him that someone had just come in. Looking up, he saw a young man who appeared to be just over six feet tall, with broad shoulders and narrow hips. He was wearing a pistol, the holster low and tied down on the right. Walhausen was perceptive enough to know that this was a man who knew how to use it, but he was also intuitive enough to know that his gun wouldn't be misused.

"Yes, sir, can I help you?"

"I was told that you might be able to tell me a little about the Regulators."

The expression on Walhausen's face changed from one of benign curiosity to measured caution. "May I ask why you are interested? Are you, by chance, seeking a position with them? If so, I'm afraid I can't help you."

Matt chuckled. "Looking to join them?" He shook his head. "Mister, that's the last thing I want. I plan to help Hugh Conway get his horses to market, and I understand that the Regulators might be of some concern. Hugh suggested that I talk to you about them."

The expression on Walhausen's face turned to one of relief. "You are working for Conway?"

"It's more like I am working *with* him," Matt replied. "Mrs. Conway is the sister of a friend of mine, and that friend asked if I would help them." He extended his hand. "My name is Matt Jensen."

"Matt Jensen? So it is true."

"I beg your pardon?"

"I heard how Matt Jensen had arranged a demonstration of Ed Sanders's facility for fisticuffs upon Walter Toone and Moe Greene."

Matt laughed. "Let's say Ed got his licks in."

"You really are here. I wanted to believe it. I just wasn't prepared to accept the idea that someone like you would be inclined to visit our small town. But I can see how you might respond to the request of a friend. So you want to know about the Regulators, do you?"

"Yes, but not just the Regulators. I'm also curious about Kennedy and O'Neil and would like to see or hear anything you have on them."

"What can I tell you? Those rapacious scallywags who call themselves Regulators are the most loathsome dregs of society. And of course they are led by Tyrone DuPont, the biggest miscreant of them all. I remember him from St. Louis."

"You knew DuPont in St. Louis?"

"I knew *of* him. I didn't actually know him," Walhausen said. "I was a newspaperman there, too, working for the *St. Louis Republic.*"

"Ed Sanders, the man who works for Hugh Conway, believes that the Regulators themselves may be doing some of the horse stealing that is going on," Matt said. "Do you think that's possible?"

"Not only possible, I think it is probable that they are stealing horses and rustling cattle, but I can't print it because I have no proof. Kennedy and O'Neil would sue me in a heartbeat."

"Kennedy and O'Neil. Yes, I would like to know about them, as well."

"Garrett Kennedy and Sean O'Neil. I've done some research on them. Just a minute. Let me get my notes." Walhausen opened a drawer to his desk, then pulled out a file and began looking through it. "Ah yes, here it is. They were bankers in New York, but it wasn't the kind of bank you think of. You couldn't write a check on the bank. You couldn't deposit any money in the bank, nor could you borrow money from the bank."

"What kind of bank was it?"

"Their bank bought up loans. It specialized in purchasing loans that were in distress. That gave them title to the equity, be it a small business or property, even a private house. Then, when the loan came due they would foreclose on it, taking over the property, then selling it for gain. It was enormously profitable, but they ruined a lot of innocent lives."

Matt frowned. "Why did they give that up? Why did they come out here?"

"They made some powerful enemies in the Whyos Gang."

"The what?"

"The Whyos Gang is an Irish gang operating in New York. They are pretty eclectic, counting in their number anyone from pickpockets to murderers. They emerged from what had been the Five Points Gang and pretty quickly either eliminated or absorbed a lot of other gangs."

"And you believe that these two men, Kennedy and

O'Neil, were once a part of that gang? Is that how they wound up owning a ranch here in Wyoming? When you think about it, that seems a little far-fetched."

"It isn't so far-fetched if you know their history. Kennedy and O'Neil had ambitions to take over the gang, and they got into a fight with the two of the gang members, Lyons and Driscoll, who had the same ambition. Lyons and Driscoll won the battle, and Kennedy and O'Neil were forced to flee.

"As a result of their banking operation, they had a great deal of money when they arrived, and they bought out four or five smaller ranchers, then put together their Straight Arrow Ranch. Let me show you my morgue."

"Your morgue?" Matt replied in surprise.

Walhausen chuckled. "Nothing sinister. In the newspaper business, it's what we call old back issues. I actually have two morgues, the regular morgue that consists of only past newspapers, and a special one that has stories of particular interest.

"The first one I will show you is about Tyrone DuPont. It appeared in the *St. Louis Republican*, where I once worked. I didn't write it, and it's just as well I didn't, for if I had, and he had been able to make the connection, I would be at great risk now.

"I'll get the St. Louis paper first, and while you're reading the story, I'll get the others."

St. Louis Police Officer
Found Guilty of Fraud

Tyrone DuPont, a five-year member of the metropolitan police force, has been indicted on charges of bribery and conspiracy to commit bribery following an internal affairs investigation into a scheme where he accepted bribes to turn his back on crimes being committed by local citizens.

The alleged scheme worked like this: DuPont would find violations of laws and ordnances, then, for a price, promise the perpetrator no information that would lead to a charge would be turned in. The payments to DuPont were always in the form of cash so as not to have any evidence of his malfeasance. DuPont allegedly made over two thousand dollars in payoffs.

Chief of Police Arthur Bruce criticized the behavior detailed in the indictment as "disgraceful," asserting that it amounts to an abuse of authority. "The most important thing any police officer strives for in their career is earning the trust and confidence of the people they serve," Chief Bruce went on to say.

In order to prevent the adverse publicity that would befall the St. Louis Police Department in a trial, DuPont has agreed to a plea bargain where he will be stripped of all police powers and removed from the force.

By the time Matt finished the article, Walhausen had returned from the morgue file, bringing ten newspapers back with him.

"I see where he was kicked off the force," Matt mentioned. "Is that why he left St. Louis?"

"Not immediately. For a while he became a gambler on riverboats headed for New Orleans, and from all that I heard, he was doing quite well. But I lost track of him until he showed up here."

"What did he think about seeing you here?"

Walhausen smiled and shook his head. "As far as I know, he hasn't given me a second thought. I was not a well-known journalist while I was in St. Louis and, as I told you, we had never met, so I'm sure he had never even heard of me."

Matt had more questions. "How many Regulators are there?"

"As of now, at least to the point I have been able to keep up with it, there are eight. Nine, counting DuPont."

"What about Angus Shardeen? Is he part of the Regulators?"

"You know Shardeen?"

"I know of Shardeen, but I've never met him."

"That little tour-de-force demonstration he gave in the Wild Hog is indicative of his position as the puissance of the Regulators," Walhausen said.

Matt laughed out loud. "I have no idea what you just said, but I'm going to take it to mean that yes, Shardeen is part of the Regulators."

"He is indeed."

"What about Sheriff Clark? Have you told him about your suspicions?"

"I don't need to tell him. He knows all about it," Walhausen said.

"Are you saying that Clark is behind this? That he is actually a part of it?"

"No, I'm not saying that, exactly. He isn't involved with Kennedy and O'Neil, nor even directly involved with the Regulators, for all that he has deputized DuPont. I think Clark is basically an honest man, but he is a weak man who lacks the initiative and the backing to challenge the Regulators."

"And yet he is the one who made them all deputies."

"I suppose that's true, but I'm convinced that when he did it, he truly believed that they would be helping him, and that it would be for the good of the town and county. Now things have gotten out of hand, and he is too frightened to oppose them."

"I think I'll pay the good sheriff a little visit," Matt said.

"Go easy on him, Mr. Jensen. As I said, I believe Sheriff Clark is an honest man—just in well over his head."

Matt's only reply was a nod before he left the newspaper office.

Chapter Nine

Sheriff Davey Clark was about five feet nine, a slender man with gray hair and a gray, bushy moustache. Matt figured he was in his late sixties, maybe even a little older.

"You're Matt Jensen, aren't you?" Clark said when Matt stepped into the sheriff's office.

"I am."

"What can I do for you, Mr. Jensen?"

"Is it true you have deputized the Regulators?"

"Yes."

"Why would you do that?"

"Jensen, I am supposed to police over ten thousand square miles. I can't do it by myself, and the county won't authorize the funds to pay for but one deputy. I've appointed DuPont as my deputy, and he has come up with a group of men who have volunteered to be deputies without pay. That means I don't have to come up with money the country doesn't have, because the Regulators work for nothing."

Matt shook his head. "No, they don't work for nothing, Sheriff, and you know that."

"If they round up a stray horse or cow now and then, it's nothing ranchers haven't always done."

"And if the horse or cow isn't exactly a stray?"

"It's called taxes," Clark said.

"Taxes? My friend Hugh Conway is on the verge of losing his ranch to the roundup of the *stray* horses he has in his own pasture. And you call that taxes?" Matt emphasized the word *stray* to make a point.

Clark closed his eyes and pinched the bridge of his nose. He was quiet for a long moment.

"Jensen, I am seventy-one years old. There is no way I can actually deal with this. My term will be up at the end of this year and, believe me, I will not be seeking reelection. My primary goal is to live until then, and I don't think going up against Tyrone DuPont is a good way of doing that."

"Let me ask you this, Sheriff. Will you get in my way if I deal with it?"

"You're one man. How would you deal with it?"

"Leave that up to me. I do have a favor to ask of you, though."

Clark frowned. "What sort of favor?"

"Make me a deputy."

"What good would that do? I've got too many deputies now. That's the problem."

"No, you have the wrong deputies, and *that* is the problem. Deputize me, and let me take care of it."

"I don't have any money to pay you."

"I'll do it as a public service."

"Jensen, I know about you. I've heard all about you. I know that you are exceptionally good with a gun, and it would be good to have you on my side.

But if DuPont starts giving me any trouble over this, I'm going to count on you standing between him and me."

"I'll be there," Matt promised.

All eight men in the Regulators were wanted men. That fact was one of the inducements DuPont had used in recruiting them.

"This is the best way to avoid any paper that might be out on you," he'd told each of them. "If you *are* the law, you won't be coming after yourselves, will you?"

The Mason brothers were his first recruits. John and Lem were from Missouri and, for a while, they had ridden with Frank and Jesse James. After the James Gang broke up, John and Lem formed their own gang and with three others tried to hold up a stagecoach between New Madrid and Sikeston, Missouri. They hadn't counted on six armed men inside the coach, in addition to the shotgun guard. Two of the gang members were killed outright and the third badly wounded. John and Lem Mason got away but without any money, then fled Missouri.

Asa Carter was originally from Ohio, but more recently he had been in the army at Fort Riley, Kansas. Three years ago he'd murdered his first sergeant, then deserted the army and changed his name from Private William Dudley to Asa Carter.

Walter Toone and Moe Greene had been cowboys down in Texas. One night they murdered the foreman when he was coming back from the bank with the monthly wages, stole the four hundred dollars he was carrying, and went on the run.

Luke McCoy was from Arizona. He had held up a stagecoach outside Flagstaff, got forty dollars and his name on a wanted list. Nobody had been hurt in the holdup.

Isaac Newton was DuPont's final recruit. He was an unusual recruit in that he was a black man. He didn't speak like any black man DuPont had ever known. As a matter of fact, DuPont knew very few men, black or white, who had as good a command of the English language as did Isaac Newton. His grammar was excellent, and his enunciation was clear and precise. At first DuPont passed it off as Newton being from Boston because he could believe that all Bostonians spoke in such a fashion.

But DuPont quickly learned that Newton was well educated.

"Why did you go to school?" DuPont asked. "I mean, you bein' a man of color 'n all, there ain't that many places you can work that you'd be needin' schoolin' for, is there?"

"I taught school," Newton replied.

"Yes, well, I suppose the little colored children need schoolin', too, 'n who would teach 'em, if not somebody else who's colored?"

"Precisely," Isaac agreed without further explanation.

After listening to Toone and Greene give their reports on Matt Jensen, DuPont said, "Yeah, I've heard of him. What I want to know is, what is he doing here?"

"I expect he's just passin' through," Toone said.

"No, he ain't just passin' through," Greene said. "Don't you recall him a-sayin' he was a-goin' to be workin' for Conway?"

"Yeah, but I think he was just sayin' that so as to get our goat," Toone replied.

"I need to know if he really is workin' for Conway," DuPont said.

"All right. We can go back inter town 'n find out for sure," Toone suggested.

"No, I'd rather you not go back so soon. I'll send someone else."

"Who?" Toone asked.

The benign expression on DuPont's face was replaced by an expression of irritation, almost of anger. "It ain't none of your business who I plan to send," he snapped back

"No, I reckon it ain't," a cowed Toone replied. "I was just curious, is all."

Rongis

Luke McCoy and Isaac Newton were sharing a table at the Wild Hog. Newton wasn't the only black customer. There were at least three others. About one out of four of the valley cowboys were black, a couple of blacks worked for the wagon freighter, and one worked at the livery stable. The Wild Hog catered to them.

"A lawyer? Who are you kidding? I thought you said you was a schoolteacher," McCoy said.

"I have taught school, that is true, but I am also an attorney."

"I can believe maybe you was a schoolteacher oncet. I mean, teachin' in your kind o' schools, them students bein' colored 'n all. But I cain't hardly believe that you're a lawyer."

"I have a certificate proving that I have passed the bar," Isaac said.

"Passed the bar?" McCoy laughed. "Yeah, I reckon you did pass the bar, seein' as most bars I know won't let no nig—"

"Don't say it!" Isaac demanded, a pistol appearing quickly in his hand.

McCoy blanched. "Yeah, look here, Isaac, I didn't mean nothin' by it. I mean, you been ridin' with us for more 'n two months now, 'n there ain't none of us took no notice a-tall that you was a colored man. I was just sayin' that there ain't hardly many bars I know will let you come in, is all. Yeah, the Wild Hog will, but they don't care none iffen you're colored or not, 'n they even got 'em a couple o' colored girls that work here. But I bet you a dollar they wouldn't let you in the Pair O' Dice."

Newton smiled, then slipped his pistol back into his holster. "Someday I may just take you up on that bet. But we came to town today to have a few drinks in the Wild Hog, didn't we?"

"Yeah, that's why we come to town all right," McCoy said. "Oh, 'n to try 'n find out somethin' about Jensen."

"I almost made you pee in your pants, didn't I?"

Seeing now that his life was in no real danger, McCoy laughed. "Yeah, you damn near did. But tell me, what do you mean you passed the bar?"

"That's what you have to do in order to become a lawyer. You have to study for the law, then you have to pass a test that's called the bar exam."

McCoy was confused. "Bar? You mean like the Wild

Hog? Why for would you have to take test in a bar in order to be a lawyer?"

Isaac shook his head. "It isn't that kind of a bar. The term originated from the existence of an actual railing or bar in old courtrooms. The bar was in front of the judge's bench, and when a case was being heard, only licensed lawyers could go inside the bar railing to approach the judge with their arguments."

"I'll be damned. That sure sounds like you know what you're talkin' about all right. But look here, how did you become a lawyer? I mean ain't most of the schools set up so as coloreds can't get into 'em?"

"I read for the law under Robert Morris, who was one of the first black lawyers in America."

"Well then how come it is that you ain't actual lawyerin'? I mean, how come it is that you're ridin' with the Regulators?"

Isaac shrugged. "The Regulators are supposed to be officers of the law, aren't they?"

"Well, yeah, I reckon we're officers of the law, least-wise, we're s'posed to be. Only, you're a pretty smart man for all that you're uh . . . well, what I'm tryin' to say is, you're smart enough to know that we're actual more outlaws than we is lawmen."

Isaac chuckled. "Can you think of anyone else who might have a greater need for a lawyer than outlaws?"

McCoy chuckled, too. "No, now that I think about it, you got that right. There don't nobody need lawyers any more 'n outlaws do. I ain't all that sure that any of the other 'ns would let you be their lawyer. But I would let you be mine."

"What makes you think I would want to represent any of the other Regulators?" Isaac smiled. "But I would represent you."

As Isaac and Luke were talking, two of the bar girls approached, one black and one white. Both shared the common denominator of being attractive and seductively dressed.

The young black girl who called herself Fancy stepped up to Isaac, put her fingers on his cheek, and smiled up at him. "Here's my good-lookin' man. I ain't seen you in a while. You ain't been over in the Pair O' Dice sniffin' 'round them trashy white girls that works there now, have you?"

"That isn't very likely, Fancy, as the proprietors of that establishment have made it abundantly clear that those of my particular genus—that is to say, with my pigmentation and African heritage—are persona non grata within the confines of the Pair O' Dice Saloon."

"Oh, Lord, honey, I don't have no idea what you just said, but you shore did say it pretty!" Fancy gushed.

"They don't allow coloreds in that place," Isaac explained.

"Well, yeah, I know that. Ever'one knows that. I just ain't never heard it said that way before."

"Do you want me to buy you a drink, or are you going to just stand here and engage in a meaningless dialogue?"

Fancy leaned into him and gave him a brief kiss. "I'd be proud to have you buy me a drink."

"'N darlin', I'd be mo' 'n proud to be buyin' one fo' you, 'n that's for sho'," Isaac said, slipping into a heavy dialect.

Fancy laughed. "See there. You can talk normal if you want to."

"Yes'sm, I sho' can," Isaac responded with a laugh.

* * *

"You was wantin' to know somethin' 'bout some o' the men that rides with the Regulators?" Cheatum asked as Matt came into the Pair O' Dice and stepped up to the bar.

"Yes, why do you ask? Do you have some information for me?"

"I don't actual have nothin' new 'bout 'em, but I seen two of 'em come a-ridin' into town not more 'n half an hour ago. I expect you can find 'em over in the Wild Hog."

"Well, I appreciate your tip, Mr. Cheatum, but it looks like you just lost the sale of a beer. I'll be stepping across the street for one. How will I know them?"

The bartender chuckled. "It won't be hard. One of 'em is a colored fella."

When Matt stepped into the Wild Hog a few minutes later, he saw a white man and a black man sitting together at a table near the grandfather clock on the wall farthest from the bar. Although at least three other blacks were in the room, only one was wearing a pistol and sitting with a white man. Matt was sure they were the two men that Cheatum had told him about.

Matt also made a quick perusal of the saloon, satisfying himself that none of the drinkers would pose a problem. From all he could tell, only cowboys and drifters were there, and less than half were wearing guns. A couple of the cowboys were wearing their guns low and kicked out, gunfighter style, but he could tell at a glance that it was all for show. He was certain they had never used them for anything other than target practice, and probably were not very successful at that.

The bartender stood at the end of the bar, wiping

the used glasses with his stained apron, then setting them among the unused glasses. When he saw Matt step up to the bar, he moved down toward him.

"Do you see those two men?" Matt asked, pointing to the two who had caught his attention when he came in.

"Yeah, I see 'em," the bartender answered suspiciously. "What about 'em?"

"I want to buy a second round of whatever it is they're drinking," Matt said. "And I'll have a beer."

"You want to take their drinks to them?"

Matt saw a young black girl standing nearby, and he crooked his finger toward her. "What's your name?" he asked when she stepped in front of him.

"My name is Fancy."

The bartender put three drinks on the bar—two beers and a whiskey.

Matt picked up one of the beers, then handed the girl a dollar. "Fancy, I would like for you to take these two drinks over to the two men sitting at that table. And tell them that I bought them. My name is Matt Jensen."

"Yes, sir," Fancy said with a broad smile.

Matt turned his back to the bar and watched as Fancy took the two drinks over.

"What's this? We didn't order no drinks," McCoy said.

Fancy nodded her head in Matt's direction. "That gentleman standing by the bar bought them. He said to bring them to you."

McCoy looked toward the man Fancy had pointed out. "I don't know him. Isaac, do you have any idea who that man is?"

"I don't have any idea," Isaac replied.

"I know who he is," Fancy said.

"Who is it?" McCoy asked.

"His name is Matt Jensen," she said, enjoying being the purveyor of information.

"Matt Jensen?" Isaac asked. "I wonder what he wants with us."

"Hell, it don't matter none what he wants with us. He's the one DuPont wanted us to find out about. Tell 'im to come over," McCoy said to Fancy.

"I don't know," Isaac said. "This seems more than a mere coincidence."

"You worry too much," McCoy said.

Chapter Ten

"They said for you to go on over 'n see 'em," Fancy said to Matt when she returned after delivering the drinks.

"Thank you."

As he approached the table, Matt was aware that the scrutiny he was under was considerably more than mere curiosity. "May I join you two?"

McCoy pushed out a chair with his foot. "Have a seat," he invited.

"If you don't mind, I'll sit over here," Matt said, choosing the chair that would put his back to the wall rather than the offered chair, which would put his back to the room.

"Careful feller, ain't you, Mr. Matt Jensen?"

"I try to be," Matt replied. "And more properly I would be addressed as Deputy, rather than Mister, but I won't make a point of it."

"Deputy? Deputy what?" McCoy asked.

"Why, I'm a deputy sheriff, of course, just as you two are. You are both deputies, aren't you? With the Regulators?"

"Yeah. Are you a-sayin' that you're plannin' on joinin' up with the Regulators?" McCoy asked.

"I didn't get your names," Matt said without responding to the question.

"My name is McCoy. Luke McCoy. This here feller is Isaac Newton."

"Isaac Newton? Seems to me like I've heard that name before," Matt said.

"Are you an educated man, Mr. Jensen?" Isaac asked.

Matt had had some formal education before he left Kansas with his parents on that fateful wagon trip west, but he had been only ten years old at the time. He'd received virtually no education while he was in the orphanage, and his subsequent education had been a result of a self-study program.

"I don't have much of a formal education," Matt replied. "Why do you ask?"

"Your reaction to my name, *Isaac Newton,* suggested that perhaps you were educated. Sir Isaac Newton was a renowned physicist. I would say that I was named after him, but the fact that we share the same name is strictly a coincidence. I'm quite sure that my mother had never heard of him."

Matt chuckled. "Now that you mention it, I have heard of Newton. He invented gravity, didn't he?"

Isaac chuckled. "He didn't invent it. It was already here and has been since the dawn of existence. He did quantify it, though."

Matt was intrigued by Isaac. "You are quite a man of words, Mr. Newton."

"He's a lawyer too," McCoy said. "Leastwise, he says

he's a lawyer. I can't hardly picture no colored man as a lawyer, though."

"Evidently not many can," Isaac replied. "That is the problem."

"If you are a lawyer, why are you with the Regulators?" Matt asked.

"I asked him that selfsame thing," McCoy said.

"Why? Do you want to join the Regulators?" Isaac asked, leaving Matt's question unanswered.

"What makes you think I would want to join the Regulators?"

"Why, you said it your ownself," McCoy said. "You said you was a deputy, just like we are."

"I'm not exactly just like you are," Matt explained. "My deputy duties won't have anything to do with the Regulators."

"Is it true that you'll be workin' for Hugh Conway?" McCoy asked.

"You do get right to the point, don't you?"

"Well, is it true or ain't it?"

"I will be working with Mr. Conway, yes," Matt said.

"I thought you said you was goin' to be a deputy sheriff. How is it you're goin' to be a deputy 'n also workin' for Conway?"

"Oh, my working with Mr. Conway will be part of my duty as a deputy sheriff. Apparently he has been having to deal with a lot of horse stealing, and he fears he may wind up losing so many horses that he will be unable to get enough to market to enable him to pay the note on his ranch."

"So, what does he want you to help him do? Steal

some horses, maybe?" McCoy asked. "Hell, ain't that what the Regulators is for?"

Matt laughed. "So you are confessing that, are you?"

"Confessin' what?" McCoy asked, clearly confused by Matt's reply.

Unexpectedly, Isaac laughed as well. "It looks like he got you on that one, Luke."

"What do you mean? What is it he got me on?"

"Never mind," Matt said. "Tell me about Tyrone DuPont."

"He's our boss," McCoy said.

"I knew that already. What else can you tell me about him?"

"Well he's—"

Isaac interrupted McCoy with a raised hand. "I must say, Deputy Jensen, that I'm a little uncomfortable with the tone of this conversation."

"Well, it's just that I'm new in town, and now that I'm a deputy, I'm trying to get the lay of the land, so to speak."

"I'm sure you will be able to learn much more by observation than by interrogation," Isaac said.

"You may be right," Matt agreed. He finished his beer then stood up. "Gentlemen, thank, you for inviting me to join you. Try to stay out of trouble while you are in town."

Isaac and McCoy watched Matt as he pushed through the batwing doors and stepped outside.

"He's kind of a strange 'un, ain't he?" McCoy said.

"He may be trouble for DuPont and the Regulators," Isaac observed.

"Ha! How can he be? He don't seem to me like he's all that smart."

"He *don't* seem smart?" Isaac asked.

"You seen it, too, didn't you?"

Isaac chuckled at his private joke. "Yes, I *seen* it, too."

"What did you find out about Jensen?" DuPont asked when Isaac and McCoy returned to the Purgatory Pass headquarters.

"Hell, he ain't nothin' to worry about," McCoy said. "He don't have no idea what's goin' on."

"Newton, do you agree with McCoy?"

"Not exactly," Isaac said. "I think Jensen could mean trouble for us."

"Why do you say that?"

"He is going to be working with Conway, and because he is a deputy, he will have the authority of the law on his side. It might be a good idea to suspend our horse acquisition operations for a while."

DuPont shook his head. "I don't agree. If we can run Conway out of business, Kennedy 'n O'Neil can take over his ranch. And those horses would pay more than any of the other jobs we have done."

"But to whose benefit? Would the profits accrue to the Regulators or to Mr. Kennedy and Mr. O'Neil?" Isaac asked.

"That is not for you to worry about," DuPont said. "Besides, if Jensen is going to be a problem like you say, then we're goin' to have to deal with him before we go any further."

"Deal with him how?"

"Deal with him permanently."

"Mr. DuPont, there is a most ominous connotation to that remark. You may want to rethink it."

"Why would I want to do that?"

DuPont's response was provocative enough to cause Isaac to withdraw his objection. "No reason," he said, not wanting to get into a confrontation with DuPont. Isaac smiled. "You might just say I was making conversation."

"Yeah, well, you can make all the conversation you want, so long as you know I'm the one that makes the decisions."

"Of course you are, and I would never suggest otherwise."

"Hello, Matt. Won't you come in?" Lisa invited, stepping out onto the front porch as Matt rode up to the Spur and Latigo ranch house. "I just made a pot of coffee."

"Thanks, that sounds good," he said as he dismounted and wrapped the reins around the hitching post. "Where's Hugh?"

"He's out in the bunkhouse talking to the new hands."

"New hands?"

Lisa smiled. "Yes, thanks to the loan from my sister we were able to hire two more men. Hugh says they'll be able to help us move the horses to Bitter Creek."

"I'm sure they will. Maybe I should go out—" Matt started toward the bunkhouse.

Lisa called out to him. "There's no need. He's coming right back. Why, he's the one who asked me to put on a pot of coffee in the first place."

"All right," Matt agreed.

Stepping inside, he could smell the aroma of Arbuckles' with a hint of cinnamon. Although there was a large dining room with a great table, there was also a very small table in the kitchen that had only two chairs.

Lisa made a motion toward it. "We can sit here for our coffee," she suggested.

Matt was sure that this was where Hugh and Lisa took their meals when they were alone, and he felt uneasy about invading that private space.

"Are you telling me that you don't trust me to take my coffee in the keeping room?" Matt asked, making a joke of his declining the offer. "Are you afraid I will spill my coffee on your furniture?"

Lisa laughed. "No, of course not. Go on in, and I'll bring it to you in a moment. How do you like it?"

"Black."

"Yes, I would have guessed as much."

Matt stepped into the keeping room and had a look around. A highly polished baby grand piano stood in the room, and a large oil painting of Hugh wearing tails and striped pants hung from the wall. The sofa was leather covered, but the three chairs were all of fabric.

"Here's your coffee," Lisa said, coming into the room carrying two cups.

"I didn't know you played the piano," Matt said.

"I don't. Hugh does."

"Hugh?"

"Hugh was a concert pianist before we were married. He has played in London, Paris, Vienna, and Rome, as well as New York, St. Louis, and San Francisco."

"I don't understand. If he has done all that, how did he wind up on a horse ranch?"

"Because I got tired of spending so much of my time on ships and in trains," Hugh replied.

Matt turned to see him standing in the arch of the doorway, holding a cup of coffee.

Chapter Eleven

"Hello, Matt. I saw your horse tied up out front," Hugh said as he came on into the room. "Is there a problem?"

"No, no problem," Matt replied. "I met a couple of DuPont's men, and I just wanted to know if you knew them."

"I know all of them," Hugh said. "Who did you meet?"

"Luke McCoy and Isaac Newton."

"Ah yes," Hugh said. "I know them both. Isaac Newton is a particularly interesting man, surprisingly articulate."

"I had the same impression," Matt said. "But the real reason I came out here was to tell you about this."

Matt reached into his pocket and pulled out a star to show to Hugh.

"What is that?" Hugh asked.

"Sheriff Clark has hired me as his deputy. Well, he hasn't actually hired me since he doesn't have the money to pay me. But I am a duly authorized deputy sheriff."

"Why did you do that?" Hugh asked. "I don't understand."

"Hugh, I'm quite sure that we won't be able to get your horses to market without some conflict, and it could be that the conflict will lead to someone getting shot. And since I don't intend to be the one getting shot, it stands to reason that I will be the one doing the shooting. If I'm going to shoot someone, I would like the cover of being a deputy sheriff."

"But aren't all the Regulators deputy sheriffs as well? Won't they have as much legal justification as you?"

Matt smiled. "Only DuPont has been officially designated as a deputy. The others have no more authority than someone who has been temporarily appointed as a posse member."

"But they aren't temporary. The Regulators have been around for several months now," Hugh said.

"They may still be around, but according to Sheriff Clark, their actual appointments as deputies expired thirty days after DuPont issued them. They have no legal authority anymore."

"But won't DuPont get them all reappointed once he finds out that the appointments have expired? What will keep him from just renewing them?"

Matt shook his head. "He can't renew them. Only the sheriff can. The last time DuPont issued the appointments, he did so with Sheriff Clark's authorization. The sheriff has no intention of authorizing them again."

"I thought Sheriff Clark was in DuPont's hip pocket," Hugh said.

"That was a matter of interpretation. No, it was more a matter of intimidation. But Sheriff Clark is no longer intimidated."

"I'll be. Well, I'm glad to see that the sheriff has gotten a backbone, even if he is borrowing it from you."

"Hugh, won't you play something for us?" Lisa asked.

"Yes, Hugh, please play," Matt invited.

"I, uh, was always pretty much of a perfectionist when I was on tour," Hugh replied. "I took myself to task if I didn't play the very best, and I practiced every day. I no longer maintain the schedule it takes for perfection, so if I play, I must apologize in advance, because I'm sure it won't be a polished performance."

"It will be beautiful, Hugh, as it always is," Lisa insisted.

"All right," Hugh agreed. He walked over to the piano and ran his hand across the smooth, ebonized rosewood. Pulling the bench out, he sat down between the carved cabriole legs, then lifted the lid and supported it with the fretwork music rack.

He hit a few keys and was rewarded with a rich, mellow tone. Then he tilted his head and paused for a long moment. At first Matt wondered if Hugh might not be having second thoughts about playing. Then he realized that Hugh had just transported himself to another time and another place.

Fifteen hundred people filled the Crystal Palace in London, England, to hear the latest musical sensation from America. When the curtain opened, the audience applauded as Hugh Conway walked out onto the stage, flipped the tails back from his swallowtail coat, then took his seat at the piano.

The auditorium grew quiet and Mr. Conway began to play Beethoven's Concerto no. 5 in E-flat Major. The music filled the concert hall and caressed the collective soul of the audience.

One review read, *"It was something magical. The brilliant young American pianist managed, with his playing, to resurrect the genius of the composer so that, to the listening audience, Hugh Conway and Ludwig Beethoven were one and the same."*

Matt's music appreciation was pretty much limited to a cowboy or cowboys who sang, sometimes to the accompaniment of a mellow guitar. He had also heard a few city bands and, of course, the ubiquitous saloon piano. But he felt himself caught up in the music, and when he glanced over at Lisa he saw that she was looking at him with such intensity that he couldn't look away. Then he saw a tear sliding down her cheek.

He held her gaze until the last note of music drifted away.

Lisa sniffed, wiped her eyes, and smiled. "That piece of music always makes me cry."

"Why did you quit the concert stage?" Matt asked again. "And don't say it's because you got tired of traveling."

Hugh closed the piano and sat there for a moment, then got up and moved to the sofa to sit beside Lisa. He was still quiet, but deep in thought. Finally, he spoke. "I had my reasons."

"Good enough," Matt said without pressing him for any further explanation.

As if forcing a mood change on himself, Hugh smiled, then stood. "Come, I would like you to meet the two new men I hired. I was able to do that thanks to you."

"You mean thanks to Meagan, don't you?"

"Yes, but in truth, it is thanks to both of you. You're the one who brought the money."

When Matt and Hugh stepped into the bunkhouse, Ed Sanders had the two new men standing at attention as he was giving them instructions.

"Ed used to be a first sergeant," Hugh said with a little chuckle.

"No sir, I didn't *used* to be a first sergeant. I still am," Sanders replied. "Once a first sergeant, always a first sergeant."

"I thought you two new men might like to meet Matt Jensen," Hugh said.

"Wow! You're Matt Jensen? Really?" the younger of the two asked.

"This is him, all right," Sanders said. "Introduce yourselves."

"My name is Jake Haverkost," the younger one said, extending his hand.

"I'm LeRoy Patterson," the other said.

Matt shook hands with both of them. "Have you two boys ever worked with horses before?"

"Horses, cows, sheep, you name it, I've worked with 'em," Patterson said.

"That's quite a background for someone your age," Matt said.

"Yes, sir, I s'pose it is, but I didn't have no choice,

seein' as I've been on my own since I was twelve years old 'n had to work to eat."

"I joined up with LeRoy last year," Jake said. "And ever since then where he's gone, why, I been. 'N me bein' a orphan, too, why you might say me 'n him is most like brothers."

Matt knew what it was like to be on his own early in life, and he related quickly to the two young men. He turned to Sanders. "Have you told them about DuPont?"

"Are you talkin' about that group of outlaws that calls themselves the Regulators?" Patterson inquired.

"You call them outlaws?" Matt asked.

"Them Mason brothers is outlaws, 'n I know that for a fact, on account of me 'n them oncet—" he stopped in midsentence, then realized everyone was waiting for him to complete his sentence—"uh, me 'n them oncet held us up a grocery store. Onliest thang is, I didn't know what we was goin' to do was actual go in 'n hold it up. I thought we was just goin' to break in after they closed 'n steal some whiskey. But John 'n Lem, what they done was hold a gun on them two old people what was runnin' the store 'n stole all their money. After that, I didn't want nothin' no more to do with 'em.

"Anyway, that's how come I know them to be real outlaws."

Matt nodded, then looked over at Hugh. "I'm just guessing, of course, but I'd be willing to bet that these two young men are going to make you a couple of fine hands."

"Yeah," Sanders said with a smile. "They'll be just fine as long as they listen to me so's I can get 'em shaped up."

"Suppose we start now," Hugh suggested. "Let's take them around the ranch and show them the pastureland and horses."

"All right. I'll get your horse saddled for you, Mr. Conway, 'n give you a call when we're ready."

Hugh chuckled. "I can get my own horse saddled. Matt, do you want to come along with us?"

"I'd like to, but being as I'm a new deputy, I really think I should get back to town. I want to establish my position with everyone, and I particularly want them to know that I have nothing to do with the Regulators."

Hugh nodded. "Yes, that's probably a pretty good idea."

Matt waited around, talking and joking with Hugh and the others until they rode away. Then he started back to the hitching post in front of the house, where Spirit had been waiting patiently.

"Matt?" Lisa said, stepping out onto the porch as he started to unhitch his horse.

"Yes?"

"You and Hugh left before I was able to offer you any of the cake I baked this morning. Would you like to come in and have a piece now?"

From the tone in her voice and the way she held Matt with her eyes, he got the distinct impression that there was more to the invitation than a piece of cake. "I, uh, had better not."

"You feel it too, don't you, Matt?"

There. It was out in the open, and by her words Matt knew that this wasn't something he was just imagining. "Lisa, I . . ."

Lisa shook her head and held up her hand, palm toward Matt. "No!" she said resolutely. "Oh, Matt, please forgive me, and forget that I even said such a thing. I-I don't know what has gotten into me."

"Perhaps it would be better if I didn't come around anymore," he said.

"No, please, don't do that. Hugh is counting on you. I am counting on you to help us get through this trouble we're facing. If you would suddenly disappear, Hugh would wonder why, and he would start asking questions. Matt, I'm not sure I could deal with that."

"But can you . . . can we, deal with this, this thing that is trying to come up?"

Lisa shook her head. "It won't happen again. We can deal with it. We *must* deal with it. And I promise, I'll never say another word that will make you feel uncomfortable."

Matt swung into the saddle, then looked at Lisa for a long moment. "Good-bye."

"Matt, you'll come back?" Lisa asked in a pleading voice.

He nodded. "I'll come back."

As Matt rode away from the Spur and Latigo, he fought hard to push back the thoughts he was having. Lisa was a beautiful woman, yes, though he couldn't say that she was the most beautiful he had ever seen. But there was something else about her, some visceral attraction that he couldn't deny. Even as he realized that, he promised himself he would deny it. He had no other choice.

Chapter Twelve

Ed Sanders and Jake Haverkost found four Spur and Latigo horses confined in a hastily constructed corral on Soda Creek about five miles northeast of the ranch.

"Well, look here," Sanders said with a broad smile. "Mr. Conway is going to be happy to get these critters back."

"It's funny them just bein' left out here like this," Haverkost said cautiously. "It's almost like they wanted us to find them."

"Whoever it was that stole 'em prob'ly just put 'em here till they could get 'em sold somewhere," Sanders said. "Only they ain't a-goin' to be sellin' these horses, 'cause we're goin' to take 'em back. You keep a look-out while I go down there 'n get 'em."

"All right," Haverkost said, standing in his stirrups as if by increasing his height by six inches he would have a better view.

"Hey, Moe, do you see what I see?" Walter Toone asked as he pointed toward the single rider. "Looks like Sanders has found our horses."

"He ain't only found 'em. Looks to me like he's fixin' to take 'em back," Moe Greene replied.

Toone, Greene, and Asa Carter had been keeping an eye on the corralled horses.

"You mean he's goin' *to try* 'n take 'em back." Carter pulled his rifle from the saddle holster. "We can take care o' that right now."

"No," Toone said, holding up his hand. "Don't shoot 'im."

"Why not? We're deputies, ain't we? 'N he's stealin' horses, ain't he?" Carter laughed. "Even if it's horses we done already stoled first."

"No, shootin' 'im is too good," Toone said. "Me 'n Moe owe him somethin'."

"What do we owe 'im?" Moe asked, confused by Toone's comment."

"Maybe you don't 'member how he beat us both up while Jensen was a-holdin' his gun on us so we couldn't fight back," Toone said, using the story he and Greene had told the others to explain the beating they had taken from the foreman of Spur and Latigo.

"Oh yeah," Greene said. "Yeah, I remember that."

"What you got in mind, Walt?" Carter asked.

"What do they generally do with horse thieves?" Toone replied.

Carter smiled cynically. "They hang 'em."

"Yep. 'N that's just what we're a-goin' to do."

"How we goin' to hang 'im?" Greene asked. "They ain't no trees 'round here."

"We'll take 'im back to DuPont," Toone said easily. "Then we'll find us a good tree."

* * *

Matt had discovered long ago that one of the easiest ways of keeping abreast of everything that was going on was to monitor the conversations in a popular saloon. Of the two saloons in town, the Pair O' Dice was the most popular. At the moment he was having a beer with Art Walhausen.

"Mr. Jensen! Mr. Jensen!" a young man called out, rushing into the saloon then hurrying back to the table occupied by Matt and Walhausen.

"Haverkost, isn't it?" Matt asked, recognizing him as one of the two new hands Hugh Conway had hired.

"Yes, sir, Jake Haverkost. Come quick, Mr. Jensen. They've catched 'im, 'n I don't know what it is they aim to do with 'im, but I'm plenty a-scairt. Please, hurry!"

"Who have they caught?"

"Mr. Sanders. The Regulators has catched Mr. Sanders for horse stealin', only we warn't stealin' no horses, 'cause them horses already belong to Mr. Conway. Mr. Sanders was just tryin' to get 'em back, is all."

"Where have they taken Ed?"

"Looks to me like they was a-headin' toward the Rattlesnake Mountains."

"Are you certain that the men who have Mr. Sanders are members of the Regulators?" Walhausen asked.

"Yes, sir, I'm real sure. I recognized Greene 'n Carter, 'n I know them two is Regulators. I didn't get me a close enough look at the other 'n, but they ain't no doubt in m' mind but what he ain't a Regulator, too."

"Purgatory Pass," Walhausen said. "If they were

heading for Rattlesnake Mountains, and if they were Regulators, they are taking him to Purgatory Pass. The Regulators make their headquarters there."

"Thanks, Art. All right, Jake. Let's go."

"Yes, sir, onliest thing is my horse is pretty much wore out, bein' as he was rode so hard for me to get here as fast as I done."

"You can take my horse, son," said one of the other saloon patrons. He had been close enough to overhear the conversation. "It's the bay tied up in front of Sikes Hardware, which is just next door."

"Thank you, sir!" Haverkost said. "I'll bring 'im back in good shape."

"It's more important you bring Ed Sanders back in good shape," the generous customer said. "Me 'n him been friends for a long time. Ever since we was in the army together."

Matt's horse was tied up in front of the saloon. He waited for just a moment until Haverkost had mounted the bay, then urged his horse into a gallop. Spirit started down the street as if he had been fired from a cannon. The rapid acceleration and the speed of two galloping horses drew the attention of the more than two dozen pedestrians who were tending to their business, unaware of the drama behind the rapid departure.

Purgatory Pass

The arrival of Greene, Toone, and Carter, along with a fourth man tied up, drew the attention of the remaining Regulators. DuPont had been eating some beef from a stolen cow when he heard the commotion out front, and still chewing the last bite, he went outside to see what was going on.

"That's Ed Sanders, ain't it?" DuPont asked.

"Yeah, it's him, all right," Toone said with a triumphant smile.

"Ain't he the one who beat you two boys up?" McCoy asked.

"Yeah, but he wouldn't a-done it iffen Jensen hadn't held his gun on us the whole time so's that we couldn't fight back," Greene said.

"Why did you bring 'im here?" DuPont asked. "I hope it's not just because he's the one that beat you up."

"No, that ain't the reason we brung 'im here," Carter said. "We brung 'im here 'cause we caught 'im stealin' our horses."

"They wasn't your horses," Sanders said, speaking for the first time. "Them horses belong to Mr. Conway. I found 'em 'n was takin' 'em back where they belong, is all."

"Where at did you find 'em?" Greene asked. "They wasn't just a wanderin' around, was they?"

"No, they were in a corral. All four of 'em."

"Then if you took 'em from a corral, you was stealin' 'em," Lem Mason said.

"What are we goin' to do with 'im, Mr. DuPont?" Lem's brother, John asked.

"Lock 'im up in the granary till I figure somethin' out," DuPont replied.

Matt and Jake covered the fifteen-mile distance from Rongis to Purgatory Pass in just over an hour, but the horses were breathing heavily when they stopped to let them drink deeply from the Sweetwater River.

"Do you know where Purgatory Pass is?" Matt asked.

"Yes, sir, I know. It's right over there," Jake said, pointing. "But we won't be able to ride right up to it, on account of most o' the time they got someone a-lookin' out for people that come without being invited."

"All right then. We'll just have to look for another way in so the lookout won't see us."

"I don't know no other way in," Jake said.

Matt smiled. "That's why I said we'd have to look for another way."

Inside the Regulators' Purgatory Pass headquarters, Tyrone DuPont had made up his mind as to what they would do with their prisoner. Back out on the porch of his cabin about half an hour later, he ordered that the prisoner be brought to him.

Greene and Toone, who were taking particular pleasure from the situation, brought the Spur and Latigo Ranch foreman out with his hands tied behind his back and stood him before DuPont.

Every other Regulator was present—Angus Shardeen, the Mason brothers—John and Lem—Asa Carter, Isaac Newton, Luke McCoy, and of course, Toone and Green.

Sanders stood before them all, obviously apprehensive about what was about to happen to him, but equally defiant. He glared at DuPont with an unwavering stare.

DuPont cleared his throat. "Ed Sanders, as duly appointed deputies of Laramie County, we are about to hold court to try you for horse stealin'."

"This here ain't no court," Sanders replied.

"It's a court because I'm callin' it a court," DuPont said. "'N since we don't have no judge or prosecutor out here, I'll be doin' both jobs."

"You not only don't have a judge or a prosecutor, you also don't have no jury," Sanders said. "I seen me enough court-martials in the army to know what a court is like. 'N unless you waive your rights to a trial by jury, you got to have one."

"Oh, we'll have a jury all right," DuPont said. "These men will be the jury, and you're even goin' to have your own lawyer to defend you." DuPont pointed toward Isaac Newton. "This is here is Newton, 'n he tells us he's a real lawyer."

Newton shook his head. "No sir, I don't know where you get that from, but I have no intention of defending him."

"Why not? You said you was a lawyer. Was you lyin' about that?"

"I wasn't lying. I am a lawyer. But Mr. Sanders is right. This is not a legally constituted court of law, and no matter what decision this court might reach, that decision is invalid. Any attempt to apply the results of the decision would be a violation of the law. I caution you that such a contrary decision will put into jeopardy anyone who participates in the travesty, and we could all be charged with conspiracy to murder."

"You don't think we should hang 'im?" DuPont asked.

"I do not."

"Then it's up to you to defend him. 'Cause if he

don't have no defense, there ain't no way a-tall that he'll be found innocent. What we'll more 'n likely do is, we'll find 'im guilty 'n we'll hang 'im."

"Mr. DuPont, I'm quite sure that it is your intention to declare him guilty and to hang him, whether I defend him or not."

DuPont laughed. "You're pretty smart, ain't you?"

"If I take part in this sham of a trial, even if it is to defend him, my mere participation will be bona fide evidence of my countenancing the act. And that would make me as guilty of murder as any of the rest of you."

"Well, Newton, it don't make me no never mind whether you defend him or not," DuPont said. "It's like you said, we're goin' to find him guilty of horse stealin', 'n we're goin' to hang 'im for it."

Isaac sighed and looked over at Sanders. "Mr. Sanders, my participating in this would mean that I accept the legitimacy of this trial. And I definitely do not accept that. Also, you do see how useless any attempt on my part to defend you would be, don't you?"

"What you're sayin' is, they're goin' to hang me no matter what," Sanders said.

Isaac nodded. "Yes, sir, I'm afraid that is exactly what I'm saying."

"Then I don't see no need in you a-doin' it. 'N I'm thankin' you for speakin' up for me," Sanders said.

"Let's get this trial started," DuPont said. "Sanders, you was seen tryin' to steal four horses. What do you say to that?"

"I wasn't stealing those horses," Sanders said. "I was takin' 'em back to the Spur and Latigo Ranch, which is where they was stole from in the first place."

"Jury, you've heard the charge that Sanders was stealin' horses, 'n you've heard Sanders say he wasn't doin' that, even though Greene 'n Toone, 'n Carter caught him in the actual act of stealin'. So what do you say? Is he innocent or guilty?"

"Guilty!" the others called out as one.

"All right. Let's get 'im up on his horse 'n get 'im hung."

Sanders's hands were already tied behind his back, so it was necessary for Toone and Greene to help him into the saddle. A noose was hanging from the limb of a tree, and DuPont, who was now mounted, rode up beside Sanders and fitted the loop around his head.

"You got any last thing to say?" DuPont asked.

Sanders looked into the faces of every man present. All except Isaac Newton were staring at him with an expression of morbid excitement. Isaac wasn't looking at him at all.

"Yeah, I got somethin' to say," Sanders replied. "Someday every last one of you sons of bitches is goin' to die. And when you do die and wind up in hell, I'll be waiting for you. By then, me 'n ole Satan will be friends, 'n I'll make sure you get a particular welcome. Now, do your damndest."

Suddenly there were two rapid shots fired, and the rope that hung from the tree was cut in two. The horse Sanders was on was his own horse, and it dashed away.

Matt, who had fired the two shots, was mounted, and in position to grab the reins of Sanders's horse as it galloped by. He stopped the horse just long enough to allow Jake to cut Sanders's wrist restraints.

"Let's get out of here before they can get mounted," Matt shouted, and he, Sanders, and Jake galloped away.

"Haverkost, I was pure-dee hopin' you had gone for help, but son, you need to learn a little more about gettin' somethin' done in time. You was about one second away from bein' too late."

"Yeah, but I was on time, wasn't I?"

Sanders laughed out loud. "Yeah, Jake, I have to give you credit for that, you was on time. Barely, but you was on time."

"Who was that?" DuPont shouted. "Who was it that shot that rope in two like that?"

"Onliest one I know of who can shoot like that, other 'n me, would be Matt Jensen," Shardeen said.

"Matt Jensen," DuPont said with an angry growl. "I knew it soon as I heard he had come here. That sidewinder is going to cause us problems. Big problems."

"What would it be worth to you to make the problem with Jensen go away?" Shardeen asked.

"It won't be easy," DuPont said. "From ever'thing I've heard about him, he is one tough son of a bitch. Hell, we all seen what just happened. I mean him shootin' that rope in two like he done. Do you think you can handle him, Angus?"

The ugly little man tapped the pistol by his side. "I can handle him."

"If you really do think you can handle him it would be worth—"

Isaac held up his hand to stop him in midsentence. "Mr. DuPont, I would advise you not to make a monetary connection between this discussion of Jensen and anything Shardeen might do, nor even to give an affirmation of his plans."

"Why not?"

"If Shardeen is successful and Jensen is killed, a court of law could find you guilty of conspiracy to murder. It would be better for you, and as you are our leader, ultimately better for all of us, if you could avoid any such conspiratorial entanglements."

"That's the second time today you've used the word *conspiracy*. You're big on that, ain't you?"

"I'm just trying to keep you, all of us actually, but you in particular, out of trouble," Isaac said. "You were a policeman once, so I'm sure you are aware that conspiracy to commit murder carries just as stiff a penalty as committing the murder yourself."

"Yeah, of course I know that. But I also know that if Shardeen has it in mind to kill Jensen, there ain't no need for me to try 'n talk him out of it."

"How can you try and talk me out of it, when you don't have no idea what it is I plan to do?" Shardeen asked with a smile

"But I do know. What do you think we've been talking about?" DuPont asked, confused by Shardeen's comments.

"No you don't. You don't have no idea what it is I'm planning to do," Shardeen said a second time. "Oncet Jensen is dead, you won't know nothin' 'bout how it was done, but you'll just be givin' me five hunnert dollars to keep me on with the Regulators."

"Oh," DuPont said, understanding now what Shardeen was saying. "Yes, I understand. Now that you mention it, I don't have no idea what you got in mind. On the other hand I do have five hundred dollars that I would be willing to offer as a reward for anyone who might come up with an idea to make things easier for us."

Shaking his head, Isaac walked away. He didn't say anything about the conversation he had just overheard.

Chapter Thirteen

"I'll tell you the truth. I thought I was a goner," Sanders said. He Patterson, Haverkost, Hugh, and Matt were sitting on the porch of the main house. All were drinking coffee and enjoying a piece of the apple pie Lisa had baked for the occasion.

"The only thing I regret is that they caught me before I could get the four horses back to the ranch."

Hugh smiled. "You don't even have to regret that. They came back on their own."

"They did? Damn, I wish now we had found more than four of them."

"That doesn't leave any doubt as to who has been stealing them, though, does it?" Hugh asked.

"They were being held in a corral that was out in the open, weren't they? They weren't at the Regulators' Headquarters in Purgatory Pass," Matt said.

"What does that matter?" Patterson asked. "It was the Regulators that put 'em there. Hell, ever'body knows that."

Matt shook his head. "Everyone might know it, and I have no doubt that it is true. But I've been around enough trials to know that without any evidence to tie them specifically to the Regulators, we wouldn't be able to make a case."

"So we just let them go?" Sanders asked.

"For now," Matt said. "But they're going to make a mistake someday, and when they do, we'll be right there. In the meantime we'll make certain that no other Spur and Latigo horses leave the ranch until we are ready to take them down to Bitter Creek to ship them off to market."

"And don't forget, four of them came back," Haverkost said.

Sanders finished his pie then pushed the empty plate away. "All right, boys, we can't lollygag around here for the rest of the day. Come on. We have work to do."

"Come on, Mr. Sanders, I saved your life," Haverkost said with a big smile. "You ought to give me the rest of the day off for that."

"Son, I'll be workin' you so hard over the next few days that you'll be wishin' you had been ten seconds slower," Sanders said.

Haverkost gave a good natured groan, and the others laughed as the three hands left the house.

"Thank you, Matt," Lisa said, putting her hand on Matt's. "Mr. Sanders has come to mean a lot to Hugh and me."

"Indeed he has," Hugh said. "And you have my thanks as well."

Matt was barely cognizant of what either of them said. He was too aware of the heat of Lisa's hand on his.

"Hugh, Jim and Mary Ella are coming for dinner this evening. Don't you think it would be good to have Matt stay so he can meet them?"

"Yes," Hugh said, with a big smile. "I think that would be a great idea."

When Jim Andrews and Mary Ella Wilson arrived that evening, Hugh met them, then led them inside. Matt stood as they stepped into the keeping room.

"Jim, Mary Ella, this is Matt Jensen. He has come to help us."

"I heard how you saved Ed Sanders," Jim said.

"Really? News gets around fast, doesn't it?" Matt replied with a smile.

"Well, our place is real close, and cowboys talk. By now everyone in the valley knows what happened."

"That reminds me. Who is *everyone*? I imagine the situation here has people on both sides. Who is on our side?"

"Besides us, there are five other families, and two men who are on their own," Hugh said.

"That is, if you count Mary Ella and me as a family," Jim said.

"Of course you're a family," Hugh said. "There's no need for a preacher's affirmation to make you a family. Frank and Julia Edmonston, Bob and Sandra Guthrie, Ernest Dean and Anne Fawcett, Travis and Alice Poindexter, and Gerald and Sue Ellen Kelly are the other families in the area. Tom Percy and Elmer Grant aren't married."

Matt nodded. "It's good to know who is on our side.'

"I've heard of you, Mr. Jensen," Jim said. "How did you wind up here?"

"My sister sent him to us," Lisa said. "He's a friend of Duff's."

"Duff? Duff MacCallister?" Jim smiled and nodded his head. "Duff is a good man. I moved out here from Chugwater a few years ago, and know him well. Any friend of Duff's is a friend of mine."

During dinner and after, they discussed the other smaller ranchers. Frank Edmonston and Bob Guthrie had been cowboys down in Texas, but settled in Wyoming when they were able to homestead some land. Travis Poindexter had actually been a cowboy for the Straight Arrow, but decided to try ranching on his own. Gerald Kelly was a former soldier who had been in the Seventh Cavalry with Custer. He was with Reno in the fight at Little Big Horn. Ernest Dean Fawcett was one of the earliest settlers in the area, arriving even before Kennedy and O'Neal.

Sylvester Malcolm was also part of the group but, like Hugh, Sylvester didn't run cattle. Sylvester had moved from Missouri. He had been a farmer in Missouri and was still farming.

"They're good men, all of them," Hugh said.

"I'm afraid Malcolm might be about ready to give it up, though," Jim said. "The drought hurt him last year, and a couple of weeks ago some cattle came through one of his wheat fields and knocked it all down to stubble. Sylvester said he's sure it was Straight Arrow cattle, but Kennedy and O'Neil deny it, and Sylvester has no proof."

"Edmonston has said that he might give it up as well and go back down to Texas," Hugh said. "But Lisa and I are not leaving."

"I have no intention of leaving, either," Jim said. "I've never really belonged anywhere before, 'n until I met up with Mary Ella, I was all right with that. But Mary Ella and I are making a home here. Someday I hope we have some kids, 'n if we do, I want to have something to leave to them."

"It's good to have good friends as close neighbors," Lisa said.

"Yes, friends are good to have," Mary Ella agreed.

"Mr. Jensen," Jim started.

"It's Matt."

"Matt, what about Shardeen?"

"What about him?"

"Shardeen is one of the Regulators, and that means that you 'n he might come up against each other."

"I expect we will."

"Well, what I'm asking is, if you 'n Shardeen do wind up facing each other, how do you think it'll come out?"

"I guess we won't know about that until it happens."

"Matt, are you worried about it?" Lisa asked, showing an expression of concern.

He shook his head. "It does no good to worry about such a thing."

"But he's fast. He's very fast," Hugh said.

"So I've heard. But worrying about it will make me no faster, nor will it make me shoot straighter."

Hugh chuckled. "When you look at it that way, I guess that's right."

"Deputy Jensen, would you like to buy me a drink?" the very pretty young bar girl asked.

Matt nodded, then glanced toward the bartender of the Pair O' Dice. "Mr. Cheatum, would you please pour a drink for Jennie Lou?"

"I would be glad to," Cheatum replied, getting a special bottle beneath the bar.

"Would you like to sit at a table?" Jennie Lou asked.

In truth, Matt would have preferred to remain at the bar, but he knew that Jennie Lou spent most of the time on her feet and would probably appreciate sitting for a while. "Sure. Let's go," he said, grabbing his drink and following her to the table.

"What did you think of Mary Ella Wilson?" Jennie Lou asked.

Matt smiled. "How do you know I met her?"

"Mary Ella told me. She's my friend, you know." Jennie Lou made little circles on the table from the condensation of the bottom of her glass. "I'm glad she was able to leave the line, but I do miss her."

"She seems like a very nice person."

"She's real smart, too. Why, did you know that she used to teach school? She got fired when her no-account husband went to prison, which I don't think is fair, then she couldn't get a teachin' job nowhere else, so she wound up here, which is where I met her."

"And so now, she is married to Jim Andrews," Matt said.

"No preacher will say any words over 'em, so I guess she ain't actual married, but it's the same as." Jennie Lou chuckled. "Thing is, Mr. Andrews, whenever he would come here, he only wanted Mary Ella, 'n if she was busy, he would wait till she wasn't busy. There wasn't nobody who worked here who didn't see that them two was in love. 'N when the two of 'em decided to get 'em a ranch together, all the rest of us was real happy about it."

When Angus Shardeen rode into town, he had two things on his mind. Most important was the five hundred dollars he would get for killing Matt Jensen, but there was also the recognition he would get for killing him. Shardeen didn't plan to be a Regulator forever, and being known as the man who killed Matt Jensen would elevate his status and his earning power above almost anyone else who planned to make a living with his gun.

As a boy in Litchfield, Illinois, Shardeen was always the smallest of any of his peers. The others teased him, and called him the "runt of the litter." One boy in particular, Billy Taylor by name, had been a brutal bully, beating up on Shardeen every chance he got.

When Shardeen was sixteen he got a gun and, holding it behind his back, confronted Taylor one night as he was coming back home from working for a freight company, loading and unloading wagons.

Shardeen remembered that night.

"Taylor?" he said, stepping out from behind a tree where he had been waiting.

"Well, well, well," Taylor said, smiling. "If it ain't the little runt. You ready for another ass-whuppin', are you, runt?"

"No, you ain't goin' to whup me no more," Shardeen said, bringing the pistol around to point at Taylor.

"Ha! Am I supposed to be scared of you now?" Taylor asked confidently, defiantly.

"No. You're supposed to die," Shardeen said, pulling the trigger.

The last expression on Taylor's face was one of complete surprise.

Shardeen gave a nod. Taylor was the first man he had ever killed.

Since then Shardeen had proven his skill with the

pistol many times, as well as a propensity, almost an eagerness, to use it. He enjoyed watching bigger, stronger men quake in their boots when he addressed them. And so far he had come out on the still-standing side of every gunfight in which he had been a participant.

Deciding to have a beer before he looked up Jensen, Shardeen tied his horse off in front of the Wild Hog Saloon then stepped inside.

"There is Shardeen," said Candy, one of the girls who worked in the Wild Hog. "He frightens me."

"He's an ugly little toad," Fancy said. "But he doesn't frighten me."

"Are you saying you aren't scared of him?"

Fancy smiled. "Why should I be? He won't have anything to do with me because I'm colored."

"Ha. Then no wonder he doesn't frighten you. Oh, there goes Belle. She's new here. Let her deal with him."

"Hello, cowboy. Welcome to the Wild Hog," Belle said with a practiced smile.

"Cowboy? Do I look like a cowboy to you?" Shardeen asked, his response little more than a growl.

"Uh, would you like to buy me a drink?" Belle asked.

"No, get the hell away from me."

Belle walked away from him, a little cowed by Shardeen's unexpected reaction. "What a rude man," she said as she joined the other two.

"Be thankful that rude is all he was," Candy said.

"What do you mean?"

"A girl that worked here before you came, named Lucy, took him up to her room one night, and the next day she was covered with bruises."

"From him?" Belle asked, pointing to Shardeen.

"Lucy never would say, but everybody knows that's who did it. She was too scared to talk about it, and a couple days later she left town."

"Why doesn't somebody do something?"

"Do what?" Fancy asked. "He's a Regulator. The Regulators get away with anything they want."

"Besides, they say he's about the best with a gun that there is," Candy said.

Standing at the bar, Shardeen was unaware that he was the subject of conversation. The only thing on his mind was Matt Jensen. Shardeen knew that Jensen had the reputation of being a fast draw and accurate shooter. But he also knew that Jensen valued his reputation of always being in the right.

Shardeen wasn't burdened with the necessity of being in the right. He didn't feel a need to make the fight fair. All he intended to do was kill Jensen, and he didn't care what he had to do to get the job done.

When it's all over, Jensen, you'll be dead, I'll still be alive, 'n I'll be five hunnert dollars richer. Shardeen smiled at the thought.

He also knew that he would be known as the man who killed Matt Jensen, and nobody would give a second thought to how it was done.

"Hey," Shardeen called down to the bartender.

"Yes, sir?" the bartender replied, approaching Shardeen with apprehension.

"Do you know Matt Jensen?" Shardeen asked.

"Well, no sir, not really. I mean, not so's you could call us friends or nothin'. But I recognize him when I see him."

"Where can I find 'im?"

"Well, I s'spose he could be just most anywhere."

"You ain't helpin' out much," Shardeen said gruffly.

"Uh, no, sir, I'm sorry. But he don't spend much time in here. He's a deputy sheriff, so he might be in the sheriff's office, but the truth is, you're more likely to find 'im in the Pair O' Dice. 'N even iffen he ain't in there, why, they'd be more apt to know where he is than I would."

"Thanks."

"Uh, would you like another drink, Mr. Shardeen?"

"No."

Shardeen pulled his pistol. Frightened, the bartender stepped back from him. Shardeen opened the gate then rotated the cylinder to check the loads, then he closed the gate and slipped the pistol back into his holster.

"Did you see him check his pistol like that?" Candy asked after Shardeen left the saloon."

"Yes, I saw it," Fancy replied.

"What do you think that was all about?"

"I don't know, but if he has it 'n mind to go after someone, I'm sure glad that it ain't goin' to be in here," Fancy said.

"Yes, I am too," Candy agreed.

"I'd like to see it," Alice said.

"Why on earth would you want to see it?" Candy asked.

Alice grinned. "Maybe the miserable rat will get hisself kilt."

Chapter Fourteen

"Jennie Lou, how long are you just goin' to sit there?" someone called.

Jennie Lou smiled across the table at Matt. "I reckon I had better get back to work. Just a minute," she called. "I'll be right there, cowboy!"

"I've enjoyed the visit," Matt replied with a friendly smile. He stood as Jennie Lou did.

As she walked over toward the cowboy who had called out to her, Matt stepped up to the bar. "Mr. Cheatum, I'll have another beer, if you please."

"Yes, sir, one beer coming up."

When Shardeen stepped into the Pair O' Dice a moment later, he saw a tall, broad-shouldered man standing at the bar, holding a beer. Shardeen had never seen Matt Jensen before, but he knew about him, and he had heard him described, so he was reasonably certain this was the man he was looking for.

He decided to make sure, so he called the bartender down. "Hey, Cheatum, would that feller standin' down there be the one they call Matt Jensen?"

"Yes it is," Cheatum replied. "You want a drink?"

"I don't need no drink for what I've got in mind. *Hey you, Matt Jensen!*" Shardeen's shout was loud and angry.

Matt didn't turn.

"I'm talkin' to you, Jensen."

Matt turned his head then, and saw an incredibly ugly man standing at the other end of the bar. "What can I do for you?"

"You're going to die!"

"I expect I will," Matt replied. He smiled and lifted his beer toward Shardeen. "You know it's true what they say. No one gets out of life alive." His response was in a conversational tone.

"Did you hear me? I said you was goin' to die," Shardeen repeated.

"Yes, I heard you. Tell me, sir, is there any particular reason you would like to talk about dying?"

This was a new experience for Shardeen. At this point in any previous confrontation, his adversary was showing fear, and their fear always played to his advantage. It was quite evident that Matt Jensen wasn't afraid of him.

"Yeah, there is. The reason I brung it up is on account of you're goin' to die *today*. I've come to kill you."

"Have you now? Well, I suppose that would be information I should know, and I do appreciate you telling me. But I must ask, did you come alone? Or did you bring others with you?"

"No, why would I need anyone else? I can get the job done all by myself."

"You think so, do you? Well, when you set out to do

a job like this, I suppose it is good to be confident in one's own abilities."

While still holding the beer mug in his gun hand, Matt turned fully and faced Shardeen.

"They say that you're real good with a gun," Shardeen said. "Is that true? Are you real good with a gun?"

"Oh, I'm pretty good," Matt replied. "But then I'm also a good rider, a good roper, and I'm a pretty good at mumblety-peg." Matt chuckled. "I can't sing though. I've tried a few times, and my friends tell me I sound like a heifer with her foot hung up in a strand of barbed wire." He laughed.

"What's wrong with you? Are you some kind of a fool? Didn't you hear what I said, mister? I said I've come to kill you and all you want to do is stand there 'n talk about nonsense!" Shardeen shouted, his challenge a loud bluster.

By now the little man's belligerence told the others in the saloon that shooting was imminent, and they might be best served by making certain they weren't in the line of fire when the shooting broke out.

"May I give you a word of advice? Don't try me," Matt said.

He was still holding the mug of beer in his gun hand, and that give Shardeen a boost of confidence. "Don't try you? Don't try you?"

The saloon had grown deathly still as the patrons and the three bar girls stood well out of the way, quietly, nervously, and yet titillated by the life-and-death drama that had suddenly begun to unfold in front of them.

Shardeen turned to address the others. "Did you folks hear that? He said 'don't try me.' I suppose he thinks I should just quake in my boots because I am in the presence of the great Matt Jensen."

"Did DuPont send you here to challenge me?" Matt asked.

"DuPont? No, he don't even know I've come to town. But he'll know about it before this day is out. Ever'body will know about it, and I figure by me a-killin' the great Matt Jensen, why the price of my gun is going to go up."

"The price of your gun?"

"Yeah, I sell my gun for a livin'. 'N I do pretty good at it, too."

"You do pretty well, huh? What is your name?"

"What is my name? Are you kidding me, mister? Are you telling me you don't know who I am?"

Matt knew exactly who he was, but he also knew that Shardeen was a very vain man. To think that he wasn't recognized would agitate and unnerve him.

"No, I don't know your name. Should I?"

"The name is Shardeen. Angus Shardeen. I reckon you've heard of me."

"Yes, now that I think about it, I believe I have heard of you," Matt said.

Shardeen's smile broadened. "Yeah? What have you heard?"

"I've heard that you are an ugly, dried-up little pissant." Matt's smile was without humor. "I must say that the description of you doesn't do you justice. You are even uglier than I've heard."

Shardeen's smile quickly turned to an angry snarl. "Draw, Jensen!" he shouted, but he had given himself an advantage by going for his own gun even before he issued the challenge and while the beer mug was still in Jensen's gun hand.

Keeping his eyes on Matt Jensen's gun hand, he saw that Jensen didn't drop the beer mug, nor did he make any effort to go for his gun. Shardeen smiled in triumph as he brought his gun up, but his smile turned quickly to an expression of horror.

Matt's left hand had suddenly whipped forward and, in absolute panic, Shardeen saw a knife, point first, quickly close the distance between them. He felt the sharp pain as it plunged into his chest all the way to the hilt. With little more than muscle memory, he was able to pull the trigger, but the bullet managed to do nothing more than poke a hole in the floor.

Looking down at himself, Shardeen put his hand onto the handle of the knife as if he were going to pull it out, then he dropped his hand by his side and looked at Matt in disbelief. "A knife. You . . . you used a knife."

"Yeah, I did, didn't I? Well, I told you I was pretty good at mumblety-peg, and I don't know whether or not you know the game, but it uses a knife. Oh, but here I am trying explain a game when we should be talking about dying. That is what you wanted to talk about, isn't it?"

Shardeen coughed once, then he fell back against the bar, making an attempt to grab hold of it to keep himself erect. The attempt was unsuccessful, and he fell onto his back, his right arm stretched out beside him. His pistol was still connected to him only because his forefinger was hung up in the trigger guard.

Matt drained his mug, then set it on the bar before him. "Mr. Cheatum, I think I would like a refill."

"Sure thing, Mr. Jensen. It's coming right up, and

it's on me," Cheatum said, holding a new mug under the spigot on the keg to draw another beer.

When Sheriff Clark arrived a couple of minutes later, the bar was crowded with drinkers. A body with the knife still buried in its chest was lying on the floor.

"I'll be damned," Sheriff Clark said, surprised to see who it was. "That's Angus Shardeen."

"Yes, sir, that is the name he gave me," Matt said. "Come have a beer with me, Sheriff."

"Who killed Shardeen? Did you do it, Jensen?"

"I did."

Sheriff Clark stood there for a moment longer, looking down at the body. "I don't need to ask why you killed him. The gun in his hand is all the evidence I need, though I suppose most of you saw it."

"We all seen it, Sheriff," one of the patrons said. "'N I tell you the truth. It was the damndest thing any of us has ever saw."

"Clyde's tellin' you the truth, Sheriff. Shardeen there drawed on Jensen, 'n then, from nowhere it seems like, Jensen just kind of flung this knife . . . 'n, well, you can see what happened."

"Is that right, Cheatum?"

"It's just like Clyde and Frank is tellin', Sheriff," Cheatum replied.

Half a dozen others backed the bartender up.

Sheriff Clark shook his head slowly as he stood there staring at the body. "Angus Shardeen. I never thought anyone could beat him in a fair draw."

"Hell, there warn't nothin' fair about it," Cheatum said. "Shardeen drawed on Jensen first, 'n not only that, he done it while Jensen was still a-holdin' onto his beer mug."

"Sheriff, the invitation to have a beer with me is still open," Matt said.

"Yeah," Sheriff Clark said as he stepped up to the bar. "Lonnie, give me a beer. I'm going to have a drink with my deputy."

Circle Dot Ranch

Bob Guthrie dipped a scoop of water from Jim Andrews's water bucket, took a drink, then continued with the reason for his visit. "How many head of cattle do you have?"

"Five hundred and three head," Jim replied.

"I'm runnin' just over three hunnert head, 'n Frank has another two hunnert 'n fifty. Poindexter has near a thousand. I was thinkin' we could maybe make us a gather 'n run 'em all down to Bitter Creek. It'd be easier runnin' 'em together now, than it would for us each to try 'n do it by our ownself."

"You may be right," Jim replied.

"He's dead! He's dead! Jensen kilt 'im! He's dead!"

At first the words shouted by Frank Edmonston from the back of a galloping horse were too indistinct to be heard. But he repeated it as he dismounted in front of the two men.

"Have you heard? Shardeen is dead. Matt Jensen kilt 'im."

"I'll be damned," Jim said. "Shardeen's dead, is he? Well, I don't think anyone will be mourning over that no-account little varmint."

"Was it a shoot-out?" Ernest Dean asked. "I sure woulda liked to seen that."

"Well, it warn't exactly a shoot-out," Edmonston said as he explained the details.

"I don't care if Shardeen got hit in the head with a shovel full of it," Jim said. "We're all a lot better off with him dead."

Straight Arrow Ranch

Sean O'Neil pulled the cork on a bottle of Glenlivet Scotch and poured a glass for Garrett Kennedy and himself. "According to everything we've been told, Shardeen was supposed to be the most deadly of all of DuPont's men. And yet this Jensen person made rather quick work of him."

"Yes, but apparently he tricked him," Kennedy replied. "He had a knife hidden, and he used it when Shardeen was expecting him to draw his gun."

"The result is the same," O'Neil said. "Shardeen is dead, and Jensen is alive."

"If this man Jensen was able to get the better of a killer like Shardeen, he may become quite a thorn in our side," Kennedy said.

"I think we are in no danger from him at the moment," O'Neil replied. "I'm sure he is more concerned with the Regulators than he is with us."

"But we use the Regulators."

"Yes, we *use* the Regulators, but we don't identify ourselves with them, and I think it is better if we keep as much separation between us and DuPont as we can. And as far as Shardeen is concerned, he did exactly what he was supposed to do."

"What do you mean, he did just what he was

supposed to do? He tried to kill Jensen, but wound up getting killed himself."

O'Neil smiled. "That is exactly my point. One of the reasons we accepted the offer of DuPont and the men of the Regulators to become our allies was so that that any actual confrontation that resulted in someone dying, the someone who died would be a Regulator instead of us. Shardeen is dead. We're not." He lifted his glass of scotch. "To Angus Shardeen."

Kennedy laughed out loud and lifted his own glass. "To Shardeen."

"You know, Garrett, it might not be a bad idea for us to find a replacement for Shardeen," O'Neil said.

"Oh, I'm sure DuPont will find one."

O'Neil shook his head. "No, I don't want DuPont to find one. I mean *we* should find Shardeen's replacement—not for DuPont, for us. I want someone who is as skilled with a gun, or perhaps even more so, and I want him answerable only to us. When the time comes for us to separate our interests from the Regulators, it will be easier to do so if we have such a man in our employ."

"Yes," Kennedy said. "Yes, I see what you mean. Do you have anyone in mind?"

"As a matter of fact, I do. The last time I was in Cheyenne I heard of someone called the Undertaker. He might just be our man."

"Wait, are you saying you want to hire an undertaker?" Kennedy asked.

O'Neil chuckled. "Not *an* undertaker, *the* Undertaker. His real name is Merlin Boggs, but he is a gunman and so proficient at his profession that many of his opponents wind up needing an undertaker, so people have taken to calling Boggs the Undertaker."

"Do you think we can get him to join us?" Kennedy asked.

"Yes, everyone has his price. But I'll have to go to Cheyenne to find him and find out just what his price might be."

"All right. You go see what you can do about getting him to come work for us. I'll take care of things here while you're gone."

Chapter Fifteen

"Papa, you're going to Cheyenne?" Colleen asked.
"Yes."

She smiled. "Please take me with you. It would be nice to get away for a few days."

O'Neil was packing his grip. "It's going to be business and you would just be in the way."

"I'm a grown woman, Papa. I won't be at your heels all the time. Please take me with you."

"No."

The disappointment showed on Colleen's face as she turned away from her father. Then she thought of Cooter. Without her father there to show his disapproval, she and Cooter could go riding together.

Two days after his confrontation with Shardeen, Matt returned to the Spur and Latigo Ranch. He was just dismounting when Lisa stepped out onto the porch to greet him.

"Hello, Matt, you're just in time for lunch," she invited.

"Is Hugh here?"

"No, he and the others are out on the South Range."

"Oh, uh, then I'd better not come in."

"Are you afraid of me, Matt?"

"What? No, I— Why would you ask that?"

Lisa laughed, and with a toss of her head and a brush of her hand, moved a fall of hair back from her face. "I'm teasing you. I have lunch ready to take out to the South Range for Hugh and the others. I thought you might like to come along and join us."

It was Matt's time to smile. "Well, if you put it that way, yes, I would like to ride out to the range with you."

"You could help if you would like, by hitching up the buckboard and bringing it around. By then I'll have my bread out of the oven."

Matt took the saddle off Spirit then turned him out into the corral. By the time he brought the buckboard back up to the main house, Lisa had stepped onto the porch, carrying two large baskets.

"Well, that was good timing," she said as she passed the baskets down to Matt, who put them in the back of the buckboard.

It was just under a mile from the house to where the men were working, and though there were no roads, the ground was flat and without obstructions so the buckboard rolled easily, making the trip in under ten minutes.

Matt was very aware of Lisa's close proximity to him. *What is wrong with me? Why am I reacting like this around Lisa? She's married, for crying out loud!*

"How long have you known my sister?" she asked.

It was an innocent question, but her voice was low, and though Matt wasn't familiar with the term *sensual*, he was certainly aware of the results that were generated by a sensual voice. Was she purposely using that tone of voice?

No, if Matt was honest with himself, he would say that this was no different from the way she always spoke. It was just that intimacy of their sharing the seat of the buckboard that made him much more aware. And he couldn't help but recall the other day when, just before he left, she had said, "You feel it too, don't you, Matt?"

He had not answered her question that day, but he was aware that his silence in response to her current question was getting uncomfortably long.

"Well, I met your sister very soon after I met Duff, and he and I have been friends for quite a while."

"How did you meet Duff?"

"I met Duff through Smoke."

"Smoke?"

"His real name is Kirby Jensen, but everyone calls him Smoke."

"Ahh, his name is Jensen. So you are related then."

"Not really. Smoke is a friend. My best friend, actually. He took me in when I was a young orphan, and he taught me everything I know. When I went out on my own, I took the name Jensen as my own name. I did it as a way of honoring him."

"Oh, what a wonderful thing for you to do," Lisa said, putting her hand on his arm.

The tips of her fingers burned him through his shirtsleeve.

"There they are," he said, glad to be able at that moment to point out Hugh and the others.

Ed Sanders was the first one to see them coming,

and even as they were driving up, they heard him call out, "Grub on the way!"

He, Hugh, Haverkost, and Patterson walked toward them.

"Look who showed up," Lisa said as she hopped down from the buckboard. "He was just in time for lunch, so I invited him to join us."

"Ha. If you ask me, he was just looking for a free meal," Haverkost teased.

As the men exchanged jocular comments, Lisa took a bedsheet from the back of the buckboard, unfolded it, and spread it out on the ground. A moment later, she had fried chicken, sliced bread, German potato salad, and a chocolate cake laid out for everyone.

"Have you heard anything from any of the Regulators about what happened between you and Shardeen?" Hugh asked as he took a piece of chicken. Because he was the boss, the others had waited patiently for him to get the first pick.

"No, nothing since the incident," Matt said.

"Well, I'll tell you what I've heard. I was in the mercantile yesterday 'n ever'one was talkin' about it." Sanders chuckled. "'N ever'one of 'em, to a man, was a-sayin' that Shardeen gettin' hisself kilt is 'bout the best thing to happen around here in a long time. 'Bout the only one upset about it is DuPont."

"Hugh, have you ever met Tyrone DuPont?" Matt asked.

"Yes, I've met him." Hugh tore off a piece of bread "I met him long before either one of us moved here."

"Really?" Matt said, surprised to hear that. "You mean you knew him from somewhere else?"

"I didn't say I knew him. I said I met him. It was three years ago on board the Mississippi riverboat *Delta Mist.* I had been hired to play the piano from St. Louis to New Orleans. Tyrone DuPont was a passenger on the boat, but he wasn't just a passenger. He was a gambler, making his living by fleecing the other passengers. He called it a game of chance, but there was very little chance involved. As it turned out, he was a notorious cheat and had already been banned from just about every boat on the river. I don't know how he came to be aboard the *Delta Mist.*

"At the time, though, we didn't know anything about him, and I say *we* because one of the people who played cards with him was Jason Stone, my manager. Jason got caught up in the game, and he wound up losing every cent we had been paid on the contract for me to play the piano." Hugh was quiet for a moment as if gathering his thoughts.

"Jason came to my stateroom to apologize," Hugh continued, "and he swore that he had been cheated. I believed him but I also—" Hugh stopped in the middle of his sentence and was quiet for a long moment. "I, uh, chastised him for it and pretty severely, too. After all, his intemperate actions had left us totally without funds.

"Oh, he was overcome with guilt, of course, and he apologized again, and I met this apology with absolute silence. When he saw that I couldn't be placated by anything he said, he quit trying, then he went to his own room."

Again, there was a long period of silence before Hugh resumed his story.

"The purser found him the next morning with a pistol in his hand and a bullet hole in his head. He had committed suicide in remorse, a remorse that his best friend had only intensified."

"Oh, Hugh," Lisa said, her face reflecting compassion for what he was sharing with them. She laid her hand on his arm. "Oh, Hugh, I'm so sorry. You've never told me that story."

"This is the first time I've ever told anyone the story. I've never had the courage to speak of it before. If I had been more sympathetic, if I had accepted his apology, I am convinced that he wouldn't have killed himself. He felt guilty for betraying my trust and yet, by far, the biggest betrayal was of my doing."

There was another long period of absolute silence as they all looked at Hugh, aware of the pain he was reliving in the telling of the story.

"Matt, the other day you asked me why I left the concert tour," Hugh said. "From the day I left that boat, I have never played professionally again."

"Hugh, I know that had to be hard on you. But it wasn't your fault," Matt replied.

"Yes, I know that Jason was responsible for his own fate, both the gambling and committing suicide. But I can't put the feeling of guilt aside."

Lisa lifted Hugh's hand and kissed it. "I'm so sorry."

There was a long moment before anyone spoke again.

It was Patterson who broke the extended silence with a question. "Do you think DuPont will get someone to replace Shardeen?"

"It looks to me like he's going to have to," Sanders said.

"I'm not all that sure that he will," Matt said.

"Why not?"

"A big part of DuPont's plan is to make everyone think that he and the Regulators are upholding the law. Shardeen was the total opposite of that. He was known far and wide as someone who sold his gun. That was the total opposite of how DuPont is trying to portray himself."

"But ain't you sold your gun to us?" Haverkost asked.

"Jake!" Patterson remanded him sharply.

"Well I don't mean nothin' bad by it, Leroy. I was just asking is all. I don't mean no offense, Mr. Jensen," Haverkost said quickly.

"No offense taken, Jake. Yes, I suppose some may call me a gunfighter, and I have often put my gun to use. But in every case, I have made certain that I chose the right side. You've been here for a while. You know what's going on around here. If you had to choose which side is in the right, and which side is in the wrong, which side would you choose?"

Jake smiled before he answered. "There ain't no need for me havin' to make a choice like that. I've done made that choice, 'n you have, too. 'N we both chose the right side."

Sanders laughed. "Haverkost, when I was in the army I seen privates try 'n get themselves out of situations that they let their big mouths got 'em into, but damn me if you didn't get yourself out of this 'n just about as slick as any private I've ever seen."

"What do you think is the most likely reaction DuPont will have over the loss of his gunfighter?" Hugh asked.

"I'm not sure," Matt replied. "But if I had to guess, I would say that he is going to try and do something to prove that he is still in control, even if he doesn't have Shardeen around anymore.

"This is the prettiest part of the whole ranch," Colleen said as she spread out the picnic lunch on a precipice that overlooked the twisting river.

"Nah, it isn't the prettiest," Cooter said.

"Really? Well, I would like to know what part of the ranch is prettier."

A broad smile preceded Cooter's reply. "That's easy. Anyplace you are is the prettiest place on the ranch."

Colleen's laughter reminded Cooter of tinkling wind chimes. "Now, Cooter Gregory, just what do you expect to get from such flattery?"

"A piece of that apple pie you brought?" Cooter said.

"Oh? Well, I must say that I'm disappointed."

"Why are you disappointed?"

"I thought maybe you might want a kiss."

"Oh, Miss O'Neil . . ."

"Cooter, if you are going to kiss me, don't you think it's about time you started calling me Colleen?"

"Colleen," Cooter said, though the word was smothered by the kiss.

Chapter Sixteen

Morning Star Saloon, Cheyenne, Wyoming

"Boggs!" The name exploded in a loud shout, and with enough provocation to get the attention of everyone in the saloon. The piano player turned away from his keys, and not only did the music stop, but so too did all conversation. The bartender who had just taken down a bottle to pour a drink stood still.

Boggs, who was the target of the shout, was standing at the bar, and he made no reaction to the challenge.

"I'm what you might call a bounty hunter, Boggs, 'n there's paper out on you. A thousand dollars it is, for anyone that brings in the feller they call the Undertaker. That's you, ain't it Boggs? You're the Undertaker, 'n I aim to collect on it. Take out your gun real slow 'n let it drop to the floor, 'n I'll let you live. Try anythin', 'n I'll kill you right there where you stand."

Merlin Boggs was leaning on the bar with his back to the man who had just challenged him. He didn't have to turn around. He could see the bounty hunter in the mirror.

"And who might you be?" Boggs's voice was low

and sibilant, once described as sounding like the hiss of a rattlesnake.

"The name is Rufus Stallings. I reckon you've heard of me."

"I reckon I have," Boggs replied.

"But it don't really make no never mind what my name is. When I go to collect my reward, your name is all that is important."

"Your name is important too," Boggs said. "I expect the undertaker will need to know what name to put on your tombstone."

Stallings laughed, though it was a forced laugh. "The Undertaker talking about an undertaker. That's just real funny. But you know what's even funnier? The Undertaker bein' buried by an undertaker."

In the mirror, Boggs could see that many of the other saloon patrons, having overheard the chilling conversation between the two men, were beginning to move toward the sides of the room. One of the saloon patrons wasn't moving, though. He was standing back as if he were an observer only, but Boggs saw that, like Stallings, he was holding a gun in his hand. The only difference was that Stallings was pointing his gun directly at Boggs's back, while the other man was holding his gun down by this side, doing so in a way that it wouldn't be obvious.

"Are you plannin' on shootin' me in the back?"

"You don't understand, do you Boggs? You're wanted dead or alive. It don't really make no never mind to the law how you're kilt, just as long as I bring you in."

"Can I turn around?"

"Are you sayin' you'd rather be a-lookin' at me when I kill you?" Stallings asked.

"Yeah, somethin' like that."

"Sure, turn around. I don't mind bein' the last thing you'll look at on the face of this earth."

Boggs turned to face his adversary.

"Put your hands up," Stallings ordered.

"Why? You're going to shoot me anyway, aren't you?"

Stallings chuckled. "I am at that."

Stallings lifted his hand slightly and started to pull the hammer back. Then to the shock of Stallings and everyone else in the room, Boggs drew and fired. Even as the first bullet was plunging into Stallings's chest, Boggs whipped his gun around to aim at Stallings's partner, who, astonished by what he had just seen, was just raising his own pistol, thinking to have the advantage of surprise.

Boggs fired a second time and Stallings's partner went down, as well.

For a long moment Merlin Boggs stood there holding the smoking gun, studying the faces of all the others. Seeing awe and fear, but no challenge, he returned his pistol to his holster, then turned back to the bar to pick up his drink.

"Mr. Boggs, that's the damndest thing I've ever seen in my entire life." The bartender smiled. "Why, what you just done will make the Morning Star Saloon famous. I'll sell twice as many drinks in here."

"Anyone want to tell us what all the shootin' was about?" someone asked loudly. Looking toward the questioner, Boggs saw that two men wearing the uniform of the Cheyenne Police Department had just entered the saloon.

"Hello, Sergeant Martel." The bartender pointed to the two men on the floor. "That one is Rufus

Stallings. I don't know the name of that one over there, but since Stallings is . . . that is . . . *was* a bounty hunter, I expect that one is, too. Anyhow, both of 'em tried to shoot Mr. Boggs in the back."

"Yeah, bounty hunters like to do that, I hear. You got paper out on you, Boggs? Not that it would matter none to Enos or me," he added, indicating the other uniformed officer who had come into the saloon with him. "Bein' as we're policemen, we couldn't collect anything anyway."

"Who drew first?" Enos asked.

"I would say Stallings," the bartender said. "Only he didn't draw, seein' as he already had his gun out. That one over there, too, both of 'em already had their guns in their hands before Boggs drew."

Enos nodded and looked over toward his partner. "There's nothin' for us here."

The two policemen left the saloon, and as Boggs drank quietly, the other patrons buzzed in excitement.

Sean O'Neil had been in Cheyenne less than two hours before he heard the story of the shoot-out between Merlin Boggs and Rufus Stallings and Aaron Till.

"Bam, bam," the speaker was saying in his animated telling of the story. "I mean them two shots was right on top of one another, 'n the next thing you knowed, why Stallings 'n Till—Till, that was the other feller's name—they was lyin' stretched out on the floor, both of 'em deader 'n doornails. 'N they wasn't standin' right next to each other when the shootin' commenced, neither."

"Who was the shooter?" O'Neil asked, imposing himself into the conversation even though the dialogue was between two men who were standing together several feet down the bar from him.

"What?" one of them asked.

"The shooter you were talking about. Would that have been the one they call the Undertaker?"

"Yeah, it was. Do you know him, mister? I swear I ain't never seen nothin' like it."

"Is he still in town? I like to keep up with old friends."

"Yeah, just before I came in here I seen 'im a-goin' into the Palace Café to take his supper. More 'n likely he's still there."

"Thank you," O'Neil said. He put a dollar on the bar. "Barkeep, give these two gentlemen free drinks as long as the money lasts."

"Why, thank you, mister!" the informative one replied happily.

When O'Neil stepped into the Palace Café a couple of minutes later, he had planned to ask around to locate Boggs, but he didn't have to. Sitting at a table in the far corner of the room with his back to the wall was a slim, wiry man. He was better dressed than most of the others in the café, with black polished boots and large-roweled Mexican spurs.

O'Neil instinctively knew this would be the man he was looking for. When he approached the table the man looked up, appraising him with cool, green eyes.

"You got somethin' in mind?"

The hissing sound of his voice so unnerved O'Neil that he hesitated for just a second before he spoke. "Would you like a job?"

"I ain't particular lookin' for work."

"There's no work involved."

"What kind of job is it where there's no work?"

"One that pays well," O'Neil replied. "It is a job that I believe you would be very good at, Mr. Boggs."

"You're hiring my gun, ain't you?"

"Yes."

"You said it pays well. I don't come cheap, so just how well is *well*?"

"The pay is fifty dollars a week, and bonuses."

"Where is this job?"

"Up on the Sweetwater."

"What's your name?"

"I'm Sean O'Neil. My partner Garrett Kennedy and I own the Straight Arrow Ranch there."

"Do I have time to finish my supper?"

O'Neil nodded. "Yes, the next train doesn't leave for another hour."

"Go buy me a new hat. I'll meet you at the depot before the train leaves. You can give me my hat then."

"You want me to buy you a new hat?" O'Neil was surprised by the request.

"Yeah, you can call it one of them bonuses you was talkin' about."

"All right. I'll buy you a new hat."

"I want it black with a low crown, sorta like this 'un," Boggs said, picking up a hat that had obviously seen better days. He removed the silver band and handed it to O'Neil. "Put this around it."

O'Neil started to leave, then turned and looked back at Boggs. "Before we close this deal, I need to ask you about a couple of men—Matt Jensen and Tyrone DuPont. Have you ever heard of either of them?"

"I ain't never heard of DuPont, but I have heard of Matt Jensen."

"What have you heard about Jensen?"

"I've heard that he's damn good with a gun."

"Are you as good as he is?"

"I may be."

"I need you to be as good as he is. Actually, I need you to be better than he is."

Boggs chuckled. "No, you don't."

"What do you mean, I don't?"

"If you're plannin' on me goin' up agin Jensen, then *I* need me to be better 'n he is."

"Yes," O'Neil said. "I see what you mean."

"Who is this DuPont feller? Will I be goin' up agin him as well?"

"I don't know," O'Neil said. "He is supposed to be our friend, but conditions might change. If our relationship becomes adversarial, then I shall expect you to be the advocate of my partner and me. But should that happen, I think you'll have no problem with him."

"You got fifty dollars on you now?"

"Yes, I have fifty dollars. Why do you ask?"

"I'd like my first week's pay now. Just to show me that you can pay me what you're offerin'."

O'Neil nodded, then drew his billfold from his pocket and pulled out two twenties and a ten and handed the money to Boggs.

"You ought not to walk around a-carryin' so much money," Boggs said. "I could kill you 'n take the rest."

"You would be a very foolish man to kill the goose that lays the golden eggs," O'Neil said with an easy smile.

Boggs chuckled. "Yeah, I would, wouldn't I?"

Chapter Seventeen

Spur and Latigo Ranch

"I haven't seen Jim so excited over anything in a long time as he is over this horse he is getting from Hugh," Mary Ella said.

Mary Ella and Lisa were having coffee together on the small table in the kitchen. Jim had declared his intention of buying a horse, and he and Hugh were out looking at them.

"Hugh is excited about it as well." Lisa chuckled. "He almost always finds a horse that he particularly likes, then when we have to take them to market, he worries that the horse will find a good home. With Jim, he knows this horse will find a good home."

"Hugh has been a good friend to Jim, and you have been a good friend to me." Mary Ella sighed and shook her head slightly. "The funny thing is, when I was a schoolteacher and my husband was vice president of the bank, we had people that I thought were my friends. We took part in all the social functions. I was even president of the Women's Club of Hays City, if you can believe that. Then, when Garland did what he did, well, you know what happened.

Everything went downhill from there until I wound up a common whore."

"Trust me, Mary Ella, you may have been a prostitute, but there's nothing common about you. And don't think that I'm your only friend here. I know for a fact that the other ranchers' and farmers' wives consider you a friend. It's just the so-called *ladies* of the town who look down their noses at you."

"Thank you for saying that."

"Besides, I may wind up in the same boat as you." The tone of Lisa's voice had gone from uplifting to somber.

Mary Ella got a confused expression on her face. "Lisa, what on earth are you talking about?"

"I'm talking about Matt Jensen."

"What? What about him?"

"I . . . oh, Mary Ella, I love Hugh, I really do. But there is something about Matt Jensen that—I can't explain it, but I am so drawn to him."

"Lisa, I'm older than you are, and I think you will be the first to admit that I have a lived a life that, well, let's just say that I am a lot more experienced than you are. Life is sometimes difficult and we are often faced with temptations, temptations to do something that is not like who we really are. You are only human. Hugh is considerably older than you are, and, let's face it, Matt is a very handsome young man. Even I can see that.

"All I can say is, don't feel guilty for having thoughts and feelings, but please take my advice and *don't give in to them.*" Mary Ella said, stressing the last five words. "Remember, Hugh loves you, and you have said yourself that you love him. A good marriage is much too valuable a commodity to throw away."

Mary Ella reached across the table to take Lisa's

hand in hers. Mary Ella's eyes filmed with tears. "I just wish I had the opportunity to have one."

"You can." The tone of Lisa's voice was once again more upbeat. "I know how you can do it, and we'll plan it together."

It was about an hour before Hugh and Jim returned to the house, and during that hour Lisa had not only explained her idea to Mary Ella, but the two women had expanded upon the idea until they came up with a proposal to which both had agreed.

"Mary Ella, I have found the most wonderful horse!" Jim said excitedly when the two men came in. "He's a chestnut, with a graceful neck and eyes that can look right into you. I've already picked out a name for him. I'm going to call him Bosun, as in Boatswain's Mate."

"Oh, what a wonderful name for him!" Mary Ella said.

"I thought you might like it," Jim said with a proud smile. "So, what have you ladies been doing while we were gone?"

"Before I answer that, I have a question for you," Mary Ella said, with a pensive look on her face.

"Oh, you look serious."

"It's a serious question."

"All right, what is the question?"

"Will you marry me?"

"What?"

"It's a simple question, Jim, and it requires only a yes-or-no answer. Will you marry me?"

"Yes, of course I'll marry you!" Jim literally shouted with a broad, happy smile on his face. But the smile quickly faded, to be replaced with a questioning expression. "But how can we?"

"Oh, don't you worry about that," Lisa said. "Mary Ella and I have got it all worked out."

Jim turned to Hugh. "Hugh, do you have any idea what this is about?"

"No," Jim said. "But Lisa says she has it all worked out, so if I were you, I would start deciding on what to wear for the wedding."

Straight Arrow Ranch

Shortly after O'Neil returned from Cheyenne, he and Kennedy sent one of their ranch hands out to Purgatory Pass to take a message.

Rodney Gibson was getting twenty dollars to deliver the message, and though twenty dollars was a goodly sum, he wasn't all that comfortable with the job. He had been told exactly how to approach the hideout so that he wouldn't be shot. Of course, technically it wasn't a hideout. The Regulators were supposed to be lawmen, and O'Neil had referred to the place where they were staying as a *headquarters*, not a hideout.

Gibson rode east for several minutes after the *V* of Purgatory Pass came into view, then he stopped and held his arms out straight to either side. He held them there until it began to hurt, but just when he felt he couldn't hold them any longer, a rider came toward him. He recognized the rider as Moe Greene.

"Hello, Moe."

"What are you doin' out here?"

"I've brought a message from Mr. Kennedy and Mr. O'Neil to give to Mr. DuPont."

Moe Greene extended his hand. "Give it to me. I'll give it to him."

"No, sir," Gibson said, drawing the message back. "They said for me to give it to 'im personal."

"If you don't give me the message, he won't get it."

"That don't matter none to me," Gibson said. "I've already been give my twenty dollars for comin' out here. I'll just go back 'n tell 'em you wouldn't let me come in." He turned to ride away.

Greene called out to him. "No, wait. There ain't no need in you goin' back. Come on, I'll take you in."

Of the two buildings inside the gorge, the seven Regulators who remained after the death of Shardeen shared the larger building. DuPont had the smaller building all to himself. He was drinking coffee when Greene brought Gibson in to see him.

"You're one of the Straight Arrow riders, ain't you?" DuPont asked.

"Yes, sir."

"What are you doin' out here?"

"Mr. Kennedy 'n Mr. O'Neil wanted me to bring you a message."

"Yeah? What is it?"

"I don't know. He wrote it out 'n put in in this envelope. I didn't figure it was my place to read it."

"You prob'ly figured right," DuPont said, holding out his hand for the note. He read the message.

It is imperative that you come see us as soon as possible.

Kennedy and O'Neil

To DuPont that had the feel of being summoned, and he had no intention of being summoned by anyone. "You go back and tell Kennedy 'n O'Neil—" He stopped in midsentence. He had a good thing going with the two ranchers, too good to let it go just because he was irritated with them.

"Never mind. I'll tell them myself. Wait until I get my horse saddled."

"Yes, sir, I'll wait," Gibson said.

For some reason DuPont seemed irritated by the note. Whatever the note said was of no concern to Gibson. He was just a cowboy, drawing twenty and found. It would be best to let the highfalutin people like DuPont, Kennedy, and O'Neil work it out among themselves.

"They want me to come see 'em," DuPont said half an hour later as the two men were riding back to the Straight Arrow Ranch. "What's this about, Gibson?"

"I don't have no idea," he replied. "Like I told you, I didn't even know what was in the note. All I know is they give me twenty dollars to carry it out here to you."

"What if I had decided I didn't want to come in?" DuPont asked.

"Iffen you hada decided that you wasn't goin' to come, all I woulda done was ride back 'n tell ''m I give you the note like I was s'sposed to 'cause it don't matter none to me, personal, whether you come see 'em or not."

"I reckon you're right about that. But I'm sort of a curious kind of a feller, so I guess I woulda come anyhow just to see what this is all about. Which is just what I'm a-doin'," he added.

When they reached the big house of the Straight Arrow Ranch, Gibson held his hand out toward DuPont's horse. "I done got my twenty dollars, so there really ain't no need for me to be a-goin' in there to talk to the bosses. Iffen you'd like me to, I'll see to your horse to get 'im some food 'n water."

"Yeah, thanks," DuPont said as he dismounted.

His first thought once he stepped into the office was to let Kennedy and O'Neil know that he did not appreciate being summoned like a schoolboy. He held that thought in check when he saw a third man.

Something about him activated the old policeman instinct in DuPont. He stared at the man, who returned the stare with unblinking eyes.

"Mr. DuPont, thank you for coming," Kennedy said.

DuPont tried to read the faces of Kennedy and O'Neil, but their expressions told him nothing. The expression on the face of the third man was a little easier to read. It was one of smug confidence.

But smug confidence about what? he wondered.

"Is there any need for this man to be here listenin' in to whatever it is we got to talk about?" DuPont asked, nodding toward the third man.

"He is the reason we asked you to come meet with us," Kennedy said. "Mr. DuPont, this is Merlin Boggs."

"Boggs? Is he the one they call the Undertaker?"

"Indeed he is. I thought it would be a good idea for the two of you to meet."

The expression on Boggs's face didn't change, and he made no effort to extend his hand in welcome.

"Yeah, I've heard about him. He's a gunfighter, ain't he?" DuPont asked, purposely talking about him as if he weren't in the room.

Boggs made no show of irritation over the obvious snub.

"He is indeed a gunfighter, and quite a good one

at that," Kennedy said. "And that's why he's here. I think you would agree that with Shardeen gone, we are quite likely at a disadvantage as it might relate to this new champion of Hugh Conway and the small ranchers. That's why Mr. O'Neil and I have just hired Boggs."

"Yeah, well if it's all the same to you, I'll do m' own hirin'. I'm lookin' for someone to replace Shardeen, that's true enough, but there ain't no need of you a-doin' it."

"Oh, by all means, Mr. DuPont, yes, do find your own replacement for Shardeen, but I think you may have misunderstood what I'm saying. Mr. Boggs isn't a replacement for Shardeen, and he won't be working for you, nor will he, in any way, be answerable to you and the Regulators. Merlin Boggs is an employee of the Straight Arrow Ranch and, as such, he will be answerable only to Mr. O'Neil and me."

"Yeah, you're right I don't understand," DuPont said. "Why would you want to hire a gunfighter like Boggs? I mean if it's for protection, ain't that what you got the Regulators for?"

"Indeed it is," Kennedy said. "But you might say that Mr. Boggs is just a second layer of protection, so to speak."

DuPont was quiet for a long moment, then he glanced over at Boggs again. The gunfighter had not spoken a word, changed the expression on his face, nor given any indication that he was paying attention to the discussion, even though it was about him.

"Is this the only reason you asked me to come in to see you?" DuPont asked.

"Yes. I wanted to extend you the courtesy of letting you know about our newest employee."

"Courtesy?"

"Yes, of course."

DuPont gave a curt nod of his head. "All right, I know."

"That was DuPont?" Boggs asked after DuPont left.

"Yes, Tyrone DuPont," Kennedy said.

"He don't seem like all that much to me."

"Individually, I'm sure he isn't very much. He is certainly not good enough to be of any worry to you," O'Neil said. "But you can't think of him as an individual."

"What are you talking about?"

"DuPont has a group of men riding for him. They can be quite deadly, and they are intensely loyal," Kennedy said.

"That's the Regulators you are talking about?"

"Yes," Kennedy replied. "And though not a single man among them can hold a match to you, every one of them is experienced in, let us say, armed confrontation. And all of them together would be most formidable, especially as they are quite well led. Mr. DuPont was once a police officer in St. Louis, so he is well schooled in the concepts of leadership and discipline."

"So what you have to do is make certain you don't ever have to face any more than one of them at a time," O'Neil added.

"If they're workin' for you, why is it I'd ever have to face any of 'em, even DuPont?" Boggs asked.

"Why indeed?" Kennedy asked. "Let us hope that you never will have to. It's just that the first loyalty of every one of the Regulators is to DuPont. And the first loyalty of DuPont is to himself. I want someone whose first loyalty is to Mr. O'Neil and me."

"You'll have my third loyalty," Boggs said.

"Third?" Kennedy asked with an expression of surprise and disapproval on his face.

Boggs smiled, the smile making him appear even more evil. "My first loyalty is to me, my second is to the money you will be paying me, and my third loyalty will be to you."

Kennedy laughed. "All right, Mr. Boggs. I think that arrangement would be quite acceptable."

Later in the day, O'Neil found the occasion to be speaking with his daughter. "Is it true what I have heard about you and Cooter Gregory?"

"I don't know whether it's true or not. It depends on what you've heard."

"I've heard that you have been keeping company with him."

"I have."

"I would rather you not spend time with a common cowboy."

"There is nothing at all common about Cooter. He is very smart, I would trust him with my life, and he is one of the nicest men I have ever known. Besides, he isn't just a cowboy. He is the foreman of the largest ranch in the valley. The truth is, you and Mr. Kennedy own the ranch, but Cooter is the one who actually runs it."

"I'm sure you can find someone more appropriate."

"Where? Who in town would be a more appropriate person for me to keep company with?"

"I . . . I don't know."

"Then I shall continue to keep company with Cooter," Colleen said defiantly.

Chapter Eighteen

Rongis

"His name is Merlin Boggs," Sheriff Clark told Matt. "But they call him the Undertaker. Have you ever heard of him?"

"Yes, I've heard of him."

"I thought maybe you had. I figure that all you fellas that's really good with a gun prob'ly sort of keep up with one another. Have you ever seen or met 'im?"

"I've never met him, and if I've ever seen him, I'm unaware of it."

"Well, I expect you will meet him soon enough. He's come to the valley."

"Is he the one DuPont got to take Shardeen's place?"

"Uh-uh," Clark said as he shook his head. "And that's the strange of it. Boggs won't be ridin' none with DuPont. He'll be working for Kennedy and O'Neil."

"That *is* interesting."

"Yeah, but you got to wonder why that is. I mean what will he be doin'? Anything that Kennedy or

O'Neil need done with guns or just plain bein' rough on someone can be done by DuPont and The Regulators."

"Perhaps Kennedy and O'Neil feel control slipping away from them," Matt said. "There's a story about a man that got on board a bucking bull. 'Why are you ridin' that bull, John?' someone shouted at him. "I'm ridin' this bull 'cause I can't get off,' John yelled back."

Sheriff Clark chuckled. "I see what you mean. What you're sayin' is, Kennedy and O'Neil might be havin' second thoughts about gettin' hooked up with DuPont, but they can't figure out a way to let go. So they got this Boggs feller to be on their side just in case DuPont and his boys starts a-turnin' on 'em.

"But the truth of it is, I reckon you could be tellin' that about me, couldn't you?" Clark added. "I mean here I was, hooked up with DuPont 'n all them men he's got a-ridin' with him, 'n there didn't seem like nothin' I could do about it till you come along. Kennedy 'n O'Neil have got Merlin Boggs, 'n I have you."

"You've got me," Matt said with a little chuckle.

"But you've also lined yourself up with the small ranchers and farmers, and Boggs is with the biggest landowner in the county. That sort of puts you 'n the Undertaker at cross-purposes, don't it?"

"I suppose it does," Matt admitted.

"Which means there ain't hardly no way that you 'n Boggs ain't goin' to come agin each other. So, here is my question for you. If it comes down to a fight betwixt you 'n Boggs, do you think you can handle 'im?"

"There's only one way to answer that question. If it

comes to a confrontation between us, I'll *have* to handle him, won't I?"

"Yeah," Sheriff Clark said. "Yeah, I reckon you will at that."

The next morning a slight breeze filled the muslin curtains of the open window and lifted them out over the wide-planked floor of the hotel room. Matt moved to the window and looked out over the town, which was just beginning to awaken. Water was being heated behind the laundry, and boxes were being stacked behind the grocery store. A team of four big horses was pulling a fully loaded freight wagon down the main street.

From somewhere, Matt could smell bacon frying and his stomach growled, reminding him that he was hungry. He splashed some water in the basin, washed his face and hands, then put on his hat and went downstairs. There were a couple of people in the lobby, one napping in one of the chairs, the other reading a newspaper. Neither of them paid any attention to Matt as he left the hotel.

The morning sun was bright, but not yet hot. The sky was clear and the air was crisp. As he walked toward the café, he heard sounds of commerce—the ring of a blacksmith's hammer, a carpenter's saw, and the rattle of working wagons. That was opposed to last night's sounds of liquor bottles, off-key singing, laughter, and boisterous conversations. How different the tenor of a town was between the business of morning and the play of evening.

Half an hour later, Matt was enjoying a breakfast of

bacon, eggs, fried potatoes, and biscuits and gravy when a boy of about sixteen came to his table.

"Mr. Jensen, I got your horse saddled 'n brung 'im here to the café like you asked." The boy smiled. "Spirit sure is a good horse."

"Yes, he is. Thank you, Joey," Matt said, giving the boy a fifty-cent piece.

"Thank you!" Joey replied with a happy smile.

"I've noticed you over at the livery stable. You're very good with horses."

"Yes, sir, thank you. I reckon I'm good with horses on account of I've been around them most of my life."

"You've worked at the livery that long?"

"No, I ain't always worked for Mr. McGill. Time was when my pa and ma and me run a ranch. It wasn't a very big ranch, but since Pa and me didn't have no hands, it was just the right size for us to run alone. But that's all gone now. Pa couldn't pay the loan at the bank, 'n somehow Mr. Kennedy 'n Mr. O'Neil wound up with the ranch. My pa got so upset he died of the apoplexy. It warn't long after that before my ma died of a heart that was broke."

"I'm real sorry to hear that, Joey."

"Yes, sir, me too. But Mr. McGill has give me a job, 'n he's been just real good to me, so I reckon things could be worse."

After breakfast, Matt got a haircut and a bath, changed into his clean shirt and pants, then took the ones he had been wearing to the laundry. Lisa had offered to do his laundry for him, but he had declined.

"Matt, it means nothing," she'd told him. "I do the laundry for Mr. Sanders, and for Patterson and

Haverkost, as well for Hugh. One more set of clothes wouldn't matter."

"I can get them done in town," Matt had said.

He knew that Lisa was right, if she did the clothes for the hired hands, doing his might not mean anything to her. But it would be one more connection that might further complicate a situation that was already somewhat problematic.

Lisa was too vulnerable right now, and Matt knew that even if she wasn't married, there would be no chance for any kind of a real relationship between them. He was a drifter; his lifestyle didn't lend itself to marriage. Eventually he would ride on, and when he did, she would be hurt.

He also had to think about the man they called the Undertaker. Matt knew that Boggs hadn't been hired as a cattle hand. He was here for one reason, and everyone in Sweetwater Valley knew what that reason was. He was here to kill Matt.

Matt had asked Joey to bring Spirit to him this morning because he planned to ride out to the Spur and Latigo to see how things were going. Hugh's horses would be moved to Bitter Creek when the time came, and once that was done he would make enough money to pay off all his debts, including the mortgage on his ranch. After that, Matt would be riding on to somewhere else.

Sanders greeted him when he rode into the yard. "Hello, Matt. Mr. Conway ain't come out yet this mornin'. You can go on in, I'll take care of Spirit for you."

"Thanks. You and Joey."

"Joey?"

"The young man who works for Maurice McGill at the livery," Matt said.

"Oh, yes, that would be Joey Dunaway."

Sanders led Spirit off to the barn and Matt started toward the house, met on the front porch by Hugh.

"Keith Dunaway was a good man," Hugh said after Matt told him of his conversation with Joey. "It's a shame what happened to him. He had a small ranch, Tumble D, where he ran about six or seven hundred head of cattle. Rustlers took half of his herd, his barn burned down in a mysterious fire, and then nature took over.

"A few years ago, beef prices began falling and much of the range was overgrazed because the Straight Arrow had built up a herd too large for the land. The summer was unusually hot and dry, and a drought hit. Even on ranges that hadn't been overgrazed, the grass died. Brushfires burned off even more. Water sources dried up.

"Then in November, the snow came. Day after day the snow came down, and the weather stayed so cold that there was little thawing, so the snow just kept piling higher and higher. By January, the drifts had filled the ravines and coulees to almost level. Temperatures dropped to thirty below, and it was even colder the next month.

"By spring, when it thawed, it was too late for Keith. He had so few cows left that even if he had been able to sell them at top dollar, he wouldn't have been able to make the payment due. That was when he learned that Kennedy and O'Neil were holding the mortgage to the Tumble D. They foreclosed, and Keith was dead within a month. Mrs. Dunaway died two months after that.

"Joey was fourteen then, and McGill gave him a job at the livery. He's been working there ever since." Hugh laughed. "He says that when he's older, he's going to buy back the Tumble D."

"You know what? I think he just might do that," Matt replied.

"Matt, you are going to the celebration at the Circle Dot, aren't you?" Lisa asked, joining the men.

"What celebration?"

"Jim and Mary Ella are getting married next week," she said with a broad smile.

"Well, good for them. They found a preacher who would read the words over them, did they?"

"No."

"Then I don't understand. How is it that they are getting married?"

Hugh laughed. "You can thank Lisa for that. She figured out how they could do it."

"They are just going to declare themselves married in front of all their friends."

Matt laughed. "Why not? It works for me."

"Hugh is going to play the piano for them."

"That is, if we can get the piano moved over there. It's pretty heavy," Hugh said.

"Can you count on Ed, LeRoy, and Jake?" Matt asked.

"Yes, of course."

"Well, I'll help too, and that'll be four of us."

"No, five of us," Hugh said.

"You're the piano player. You're the one who should be directing us on how it should be done."

Chapter Nineteen

From the *Red Desert Gazette:*

**NUPTIALS TO BE SPOKEN
THURSDAY NEXT**

*Jim Andrews and Mary Ella Wilson
to Be Wed*

Friends and neighbors are invited to the Circle Dot Ranch for the purpose of celebrating the marriage of Jim Andrews and Mary Ella Wilson. While this may not be a traditional marriage in that unique circumstances will not permit it to be celebrated by a man of the cloth, it will be validated by the expressions of love that the two will share.

Those who attend the wedding, for a wedding it shall be, will be treated to music appropriate to the occasion as performed by Mr. Hugh Conway, who has been acclaimed as one of the finest concert pianists in America.

This editor is pleased to use the GAZETTE

as a means of publicly expressing his congratulations and best wishes to the couple.

As Art Walhausen was having his dinner in the Palace Café, he looked up to see three women coming toward him. He recognized one of them as Marie Goodbody, who was the president of the Ladies League. She was a frequent visitor to the newspaper, generally with complaints. She was opposed to the saloons, to the dance hall, to any visiting theatrical group, and even to the annual Founders Day parade. The expression on her face was a clear indication that she had something else to complain about, and Art was pretty sure he knew what the complaint would be.

"Hello, Mrs. Goodbody. What's on your mind?" he asked as she and the other two women stormed through the restaurant, stopping at his table.

"This!" Mrs. Goodbody said, dropping the newspaper on the table. It was folded in such a way as to show the article about Jim and Mary Ella. "How dare you write such a glowing article about this . . . this perfectly disgusting event that is going to take place out at the Circle Dot next Thursday? I don't know what to call it when a man and his whore make some sort of public declaration that they are going to live together, but you certainly cannot call it a wedding."

"Am I to take it by your comment that you won't be coming to the marriage ceremony? Would you like me to give them your regrets?" Art asked.

"What? Why . . . I never!" Mrs. Goodbody exclaimed angrily. "Come, ladies!"

The three women turned sharply, then walked briskly from the restaurant with as sour an expression on their faces as they had been wearing when they came in.

Art couldn't help but chuckle.

"Good for you!" a young woman's voice said, and she augmented her comment by applauding lightly.

Looking up, Art saw Jennie Lou Jones—or at least, that was the name she was known by at the Pair O' Dice.

"Hello, Jennie Lou. If you are here for dinner, I would love to share my table with you. I don't often get to eat with a pretty young woman."

"Thank you. I've already eaten, but I would be happy to sit with you for a minute or two. And you don't even have to buy me a drink," she added with a broad smile.

"Your company is always pleasant, Jennie Lou, whether I have to buy you a drink or not."

She chuckled. "Why, thank you. And thank you for writing that story about Mary Ella and Mr. Andrews."

"They're good people, and I was pleased to do so."

"I don't think, no, I *know* that the average person has no idea what a good person Mary Ella is. Why, I've seen her write letters for poor cowboys who don't know how to read or write. And last year when Linda was sick and nobody would go into her room because they were afraid they would catch it, why, Mary Ella took her food and stayed in her room to take care of her."

"Yes, I've heard of some of the good deeds she has done," Art said. "And I know that she helped some people of the town without them even knowing she had helped. Mary Ella came to the newspaper office with money for me to give without letting anyone know where it came from."

Art was silent for a moment. "The bitter irony of that story is that, in some cases, the people she helped in such a way are the very people who are turning against her now."

"You should tell them what Mary Ella has done for them."

Art shook his head. "No, Marry Ella asked me to keep it secret, and I won't betray her confidence."

"Mr. Walhausen, are you going to the wedding on Thursday?" Jennie Lou asked.

"Yes, I am."

"Would you please take me with you?"

Art smiled. "Why, Miss Jones, I would be pleased to take you with me."

On the day of the wedding, Hugh and Lisa drove over to the Circle Dot in the surrey. Matt rode Spirit alongside them, and Ed Sanders, LeRoy Patterson, and Jake Haverkost followed in the wagon that hauled the piano. Because they were bringing the piano and Hugh was going to play for the wedding, they were practically the first ones to arrive. Joey Dunaway had gotten there earlier and he came out to meet them.

"Good, you did bring the piano! Me 'n Mr. Andrews built a little platform where we can put it, 'n I'll help you unload it."

"Thanks, Joey, we can handle it," Ed said. "You just show us where this platform is, and tell us how close we can get the wagon to it."

"Why, you can back right up to it with no problem a-tall. Come on. I'll show you."

"While you men get the piano unloaded, I'm going to go see if Mary Ella needs any help," Lisa said.

* * *

The bride to be was sitting at the dresser, and she greeted Lisa with a warm smile. "Thanks for coming early."

"We had to come early to get the piano in place, but I would have wanted to come early anyway. Oh, Mary Ella, you look beautiful!"

"Thank you. It's not the traditional wedding dress." Mary Ella chuckled. "But then, what is traditional about this marriage? No church full of people, that's for sure."

"No church, that's true, but you are going to have a lot of guests today. I've already spoken with many of them."

"Is it safe to assume that Mrs. Goodbody won't be one of them?"

Lisa laughed. "Yes, I think that would be a safe assumption."

Guests began arriving over the next hour, mostly from the neighboring ranches and farms, but there were a few from town. Art Walhausen arrived not only with Jennie Lou but also with Lonnie Cheatum and Missy Crews from the Pair O' Dice. To the surprise of several, Sheriff Clark arrived as well.

It was no surprise that neither Kennedy nor O'Neil nor any of the Regulators arrived, but it was a surprise to see Colleen O'Neil, who arrived with Cooter Gregory.

"Miss O'Neil, you have come?" Lisa said.

"If my being here will make everyone uncomfortable, I'll leave," Colleen said. "But I saw the story in the paper, and I thought I would like to come and offer them my best wishes."

Lisa smiled. "You're welcome, and so is Mr. Gregory."

"Thank you," Colleen said, the expression in her voice showing her relief at being welcomed.

For the first several minutes, the ranchers and farmers discussed the current situation.

"This will be my last gathering," said Sylvester Malcolm, one of the area farmers.

"Sylvester, no. Try to stick it out just a little longer," Gerald Kelly said. "Things are going to get better. I know they will."

"I've got no way to stick it out, Gerald," Sylvester said. "My wheat was destroyed, and I don't have time left to get in another crop. I've got a wife and two kids to support, and I've got no way of making a living."

"Stick around, please. I'm sure we can work something out," Gerald said.

Malcolm shook his head. "I won't take charity. I don't take money I haven't earned."

"Earn it, then, by working for us," Darrel Pollard suggested.

"Darrel, you've already got three men working for you. I know you can't afford another one."

"No, when I say *us*, I mean us," Pollard said, taking in everyone else with a circle of his hand. "Work for me a little, work for Travis some, work for Gerald. We'll spread you around, and that way you won't cost any of us too much, but you could make enough to hold on until you get your next crop in."

"You men would all go along with something like that?" Sylvester asked.

"Yeah, I would," Poindexter said, and every other rancher present agreed.

"That would be very good of you all to do that."

"That's what neighbors are for, isn't it?" Poindexter asked.

"So now the question is, will *you* do it? Will you stick around and work for us?" Kelly asked.

A broad, happy smile spread across Malcolm's face. "Yes! Yes, I'll do it! And thank you, men. I thank you, and Marjane will thank you, too, as soon as I tell her."

"Ladies and gentlemen, if you would all find a seat, Hugh Conway is going to honor us with some music before the ceremony gets underway," Art Walhausen called out to the others.

When all were seated and quiet, he stepped out in front of the assembly. "And now, if you would, join me in welcoming Professor Hugh Conway."

Art stepped to one side and began to applaud. The others applauded as well, the applause polite but not exuberant.

"Oh, my, would you look at him?" Jennie Lou said as Hugh stepped out from the house. "I've seen him many times, but I never had any idea he was such a handsome man."

What had drawn that response was the way Hugh was dressed. Though most who knew him were used to seeing him in denim and work shirts, the same apparel that they wore, today he was wearing a cut-a-way and tails, with white tie and a silver silk vest.

Hugh bowed to the audience, then, with a practiced sweep of his tails, took his seat on the piano bench. He stared at the keyboard for a moment, then, with a flourish, began playing Beethoven's Piano Concerto no. 3.

Most were used to hearing the piano at the Pair O' Dice or the Wild Hog. But the music coming from this piano was so rich and deep that it was almost as great as the difference between the voice of a solitary singer and a full chorus.

Matt looked over at Lisa and could see by the gleam in her eyes and the expression on her face how much she was enjoying it and how proud she was of her husband. Having the concert in conjunction with the wedding had been Lisa's idea, and the reaction of the others told Matt that it was a very good one.

If the applause had been rather restrained when Hugh first made his appearance, it was loud and enthusiastic at the conclusion of the piece. He stood, and with a broad smile on his face, bowed to the audience. Then he sat back down and played Mendelssohn's Wedding March.

Mary Ella came up the aisle between the seats on the arm of Lonnie Cheatum.

Some might have questioned her choice of Lonnie as a surrogate to "give away" the bride, but Matt didn't. He knew Lonnie as a good man who didn't mistreat the women who worked for him.

Jim stepped to meet them, then rather ceremoniously, Lonnie took Mary Ella's hand from his arm and gave it to the man who would be her husband.

Art stepped out to address the gathering again. "Ladies and gentlemen, as you are already aware, a unique set of circumstances have prevented Jim and Mary Ella from having a conventional wedding. However, they have something planned that I am sure you will all be able to recognize as an affirmation of their love and a commitment of their lives to one another.

There will be none who can doubt that this will be as binding as any church wedding that has ever been performed. I will step aside now, and let this celebration begin."

After Art sat down, Jim and Mary Ella faced each other and held both hands as they looked into each other's eyes.

Jim spoke first. "Mary Ella, there may be some who would suggest that the lack of clergy or a legal document would mean that we are not actually married, that a ceremony such as this, without some sort of contract, is invalid."

Jim reached into his inside jacket pocket and removed a document. "This document will take care of all legalities dealing with our cohabitation. It is a business partnership declaring that we own, jointly, the Circle Dot. It also gives us the right to sign for each other, to speak for each other, and to act on behalf of and for each other in every way that those who are married can do. In addition I have filed with the territorial government in Cheyenne for you to legally change your name to Andrews, needing only your signature to complete it.

"That leaves only the commitment of love that is expressed when two people exchange vows. I believe all that is really needed to be married is for two people to say that they love each other, and if we make a public pledge of our love for one another, and if we say in public that we want to be married, then I can see no reason why that wouldn't be so. Mary Ella, I love you with all my heart and with all my soul, and I want us to be married."

"Jim," Mary Ella replied, "before I met you, I was

what many people would call a fallen woman. I was ostracized by the 'good' people of town, and counted among my friends only those who were of my same station.

"But then something totally unexpected happened. A wonderful man came into my life. That man was you, Jim. You looked past what I was presenting to the world, and you saw *me*, the real me.

"So now, Jim Andrews, it is with tremendous gratitude and much love that I publicly declare my love for you, and state my intention for us to be married."

Jim smiled. "Well then, it looks to me like all we got to do now is kiss one another in front of all these witnesses present, and we'll be as married as if we had stood up in church."

Jim and Mary Ella kissed.

"Ladies and gentlemen, may I introduce Mr. and Mrs. Jim Andrews?" Art called out, and the others applauded.

Chapter Twenty

After dinner, a place was cleared away for dancing and, with Ernest Dean Fawcett, Frank Edmonston, and Travis Poindexter providing the music, the dancing began.

The newlywed couple led the dance while Jennie Lou and Missy danced with some of the cowboys and Colleen danced with Cooter. Matt leaned against the gate to watch the proceedings.

After a few dances, Hugh came over to the gate to speak to Matt. "Whew," he said in an exaggerated whistle. "Lisa is a lot younger than I am, and she has about worn me down to a frazzle with all the dancing, especially with this formal wear I've got on. Matt, how about you spelling me for a while?"

"Well, I don't know. What does Lisa say about that?"

Hugh chuckled and pointed. "What do you think?"

Lisa was holding her hand out toward Matt.

The first dance after Matt joined was the polka, and because it was a rather brisk dance with intricate steps, Matt felt no anxiousness. But the next dance was different, a slow waltz. Knowing that he would be holding her close to him, he was more than a little apprehensive about it.

To Lisa's surprise, Matt turned out to be an excellent dancer, and with him leading, the steps seemed to fall into place. So easily did the movement come that she found herself concentrating less on the dance and more on the dance partner.

As they danced, he looked into her face and she found the smoldering fire in his eyes to cause a dizzying current to race through her. There was the tiniest trace of a smile on his lips, as if he could read her thoughts, but he neither said nor did anything that was, in the slightest, untoward.

Concentrating on keeping her own feelings in check proved to be much harder than she would have imagined. As the dance continued, the physical contact seemed to grow much closer and more intense.

The music ended, and the moment of intimacy dissipated with the dancers' applause in appreciation of the music.

Without saying anything, Lisa hurried over to the gate, where Hugh was standing with Ernest Dean Fawcett. Ernest Dean's wife, Anne, had agreed to dance with rancher Tom Percy, who was single.

"Hugh, I do hope you rested enough to have the next dance with me," Lisa teased. "Or would you farm me out for the rest of the night as if lending one of your horses?"

"I'm ready," Hugh said. "Do you think I'm an old man?"

Lisa laughed appreciatively. "Then come ahead.

The night is young." She looked over at Matt. "Thank you for coming to the rescue of my husband."

"And thank you for the dances," Matt replied.

As the next dance got underway, Matt turned to Ernest Dean. "Would you do me a favor and tell Hugh that I've gone back into town?"

"Are you sure you want to do that, Matt? There's a lot of pies that ain't been et yet."

"Yes, I'm afraid I need to go. Oh, and give my regards to Jim and Mary Ella as well."

"All right. I'll do that."

As Matt rode through the night, heading back to town, he thought of the dance he had shared with Lisa, and he chastised himself for the feelings he had experienced. He would not put himself in such a position again.

But wait. Hadn't he made that vow once before?

Straight Arrow Ranch

"Did you know that Colleen and Cooter went to that . . . that wedding held over at the Circle Dot?" Kennedy asked O'Neal.

"Yes, she told me she would be going."

"And you were all right with that?"

"She's a young woman with very little social life," O'Neil replied. "That wedding was the closest thing to a social occasion we've had around here in a while."

"They aren't actually fooling anyone, are they?" Kennedy asked. "I mean everyone knows they can't really be married."

"It doesn't make any difference whether they are legally married or not," O'Neil said. "As long as everyone thinks they are married, and treats them as they are married, then it has the same effect. And that effect is bad for us."

"Why is it bad for us?"

"Because Andrews with the Circle Dot, and Conway with the Spur and Latigo, are the two strongest ranchers in the valley. As long as they hold out, the others will hold out, as well. With Andrews and the whore married, it just gives him more reason to stay here."

"Maybe we should send Boggs with some of the Regulators to pay them a visit," Kennedy suggested.

O'Neil shook his head. "No, I don't intend to connect Boggs with the Regulators in any way. He is here for our protection against Matt Jensen—and possibly Tyrone DuPont."

"Well, if that's the case, why don't we just turn Boggs loose on him now?"

"When the time comes," O'Neil said. "When the time comes."

A few of the Regulators rode into town and went into the Wild Hog, where they were greeted by three of the girls, Fancy, Candy, and Belle.

"Well now, tell us," Candy said. "Did you boys go to the big, fancy wedding?"

"What weddin'?" McCoy asked. "I don't know nothin' 'bout no weddin'."

"Why, Jim Andrews and Mary Ella Wilson got married," she said.

"I don't never go to no weddin's anyhow," McCoy said. "I'm always afraid some woman might trap me into marryin' 'er."

"Honey, I'd like to see the woman who couldn't do any better 'n you," Belle said, making the other girls laugh.

"Yeah, well, what are you three talkin' 'bout gettin' married anyway?" Carter asked. "All three of you is whores, 'n they don't nobody ever marry no whores."

"Andrews is a-marryin' one," Greene said.

"Hell, Andrews don't count," Carter said as if that validated his point.

"I might get married someday," Fancy said, looking directly at Isaac. "Can I get you something, Isaac?"

"A beer would be nice," he replied as he, McCoy, Greene, and Carter took a table.

"Hey, how come you ain't asked if we want somethin'?" McCoy asked.

"What do you want?" Candy asked.

"A beer, just like Isaac."

"Me 'n Greene will have a beer, too," Carter added.

"I been thinkin' 'bout Shardeen," Greene said after the drinks were delivered.

"What's there to think about?" McCoy asked. "He's dead."

"Yeah, that's what I'm thinkin' about. Shardeen is dead, 'n that means we're goin' to need us another gun as good as he was," Greene said.

"Well hell, we got one that might even be better 'n Shardeen was," Carter said. "This new feller we got, the Undertaker, is ever ever' bit as good as Shardeen was, 'n they's some that will say that he's even better."

"Yeah, but the only thing is, we don't have 'im," Greene said.

"Yes, we do. DuPont seen 'im over at the Straight Arrow," Carter said.

"That's what I'm talkin' about. He's workin' for Kennedy 'n O'Neil. He ain't ridin' with us."

"That's the same thing, ain't it?" Carter asked.

"No, it ain't. What if Kennedy 'n O'Neil decide they don't need us no more? If that happens, the money will more 'n likely dry up on us."

"Damn, I hadn't thought of that. I wish Boggs was with us instead of the Straight Arrow," Carter said.

"Why?" Isaac asked.

"Why? What do you mean, why? On account of we got us a good thing a-goin' here, but if we ain't got somebody like Shardeen or this Undertaker feller on our side, why, that could mean trouble."

"No, it's just the opposite. As long as we had Shardeen he was potential trouble, and it would only be exacerbated with Boggs," Isaac said.

"What's that word you just said? *Exzer* somethin'?" Greene asked.

"The word is *exacerbated*, and it means that if we had Boggs with us, he could wind up causing us a lot of trouble."

"Why are you sayin' havin' Boggs would be trouble?" McCoy asked.

Isaac finished his beer before he responded. "I was worried all the time we had Shardeen that he might kill someone during one of our jobs. Had he done so, the entire complexion of our operation would have changed. Instead of merely being a group that occasionally cast a long rope, we would have become a pack of murderers. If we acquire another person who is just as prone to killing as Shardeen was, and apparently this man Merlin Boggs is, then we would again have to deal with the potential of facing a charge of homicide."

"Uh-uh. You're a-worryin' too much," Moe Greene said. "If we was to have the Undertaker ridin' with us, 'n if he would happen to kill someone, it'd be him that has to pay for it, not us."

"I'm afraid you have very little understanding of the law," Isaac said. "If someone is killed in the commission of a felony, the charge of murder will apply to all who are participating in that felony. And armed robbery, regardless of the amount stolen, is a felony."

"There you go. We don't have nothin' to worry about, boys. If we get into trouble, Isaac will help us out," McCoy said. "Maybe you fellers don't know it, but ole Isaac here is a lawyer."

"That ain't true," Asa Carter said. "He's colored. There ain't no lawyers that's colored."

"That don't make no never mind whether he's colored or not," McCoy said. "He's a lawyer. Tell 'em, Isaac."

Isaac started to reply, but what could he say?

He gave that some thought then said, "Technically, I suppose one must actually be practicing law to be an attorney. And as I'm sure it is obvious to all that I am not practicing law, then I would not be considered an attorney."

"See, what did I tell you? Newton ain't no lawyer," Carter said.

"But you are a lawyer, right?" McCoy asked. "I mean

ain't that what you done told me? Somethin' about goin' into a bar 'n gettin' your license?"

"I have been admitted to the bar, that is true."

"Ha! Only this one, though," Greene said. "They more 'n likely wouldn't even let you in to the Pair O' Dice."

"Yes, only this one," Isaac said without further explanation.

Chapter Twenty-one

As the conversation in the saloon returned to the skills of various gunfighters the others had seen or heard of, Isaac let his thoughts drift back to the last time he had actually practiced law.

After proving that he was a member of the bar, duly licensed to practice law in Texas, he was hired to do legal work for the Texas and Pacific Railroad. His legal work was restricted, however, to the mundane tasks of dealing with records research. Filing for land grants and route right of-way clearances, as well as all actual court appearances, were handled by the white lawyers.

Isaac was looking over some papers at the railroad office in Spring, Texas, one day when a black soldier came in to see him. The soldier was wearing sergeant's stripes and he was a member of the Tenth Cavalry, which was stationed at nearby Fort Davis.

"Mr. Newton?"

"Yes?"

"Mr. Newton, is it true that you're a lawyer?"

"I am."

"Mr. Newton, my name's Sergeant Potter. My officer's bein' accused of somethin' that he didn't do 'n I want you to get him out of trouble."

"How do you know he didn't do it?"

"'Cause he told me he didn't do it, 'n I believe him. Will you help 'im?"

"I'm not sure why you would come to me. Doesn't the army have a Judge Advocate Corps?"

"Yes, but I'm a-feared they won't be fair to Lt. Flipper, him bein' colored 'n all."

"He's colored? I didn't know the army had any colored officers."

"He's the first one they've ever had, 'n he's the only one they got. That's why I come to you, you bein' a colored lawyer."

Before agreeing to take the case, Isaac went to the base headquarters at Fort Davis to learn what he could about Lt. Henry O. Flipper. He'd discovered that Flipper was the first black graduate of West Point and was assigned to the Tenth Cavalry, an all-black regiment known as Buffalo Soldiers. Except for Flipper, the officers were white, and they resented his intrusion. Despite a record of honorable service, Flipper had been accused of embezzling a large amount of money from the Fort Davis commissary.

After Isaac read the reports and files, he indicated by a nod of his head that the sergeant should step outside with him so they could speak in privacy.

"He didn't do all that, Mr. Newton," Sergeant Potter said. "Will you be his lawyer?"

"Where will I find him, Sergeant? Is he in jail now?"

"No, sir, he ain't in no jail. Him bein' an officer, even though he's colored, what they done was, they just said he can't leave his quarters. I'll take you to talk to 'im if you'd like. 'Cause oncet you talk to 'im, I'm just real sure that you'll decide to be his lawyer. Mr. Newton, Lieutenant Flipper is a real good man, despite his bein' an officer."

"Is the lieutenant expecting me?"

"No, sir, I don't know that he is 'cause I ain't told 'im nothin' 'bout you yet, me not knowin' whether or not you'd say that you'd be his lawyer. But if I take you out to see him, he'll be happy to talk to you. The reason I know that is, 'cause he needs a lawyer real bad."

The post was a busy place with some soldiers participating in mounted drill and others at various tasks from polishing the signal cannon to doing repair work on a couple of buildings. All the soldiers were black, though there were a few white officers in supervisory positions, and they cast curious glances toward Isaac as he followed the sergeant to one of the buildings the sergeant identified as bachelor officers' quarters. Stepping into the hallway inside, Sergeant Porter knocked on the door.

"Who knocks?" a voice called from within the room.

"It's Sergeant Potter, Lieutenant. I've got someone here to meet you, sir."

"Enter."

Sergeant Porter opened the door and stepped aside to invite Isaac in.

Isaac saw a handsome young man in uniform sitting at a table. He had an open ink bottle and he was writing on some papers that were spread out on the table. He looked up at Isaac, the expression on his face displaying his curiosity. "Who are you?"

"Lieutenant, this here feller is a real lawyer, even him bein' colored 'n all, 'n what I done is, I asked him to be your lawyer."

"Have you agreed to do so?" Flipper asked.

"I'm not even sure I will be allowed to defend you, Lieutenant," Isaac said. "I'm a civilian, and I don't know what the army will say about that."

"You can defend me. According to the Articles of War, any soldier being court-martialed is entitled to a civilian lawyer if he so wishes," Flipper replied. He smiled. *"And under the circumstances, you might be a better advocate for my case than a white JAG officer."*

"I'm honored that you would think so."

"Will you take the case?"

"All right. I'll do the best I can."

Lieutenant Flipper chuckled, the laugh surprising Isaac, given the amount of trouble he was in.

"I was just thinking," Flipper said. *"A colored lawyer defending a colored army officer. We'll get the court's attention if we don't do anything else."*

Colonel William Shafter was an oversized man with a round face, flushed cheeks, and a full gray moustache. He stroked his moustache subconsciously as he studied Isaac Newton.

"Are you sure you're a lawyer? Lieutenant Flipper might be colored, but he is still one of my officers, and I want to make certain he is ably defended."

"Colonel, it was my impression that he was to be defended by one of your officers who isn't a lawyer."

"That doesn't matter. He can be defended by an officer whether he is a lawyer or not. Only the Judge Advocate has to be a lawyer."

"A white officer."

"As Lieutenant Flipper is the only colored officer in the entire United States Army, it stands to reason that any officer who defends him would be white," Shafter said.

"Lieutenant Flipper has asked that I defend him, and I am now petitioning you to allow me to do so. I understand that the Articles of War will allow me to represent a soldier if

that soldier makes such a request. Lieutenant Flipper has made that request."

"You have some proof that you are actually a lawyer?"

Isaac showed Colonel Shafter his law license. Shafter looked it for a moment, then nodded.

"All right. The court-martial convenes on the fifteenth, that'll be Thursday, three days from now. Captain Merritt Barber will be the court-appointed counsel, which means that, technically, he will be in charge of the defense. However, I will see to it that you are allowed to present the case. Captain Barber will be there to assist you on all things military."

"Thank you, Colonel."

On the day of the trial, Isaac and Lt. Flipper walked together from the BOQ to the post chapel where the court-martial was to be held. Isaac thought the post chapel was a strange place to hold the court-martial, but it was the only place with seating enough to hold the people who wanted to attend. The first person he saw as he entered was Sergeant Potter, who was sitting with many of the men from Lt. Flipper's company.

Because nobody below the rank of the accused can be seated on the court-martial board and Flipper was the only black officer in the entire army, the "jury" was composed of eight white officers. The "judge" or presiding officer was Colonel George Pennypacker. The prosecutor was the judge advocate, Captain John Clous.

Captain Barber was already seated at the defense table, and he stood and greeted Isaac and Lt. Flipper with a smile as they approached. "How are you feeling, Lieutenant?" Barber asked.

"A little nervous. Thank you for asking, sir," Flipper replied.

"Well, that's to be expected. Mr. Newton, the case is in

your hands, but I will assist you with regard to anything in the trial that is specifically of a military nature."

"Thank you, Captain," Isaac said.

When the court was seated, Colonel Pennypacker glanced over at Captain Clous. "Captain, what are the charges?"

"Lieutenant Flipper is charged with embezzlement. He is also charged with conduct unbecoming, in that he wrote a check for which there were insufficient funds."

"Very well, Captain, you may make your case."

Captain Clous turned toward the board to begin his presentation. "Lieutenant Flipper had, before he was relieved, the position of commissary officer. That is a position of great trust in that he was responsible for all the money that comes through the commissary. An audit disclosed a shortage of three thousand, seven hundred, and ninety-one dollars and seventy-seven cents.

"Gentlemen, that is your money, it is my money, and more important, it is the money of the soldiers under us, the soldiers for whose welfare we are responsible.

"In addition to embezzlement, he also wrote a check for two thousand five hundred dollars, no doubt in a vain attempt to repay the money he stole."

Clous turned away from the board and looked toward the presiding officer. "Sir, I call Mr. Phil Shy, the civilian commissary, as my first witness."

The civilian commissary was a very slender man with a closely cropped moustache and thin blond hair. After he was sworn in, he took his seat in the witness chair.

"Mr. Shy, you are the one who reported the shortage in the commissary funds, are you not?"

"Yes, sir, I did. But since that time—"

Clous interrupted him. "Please add no comments other than in response to my questions. When you first noticed the shortage, what did you do?"

"I told Lieutenant Flipper about it."

"And what did Lieutenant Flipper say?"

"He said don't worry about it. That he would take care of it."

"He would take care of it? What do you think he meant by that?"

"That he would take care of it. And he did, because—"

"Please, speak only in response to my questions. Did he show you a check that he had written?"

"Yes, sir, he did."

"And for how much was the check written?"

"Twenty-five hundred dollars."

"Thank you, no further questions."

Isaac walked halfway between the witness and the defense table. "Mr. Shy, is the commissary still short the money?"

"No, sir."

"Where did the money come from?"

"Well, it's like I was going to say, Lieutenant Flipper said he would take care of it and he did. But to tell the truth, I don't know where the money came from."

"You said he showed you a check for twenty-five hundred dollars. Did he give you that check in repayment?"

"No, he didn't."

"No further questions."

The prosecutor's next witness was Charles Roberts, the post banker.

"Mr. Roberts, does Lieutenant Flipper have twenty-five hundred dollars in his bank account?"

"No, sir, he does not."

"Has he ever had twenty-five hundred dollars in his account?"

"No, sir."

"No further questions."

Isaac stood, but didn't leave the defense table. "Mr.

Roberts, did you refuse payment on Lieutenant Flipper's twenty-five-hundred dollar check?"

"No, I never refused payment on that check."

"Why didn't you? I mean you testified that never, at any time, has Lieutenant Flipper had that much money in his account. Why didn't you refuse payment when the check was presented?"

"There was no need to refuse payment, because the check was never presented."

'Thank you."

When Lieutenant Flipper took the stand, Isaac asked him about the twenty-five-hundred dollar check. "Why did you write the check, if you didn't have the money?"

"I don't have the money yet, but I will soon," Lieutenant Flipper said. He smiled. "My book, A Colored Cadet at West Point, *will soon be published by Harper Lee and Company, and they are paying me twenty-five hundred dollars."*

There was a gasp of surprise, and even shock, from the others in the court and in the gallery.

Isaac returned to the table and picked up a piece of paper. "Your Honor, here is a letter from the publisher, verifying Lieutenant Flipper's claim."

In Captain Clous's closing remarks, he added one more piece of evidence. "I would like to point out that the conduct unbecoming does not refer only to the check, but to the fact that Lieutenant Flipper has been often seen riding with Miss Mollie Dwyer. Miss Dwyer is a white woman. Prosecution rests."

Captain Barber said that he would like to give the closing argument for the defense, and Isaac, after consulting with Lieutenant Flipper, agreed.

Barber approached the board, and in the most eloquent and flowery prose, made his petition. "May we not ask this court to take into consideration the unequal battle my client

*has to wage, poor, naked, and practically alone, with
scarce an eye of sympathy or a word to cheer, against all
the resources of zealous numbers, official testimony, official
position, experience and skill, charged with all the ammunition which the government could furnish from Washington
to Texas, and may we not trust that this court will throw
around him the mantle of its charity, if any errors are found,
giving him the benefit of every doubt . . . and giving him
your confidence that the charity you extend to him so generously will be as generously redeemed by his future record in
the service."*

Lt. Flipper was found innocent of embezzlement, but
guilty of conduct unbecoming, and was dishonorably discharged from the army.

After the trial, when Isaac returned to his job at the railroad, he learned that he had been fired "for bringing dis-
credit upon the railroad" for his defense of Henry O. Flipper.
His firing had even further implications in that his "poor
record with the railroad" reflected with disfavor upon the
legal profession.

As a result, Isaac was disbarred.

That had been four years ago. Since then, he had drifted
from place to place throughout the West, doing odd jobs here
and there, but the big turn came when he held up a Texas and
Pacific train. He believed that by firing him the Texas and Pacific Railroad had destroyed his career and ruined his life.
He got less than five hundred dollars in the robbery and used
the money to leave Texas.

A few more minor holdups and burglaries here and there
made him sink deeper into the outlaw life. Then, to his surprise and advantage, when people began speaking of the

colored outlaw, they were ascribing all the jobs Isaac was doing to the better-known black outlaw Isom Dart.

A few months ago Isaac had joined with DuPont and the Regulators.

"Well, honey, are you just goin' to sit there, starin' off into nowhere like that?"

The woman's voice brought Isaac back to the present and he realized that he was sitting with Fancy, she being the only other person at the table.

"What?" He looked around. "Where are the others? McCoy, Greene, and Carter?"

Fancy laughed. "Honey, you really was asleep with your eyes open, wasn't you? They's all done got 'em a girl 'n gone."

"What are you doing still here?"

"Well, ain't I your girl?" she asked, her big brown eyes opening wide.

Isaac smiled. "Yes. Yes, indeed you are."

"Well, don't you think maybe we ought to do somethin' about it?"

Isaac stood and held his hand out toward her. "I think that would be a very good idea."

Chapter Twenty-two

Sean O'Neil, who was the president of the Sweet-water Ranchers' Association, had called for a meeting to be held in the Rongis Hotel. O'Neil's partner Garrett Kennedy was there as well.

Matt had come to the meeting with Hugh Conway. In addition to Hugh, several other area ranchers were present—Jim Andrews, Frank Edmonston, Bob Guthrie, Travis Poindexter, Gerald Kelly, Darrel Pollard, Norman Lambert, Eddie Webb, and Ernest Dean Fawcett. Sylvester Malcolm was there as well, though technically he was a farmer, not a rancher.

A few of the ranchers were dressed as business-men, but most of them, Matt realized, would have felt much more at home dressed exactly as he was. They were used to the saddle and to range clothes, and they pulled at their collars and tugged at their sleeves as they sat uncomfortably in the hard chairs around the long conference table.

Besides Matt, the only nonproperty owners present were Sheriff Clark, Tyrone DuPont, and Merlin Boggs.

A hotel employee came into the meeting room, carrying a tray with a couple of bottles of wine. Wine-glasses were already in front of those present, and as the wine steward passed by, Matt held out his glass to be filled.

"Gentlemen, if all your wineglasses have been charged, may I propose a toast?" O'Neil said, holding up his own glass. The red liquid in his glass caught a beam of light from the overhead gas lanterns and gave off a bright crimson flash.

"To cooperation among all the ranchers of the valley, whether your stock be cattle or"—he paused to look directly at Hugh—"horses. May we have a profitable year, free from the menace of rustlers."

"Hear! Hear!" Kennedy said loudly, and all lifted their glasses to drink.

"And, while we are here gathered, I would also like to propose an official congratulation from the Sweetwater Ranchers' Association be extended to our member Jim Andrews on the occasion of his recent marriage."

"Hear! Hear!" Hugh said, mimicking Kennedy's earlier comment.

Every member of the association held their glass out toward Jim in salute.

"Now," O'Neil said. "Let us get on with the meeting, shall we? I think I can speak for everyone here when I say that rustling has been the scourge of all of us."

"If this goes on any longer, it's going to drive me out of business." Ernest Dean Fawcett was a big man with an easy smile and thinning hair.

"And not only Fawcett, but me 'n Guthrie, too," Edmonston added.

Hugh remained silent.

"My problem ain't with rustlin'," Sylvester Malcolm said.

"I don't hardly see how it could be, seein' as you aren't running any cattle," DuPont said.

"No, I'm a farmer, and I raise wheat. That is, I was raising wheat until a bunch of cattle was drove through my wheat field, smashing it all down."

"Well then, Mr. Malcolm, your problem might very well be cattle rustlers same as the rest of us," O'Neil said.

"What would make you say something like that?" Malcolm asked.

"Well, think about it. What cattle would be coming across your wheat field except for stolen cattle? And if there were enough cattle to destroy your wheat crop, they were probably from the Straight Arrow."

"The Straight Arrow is 'bout the only ranch stout enough to keep goin'," Edmonston continued. "In fact when I got hit so hard last year, if I hadn't been able to get a loan from the bank, I wouldn'ta been able to keep goin'.

"At least you're tryin'," Fawcett said. "You might notice by lookin' around the table that two men who used to be members of the Ranchers' Association, them bein' Tucker 'n Woodward, ain't here no more. They just give up, is what they done." He looked over at DuPont. "They was both all in favor of havin' the Regulators come in 'n take care o' things. Now they's gone."

"The truth is, gentlemen, that I'm afraid they were too small to survive," O'Neil said.

"They tried though," Travis Poindexter said. "You sure as hell can't say they didn't try 'n hang on."

"Yes, well, they are both good men, and of course their instinct was to fight back when the rustlers started hitting them," O'Neil said. "Their problem was that they didn't have anything to fight with, and the rustlers didn't leave them enough cattle to even make all the ends meet, so they went under."

"Where were the Regulators?" Matt asked, speaking for the first time.

"I beg your pardon?" Kennedy replied.

"I've been led to believe that the purpose of the Regulators was to prevent such wholesale rustling." Matt looked directly at DuPont. "I'm asking you, DuPont. Where were you and all your deputies when Tucker and Woodward were being so hard hit by the rustlers?"

"I know you asked the question of Mr. DuPont, but I would like to answer that," Kennedy said. "To be fair to Mr. DuPont and his Regulators, they were just getting formed and weren't ready yet to fight off the rustlers. And unfortunately Tucker and Woodward were too weak to survive until Mr. DuPont and his deputies were sufficiently organized to be effective in their campaign against the rustlers."

"It could've been worse, though," Guthrie said.

"How could it have been worse?" Matt asked. "Neither one of them are here anymore."

"The Straight Arrow bought both of 'em out," Guthrie explained.

"You mean you have their ranches now?" Matt asked, looking at Kennedy and O'Neil.

"Yes, but we didn't maintain them as individual ranches," O'Neil explained. "We have incorporated their land into the Straight Arrow."

"I see," Matt said

"No, Jensen, I don't think you do see," Kennedy said. "It was not necessary that we *buy* them out, because it had been homestead property. Once they abandoned their ranches, the land was out there, just for the taking. Mr. O'Neil and I paid them for it when, by law, we didn't have to pay them a cent."

"I couldn't see us just taking over," O'Neil added. "I wouldn't have felt good about that. After all, both men did have families to support."

"What about Keith Dunaway? He had a family to support as well, but it is my understanding that you made no such generous offer to him," Matt said.

"Mr. Jensen, I'm not sure what you have heard, or what you think you may have heard," O'Neil replied, "but the Tumble D was the very first piece of property we acquired, and we tried to deal with Mr. Dunaway. Unfortunately he was obdurate, and unwilling to make any sort of compromise. As a result he lost his ranch, and it only made good business sense to acquire it."

"His ranch and livestock was worth more than the amount of the note due, wasn't it?" Ernest Dean Fawcett asked. "He came to me for a loan and showed me the equity."

"And yet, you didn't help him," O'Neil said.

Fawcett shook his head. "I wanted to, I truly did, but I was strapped for cash at the time, and I had my own note due. You might remember, all that happened just after the big freeze-out."

"Gentlemen, that is all old business and is behind us now," O'Neil said. "The purpose of this meeting is to see what we can do to keep such a thing from happening to anyone else. That's why the Regulators have come into being."

"Well, I'm still around, and despite the presence of the Regulators, I am still having to deal with rustlers," Hugh said.

"Yes, but your situation is a little different from the others," O'Neil said. "You are raising horses, and because horses are easier to take than cows, they would always be a prime target for rustlers. Also they are worth more money per head, and they are much easier to sell."

"I'm sorry 'bout all the rustlin' that's goin' on at your place, Conway, but we're spread pretty thin now, 'n if I'm goin' to defend ever'one, I'm goin' to need some more men," DuPont said.

"And yet, you were about to hang one of my men for attempting to recover four of my horses," Hugh challenged.

"We was just doing our job," DuPont replied. "We caught a man, red-handed, herding four horses. We knew those horses were yours, and we thought he was stealing them from you. We were merely trying to recover your stolen property, that's all."

"How could it be stolen property if it was my man with the horses?" Hugh asked.

"Well, that's the problem, you see. We knew he was your man, but the horses weren't on your property. So it's like I say, we thought he was stealin' from you.

It wouldn'ta been the first time someone stole from the person he was workin' for. Anyway, all we did was try 'n stop it."

During this discussion and throughout the meeting Matt and Boggs continued to study each other, neither of them looking away. Sheriff Clark had pointed him out to Matt when he arrived.

"What do you mean you're going to need more men?" Fawcett asked.

"It's like I said, seein' as Shardeen got hisself kilt by Jensen there"—DuPont nodded toward Matt—"I've only got seven men left in the Regulators."

"Now, DuPont, I looked into that killin'," Sheriff Clark said. "They was plenty of witnesses to it, 'n ever'one of 'em told the same story. Shardeen was the one who started that fracas, 'n when Jensen kilt 'im, it was in self-defense."

"Yeah, well I admit that Shardeen may have been out tryin' to prove somethin', so I ain't a-sayin' it warn't in self-defense. But what I am sayin' is that since Shardeen got hisself kilt, I only got seven men left," DuPont said, replying to the challenge. "'N I already didn't think I had enough, which you men have pointed out by tellin' me how all the rustlin' is still goin' on 'n all."

Hugh looked over toward Clark. "Sheriff, it was my impression that you had suspended the position of deputy for the existing members of the Regulators. Surely you won't be appointing anyone new."

"I have suspended all the Regulators from their positions as deputies, and I won't be makin' 'em deputies again, 'n I won't be makin' no more, neither," Sheriff Clark said.

"Yeah, but what none of you understand is that it don't make no difference whether my men are deputies or not," DuPont said. "'N I don't need to be a deputy no more neither, which is why I'm about to give my badge back to you."

"So do you plan for the Regulators to just be a bunch of vigilantes?" Poindexter asked. "I mean having that many deputies running around was a little disturbing in itself, but having vigilantes is even worse."

"Oh no, it won't be nothin' like that 'cause we ain't goin' to be vigilantes. What I've done is, I've gone to the Union Pacific Railroad 'n I got them to appoint me as a railroad detective. I can hire as many as I want to help me out, which'll be the men I already got in the Regulators 'n maybe a few more. That way we can keep an eye on all the ranches."

"What does the railroad have to do with ranchin'?" Guthrie asked.

"Oh, it has plenty to do with ranchin'," DuPont replied. "Why, if the rustlin' don't stop, you ranchers won't have no horses or cows to ship out on the railroad, 'n if the railroad don't have no livestock to ship, why that'll wind up costin' them lots of money. 'N bein' as I was oncet a police officer before I was even a deputy, I have lots of experience at bein' a lawman, which is what I told the folks at the railroad when I went to talk to 'em. 'N that's why the Union Pacific hired me as a railroad detective."

"Is the Undertaker goin' to be one o' your new men?" Poindexter asked.

Boggs, whose staring at Matt had been without remission, turned to look at Poindexter. Made nervous by the scrutiny, the rancher used his forefinger to pull his collar away from his neck.

"I can answer that," O'Neil said, speaking quickly before DuPont could respond. "Mr. Boggs is not a member of the Regulators, nor is he any kind of a lawman. Mr. Boggs is in the employ of the Straight Arrow Ranch."

"There's nobody who hasn't heard of Merlin Boggs," Fawcett said. "And from what we have heard, and know, it's clear that you didn't hire someone who is called the Undertaker to punch cows for you. So why do you need someone like him?"

O'Neil forced a smile. "Why, you might say that Mr. Kennedy and I have hired Mr. Boggs for much the same reason that Mr. Conway of the Spur and Latigo has hired Matt Jensen. We believe that someone with Mr. Boggs's unique skill will be able to provide the protection an operation like ours needs."

"When you say *skill*, you mean his skill as a gunfighter," Fawcett challenged.

"As I just told you, Mr. Fawcett, Mr. Kennedy and I have hired Mr. Boggs for our protection. And for that matter, isn't Mr. Jensen known primarily as a gunfighter?

"We represent no challenge to Mr. Conway, but given the situation that we both face, we would hardly hire a bookkeeper for protection now, would we?"

"No, I reckon not."

"Gentlemen, let's get on with our meeting. We've many things to discuss, from water usage to grazing procedures," O'Neil said.

Chapter Twenty-three

After the meeting, Matt, Hugh, Jim Andrews, Ernest Dean Fawcett, and Bob Guthrie were having lunch at the Palace Café.

"Jim, I'm surprised Mary Ella wasn't at the meeting," Fawcett said.

"Why are you surprised? None of the other wives were."

"It's just that Mary Ella has taken more of an interest in ranchin' than the other wives," Fawcett said. "I mean, even before you 'n Mary Ella was married, she was a partner in the ranch the two of you put together."

"That's true," Jim replied. "But we figured there was no need for both of us going to the meeting."

"Yeah, I reckon that's true," Fawcett agreed.

"Say, Matt, I seen that you 'n Boggs seemed to be starin' at each other for 'most the entire meeting," Guthrie said.

"I had to do something, Bob," Matt said. "The meeting was about the most boring thing I've ever sat through."

The others laughed.

"It was pretty boring, all right," Jim agreed. "Now you know why Mary Ella didn't go."

"Matt, what do you know about Boggs?" Fawcett asked.

"I know that he's someone who sells his gun to the highest bidder."

"Sells his gun? I'm not familiar with that term," Hugh said.

"Hugh, when you were giving concerts, you were being paid for your skill and talent to play the piano. You used that skill to make music for people. Merlin Boggs is paid for his skill and talent with a gun, and he uses that skill to shoot and often to kill people."

"Matt, are you saying that Kennedy and O'Neil have hired Boggs to kill people?"

"They didn't hire him to play the piano."

"I'm having a hard time accepting that," Hugh said. "I mean, yes, Shardeen was a known killer, but he was working for the Regulators, and that entire membership is composed of men with questionable backgrounds, starting with DuPont himself. Kennedy and O'Neil are ranchers and supposedly respectable businessmen. The thought that they would hire a known killer is quite disconcerting."

"Who is it, do you think, that they want this Boggs person to kill?" Fawcett asked.

"I expect that would be me," Matt said easily as he buttered his biscuit.

After returning to Purgatory Pass from the Sweetwater Ranchers' Association meeting, DuPont called a few of his men together. "Being as we're now private detectives for the railroad, we need to find some cattle rustlers."

"Well hell, we don't have to look very far," Carter replied with a little laugh. He made an encompassing motion with his hand. "Here we are."

The others laughed as well.

"No, we need to find someone else who is rustling," DuPont said.

"That's goin' to be kind of a problem, on account of there prob'ly ain't nobody else that's doin' any real rustlin'. That is, unless you count catchin' mavericks as rustlin'," Moe Greene said.

"I'm sure we can find someone if we look hard enough," DuPont said.

"Well, I sure got no idea where to start," Walter Toone said.

"Jim Andrews 'n that whore that's livin' with him would be a good place to start," DuPont said.

"You think they're rustlin' cattle?" Carter asked.

"We can make sure that they are," DuPont said.

"What do you mean?"

"Use your head, Carter," Greene said. "How hard would it be to find some rustled cows over at the Circle Dot?"

Carter smiled, finally getting the point. "It won't be hard at all, iffen we was to put some of 'em there."

"Now you're getting smart," said DuPont.

"Where are we goin' to get the cows that we put there?" Greene asked.

"If the rustled cows that you found there happened to belong to the Straight Arrow Ranch it would prove that Andrews has been rustlin' and it would serve a purpose for Kennedy and O'Neil," DuPont said.

"Yes, I see what you mean, now," Greene said.

"Carter, you'll be in charge." DuPont took in the others with a small wave of his hand. "Moe, you, Walter, John, 'n Lem will be going along as well."

"All right." Carter looked at the others. "They don't none of you have no problem with me bein' in charge, do you?"

"I ain't got no problem with it," Greene said.

There was a general assent from the others to following Carter.

"Oh, and Carter?" DuPont continued. "It isn't just a matter of finding stolen cows on the Circle Dot. Finding them there is only a means of justifyin' what you're going to do about it."

"Do about it?" Carter replied, not understanding what DuPont was suggesting.

"Yes, do about it. Andrews and the whore need to pay for stealing Straight Arrow cows."

"Pay? What is it you're a-wantin' 'em to pay?"

"They . . . need . . . to . . . pay . . . for . . . it," DuPont repeated, setting the words apart and giving them a very ominous tone.

"Both of 'em? The woman, too?" Carter asked.

"Yes, both of them," DuPont said.

Isaac Newton had not been a part of the discussion among DuPont, Carter, and the others, but he had been close enough to overhear every word spoken. His proximity to the meeting was unnoticed because he had been standing just around the corner of the building to avoid being seen. The portentous tone of the meeting gave Isaac pause.

What had DuPont meant when he'd said that both of them must pay, including the woman?

Isaac had not been asked by DuPont to be a part of the meeting, and he was certain that it wasn't just an oversight. On more than one occasion, Isaac had put forth a cautionary comment when he thought DuPont might be pushing the Regulators into a position that was more vulnerable. Isaac wasn't sure what DuPont had in mind, but he didn't like what he had heard, and though he not been one of those selected to carry out the task DuPont had in mind, he planned to go with them. Actually, he wouldn't be *with* them, as he intended to make certain that neither Carter nor any of the others were aware that he was following.

When Jim returned home, Mary Ella stepped out onto the porch to greet him. "Did you have lunch?"

"Yes, I ate at the Palace Café with Hugh and some of the others."

"But, did you have chocolate cake?"

Jim smiled broadly at Mary Ella's question. "By asking me that, am I to assume that you have baked a cake?"

"For you, I have baked a cake and I have made some buttermilk."

Jim stepped over to wrap his arms around her. "You know what? If you weren't already married, I would ask you to marry me," he teased.

"Oh, my, if I had known that all it would take to get you to marry me was to bake a cake and make some buttermilk, I would have done that long ago."

Over the chocolate cake and buttermilk, Jim began

sharing with Mary Ella some of the details of the meeting of the Sweetwater Ranchers' Association. "DuPont and his group are no longer deputies."

"That's good. I never felt that good about all those men running around as deputies anyway," Mary Ella replied. "As far as I'm concerned, they never were anything but a bunch of crooks wearing badges. I'm glad they're gone."

"Yes, that would be good if they were really gone. But they aren't gone. Now they are passing themselves off as railroad detectives."

"Railroad detectives? How can that be? We're at least a hundred miles from the nearest railroad."

"Yes, well, DuPont explained it by saying that the railroads need us to use them for shipping our stock."

"That's a pretty far-fetched justification for being a railroad detective, if you ask me."

"Oh, I don't think there was anyone present at that meeting who wouldn't agree with you."

Jim poured himself another glass of buttermilk. "The Undertaker was there."

"Mr. Prufrock? What was he doing at a stock meeting?"

"Not Prufrock, Merlin Boggs," Jim said as he took another drink of his buttermilk. He wiped the white residue from his upper lip before continuing. "He's a gunfighter who has killed so many men that they call him the Undertaker."

Mary Ella shuddered. "Good heavens. Why is he here?"

"He has come to kill Matt Jensen."

"What?"

"But not to worry. I'm pretty sure that if and when they meet, Matt Jensen will come out on top."

Mary Ella was quiet for a long moment before she spoke. "Jim, what are we doing here?"

"What? What do you mean, what are we doing here?"

"We don't have to be here, you know. We could leave. Jim, why don't we just leave here?" Mary Ella asked.

"Leave here and go where?"

"I don't know. We could go anywhere, California maybe."

"We don't have enough money to start over."

"We could sell the Circle Dot."

"No, the only people with enough money to buy it would be Kennedy and O'Neil, and if they got wind that we wanted to sell, why they wouldn't give us a plug nickel for the place."

Their conversation was interrupted by the sound of approaching horses.

"What is that?" Mary Ella asked, showing some concern. "Who do you think would be coming here?"

"I don't know. It could maybe be Conway, Fawcett, Edmonston, and some of the boys. Maybe Jensen has something in mind that he needs some men for." Jim started toward the front door.

"Jim, no. Don't go. Don't go out there." There was a sense of urgency in Mary Ella's voice.

"What do you mean? If they've come all the way over here, the least we can do is see who it is and what they want."

"I . . . I just don't have a good feeling about it."

Chapter Twenty-four

When Jim stepped out onto the front porch, Mary Ella went out with him. Jim, too felt a sense of apprehension. These weren't his fellow small ranchers. These men were Regulators, five of them—Asa Carter, Moe Greene, Walter Toone, John and Lem Mason. Greene, Toone, and the Mason brothers were on horseback. Carter was driving a tandem seated surrey. Oddly enough, they had four cows with them.

"What do you men want?" Jim asked. He had not brought his gun out with him.

"You recognize these here cows, Andrews?" Carter asked.

"How am I supposed to recognize cows unless I can see the brand?"

"Your brand is a circle with a dot in the middle, right?"

"Yes, that's why it's called the Circle Dot. What's this all about, Carter?"

"Let me describe the brand on these cows to you. It's two straight up-and-down lines with an arrowhead on top. You have any idea what brand that would be?"

"Of course I know. It's the Straight Arrow brand. Would you mind explaining to me what cows belonging to Kennedy and O'Neil are doing here?"

"Now it's just real funny that you ask that question, Andrews, seein' as that's just what we're wantin' to ask you," Carter said. "What are they a-doin' over here? It ain't likely that they wandered this far away 'n just happened to turn up here, is it?"

"I wouldn't think so. But if you've brought them here to show me that they aren't my cows, I can see that they aren't, so go ahead and take them back to Kennedy and O'Neil. You'll get no squawk from me."

"Uh-uh. You ain't a-goin' to get off that easy. You can't just take another man's property 'n when you get caught give 'em back 'n think that will be the end of it," Carter said.

"Take another man's property? Wait a minute. Are you saying I stole those cows?"

"No, it ain't hardly likely that you stoled' 'em. What's more 'n likely is that your woman is still whorin' 'n she was willin' to spread 'er legs for whoever it was that actual stoled 'em, 'n she was paid for her whorin' by these here cows. 'N the law's pretty clear that if you take stoled property, why it's the same as if you stoled it yourself."

"Get off our property," Mary Ella said angrily.

"You heard what my wife said." Jim's words were just as angry. "Get off our property, *now*."

"Ha. That's just real funny, you a-claimin' that that whore is your wife, when ever'body knows that you two ain't really married. You can't be married on account of she's got a husband already, only he's in prison."

"I'm telling you for the last time to get off our property!" Jim said, shouting the words this time.

Carter looked over at two of his men. "Get 'em in the surrey."

Lem and John Mason rode right up to the porch, and it wasn't until then that Jim noticed each of the two brothers were holding an open-looped lariat. Even as he was wondering what that was for, the two loops were dropped simultaneously over him and over Mary Ella.

"Here, what is—" Jim started, but his protest was ended abruptly when Lem and John backed their horses up quickly.

The effect was to jerk both Jim and Mary Ella off the porch so abruptly that both fell to the ground. Then, as if tying up roped calves, both Jim and Mary Ella were secured by looping the ropes around them a few times. Once secured, they were put in the back of the surrey.

"What's going on?" Jim asked.

"We have a warrant for your arrest," Carter said. "We are taking you to jail."

"Where is your warrant?" Jim asked.

"Moe, show 'em our warrant," Carter said.

Moe held up his pistol. "This here is our warrant."

From his concealed position behind the barn, Isaac Newton saw the abduction, and though he stayed back far enough not to be noticed, he followed them when they left. He saw the surrey with Carter driving, and with Andrews and the Wilson woman riding in the back seat. Moe, Walter, John, and Lem were riding alongside as they departed from the Circle Dot Ranch.

For a moment Isaac had the idea that he should tell someone about this, perhaps the sheriff or even Matt Jensen. But what would he tell them? Where did Carter intend to take them? Isaac knew that he would have to know where the two were being held before he could tell someone where to go to rescue them.

He was left with no choice but to follow them.

Not too long after leaving the Circle Dot Ranch, the surrey left the road and began bouncing out across the sagebrush. Here the vegetation thinned out so that there were spots of bare land as big as a washtub between the clumps of grass. Arroyos and coulees spread out like fingers, and though there were no trees, Isaac was able to use rock outcroppings for concealment as he continued to follow. He didn't know for sure what Carter had in mind, but he didn't feel good about it.

When they reached Sawmill Creek, they drove right across it.

"Where are you taking us?" Jim demanded. "What the hell is going on here?"

"If you don't shut up, we'll drown the both of you in the crick," Carter said.

"That isn't likely, since there is insufficient water in this creek for a person to have a decent bath," Mary Ella said. "I don't know what you have in mind, but if you are trying to frighten us into leaving, it isn't going to work."

"We'll just see about that," Carter said as the surrey left the creek and climbed up the bank on the opposite side.

The surrey continued on across the desert ground with neither Carter nor any of the other riders saying anything.

"Jim, what's going to happen to us?" Mary Ella asked quietly. "What do you think they intend to do?" Neither of them had been secured and she was able to put her hand in his.

He squeezed it, hoping to comfort her. "I expect they're just goin' to carry us on a few more miles out into the desert then turn us loose and make us walk back."

"But why? Why would they do something like that?"

"It's like you said earlier, they just want to frighten us. I'm sure Kennedy and O'Neil are behind this, wanting to buy our ranch. I guess they figure that if they can frighten us enough, we'll be more in the mood to sell."

"No," Mary Ella said. "No, we won't sell to him. Promise me that no matter what they do, that we won't sell to them."

Despite their situation, Jim was able to laugh. "I thought you said you wanted to sell out and go to California."

"Only if it's our idea."

Jim squeezed her hand. "I love you, Mary Ella."

"I love you too, Jim," Mary Ella said, returning the hand squeeze.

After riding and bouncing across the sagebrush for at least an hour longer, they stopped near a copse of trees. The four riders dismounted, and two of them stepped up to Jim's side of the wagon while the other two stepped up to Mary Ella's side.

"Get out," Carter said as he, too, stepped down.

"Thank you, but we're both fine right here," Jim said.

Carter nodded at Greene, and he and Toone reached up to grab Jim and jerk him roughly out of the surrey. At the same time, Lem and John jerked Mary Ella down, and she let out a little cry of pain and fear as she hit the ground hard.

"Is this where you're turning us loose to walk home?" Jim asked. "Because if it is, I would appreciate it if you would point the way. You made so many twists and turns that I'm not sure where we are."

"You won't be walkin' out of here," Carter said.

The four men then half dragged and half shoved Jim and Mary Ella toward the nearby trees, and in particular toward one that was no taller than twenty feet, but had a long, protruding limb.

"Yeah," Carter said with an evil grin. "This 'un will do."

During the trek across the desert, Isaac had been following them, feeling more and more uneasy. At first he had thought they might just be taking them somewhere to hold them prisoner, but when he saw them stop he didn't see any structure that could be used for that purpose.

About five hundred yards behind them, he dismounted, tied his horse off, and began to approach on foot. Still using rocks and boulders for concealment, he got close enough to hear what they were saying.

"Are you trying to make us think you're going to hang us?" he heard Jim ask. "Well, I have no intention of selling my ranch to Kennedy and O'Neil for any price, and you can just tell them that."

Though Jim had tried to put some bravado in his voice, Isaac could tell that the rancher was actually quite frightened.

Isaac managed to advance to a boulder no more than fifty yards away, and when he took a look, he saw that Greene and Toone had already put nooses over the necks of the man and the woman and were tossing the loose ends of their ropes over the extended limb.

"Why are you doing this? We didn't rustle any cattle!" Mary Ella said. Her voice was on the edge of panic.

"Ain't you figured out by now that it don't matter none to us whether you done it or not?" Carter said.

"There is no arrest warrant, is there? You had no intention of taking us to the sheriff," Mara Ella said.

"Well now, you're pretty smart for a whore."

To the degree it was possible, Jim was struggling with the two men that were holding him. His struggles were in vain, though, and he was pushed up onto a boulder. Any further struggle could result in him hanging himself, so he was forced to stop fighting.

"What are you bein' such a coward for?" Carter asked. "Why don't you just take it like a man?"

Mary Ella was lifted up onto the boulder to stand so close to Jim that they were touching. "If you are going to do this, will you at least give me a moment so I can say a prayer?" she asked.

"Ain't no need for you to be sayin' no prayer now," Carter said with a little chuckle. "In a couple more minutes, you can just deliver it in person."

The others laughed at his cruel joke.

Good Lord, what had he gotten himself into? Isaac wondered. Stealing a few horses or rustling some cattle was one thing, but killing was another. And this wasn't just killing, this was murder! They were actually going to lynch these two people, and one of them was a woman.

Isaac could take no more of it, so he pulled his pistol and began shooting toward the five men in a desperate hope to stop it.

"What the hell? Who is it that's a-shootin' at us?" Greene asked.

"Start shootin' back," Carter demanded.

Jim and Mary Ella stood there with nooses around their necks, unable to move for fear of falling off the rock they were standing on. The exchange of gunfire continued.

Isaac was too far away for his shooting to be effective, but he continued to shoot until the cylinder rotated all the way around and the hammer fell on an already expended cartridge. He was out of ammunition, which left him no choice but to get away before they came after him.

"Who do you think that was?" Toone asked, after the shooting stopped.

"Ain't no tellin' who it was," Carter said, "but it's best we get our job done, 'n then get on outta here."

"No! No!" Mary Ella screamed.

"Damn you all to hell!" Jim shouted.

Jim and Mary Ella were pushed off the boulder, their cries of protest turned to no more than grunts by the rope. They didn't fall far enough for their necks to be broken, so they hung from the limb, not more than a foot from the ground, struggling against the ropes that were slowly strangling them.

They were so close together that during their struggles their bodies often came together. As the struggles grew less until they ceased entirely, Jim reached out to grab Mary Ella's hand. They held on as long as they could until their grip was loosened as first one, then the other, was claimed by death.

Chapter Twenty-five

Purgatory Pass

Carter reported to DuPont when he and the others returned from their job. "Someone seen us when we done it."

"Who?"

"I don't know who it was, but whoever it was, he started shootin' at us."

"Just one person?"

"I think it was just one person, but I don't know that for sure."

"Do you think he recognized you?"

"He was close enough to see us real good, but whether or not he actual knowed who we was, well, I can't say."

"If they recognized you, they will know that you are part of the Regulators."

"I'm sorry, boss. But we sure didn't know nobody was there."

"Don't worry about it," DuPont said. "This might work out better for us."

"I sure don't see how that can be. I mean what we

done is we hung a woman. Folks ain't likely to look too good on that."

"It depends on how the story is told," DuPont said. "And I know someone who can tell the story for us."

It was dark by the time Isaac rode into Rongis, though there was light from the houses and a few of the businesses that were open late. The two most brightly lit buildings were the saloons, the Wild Hog and the Pair O' Dice. He started toward the Wild Hog but changed his mind and rode onto the Pair O' Dice, instead.

Isaac had always heard it said that he wouldn't be allowed in the Pair O' Dice, but he didn't know if that was true or not. He had never tried. He was about to put it to the test, because the man he wanted to see was Matt Jensen. Isaac would either find him there or he would be able to find out where Jensen was.

Dismounting, Isaac looped his reins around the hitching rail, then pushed into the well-lit interior. He stood just inside the door for a moment, looking around at the customers, nearly all of whom were returning his gaze. Some were doing more than just staring at him, because he overheard a few of the remarks.

"What's he doing in here?"

"He's got no business in here."

"He ought to stay with his own kind."

"Yeah, well, there ain't that many coloreds in town."

"I ain't talkin' about that. He's one o' them Regulators. That's who I'm talkin' about."

Isaac stepped up to the bar, and a few of the drinkers moved aside, isolating him by their action.

The bartender moved down to confront him. "Can I help you?"

"Will you serve me a drink?"

"You have the money?"

"I do." Isaac put a nickel on the bar. "I would like a beer, please."

Cheatum drew a beer, then put it in front of Isaac. He picked it up, his hands shaking.

Cheatum reached out gently to still Isaac's shaking hands. "Mr. Newton, you don't have to be scared. As far as I'm concerned, you're as welcome as any other customer as long as you don't make any trouble."

"You know who I am?" Isaac was surprised at being addressed by name.

Cheatum smiled. "You're the educated colored man who rides with DuPont, aren't you?"

"No," Isaac replied. "That is, I don't ride with DuPont anymore."

Cheatum slid the nickel back across the bar. "In that case, this beer is on the house."

"Thank you." Isaac lifted the mug but, as before, his hands were shaking.

"Something awful has happened, Mr. Cheatum. Something unspeakable."

"What?"

"I think I should probably tell Mr. Jensen first. Do you have any idea where he is?"

Cheatum glanced toward the grandfather clock that stood against the back wall. "Right now, I would say that he is over at the Palace Café having his supper. But he generally comes in here for a few minutes afterward."

"Is it all right if I wait for him?"

"Sure. You can stand here at the bar, or if you would

rather, there's an empty table back there by the piano. Most folks don't like to sit there 'cause they complain that the piano playing is too loud for them to talk."

Isaac drained the rest of his beer, then again put forth the nickel Cheatum had returned. "I'd better have another one while I wait."

When Matt stepped into the Pair O' Dice fifteen minutes later, he was surprised to see Isaac Newton. He was sure that Cheatum wouldn't actually turn him away, but he had never seen him in here before.

"Hello, Matt," Cheatum greeted.

"Hello, Lonnie. I see you have a new customer." Matt made a nodding motion toward the table where Isaac was sitting.

"He wants to talk to you," Cheatum said, automatically putting a beer in front of Matt.

Matt took the beer back to the table. "Hello, Newton. Lonnie tells me you want to talk about something."

"I saw it happen, Mr. Jensen. I had no idea they would actually do such a thing. I thought they were going to keep them somewhere and I followed them so I would be able to tell you where they were. But they—" Isaac paused in midsentence and was quiet for a long moment.

Matt made no effort to prod him on. He knew that whatever it was had had a profound effect on him, so he waited until Isaac could gather himself.

"They lynched them, Mr. Jensen. They lynched both of them, the woman, too."

"Who?" The question exploded from Matt's mouth, but he didn't want to hear the answer. "Was it Hugh and Lisa?"

"Jim Andrews," Isaac said. "He and his woman. They were lynched."

For just a moment Matt felt a sense of relief that it hadn't been Hugh and Lisa, but just as quickly he felt guilty for being relieved. "Who did it? Are you willing to share that information?"

"Yes, I'll tell you exactly who did it. It was Asa Carter, Moe Greene, Walter Toone, and John and Lem Mason."

"Thanks."

"Mr. Jensen, I haven't lived what you would call an exemplary life since I left the legal profession. In fact I have engaged in numerous felonious acts. But I have never killed anyone, and the sight of those two struggling for their lives at the end of a rope will haunt me until my dying day."

"Why were they lynched? I mean, I could understand maybe if they broke into their house and shot them. But why lynch them?"

"DuPont set it up as if they had been rustling," Isaac said. "They brought four Straight Arrow cows with them, then said they found them on the Circle Dot."

"Straight Arrow cows, you say? Were Kennedy and O'Neil in on it?"

"They weren't there, of course, and I have no proof, nor even circumstantial evidence, that they were actually involved. But I would say that there is a significant chance that they were at least aware."

"Will you lead me to where it happened?" Matt asked.

Isaac nodded. "All right. When do you want to go?"

"Right now, if you think you can find them in the dark. No, wait. They're dead, so there's no need to hurry. I'd rather go out tomorrow morning so we can take Mr. Prufrock and his hearse with us. I intend to bring them back for burial."

"I'll meet you tomorrow morning at the mortuary," Isaac said.

Leaving the Pair O' Dice, Isaac walked down to the Wild Hog, where he was greeted happily by Fancy.

"There's my handsome man!" Fancy gushed.

"She's been wonderin' where you was," McCoy said.

"Yeah, we all been wonderin' where you was," Carter added, looking at him with what Isaac perceived as a suspicious expression.

"You wouldn't believe me if I told you," Isaac said.

"Try me."

"I was in the Pair O' Dice."

"What?" Fancy demanded. "Honey, ain't I done tole you not to go messin' aroun' with them trashy white girls? You wasn't doin' that, was you?"

Isaac forced a chuckle. "Now why would I want some white girl, when I have a sepia Nubian beauty like you?"

"Oh, honey, you talk so pretty," Fancy said.

"Why were you there?" Carter asked.

"To win a dollar from McCoy," Isaac said.

"What?" McCoy asked, puzzled by the comment.

"Do you remember when you bet me a dollar that I couldn't buy a drink in the Pair O' Dice? I told you I might take you up on it someday."

"Yeah, I remember."

"Well, I took you up on it. I bought a drink in the Pair O' Dice, and now you owe me a dollar."

"How are you goin' to prove that?"

"He done it," Carter said.

"What? How do you know?" McCoy asked.

"'Cause I seen 'im goin' in, 'n I was wonderin' why."

Isaac breathed a sigh of relief. He knew that Carter would be suspicious of everyone until he found out who had been shooting at them. And having seen him go into the Pair O' Dice would have directed those suspicions toward him.

"There you go, McCoy. Carter is all the proof I need."

"Yeah, all right," McCoy said, pulling out a dollar.

"Honey, do you plan to spend any of that money on me?" Fancy asked.

"What if I put two more with it and spend the entire night with you?" Isaac asked.

"I'll give you the best time you ever had," Fancy promised.

Isaac needed a place to spend the night so he could meet Jensen in the morning, and he could stay with Fancy without Carter or any of the others asking questions.

By midmorning the next day, Matt, Isaac, and Seamus Prufrock, the mortician, were standing at the small promontory just south of the Sweetwater River, staring at the gruesome sight before them.

The bodies of Jim Andrews and Mary Ella Wilson hung from a tree limb, turning slowly. Their eyes had bulged from the sockets, their tongues were sticking out, and their faces were beet red and contorted from the struggle.

"I couldn't stop it. I tried. I was over there." Isaac pointed to the rock he had been hiding behind. "I shot at them, hoping to at least interrupt what was going on, but I was too far away to hit anything and as soon as I fired the first time, they pushed Mr. Andrews and Miss Wilson . . ."

"Mrs. Andrews," Matt corrected.

"I'm sorry. Yes, Mrs. Andrews. As I was saying, with the first shot they were pushed off that rock." Isaac pointed to the small boulder where the two victims had been standing. "By then, it was too late for me to do anything to help them, even if I could."

Matt put his hand on Isaac's shoulder. "I know that you did all you could do, and I appreciate you coming to me to tell me what happened."

"I don't plan to go back into town with you," Isaac said. "As a matter of fact, I don't plan to stick around any longer. It isn't safe for me here."

"I understand." Matt glanced over at Prufrock, who was still staring at the hanging bodies. "Mr. Prufrock, we'll help you cut them down and load them into your hearse."

Straight Arrow Ranch

"We done somethin' last night that we'll be needin' your help for," DuPont told Kennedy and O'Neil. 'N there might be some trouble, seein' as they was some-one that seen 'em doin' it."

"Do what? What did you do?" O'Neil asked.

"You been wantin' to get the Circle Dot, ain't you?"

"Yes, we have."

"Well now you can get it, on account of Andrews 'n that whore is both dead. Only thing is, they was some-one who seen the lynchin' 'n it could lead back to the Regulators, and to you 'n Kennedy as well."

"What are you talking about? We had nothing to do with the lynching," O'Neil said.

"That don't matter none. You're goin' to wind up with the ranch, 'n ever'one is goin' to think you two was the ones that done it."

"Then I would suggest that you find out who was the witness and take care of it," Kennedy said.

"There's another way we could take care of it," DuPont said.

"And what way would that be?"

"You ever heard of Frank James? He was an outlaw we had in Missouri."

"Of course I have heard of him."

"Yeah, well, here's the thing. Frank James is about as bad a outlaw as there's ever been. Only he ain't in jail 'cause all the newspapers made a hero out of 'im. 'N you got a newspaper that's wrote some real good stories about you, ain't you?"

A wide smile spread across O'Neil's face. "Tyrone, I have to give you credit for that. You have just come up with a brilliant idea!"

Chapter Twenty-six

Rongis

The funeral for Jim and Mary Ella was held in the Pair O' Dice Saloon. The "good" people of the town were quick to criticize the fact that it wasn't being held in a church, but they were also the very ones who prevented Jim and Mary Ella's friends from using the church.

Only the braver citizens of the town, those who didn't fear being ostracized, showed up. All of the smaller ranchers and their cowboys, as well as the nearby farmers, turned out for the funeral, and for most of the women, this was the very first time any of them had ever been in the saloon. The bar girls, Jennie Lou, Linda, Carol Ann, and Edna, two of whom had known Mary Ella when she had worked in this very saloon, were sitting together quietly. Unlike their usual risqué attire, the four young women were dressed as modestly as any other woman present.

It had begun raining shortly after everyone arrived, and the storm-caused darkness in the saloon was pushed back by the same lanterns that, at nighttime, made the saloon the most brightly lit building on the street. The tables were all pushed to one side, which allowed the chairs to be lined up in rows. Matt was sitting in the same row as Hugh and Lisa, Ed Sanders, Jake Haverkost, LeRoy Patterson, Travis and Alice Poindexter, and Ernest Dean and Anne Fawcett.

Sheriff Clark was present, as were Art Walhausen and Seamus Prufrock. Colleen and Cooter were there as well, but they spoke to no one, and they sat in the very last row. None of the Regulators were present, nor did anyone expect them to be.

The two coffins, polished mahogany, were set on sawhorses in front of the chairs. The hanging had so distorted the features of the deceased that the coffins were closed.

Because he managed the saloon and had known Mary Ella and Jim very well, Lonnie Cheatum volunteered to give the eulogy. Lisa had suggested to Hugh that he might play the music, but Bill Boyce, who was the regular piano player at the saloon, asked if he could do so, and Hugh agreed that that would be appropriate.

Boyce played "Nearer My God to Thee" and "I Need Thee Every Hour." Then, to the surprise of everyone, Jennie Lou sang "Safe in the Arms of Jesus," her voice unexpectedly as pure and as sweet as the voice of an angel.

Cheatum got up to speak. "Some might think it's raining outside, but those aren't raindrops. No, sir, not a bit of it. What's comin' down outside are tears bein' shed by the angels for these two good people, our friends, who are about to be laid to rest. Some might condemn Jim for cohabitating with Mary Ella, and those same people would say that she does not deserve a Christian burial. But I ask you to remember how Jesus dealt with such a woman.

"He said to Simon, 'Do you see this woman? I entered your house; you gave me no water for my feet, but she has wet my feet with her tears and wiped them with her hair. You gave me no kiss; but she, since the time I came in, has not ceased to kiss my feet. You did not anoint my head with oil, but she anointed my feet with perfume. For this reason I say to you, her sins, which are many, have been forgiven, for she loved much; but he who is forgiven little, loves little.' Then He said to her, 'Your sins have been forgiven.'

"Now folks, that's what Jesus said, 'n if he could show love and honor for a woman who was a soiled dove, are we to do less?

"I'd like to invite you now to go outside and stand in the teardrops of angels as we put Jim and Mary Ella in the ground, where they will lie side by side for all eternity just as they did while they were here, alive amongst us."

The small ranchers lined up to act as pall bearers, and they carried the coffins out to the hearse, where they lay them side by side. The rain continued to fall on everyone as they went out to the cemetery, where dressed in black and standing under black umbrellas, they bore the rain for the graveside service.

The graves had already been opened, and when the caskets were lowered, Cheatum led everyone in the Lord's Prayer. When the prayer was concluded, the mourners left the cemetery, some on foot, a few on horseback, and the others in buckboards and wagons.

Neither Colleen nor Cooter had spoken to anyone else.

After the burial, Cheatum closed the saloon to

the public, though it was open to anyone who had attended the funeral and who wanted to have a place to visit. Hugh and Lisa went home, but Matt, Sheriff Clark, and Art Walhausen returned to the saloon.

"You know it's a hard life out here, and I've seen a lot of men and women buried," Sheriff Clark said. "I have to say that I've put a few of the men there, myself. But something about this one just gets all over me. Not just that it's a lynching. I've seen lynchings before. But to hang a man and his wife like that? I just can't come to grips with it."

"I told you who it was," Matt said. "If you would like, I can go out with you tomorrow to bring them in."

"That won't be necessary," Sheriff Clark said.

"What? What do you mean it won't be necessary?" Art asked.

"Just before the funeral commenced, Luke McCoy come into town 'n told me that the men who did this would be coming in on their own."

"That's hard to believe," Matt said.

"McCoy swore that they would come in, and I'd like to give them the opportunity to do that. You have to admit, Matt, having them come in voluntarily would be a lot better than going out to Purgatory Pass to bring them in by force."

"I'll give you that," Matt agreed. "All right. We'll wait and see what happens."

When Matt stepped to the newspaper office the next morning, Art was seething mad. "This is a setup," he said angrily. "It's all a setup and has been from the beginning."

"What's a setup, Art? What are you talking about?"

"This business about Carter and the others coming in to give themselves up is a complete setup."

"Yes, I thought it would be. But I'm going to bring them in if I have to go out there by myself."

"Oh, you won't have to do that. They'll be coming in, all right."

"They are? Then what are you talking about? What's the setup?"

"This," Art said, picking up a newspaper and handing it to Matt. "This is the *Bitter Creek Press Bulletin*. You might say that it is my competition. Read this article, and you'll see what I mean by it being a setup."

TWO NOTORIOUS CHARACTERS
HANGED FOR CATTLE RUSTLING

JIM ANDREWS AND
PARAMOUR, MARY ELLA WILSON,
FORCED TO PAY FOR THEIR CRIMES

Meet Their Fate at the Hands
of Rightfully Outraged Citizens

(SPECIAL TO THE BITTER CREEK PRESS BULLETIN) But a short time ago, Jim Andrews, a nester who had established a ranch by stocking it with ill-gained cattle, and Mary Ella Wilson, a married woman and prostitute who lived with him in sinful cohabitation, were found in possession of four illegally obtained steers. The cows bore the brand of the Straight Arrow Ranch, and for this proof of their many transgressions, Andrews and Wilson were hanged.

Our readers may be interested to know that Mary Ella Wilson is the woman who recently achieved some notoriety as Cattle Mary Ella. This villainous woman first entered the world of criminal activity with her husband, Clay Wilson, who is now serving a life sentence in the state penitentiary in Lansing, Kansas.

The lynching of the man and woman on the Sweetwater may be determined by some as deplorable. All resorts to lynch law are deplorable in a country that is governed by law, but when the law shows itself powerless and inactive, when justice is lame and halting, when there is failure to convict on downright proof, it is not in the nature of enterprising Western men to sit idly by and have their cattle stolen from under their very noses.

Rather than a lynching, the event might better be described as a legal hanging, as those who perpetrated the deed were neither a hastily formed mob nor were they vigilantes. They were duly appointed railroad detectives. These brave men, their appointments recognized by law, were acting on behalf of the ranchers of Sweetwater Valley, who for some time have had to suffer the depredations of Andrews and Wilson. Andrews, it is said, maintained a house of ill-repute using the fallen woman, Mary Ella Wilson to "offer her favors" in exchange for stolen cattle.

There had been many previous attempts to convict Andrews and Wilson, but the courts have refused to do so, regardless of the strength of the evidence. The story of Andrews's descent is an old one. It was brought about by his passion for gambling, liquor, and lewd women, such as the one with whom he was cohabitating when he met his demise.

Cattle Mary Ella is known to have killed two men, one a lover with whom she quarreled and subsequently poisoned, and a young colored man who she shot, giving as the excuse that he had attempted to steal her jewelry. Mary Ella Wilson was a tramp of the lowest sort, and Jim Andrews was the scourge of honest men everywhere.

The five men who executed Andrews and Wilson, being Asa Carter, Moe Greene, Walter Toone, and John and Lem Mason were, in many respects, doing their civic duty, and they should be lauded by all right-thinking citizens. This paper has been informed that they will be surrendering themselves soon so that their names may be cleared and that there be no shame applied to the act.

"It's disgusting!" Art Walhausen said angrily. "The *Press Bulletin* is a daily, and the *Gazette* is a weekly, but if I had known that Mike Marvin was going to print such a story I would have put out an extra to preempt him." The *Gazette* publisher stared at the copy of the *Press Bulletin* with ill-concealed contempt. "Instead, they have preempted me. Now the entire territory thinks these five men were acting on behalf of the people.

"Something like this makes me ashamed to say that I am a member of the press."

"So they really are going to turn themselves in today?" Matt asked.

"Yes, to Judge Aaron Briggs."

"Do you know Judge Briggs?"

"Oh, yes, I know him," Art said in a voice that suggested little respect for the judge. "I'm afraid our *good* judge is in O'Neil and Kennedy's hip pockets. I would be willing to bet that the men involved don't spend a single night in jail."

"You think not?"

"I know this town, I know Judge Briggs, and more important, I know Kennedy and O'Neil. It'll be a private hearing. DuPont will more than likely bring them in, present them to the judge, the judge will dismiss the case, and it'll be over."

"Well, there is one good thing about this article," Matt said, pointing to the paper.

"What can possibly be good about the article?"

"The paper has brought it out into the public, and that will make certain that it has to be a public hearing."

"Even so, we'll still have to deal with Briggs."

"No," Isaac said.

Matt had found him in the Wild Hog Saloon.

Isaac shook his head in response to the question Matt had asked. "I won't testify in court. I'm sorry. I know it is cowardly of me, but my testimony would be unverified, and because of that, the judge will give little credence to anything I have to say. Also, I'm afraid that my very appearance in court would be the same as me signing my death warrant."

"But I've been told that you were a lawyer," Matt said. "Seems to me that would count for something."

"Why would it? As I would be neither prosecutor nor defense attorney, I would have no more standing with the court than any other uncorroborated witness.

It is because I am a lawyer that I know the futility of even trying. Also, I am a colored man who left the legal profession under somewhat of a cloud, and the life I have lived since then has certainly been less than sterling.

"I wish I could help you, Mr. Jensen. Believe me, if I thought my testimony would have any impact, I would appear, despite the personal danger. But why put my life at risk when there is no possibility of a positive outcome?"

Matt nodded. "All right. I understand. But, let me ask you this. Does DuPont know you are the one who tried to stop the lynching?"

"At the moment he has no way of knowing. But he is smarter than he looks, and it won't take much for him to put two and two together and come up with the answer."

"Are you going to stay around here?"

"Not exactly."

"What do you mean," Matt asked, not understanding the rather vague answer.

"I mean I'm not exactly going to stay around here," Isaac repeated without any further clarification.

Matt nodded, then looked over toward the bar where Fancy stood, having been asked earlier by Isaac to give them a little privacy. "Does she know what you saw?"

"No, and I don't intend for her to know," Isaac said. "If she knew, it would be as dangerous for her as it is for me."

Matt nodded. "Good point. I see what you mean."

Matt left the Wild Hog, disappointed that he was unable to get Isaac to agree to testify.

"How did your visit go?" Art asked when Matt

returned to the newspaper office. Art, like Prufrock, knew that Isaac Newton had been an eyewitness to the whole thing.

"He isn't going to testify, and I can't blame him," Matt said.

"What's that?" Art asked, looking toward the front window. "What's going on out there?"

"It sounds like they might be coming in." Matt and Art could hear the shouts from the street out front.

"Here they come!"

"All five of 'em?"

"They's seven of 'em, looks like to me!"

Chapter Twenty-seven

Hearing the calls from the street, Matt and Art stepped from the newspaper office to watch the arrival of the men who had been identified as the participants in the lynching of Jim and Mary Ella.

Matt had expected only the five who had been named, but DuPont and McCoy were riding in with the ones whose names had been in the newspaper article.

Matt and the newspaper publisher weren't the only ones watching the arrival, as there were considerably more than a hundred of the town's citizens who had turned out.

"You men done good by hangin' that thievin' mongrel 'n his whore!" someone called out to the riders. "This'll teach people that they can't get away with thievin' 'n rustlin' in Sweetwater Valley!"

"Lynchin' ain't right, no matter who it is," another man called.

"You shouldn'ta hung a woman!" another called.

"Ain't no need for feelin' bad about her. She was a whore!"

"I'm going down to the courthouse," Matt said. "I want to see what happens."

"Good idea. I'm coming with you."

"There's a pretty good crowd gathering down there, so it looks like it's going to be a public hearing," Matt said.

He and Art hurried down to the courtroom, and using Matt's badge as a deputy and Art's standing as a member of the press, they were able to go in, even before the courtroom doors were opened.

Judge Briggs was a short, heavyset man who tried to fight his baldness by combing his hair over the top of his head. He wore thick glasses and had a very narrow strip of a moustache. He was sitting behind the bench when Matt and Art took a seat up front.

The courtroom was nearly filled by the time the Regulators filed into the room, and though McCoy took a seat at the rear of the room, DuPont walked down front with the five who were the subjects of the hearing.

Judge Briggs called the court to order, and all conversation ceased as DuPont stood to address the Judge.

"Your honor, allow me to introduce myself. I am Tyrone DuPont, chief of the Regulators. We're a group of private detectives employed by the Union Pacific Railroad, and we got the legal right, accordin' to the Territory of Wyoming, to do the same thing as if we was lawmen. These five men belong to that same group, 'n what they're doin' here is they've come of their own free will, to surrender themselves to the court."

"What is it you are surrendering yourselves for?"

Judge Briggs directed his question toward the five men, though not to any one in particular.

Carter answered for all of them. "We seen our names in the paper sayin' that we was the ones that hung that cattle thief and his whore."

"And, are you now confessing to that?"

"No, Your Honor, they aren't," a strong voice said.

Though Matt had not seem him earlier, the person who had spoken out was Garrett Kennedy.

"Are you acting as attorney for these men?" Briggs asked.

"No, sir, I can't do that as I am not a lawyer, but I have been asked to speak on their behalf, and with the court's permission, I shall do so."

"All right. The court recognizes Garrett Kennedy as advocate for, but not the legal representative of, the five men who are standing before me."

"Thank you, Your Honor. Your Honor, I begin my advocacy by asking if anyone present in this court is prepared to bear witness against these men?"

"That is a very good question, Mr. Kennedy, and I will now ask it from the bench. If there be anyone present who has pertinent information to offer in regard to these five men and the death, by hanging, of Jim Andrews and Mary Ella Wilson, I ask that you now present yourself and give such testimony."

No one responded.

"There is no witness to testify?"

Matt stood up.

"Yes, Deputy Jensen," Judge Briggs said. "You have testimony to present before this court?"

"Not directly, Your Honor, but you might say that I am a material witness in that I did go to the location where the lynching took place while the bodies were still hanging. In addition, I have spoken with an actual eyewitness to the murder of Mr. and Mrs. Andrews. He was the one who knew where the bodies were."

"And who was this witness, Mr. Jensen?"

Matt thought of his conversation with Isaac, and he knew that to say his name in public could put Isaac in danger. "I would rather not give his name, right now, but I would tell you, privately, and I am prepared to share with the court what this eyewitness to the lynching told me."

"If it does not come from an actual eyewitness, it would be hearsay evidence, Deputy Jensen, and as such I'm afraid that it would not be admissible," Judge Briggs said.

"But, Your Honor, I did see the two bodies hanging there, and that is not hearsay."

"We are not here to determine whether or not Mr. Andrews and Mrs. Wilson were hanged. We are here merely to establish who did it, and whether or not the hangings were justifiable."

"Your Honor, how can a lynching ever be justifiable?" Matt asked sharply.

"You are out of order, sir, and I will hear no more from you!" Judge Briggs lifted his hammer, then slammed it down sharply.

"Your Honor," Kennedy said. "As there is no one to bear witness against these men, may I ask that they be found innocent?"

"I cannot declare them innocent, as there has been no charge filed against them and no adjudication. However, minus a confession, and minus any direct testimony from a valid eyewitness to the event, I have no recourse but to declare this case *nolle prosequi.* This hearing is adjourned."

"There you have it, Matt. The best justice you can buy," Art said under his breath.

"I wish I could have convinced him to be here," Matt said. "But I can understand his reluctance."

"You're talking about Isaac Newton?"

Matt cut a quick, cautioning glance toward Art.

"Don't worry, I'm not going to publish his name nor tell anyone. I know it would be very dangerous for him if anyone else knew."

"Dangerous? It could be fatal."

Shortly after the court hearing, Art Walhausen wrote a piece in the *Gazette.*

A TERRIBLE INJUSTICE DONE

The lynching of two of the leading citizens of Sweetwater Valley by men who are members of the Regulators has been portrayed in a highly colored account in the BITTER CREEK PRESS BULLETIN. That paper speaks of Jim Andrews as a particularly tough citizen when quite the opposite is true. Mr. Andrews was well and favorably regarded and spoken of as a peaceable and law-abiding citizen.

The description of Mrs. Andrews, (portrayed as Mary Ella Wilson in the PRESS BULLETIN) is equally lurid and equally wrong. The lynching of these two admirable citizens was murder, pure and simple. And yet a farce was committed in the hearing where not one of the accused was questioned, and not one word of accusation was allowed to be entered into the record so that, in a matter of but a few minutes the case was heard and dismissed by Judge Briggs.

Is human life to hold no value whatever? Are four cows with a brand other than the Circle Dot—the only evidence stated as justification for the hanging of Mr. and Mrs. Andrews—put in balance on one side and made to weigh more than two human lives on the other? Can it be, in this age of enlightenment, in the God-favored territory soon to become a state, that the worst of all crimes can be committed and the perpetrators go free?

This scribe finds it disturbing that the PRESS BULLETIN, a newspaper that I have always respected and regarded as a companion vehicle in the effort to keep our citizenry informed, would even hint that such a crime was excusable. Shame on them for doing so.

As for the Regulators, their time has come and gone. Their position as Sweetwater County deputies has rightfully been withdrawn, which means they no longer hold any legal authority. It has become quite well known that they are now, and always have been, little more than a band of brigands. Operating under the command of Tyrone DuPont, they are dedicated not to justice, but to the private service of Sean O'Neil and Garrett Kennedy.

The murder of Mr. and Mrs. Andrews by the Regulators should energize all good citizens of the valley to rise in unison and demand that these outlaws be disbanded.

Straight Arrow Ranch

"The newspaper down in Bitter Crick, the one you talked to, give us a real good story," DuPont said.

"That is true," O'Neil replied. "But I'm afraid that the article in the *Gazette* may have undone all the good that the *Press Bulletin* story accomplished."

"If you want, I'll make certain that that newspaper don't never say nothin' no more about us or you," DuPont said.

"Who was the witness to the lynching?" Kennedy asked.

"There warn't no witness," DuPont said. "You was there in the courtroom. There didn't nobody show up to say nothin'."

"Nobody testified, that's true, but Jensen claimed to have spoken to someone who saw your men hang Andrews and Wilson."

"Oh, yeah, someone was there all right, 'cause durin' the hangin' someone commenced shootin' at 'em. But when you said who was the witness I thought you was talkin' about in the courtroom where there wasn't no witness that actual said nothin'."

"And yet he claims to have spoken to someone who did see it," O'Neil replied. "Who would that be? Who saw it?"

"There don't nobody know for sure, because there didn't nobody see who it was that was shootin' at 'em. But I got my suspicions, 'n what I'm thinkin' is that it was Isaac Newton."

"Isn't he the colored man?"

"Yeah, that's the one."

"Why do you suspect him?"

"On account of he has disappeared 'n there ain't nobody seen him in a few days."

"He could be trouble," O'Neil said.

"Yes, I was thinking the same thing," Kennedy said.

"You want me to get rid of 'im?" DuPont asked.

"You said that nobody has seen him since the lynching. Do you know where he is?" Kennedy asked.

"No, but how hard is it goin' to be to find a colored man where mostly there's only white men?" O'Neil asked.

"You have a point," Kennedy conceded. "All right. Go ahead and get rid of him."

"No, wait. He might be useful to us," O'Neil said.

"In what way could he be useful?" Kennedy asked.

"Suppose there was another rash of cattle rustling," Kennedy suggested. "And suppose the rustler was Isaac Newton. That would do several things for us. It would put more pressure on the ranchers who are struggling, increased rustling would remind everyone of the need for the Regulators, and it would provide justification for taking care of Newton when you found him."

"How are we goin' to make folks think it's Newton that's stealin' the cattle?"

"You let our friend Mike Marvin handle that," Kennedy said with a smile.

"You're goin' to put Isaac Newton's name in the paper?" O'Neil asked.

"Yes, but there must be some cattle taken before we can accuse anyone of rustling."

"You let me worry about that," DuPont said with a knowing smile. "I'll get some cows took for you, all right."

* * *

"Colleen, I don't know what's going on here, but it doesn't sound good," Cooter said later that day.

"What do you mean?"

"I think Kennedy and . . . I hate to say it . . . your father might be involved with all the rustlin' that's goin' on."

"Nonsense, why would they be involved? They've got more cattle than everyone else combined."

"I'm not sure. They've always kept me and the hands out of it, and to be honest, the pay is so good I was willing to stay out of what's going on. I don't know for sure now, what it is. But it doesn't sound good."

"I'll talk to Papa."

"No!" Cooter said sharply. "No, I think, for now, it would be best for us to just stay out of it and see what happens. Maybe I'm wrong."

Chapter Twenty-eight

From the *Bitter Creek Press Bulletin*:

Rustling Continues

NEGRO MAN SPOTTED STEALING CATTLE

Rustler Is Believed to be Isaac Newton

Ollie Lynch, a rider for the Straight Arrow brand, reported seeing the colored outlaw cutting out as many as one hundred head of cattle from the Straight Arrow herd. The theft happened Sunday night, the time carefully chosen as it would be a time when the fewest men would be patrolling the herd. The paucity of herd sentinels is the result of a policy of Messrs. O'Neil and Kennedy to give as many men time off as possible on this day of rest.

The rustler, aided no doubt by his color, was able to move as a shadow within a shadow, and wasn't detected in his nefarious activity until it was too late for Lynch to summon aid.

It has been reported that other area ranchers have also lost stock of late, no doubt to the same rustler that was spotted and identified by Mr. Lynch as Isaac Newton. That Newton has resorted to criminal activity is particularly egregious in that he had until recently, been a supporter of the law, being a member of the Regulators. Isaac Newton has betrayed the trust of the people who had counted upon him to defend their interests, and has become an outlaw of the worst sort.

Some in the town of Rongis may remember Newton as a habitué of the Wild Hog Saloon, where he often kept company with a young Negress who goes by the name of Fancy, who, as most in her profession, is not identified by a last name. Isaac Newton is a rarity among his race in that he is quite well spoken, which is indicative of his education.

Captain Tyrone DuPont, chief of the Regulators and acting on behalf of the Union Pacific Railroad, has offered a reward of five hundred dollars, dead or alive, for the capture or proven death of Isaac Newton, who is said to be five feet, nine inches tall, approximately 155 pounds, and coffee complexioned with no facial hair.

Spur and Latigo Ranch

As the newspaper had pointed out, there had been an increase in the number of cattle-rustling events over the last few days. Norman Lambert and Eddie Webb had been the victims of cattle rustling.

"Norman lost twenty-five head, but Eddy lost sixty-five head, which is near half his whole herd," Travis Poindexter told Matt and Hugh.

"They're still busy, I see," Hugh said. "I had hoped that they would slow down a bit since Jim and Mary Ella were murdered."

"Yeah, well, if nothing else, this ought to prove that it was that colored man the paper is talkin' about that's been doin' all the rustlin'. Jim 'n Mary Ella didn't have nothin' at all to do with it," Travis Poindexter said. "Onliest thing is, it's too late for it to do 'em any good now."

"I don't believe Isaac Newton has anything to do with the rustling that's going on right now," Matt said.

"Why don't you believe it? The article sounds pretty convincing," Hugh said.

"Hugh, this is the same newspaper that said Jim and Mary Ella were receiving stolen cattle, remember?"

"Yeah, 'n Jim 'n Mary Ella warn't doin' that," Poindexter said. "There ain't no doubt in my mind but that they warn't doin' nothin' like that."

"No need to tell us that, Travis. Nobody who knew them believes such a thing," Hugh said. "That whole thing was drummed up in some sick attempt to justify the lynching so that Carter and the others wouldn't be found guilty of murder."

"I'm convinced that the ones who murdered Jim and Mary Ella also knew they were innocent," Matt said. "So my question is, if they were going to murder them, why didn't they just shoot them? Why did they go to all the trouble to lynch them?"

"I'll tell you why," Poindexter said. "They done it 'cause they're just a bunch of downright evil sons of bitches. That's why they done it."

"They are evil, I'll grant you that," Matt said. "But there has to be another reason."

The three men were sitting on Hugh's front porch. Matt had been invited out for supper. The enticing aroma of Lisa's cooking wafted out from the house, and Poindexter had come over to report on the cattle losses sustained by Lambert and Webb.

"I wish we could catch some o' these thieves redhanded," Poindexter added. "I would string 'em up before you could say Jack Robinson."

"And then you would be as guilty of lynching as Carter, Greene, Toone, and the Mason brothers," Matt said. "Only, unlike them, you wouldn't be able to count on Briggs to absolve you of the crime."

"That's not the only reason I wouldn't be like them. I also wouldn't be like them, because the ones I'd be hanging would be guilty."

"Do you think Judge Briggs would see it like that?" Matt asked.

"Not hardly. That sidewinder belongs to Kennedy 'n O'Neil, 'n they 'n the Regulators have been real close from the beginnin'," Poindexter said.

Hugh chuckled. "Then, no doubt, you can see the folly of any plan to string up the rustlers if you find them."

"Yeah, I guess so. But, what are we goin' to do with 'em? I mean, if we was to catch 'em 'n bring 'em in, what would keep Briggs from just lettin' 'em go?"

"Briggs isn't the only judge in the territory," Hugh said. "If we had to, we could take them as far as Cheyenne."

"Maybe." Poindexter stood up, stretched, and stepped down from the porch. "Smellin' Lisa's cookin' reminds me that I better be gettin' on back home. I reckon Alice will have my own supper ready for me 'bout now."

"Thanks for stopping by, Travis," Hugh said. "I appreciated the visit."

"I wish we had had better things to talk about than our friends gettin' rustled."

Poindexter had just ridden away when Lisa came to the front door. "Gentlemen, supper is ready."

Matt and Hugh headed inside.

"Fried pork chops, potatoes and eggs, biscuits and gravy," Matt said, examining the meal.

"I know it's nothing fancy, but—" Lisa started to say.

"Are you kidding?" interrupted by Matt, who held up his hand. "Do you have any idea what percentage of my meals are bacon and canned beans? And when I'm not eating that, I'm eating in a saloon or a restaurant somewhere. I don't get that many home-cooked meals, and it so happens that this is one of my favorites, so I don't want to hear you putting yourself down. Just let me enjoy it.'

Hugh chuckled. "I guess he's put you in your place."

"I feel bad about not inviting Travis to stay, but I wasn't expecting him and didn't cook enough."

"That's all right. Alice is expecting him home for supper," Hugh said. "He just stopped by to tell us that Norman and Eddie had cattle rustled last night."

"Oh, that's awful."

"Hugh, how close in can you bring your horses and still have enough graze?" Matt asked.

"I can bring them in pretty close, but if they are all

bunched up, the graze wouldn't last for much over a week. But I do have everything well fenced now."

Matt nodded. "Then I expect you'll be all right as long as the fence is in place."

"Now that LeRoy and Jake have come to work for us, they, Ed, and I can keep an eye on the fence to make certain that nothing has happened to it," Hugh said.

"That's probably a good idea until we can get the horses down to Bitter Creek," Matt said.

"Bitter Creek," Hugh said in scoffing tone of voice. "Say, when we get the horses there, do you think there's any chance that they might get away from us when we're taking them through town just long enough to perhaps run over the newspaper office before we can regain control of them?"

"Why, Hugh, would you abridge freedom of the press?" Lisa asked with a whimsical smile. "Remember Thomas Jefferson said that he would rather have newspapers without a government than to have a government without newspapers."

"Yes," Hugh replied. "But did you know that Thomas Jefferson also said 'Nothing can now be believed which is seen in a newspaper. Truth itself becomes suspicious by being put into that polluted vehicle.' And clearly he was talking about the Bitter Creek newspaper."

Matt chuckled. "Hugh, if I didn't know better, I would say that you have very little love for newspapers."

"I never have cared too much for them. Except

when a newspaper would give me a favorable review for one of my concerts," he added with a smile.

"What about Mr. Walhausen? You like his newspaper," Lisa pointed out.

"Yes, I do. But his paper isn't the *Bitter Creek Press Bulletin*."

From the *Bitter Creek Press Bulletin:*

More Stock Rustling

Cattle Thievery Establishes Justification for the Regulators

One would think that executing the outlaws Jim Andrews and Mary Ella Wilson would have brought about some relief from rustling. But, sad to say, the demise of those two brigands has done little to stop the depredations visited upon the beleaguered ranchers of Sweetwater Valley.

Small ranchers Norman Lambert and Eddy Webb were visited by cattle thieves, indicating that the rustlers undoubtedly have outlets for their ill-gotten gains beyond that which was provided for them by Andrews and Wilson.

But of course theft of cattle from the small ranches isn't the only rustling taking place. Mr. Kennedy and Mr. O'Neil, being the owners of the Straight Arrow, are also victims. In an earlier story, the PRESS BULLETIN reported that the Negro Bandit Isaac Newton stole as many as 100 cows from the Straight Arrow, which is the largest ranch between the Laramie Mountains and the Wind River Range, Rattlesnake Mountains and the Seminoe Range.

It is now believed that Newton must have acquired a confederate or confederates for the most recent thievery. This supposition was arrived at because over five hundred head were taken from the most extreme western part of their ranch.

Captain DuPont, chief of the Regulators, has stated that he and his men will redouble their efforts to find Isaac Newton and rid the valley of the scourge of rustling.

Residents of Fremont County are no doubt appreciative of the fact that Messrs. Kennedy and O'Neil provide the funding which allows Captain DuPont, and the brave men of the Regulators to operate.

"How many people read this newspaper?" Matt asked, dropping it back on the counter in the office of the *Gazette*.

"I'm sorry to say that a lot more people read this paper than read mine," Art Walhausen replied. "But when I saw this story, I thought you might find it interesting."

"Five hundred head taken from Straight Arrow," Matt said.

"Well, six hundred, if you add the two reports together," Art replied. "What's funny to me is, generally Sheriff Clark keeps me apprised of what's going on, but he didn't say anything about the five hundred cows that were taken."

"I'll ask the sheriff about it, but I'm almost sure he

wasn't told about any rustling from Straight Arrow," Matt said. "Makes you wonder, doesn't it?"

"When you say, 'it makes you wonder,' are you expressing doubt as to whether or not the claim of rustling from Straight Arrow is true?" Art asked.

"Oh, I have a lot of doubt," Matt replied. "Consider this. If there really was any rustling, what happened to the cattle? How did the rustlers get rid of them? The cows that were taken from Lambert and Webb can be handled without too much problem. But five hundred, no, six hundred head, which is what Kennedy and O'Neil say they lost, would make it rather difficult to find a market, I would think."

"You have a point. There are only three railheads in this part of the country that handle stock shipments—Rawlings, Latham, and Bitter Creek—and I don't think that many head could be moved that far without someone being made aware of the operation," Art said. "If you would like, I can telegraph all three and ask them to let me know if the cattle show up there in the next week or so."

"Yes, I think that would be a good idea," Matt replied.

"Are you telling me that the Bitter Creek newspaper is reporting that five hundred head were taken from the Straight Arrow?" Sheriff Clark asked, surprised at the information Matt gave him.

"That's what it says."

"That's strange. They told me about the hundred head Newton took. I wonder why neither Kennedy nor O'Neil said anything to me about this."

"They didn't tell you anything about it, because I don't believe it actually happened."

"You mean the newspaper lied about it?"

"I'm sure the newspaper printed just what was reported. I expect the lying came from Kennedy and O'Neil."

"Why would they lie a about such a thing?"

"That's a good question," Matt replied. "Why indeed?"

Chapter Twenty-nine

"Why should we report it to you?" O'Neil asked. "When have you ever been able to deal with anything? Let the Regulators handle it. Isn't this why we funded the Regulators, so that you would have help?"

"It just seems like the theft of five hundred head of cattle would be significant enough to be reported to the law." Sheriff Clark was in the office of the Straight Arrow Ranch, having ridden out from town to discuss the newspaper article with Kennedy and O'Neil.

"You already know who took the first one hundred cows," Kennedy said. "It was Isaac Newton. Have you been able to find him?"

"No," Clark admitted.

"Then what good would it do for us to report to you that we had five hundred more taken?"

"Five hundred head is seventy-five hundred dollars," Sheriff Clark said. "It seems to me like losin' that much money would be somethin' you'd want to be reportin' on."

"We did report it," O'Neil said.

"To the newspaper?" the sheriff asked.

"And to DuPont and the Regulators."

Sheriff Clark made a scoffing sound. "The Regulators. I wouldn't be surprised if they wasn't the ones that's rustlin' your cows. That is, if any of your cows actually *is* bein' rustled."

"And just what do you mean by that?" O'Neil asked sharply.

"It's just that every time one of the smaller ranchers or farmers is forced off their property, somehow you two seem to wind up with it. And mostly the ones that loses their land loses it because they's so much rustlin' goin' on."

"If you're tryin' to say somethin', Clark, get it said," Kennedy demanded.

"Suppose, just suppose, mind you, that there was a lot of rustlin' goin' on, 'n like I said, and you was, somehow, benefitin' from all that. And maybe some folks would start wonderin' about it, and wonderin' why you wasn't gettin' none of your cows stoled, too. Wouldn't it look better for you, if you two arranged that some of your cows got took, or at least if you was able to make ever'one think that some of your cows was bein' rustled?"

"Are you accusing us of being cattle thieves?" Kennedy asked.

"No, leastwise, not so's I can actual say anythin' about it," Sheriff Clark replied. "But some of the things that's goin' on around here does kinda make a man wonder."

"Don't wonder too much," O'Neil warned. "It could be dangerous."

Sheriff Clark stared at both men for a long, penetrating moment, then he nodded. "Like I said, I was just wondering." He left without another word.

Kennedy and O'Neil remained quiet while they watched through the window and saw him mount up and ride away.

"The reason we have kept him on as sheriff is because he was dumb and a coward," Kennedy said. "When did the applehead get smart and grow a backbone?"

"Call Boggs in here," O'Neil said. "I think it might be time for us to benefit from what we are paying him."

When Boggs stepped into the office a moment later, O'Neil said, "Mr. Boggs, Sheriff Clark is getting . . . tiresome."

Boggs nodded, which was the only response needed.

Sheriff Clark was feeling pretty good about himself as he rode back to town. He had gotten lazy over the last few years, confining his police work to little more than arresting drunks for disturbing the peace, or serving warrants and court orders. He had let the Regulators take over and, though at first he had truly believed they would be honest deputies, he learned quickly that they were not.

He should have done something at the very beginning to stop them. If nothing else, revoked their appointments as deputies. In an honest self-examination, he realized that he had been too timid to do so. Well, no more. He had Matt Jensen on his side and that was all the help he needed to be a real sheriff.

Clark was halfway back to town before he noticed

that someone was on the road behind him. He wasn't all that concerned. After all, it was a public road and the route the stagecoaches took from Atlantic City to Rongis to Soda Lake. It wasn't at all unusual to see travelers on the road.

On the other hand, it could be someone following him.

But who would be following him from the Straight Arrow? Perhaps it was someone from the ranch, some disgruntled hand who had information for him. Over the twelve years Clark had been a sheriff, he had gotten a lot of information, critical information, from people who were on the inside of whatever he was investigating. Sometimes it was because they were upset with their boss, but sometimes it was just because they wanted to do the right thing.

If this was such a person, Sheriff Clark wanted to talk with him. Perhaps if he had some real information, he and Matt Jensen could get to the bottom of what was going on around here. Sheriff Clark pulled up and waited for the rider to approach. When he recognized the man coming toward him a huge knot of fear twisted in his stomach. The approaching rider was Merlin Boggs.

"What do you want, Boggs?" he asked when the man they called the Undertaker was within a few feet of him.

"Mr. Kennedy and Mr. O'Neil were upset by your visit," Boggs said, the words soft and raspy.

"If they are innocent, they have nothing to worry about."

"If they were innocent, they wouldn't have asked me to take care of you."

"Take care of me?" Clark's fear grew more intense. "Take care of me how? What are you talking about?"

"I'm talking about killing you." Boggs hadn't once raised his voice.

"No, there's not going to be any killing here," Sheriff Clark said, holding his hand out as if pushing Boggs away. "I have no intention of drawing on you."

"Oh, you don't understand, I'm here to kill you, not to fight you. I don't care whether you draw against me or not." With those words Boggs drew his gun and pulled the trigger. Sheriff Clark felt the bullet slam into his chest, then he felt nothing else.

It was actually Frank Edmonston who discovered the sheriff's body. He was driving a buckboard into town intending to pick up some supplies from Slusher's Supply when he saw a horse with some sort of bundle on it just standing on the side of the road. Looking around, he didn't see anyone who might belong to the horse.

As he got closer, he realized with a shock that the bundle was actually a body. And when he got even closer, he saw that it was Sheriff Clark.

Frank took the sheriff's body down from the horse and laid it in the back of the buckboard, then tied the sheriff's horse onto the back. He drove the rest of the way into town, stopping first at Prufrock's Mortuary.

After leaving the mortuary, Frank went down to Slusher's Supply, which was the original purpose of his visit into town. As he tied off his team, he saw

Matt Jensen a few stores down talking to a couple of the citizens and walked that way.

"Hello, Mr. Edmonston." Matt's greeting was friendly.

"Deputy, I thought you might want to know that I just brought the sheriff in."

"You brought the sheriff in? What do you mean?"

"I mean he's dead. I just left him with Prufrock."

Matt headed to the mortuary. Stepping into Prufrock's room, he realized the mortician had not yet started the embalming, but the sheriff was lying on the embalming table, bare from the waist up. A round bullet hole was visible just to the left of center in his chest.

"It's not hard to determine the cause of death," Prufrock said. "It was a bullet to the heart."

"Any powder burns on his shirt?" Matt asked.

"No, it wasn't a point-blank shot. It was from some distance away, though I have no way of determining just how far away he was. Lucky shot, I guess."

Matt shook his head. "Luck had nothing to do with it."

Two days after the sheriff was killed, Travis Poindexter sent a couple of his hands out to all the other landholders in the valley, ranchers and farmers alike, asking them to come to a meeting at his ranch.

As the nearby mountains turned from red to purple in the setting sun, Poindexter's friends and neighbors began arriving for the meeting. Wagons and buggies brought entire families across the range to gather at his house. Children who lived too far apart to play with each other on a normal basis laughed and squealed and ran from wagon to wagon to greet their friends before dashing off to a twilight game of kick the can. The women who had brought cakes and pies from home gathered in the kitchen to make coffee, thus turning the business meeting into a great social event. They visited and kept tabs on the youngest of the children while the men were conducting the meeting.

"Tell me, Hugh, where's Jensen?" Poindexter asked. "If he's s'posed to be helpin' us, don't you think he'd want to come to one of our meetings? Especially now that he's the sheriff."

"He's not the real sheriff. He is the acting sheriff," Hugh replied. "And that is only because he was Sheriff Clark's deputy."

"Yeah well, thank God for that. It coulda been DuPont as the acting sheriff if he hadn't a-turned in his badge," Kelly said.

"You got that right," Poindexter said. "Still, it seems to me like he woulda wanted to be here for the meeting."

"Travis, have you stopped to think that with all of us here, it might be the perfect time for rustlers to hit one of our ranches?" Poindexter asked,"

"What? Yeah. Come to think of it, this would be a good time, wouldn't it?"

"So to answer your question, Matt is out there riding around, keeping his eyes open for any nefarious activity that might be taking place. If the rustlers have something planned, Matt will be right on top of it," Hugh said.

Poindexter nodded. "Good, good. I hadn't thought

about that, but now that you bring it up, I'm glad Matt ain't here. That means he's out there doing his job."

"Hey, Travis, when are we goin' to get this meetin' started?" Gary Boyer asked. Boyer was a farmer, not a rancher, but he had three sections of land he had proven up, which made him one of the bigger land-holders present. The ranches themselves may have been smaller but, effectively, the cattlemen had more property than that which was deeded to them be-cause they allowed their cows to graze on unclaimed government land, or what was called free range. It was this, the graze on the free range, that most often brought the Straight Arrow and the smaller ranches into competition.

The sounds of the evening drifted across the back-yard. From the children playing, came, "I see Charley behind that trough!"

"One, two, three for Charley!" a child called.

There was a squeal, then a child's laughter.

A mule brayed. It was one of the team that had brought Boyer's farm wagon to the meeting. In a nearby tree, an owl hooted.

Inside, Poindexter said, "All right, fellas, I reckon we can get it started right now."

When all the men found someplace to sit, he stepped up before them.

"Travis," Earl Ray Underhill asked, holding up his hand.

"Damn, Earl Ray, we ain't even started the meetin', 'n you're already a-wantin' to ask a question?"

"Yeah, well, it ain't right a question. It's more like what you might call a suggestion."

Poindexter nodded. "All right. Let's hear it."

"I was just thinkin' that seein' as how the sheriff was just kilt 'n all, maybe we ought to say somethin' about 'im."

"Why?" Darrel Pollard asked. "He never done nothin' for us while he was alive. 'N most of the time he done just what Kennedy or O'Neil wanted 'im to do."

"Not toward the end there," Earl Ray said. "Toward the end, I think he had pretty much come over to helpin' us."

"I think Earl Ray's right. I think toward the end, Sheriff Clark was actually tryin' to help us. 'N most likely he was kilt because of it. Only since we ain't got no preacher with us, maybe you'd like to say some-thin'." Ollard said.

"I'd rather it be Hugh that says somethin', on ac-count of him havin' more education than most of us has," Earl Ray said.

"Hugh?"

"If you would all bow your heads, please, I could say a prayer," he said.

When everyone had done as Hugh had asked, he stood up and faced them. With his head bowed, he began to pray aloud. "Lord, Sheriff Clark was a lonely man, and because he was rather taciturn, we know very little about his past life, or even if he had a family somewhere.

"If he does have a family, I regret that we can't get word to them, so we will become his surrogate family. We will mourn for him, we will miss him, and we will remember him. Amen."

"Amen," some of the others repeated.

"Those were some mighty fine sentiments, Hugh,"

Edmonston said. "You used a couple of words there that I don't have no idea what they mean, but I reckon the Lord understood you, 'n that's all that counts."

"All right, men, now as to the meeting," Poindexter said. "I'm thinkin' we ought to form us up some kind of a group, something that all of us can belong to."

"Why, Travis, we've already got something like that, it being the Sweetwater Ranchers' Association," Ernest Dean Fawcett pointed out.

"Yes, but the Sweetwater Ranchers' Association is controlled lock, stock, and barrel by Kennedy and O'Neil," Poindexter said. "I think we should have one of our own."

"If it's just a ranchers' association, where does that leave us farmers?" Gary Boyer asked.

"It's not the same for farmers. It's not like you're having cattle rustled," Eddie Webb said.

"Ask Sylvester Malcolm if he hasn't had some dirty business done to his wheat," Gary replied.

"I've thought about that," Poindexter said, "and I think the farmers should be welcome into our group. I want this association to include all the small landowners in the entire valley."

"May I make a suggestion?" Art Walhausen asked. Even though he owned no land other than where his newspaper office sat, he was a good friend to the small ranchers and farmers. Because of that, he had been invited to the meeting.

"Sure, go ahead," Poindexter invited.

"I would suggest that you call your group the Union of Landowners of Sweetwater Valley. That will include both ranchers and farmers."

"That sounds good to me," Poindexter said.

"Should we take some steps to make that official?" Hugh asked.

"I'll be happy to take care of that. I'll have a charter drawn up for you and filed at the capitol in Cheyenne," Art said.

Poindexter smiled and addressed all who were assembled. "Gentlemen, the Union of Landowners of Sweetwater Valley is formed. Welcome to the first meeting."

Chapter Thirty

Rocking P Ranch

Darrel Pollard, his wife Ethyl, and their two children were attending the meeting but, back at his ranch, the Rocking P, the three hands who worked for him were in the small bunkhouse, where Dusty was regaling the other two with a story of his prowess with the fairer sex.

"But even though she begged me to take her with me, I told her that I wasn't the one for her. I am a man of adventure, and I just don't have a place in my life for a woman. She cried, Lord you ain't never seen no woman cryin' like she done."

The other two men laughed. "Dusty, you are as full of bull as a Christmas turkey," Billy Ray said.

"Why do people always say that?" Harley Mack asked. "I mean, who stuffs a Christmas turkey with shit?"

There was more laughter.

"You think all them ranchers is goin' to come up with anythin' at this meetin' they got goin' on over to the Poindexter place?" Dusty asked.

"I don't know. If they don't, they might all wind up

goin' out of business 'n if that happens, me 'n you 'n Harley Mack is all goin' to be lookin' for jobs somewhere else," Billy Ray suggested.

"Maybe we could wind up workin' over to the Straight Arrow," Harley Mack suggested. "Seems like ever' time someone quits ranchin', the Straight Arrow just gets bigger."

"Yeah, but if you notice, they mostly don't hire all the cowboys from the old ranches. Hell, they don't even hire half of 'em. The rest of 'em is left out in the cold," Dusty said.

"Yeah, that's true," Billy Ray agreed. "'N to be honest, I wouldn't want to be doin' no work for the Straight Arrow in the first place. I just don't like them two sons of bitches that owns it."

"Cooter's all right," Dusty said. "Me 'n him used to work together."

"Yeah, he's a good man for all that he works for Kennedy 'n O'Neil."

"You know why he works there, don't you?" Billy Ray asked. "He's sweet on O'Neil's daughter."

"O'Neil's daughter ain't nothin' like her ole man. She's nice. 'N she's pretty, too," Harley Mack said.

"Yeah," Dusty agreed. "But don't forget, that's where the Undertaker is. Why, I'd be so afraid that I might step on his toes or somethin' that I might actual do it. Then he'd more 'n likely want to shoot me for it. No, sir, if Mr. Pollard winds up goin' out of business, I'll just follow him to wherever he winds up startin' agin."

As the three young cowboys carried on their conversation in the bunkhouse, three riders outside—Stryker, Adams, and Malone—stopped on a little hill overlooking the ranch. They were the three newest recruits for DuPont's Regulators. They ground-tied their mounts about thirty yards behind them, then crawled down to the edge of the hill so they could look down toward the bunkhouse. Malone had a pair of field glasses, and he raised them to his eyes so he could surveil the bunkhouse below them.

"What do you see, Malone?" Stryker asked.

"Looks like they's only three of 'em in there. I can see 'em through the window. They're sittin' around a table."

"Eatin', are they?"

"No, it don't look to me like they're doin' nothin' but talkin'."

"Well, it don't matter none what they're doin'. DuPont said kill ever'one we find here, so let's get a little closer," Stryker said.

"Right down there," Adams said, pointing to a little open area about forty yards closer to the bunkhouse. "That looks like a good place."

They moved to the spot, and from there they had a good view of the inside of the bunkhouse. It was very dark outside, and that allowed them to come quite close without being seen, whereas the illuminated bunkhouse allowed them to see the three inside.

"Malone, you take the one on the left. Adams, you take the one on the right. I'll get the one in the center."

"I'm ready," Adams said.

The three men raised their rifles and took slow, careful aim at their targets well illuminated by the lantern that burned brightly inside the bunkhouse.

"Shoot!" Stryker said, squeezing the trigger that sent out the first bullet.

Harley Mack died instantly, a bullet coming through the window to crash into the back of his head. Dusty went down with a bullet in his chest. Billy Ray felt the pop of the bullet as it passed by his ear, and seeing what had happened to the other two, he fell to the floor.

The shooting continued for another full minute, with bullets whistling through the window, slamming into the walls and careening off the unused stove. Billy Ray scooted as far up under his bunk as he could get and lay there with his arms over his head until, finally, the shooting stopped.

"Billy Ray!" Dusty called, his voice weak and strained. "Billy Ray, I'm hit. I'm hit bad!"

Billy Ray crawled across the floor littered with shattered glass from the shot-out window. When he reached Dusty, he knew it would soon be over.

"Am I goin' to die, Billy Ray? Am I goin' to die?" Dusty gasped.

"No, you ain't goin' to die, Dusty. You ain't goin' to die." But even as Billy Ray was trying to comfort his friend, he knew he was talking to a dead man.

Billy Ray looked at his two dead friends, then thought to extinguish the lantern. With the lantern extinguished, he crawled over to the window and, cautiously, lifted his head to take a look outside. At first he saw nothing but darkness, then, with a gasp, he saw that flames were coming from the main house. He also saw three men silhouetted against the flames and, for just a second, he contemplated taking a shot at them.

He put that idea aside almost as quickly as the notion was born. There were three of them to the one of him, and he wasn't that good of a shot anyway.

What if they burn the barn and the bunkhouse? Billy Ray knew he had to get out of the bunkhouse while the getting was good. He thought of Harley Mack and Dusty, and wished there was some way he could get them out, but he was afraid to take the chance. They were already dead, anyway.

He opened the door and crawled away into the darkness while the three men continued to watch the burning flames of their handiwork.

Matt was toward the western boundary of the Spur and Latigo Ranch when he heard shooting coming from a distance. He saw flames and knew they were coming, not from the Spur and Latigo, but from the Rocking P. He put Spirit into a gallop and covered the two miles in less than four minutes. He saw three riders silhouetted against the orange glow of the ranch they had just torched. Matt moved Spirit off the trail, then dismounted and climbed up onto a rock to wait for them.

They were riding no faster than a walk, and as they came closer, Matt was able to overhear their conversation.

"We shoulda looked inside the bunkhouse to see if ever'one was kilt," one of the riders said.

"They was more 'n likely all dead," another voice said. "Hell, we didn't hear nothin' from 'em after we rode up there, did we?"

From the tone of their conversation, and seeing the men against the fire, Matt could believe that the gates of hell had opened, and three of its most evil denizens had escaped.

He cocked his pistol then stood on the rock to

confront them. "Hold it right there!" he called out to the three men.

"What the hell?" one of the men shouted. "Who the hell are you?"

"I am the acting sheriff, and you three men are under arrest."

"The hell we are! Shoot 'im down!" one of the three men shouted out.

The riders pulled their pistols and opened fire. Matt returned fire and with his first shot, one of the men dropped from his saddle and skidded across hard ground. The remaining two men returned fire, but after several seconds it was quiet again as faint echoes bounded off distant hills. A little cloud of acrid gun smoke drifted up over the deadly battlefield, and Matt hopped down from the rock and walked out among the fallen riders, moving cautiously, his pistol at the ready.

It wasn't necessary. All three men were dead, and the entire battle had taken less than a minute.

In the east the sun was a bright orange ball, a full disc above the horizon, bathing the clouds in gold. A dozen wagons were parked in the soft morning light. Nestled among quilts and blankets slept the children of the families who had come directly from the meeting to help fight the fire the night before. The light of day disclosed the damage the fire had done. The main house had been completely destroyed, but the granary, bunkhouse, and barn had been spared.

Ethyl Pollard stood next to her husband, looking at the blackened remains of the house. Their two children, Ava, age nine, and Lennie, age six, stared with wide, confused eyes.

"Mama, where will we live now?" Lennie asked. "We ain't got no house no more."

Everyone was tired and covered with a great sadness for the two young cowboys who had been killed. In addition to their deaths, the death of a home was also particularly hard, because this was an area where homes and people were few and far between.

Five bodies were lying out on the ground. Harley Mack Loomis and Dusty Waters were separated from the three outlaws Matt had killed. All five were covered with blankets so that the children wouldn't have to see them, but the men had all taken a close look at the outlaws.

"Do any of you know them?" Matt had asked.

"I've never seen any of them before," Edmonston said.

"We can get Prufrock to put 'em out in front of his place," Poindexter suggested. "Maybe somebody will recognize them."

"Travis, if we're goin' to have the mortician take care of them three lowlifes who burned my place, then I want Prufrock to take care of Harley Mack and Dusty first," Pollard said.

"Yeah, I agree that's the way it should be done," Poindexter replied.

"Mama, where are we going to sleep?" Ava asked again.

"We'll sleep in the bunkhouse until we get our house rebuilt," Pollard answered instead.

"Oh, goodie!" Lennie said. "I think it'll be fun to sleep in the bunkhouse."

"Enjoy it while you can, young man," Ernest Dean

Fawcett said. "Because we're goin' to build you a new house in no time at all."

"I thank you for that," Ethyl said.

"But, Mama, we don't have anything to put in the house when it's built. All our stuff burned up," Ava said.

"That's all right, darlin'," Fawcett said. "You've got neighbors."

Chapter Thirty-one

Rongis

By noon of that same day, three plain wooden coffins were standing up in front of Seamus Prufrock's mortuary establishment. Two of the men had their eyes closed, but one of them had one eye closed and one eye open. One of the three had an old scar on his cheek, and one of them had buck-teeth that protruded under his lips.

A printed sign was attached to the wall above them.

DO YOU KNOW THESE MEN?
<u>These</u> <u>Three</u> <u>Villains</u>
☞ *Killed* HARLEY MACK LOOMIS
and DUSTY WATERS *and*
☞ *Burned down* DARREL POLLARD'S HOUSE.
If you know who they are, please notify:
ACTING SHERIFF JENSEN.

As soon as Seamus Prufrock put the three bodies out in front of his establishment, the citizens of the town began drifting down to look at them. Some came to look at them in a genuine effort to see if they could identify them, but most were drawn by morbid curiosity.

One of those who came to view the bodies did recognize them, but he had no intention of notifying anyone. Moe Greene looked at the three men who had recently come to join the Regulators and walked down to the Pair O' Dice Saloon to have a drink.

"I don't have no idea who none of those sons of bitches is," one of the saloon patrons said. "But seein' as they kilt Harley Mack 'n Dusty, 'n they burnt down Mr. Pollard's house, I'm glad they got themselves kilt."

"Yeah, me too," one of the others said. "Only they didn't get themselves kilt."

"What the hell do you mean they didn't get themselves kilt? Why they're a-standin' up down there in front of Prufrock's place right now, just as big as life."

The second speaker laughed. "How can they be standin' up there big as life, when all three of 'em is dead? 'N the reason I said they didn't get themselves kilt, is on account of they was kilt by Matt Jensen."

"What'll it be, Greene?" Cheatum asked.

"Whiskey," Greene replied.

Cheatum poured whiskey in the glass. "You got any idea who them three are that's down at the undertakers?"

"How the hell am I supposed to know?" Greene's response was like a growl.

"Well, you're with the Regulators, 'n that's like the law," Cheatum said. "Ain't it pretty much the law's duty to keep up with such things when outlaws come around to kill folks 'n burn down houses 'n the like?

"Oh, yeah. Well, I reckon it is," Greene said. "'N that's why I've come into town like I done. I was goin' to see if maybe somebody mighta had 'em an idea as to who them three outlaws is."

Cheatum shook his head. "I ain't heard anyone say as they might know."

An hour later Moe Greene was at Purgatory Pass talking to Tyrone DuPont. "You don't have to be worryin' no more 'bout where Stryker, Adams, 'n Malone is at."

"What do you mean?" DuPont asked.

"I mean you don't have to worry none about 'em no more on account of they're dead. All three of 'em."

"Dead? Who told you they're dead? Are you sure?"

"Yeah, I'm sure. 'N no one had to tell me, on account of I seen all three of 'em out in front Prufrock's place, deader 'n a doornail."

Walter Toone laughed. "That's funny."

"What's funny?" DuPont asked.

"Doornails don't die. How can a nail die?"

A few of the other men laughed as well.

"Who killed them, do you know?" DuPont asked.

"They're sayin' in town that it was Matt Jensen."

"Yeah, it would be," DuPont said.

"They got a sign up wantin' to know who them three is," Greene said.

"Did you tell 'em who they was?"

"No, I didn't say nothin'."

"That's good. It's best to act like we don't know nothin' about 'em."

"You say it was Jensen that kilt 'em?" Asa Carter asked.

"Yeah."

"Seems to me like we're goin' to have to get rid of that man," Carter said.

"Yeah," John Mason agreed. "Onliest thing is Shardeen tried it, 'n he wound up gettin' his ownself kilt."

"Shardeen went about it the wrong way," Carter said.

"What do you mean, he went about it the wrong way?" McCoy asked.

"Hell, he wanted to prove to folks that he was better 'n Jensen. They don't none of us need to try 'n prove nothin' like that. The way to kill the dirty dog is to just kill 'im. There ain't no need for bein' fair about it. If you're goin' to kill the egg-sucker, just kill 'im 'n be done with it."

"Kill 'im 'n be done with it, huh?" DuPont said. "I've dealt with such men before, 'n it's lot easier to talk about killin' 'em than it is to actual do it."

Shortly before noon on the fourth day after Darrel Pollard's neighbors started rebuilding the house, the last shingle was put on, and the house was completed. In addition to the house being rebuilt, two wagons had been loaded with furniture to be moved in after lunch.

"We should have some sort of housewarming," Kelly said.

"No, please. The last time the house got too warm it burned down," Pollard said, and the others laughed.

The lunch turned into a genuine celebration, then

the furniture was unloaded from the wagons and the Pollard family had a home once more.

After the last piece of furniture was moved, the neighbors returned to their own homes. Matt watched them all leave, then with a final good-bye to the Pollards, he too made his exit.

It was a busy night at the Pair O' Dice Saloon. Several of the cowboys who had helped rebuild the Pollard house had come into town for their own celebration, sharing stories about the previous four days.

"Did you see ol' Logan McMurtry?" Doodle Cosby asked. "When Michaels had that long board on his shoulder 'n turned around right quick, why, ol' Mac purt near got his head bashed in."

"I ain't never seen nobody duck so fast," one of the others said to the general laughter.

"What is the house you're talkin' about that you built?" Cooter Gregory asked.

"I'm talkin' about the house that them two no-accounts that you work for had burnt down," Billy Ray Harris said. "It was the house belongin' to Mr. Pollard, who's one o' the best bosses I ever worked for."

Cooter shook his head. "I heard about that, but I don't believe either Mr. Kennedy or Mr. O'Neil had anything to do with it. Besides, they buried the three men that did do it, 'n they're lying in unmarked graves, because nobody knew who they were. I'm foreman of the Straight Arrow. Don't you think if they had been riding for the brand, I would have known them?"

"Yeah, well, I didn't say you done it. I've knowed

you a long time, Cooter, 'n I ain't never knowed you to do nothin' bad, other 'n to commence a-ridin' with the Straight Arrow outfit."

Cooter held out his hand. "Now, Billy Ray, I'm a cowboy, just like you. After Emil Tucker went broke and the T-Bar Ranch wound up as part of the Straight Arrow, I tried to get on with someone else, but none of the smaller ranchers could afford to put on another hand. I didn't have any choice but to go to work for Kennedy and O'Neil."

"You know what? Now that Harley Mack 'n Dusty is dead 'n in the ground, mayhaps you can get on with Mr. Pollard."

"Why would I do that? I'm foreman at the Straight Arrow and I'm making really good wages."

"And don't forget Miss O'Neil is there," one of the others said.

"Yeah, well, what difference does that make? She's an O'Neil just like her old man," another said.

Cooter shook his head. "No, she isn't at all like O'Neil. Colleen is as good as anyone I've ever met."

Matt Jensen stepped into the saloon then, and Billy Ray pointed him out to Cooter. "Now right there is what you would call a genuwine good man, 'n one o' these days them two you work for are goin' to get their comeuppance because of Matt Jensen. You mark my words."

"That may be," Cooter agreed. "But if he does do it, he'll have to come through the Undertaker, 'n I don't figure that's goin' to be an easy task."

Unaware that Cooter and Billy Ray were talking about him, Matt stepped up to the bar, where he was greeted by Cheatum.

"Hello, Lonnie, how about a beer?"

"Had a full day, have you?" Cheatum asked.

"It's been a busy one, all right.'

"I imagine it has been. I heard you got Darrel Pollard's house put back up," Cheatum said as he set a fill mug on the bar.

"All the neighbors and these men," Matt said, taking in several of the cowboys, "came over and pitched in to get it done. I must confess that mostly all I did was watch."

"Yes, well, out here neighbors and friends are the best insurance," Cheatum said.

Matt had no idea what made him look around at that precise moment. Maybe he saw something in the mirror, maybe he heard something, or maybe it was true what they sometimes said of gunfighters . . . that they had a sixth sense about danger. For whatever reason, Matt looked around just as one of the customers sitting against the wall suddenly stood up, his abrupt action dumping a bar girl from his lap.

Missy Crews screamed in surprise and fright as the customer came up with a pistol already in his hand.

"Matt, look out!" Billy Ray cried as he and the others at the bar dived for the floor, just as the customer fired.

The sudden move had caught Matt by surprise, and even as he was bringing his pistol up from the holster, his assailant was pulling the trigger. The bullet from the gunman's pistol hit the mug of beer Matt had been drinking, sending shattered shards of glass and a little shower of beer all over.

The cowboys weren't the only ones on the floor. Everyone else in the place had also dived for cover, leaving only Matt and the shooter still standing. But the shooter didn't stand for long. Matt fired before the other man could pull the trigger a second time. The heavy slug from Matt's gun sent the would-be gunman crashing through a nearby table. Glasses and bottles tumbled and whiskey and beer spilled out onto the table and dripped down, making a little puddle on the floor. Gun smoke drifted slowly up to the ceiling, then spread out in a wide, nostril-burning cloud. Matt looked around the room quickly to see if anyone else might represent danger, but he saw only the faces of the customers, and they showed only fear, awe, and surprise.

"Damn!" Billy Ray said into the silence that followed the two gunshots. "I wonder what made that fool think he could do something like that?"

"Is he dead?" someone asked.

"Yeah, he's dead," Matt said, even before anyone was able to check on him.

"How do you know he's dead?" Cooter asked.

"Because I didn't have time not to kill him. Do any of you know him?"

"I've seen him before," Cooter said. "His name is Asa Carter."

"What do you know about him?" Matt asked.

Cooter shook his head. "About the only thing I really know about him is that he's one of the Regulators."

Chapter Thirty-two

"Kennedy and O'Neil now own the Circle Dot," Art told Matt and Hugh. "Every acre of land, every building, and every head of stock."

"What? How did they get all that?" Hugh asked. "I know for a fact that Jim didn't have a mortgage. He owned the property free and clear."

"Taxes," Art said. "There was a five-hundred-dollar tax assessment levied against the Circle Dot with forfeiture of the property being the penalty for non-payment. Kennedy and O'Neil paid it."

"That's strange. Jim never said anything to me about owing taxes."

"Not strange at all," Art said. "He couldn't have told you, because the assessment wasn't made until after he and Mary Ella were both dead."

"Who levied the taxes?" Matt asked. "Wait, let me guess. Judge Briggs?"

"My, my, how did you guess that?" There was a clear sarcastic tone to Art's response.

Matt shook his head. "I have run across a lot of evil men in my life, but I don't know that I've ever encountered so many that it was hard to decide who among them was the worst."

"Kennedy and O'Neil got it for five hundred dollars? The stock alone is worth more than twenty thousand and the ranch is at least another ten thousand. And they got it all for five hundred?" Art asked.

Spur and Latigo Ranch

"I wonder if Gabe Short knows about this," Lisa asked later that day when Hugh told her what he had learned from Art.

"Gabe Short?"

"He's Mary Ella's brother. Don't you remember? He lives in St. Louis."

"Yes, I had forgotten about that. Mary Ella did have a brother, but they were estranged, weren't they?"

"They had been for some time, but Mary Ella told me that she and her brother had recently made up."

"I wonder why he didn't come to the funeral."

"I don't think anybody knew about him but me, and in all the confusion I forgot to get in touch with him."

"Do you know how to contact him?"

"I think so. Mary Ella said he was a dispatcher for the Missouri Pacific Railroad in St. Louis. It shouldn't be that difficult to find him."

"I think it might be a good idea to send him a telegram. There has to be some way to overturn that tax lien, and I know that Jim had no living relatives so, by rights, the Circle Dot should belong to Mary Ella's brother."

* * *

The very next day Matt was in the sheriff's office when Kenny Kern came in. Fourteen years old, he was a delivery boy for Western Union. "This here telegram is for you, Sheriff."

"Thanks, Kenny," Matt said, giving the boy half a dollar.

Kenny smiled happily. "Thanks! Most of the time I'd have to deliver ten telegrams to get this much."

"Wait. I might need to send a return telegram."

"All right."

Matt read the telegram.

WILL ARRIVE BITTER CREEK AT ONE
O'CLOCK WEDNESDAY STOP CAN I BE
MET STOP
GABE SHORT

Matt penned a quick response. *You will be met by Matt Jensen.* "Send this." He gave Kenny the message and another dollar to send it.

Two days later Matt was on the depot platform when the train arrived at Bitter Creek. It wasn't difficult to pick out the man he was to meet as only one passenger, a relatively short, thin man with glasses, left the train.

"Mr. Short?" he asked, approaching him.

"Yes, are you Matt Jensen?"

"I am. I brought a buckboard. As soon as we get your luggage we'd better get started. We won't get there until tomorrow afternoon."

During the long drive back, Matt filled Gabe in on

the situation, explaining the circumstances of the deaths of Jim and Mary Ella as well as the claim being made by Kennedy and O'Neil that they now owned the Circle Dot.

"By rights that ranch belongs to you," Matt said. "And Hugh Conway and his wife, who were very good friends to Jim and your sister, think you should fight for it."

"Oh, by fighting, I certainly hope you don't mean anything physical," Gabe said.

"It may come to that," Matt said. "But if it does, you'll have friends. In the meantime, you'll be staying with the Conways. That's where we're going now."

The day following Gabe Short's arrival, Hugh decided to take a ride around his ranch. It had become his practice to circumnavigate his ranch at least twice a day—to check the location of all his horses, and more important to check the status of the fence line. As long as fence integrity was maintained, there was little danger of any of his stock wandering off or being stolen. Happily, there had been no depredation of his horses since Matt Jensen had arrived.

He didn't plan to stay out too long. Before he left the house, he had smelled an apple pie being baked. Lisa was an excellent cook and baker, and as he thought about it, he realized the pie would already be done. He knew that she had probably planned it for lunch, but he also knew that if he was persuasive enough he would be able to talk her into a piece of pie, maybe with some cheese melted on top, and a cup of coffee as a midmorning snack.

And he knew he could be persuasive enough.

So far his ride had been uneventful, but then, to his surprise, he saw a gathering of about ten cows standing in a bunch.

"Now where in the world did you critters come from?" he asked aloud as he rode over to check them out. "Circle Dot," he said when he saw the brand.

Before his fence had been put up, it hadn't been too unusual to see Circle Dot cows on his land from time to time, as his ranch and the Circle Dot were contiguous. Seeing them again meant that there must be a break in the fence.

Hugh started back toward the bunkhouse to have Ed, LeRoy, and Jake come find the break in the fence and push the cows back onto the Circle Dot. As Kennedy and O'Neil were claiming ownership of the Circle Dot, he would just as soon not get into any trouble with them.

He felt a blow to his back.

"Who do you think that is that we just shot?" Toone asked.

"More 'n likely one o' Conway's hands," Greene said.

"Yeah? Well I hope it's Ed Sanders," Toone said. "I ain't forgot that he give the two of us a lickin' some weeks back." Subconsciously, he rubbed his chin.

"Wait. One man whupped the both of you?" Lem Mason asked, surprised by the revelation. His brother was on another errand.

"Yeah well, he would have never done it iffen Jensen hadn't held a gun on us while he was a-doin' it," Greene added quickly.

"Hey, maybe it was Jensen we just shot," Mason suggested. "They say he rides around out here to keep Conway's horses from bein' stoled. 'N after him killin' Carter, it would be good if it was. Why don't we go check?"

"We done what we was supposed to do. Looks to me like whoever it is, he's dead, 'n if he ain't, he soon will be. Let's get out of here."

"But how will we ever find out iffen this is Jensen or not?" Mason asked.

"Ain't no need to be a-worryin' none about it. If this here is Jensen we just kilt, we'll find out about it soon enough," Greene said. "Right now seems to me like the best thing we can do is just go back 'n tell DuPont that we got the cows put on Conway's ranch like he told us."

Lisa had fried a chicken for lunch. She also had made mashed potatoes and was going to have gravy, but she didn't want to start the gravy until Hugh came home. She didn't want it to get cold. She had everything ready but the gravy, so she decided to wait in the swing on the front porch. That way she could see him coming and get the gravy started so that it would be done just as he walked into the house.

As she waited, she could hear Sanders, Patterson, and Haverkost from the barn.

"Now what horse with any sense of pride would even get into that stall?" Sanders asked. "Hell, Jake, ain't you ever painted nothin' before? That's awful."

"Yes, sir, I reckon it is. But you're right. I ain't never painted nothin' before."

"You ain't?" Sanders asked. "What about you, LeRoy? You ever painted anything?"

"Yeah, sure. I've painted before."

"Good. See what you can do to clean up the mess Haverkost has made."

Lisa chuckled at the interplay of dialogue, then she saw Hugh's horse returning. The saddle was empty.

"Mr. Sanders!" she screamed in fear and dread.

"Yes, ma'am?" Sanders hurried out of the barn. Patterson and Haverkost were with him.

"There's Hugh's horse! The saddle's empty!"

"We'll check it out," Sanders promised.

The three men saddled quickly, then rode out to where they knew Hugh had gone earlier.

The first thing they saw was a black lump on the ground. Although he was still too far away to make out any actual details, Sanders knew it was Hugh Conway. The men urged their horses into a gallop and quickly covered the rest of the distance. Arriving at the scene, they swung down and hurried over to the still form.

At first, given the way he was lying on the ground, Sanders thought that he might be dead, but as he knelt beside him, he could hear him breathing. "Mr. Conway! Mr. Conway!" Sanders began patting Hugh on the cheek. "Mr. Conway, are you all right? Are you all right?"

Hugh's eyes fluttered open, and he looked up at Sanders with a confused expression on his face. "Why are you asking me if I'm all right?"

"Because you are lying on your back in the dirt."

"I am?"

"Yes, sir, you are. What happened?"

"I . . . I don't know. The last thing I remember is starting back home."

"Can you get up?"

"I suppose I can."

Hugh lay on the ground for a moment with the changing expression on his face providing the only indication that he was trying, without success, to do something. "Ed," he said in a strained voice. "I don't seem to be able to move my legs."

"We got 'im, Mr. DuPont. We got Jensen!" John Mason said excitedly when he, Greene, and Toone returned to Purgatory Pass.

"We killed his ass," Toone said.

"Killed the rest of 'im too," Greene added with a laugh.

"Good job, men!" DuPont said with a pleased smile. "We'll have to have a little celebration."

When Luke McCoy and Lem Mason rode into Purgatory Pass about an hour later, the celebration was well underway with a lot of drinks and laughter.

"Lem, you 'n Luke come grab a drink and join the celebratin'!" John Mason called.

"What is it you're celebratin'?" Lem asked.

"Yeah, that's right. You ain't heard yet, have you, brother? Matt Jensen is dead. Me 'n Toone 'n Greene kilt him," John said.

"Jensen is dead? When did that happen?" McCoy asked.

"This morning," John said.

"Are you saying that you killed Matt Jensen this morning?" Lem asked.

John frowned at his brother. "You don't seem to listen all that good, do you? Yeah, that's what I'm sayin'."

Lem shook his head. "No, you didn't, little brother. If you kilt someone this morning, it wasn't Matt Jensen."

"How the hell do you know?" Greene demanded, the tone of his voice showing his anger.

"On account of me 'n Luke just seen 'im in Rongis no more 'n a hour ago," McCoy said. "And he looked pretty healthy for someone who got hisself kilt this mornin'."

"Damn, I wonder who it was that we kilt?" Toone asked.

"Mr. Conway's been shot!" Sanders said, barging into the sheriff's office.

"Killed?" Matt asked anxiously.

"No, he ain't dead, but he's bad hurt."

"Where is he?"

"He's home. I done got the doctor 'n he's on the way out there, but Miz Conway told me to be sure 'n get you, too."

"Let's go," Matt said, grabbing his hat as he stood.

Chapter Thirty-three

Spur and Latigo Ranch

"I shouldn't have come here," Gabe said to the others as they waited outside for the doctor to examine Hugh. "This is all my fault."

"What do you mean it's all your fault?" Ed Sanders asked.

"Those awful men who stole my sister's ranch want to get rid of me. So they shot the man who is giving me a place to stay."

"Mr. Short, I've no doubt that when they learn about you, they will want to get rid of you," Matt said, "but so far there are only a few people who actually know that you are here."

"Oh, I do hope you are right. I don't want to be an imposition on Mr. and Mrs. Conway, especially since they have been so nice to me."

"Don't be foolish, Mr. Short. You're not an imposition," Lisa said, the anxiousness over Hugh showing in her voice.

"Here's the doc," Ed said as the doctor came into the room.

"He's paralyzed from the waist down," Dr. Bosch reported.

"Oh, no!" Lisa cried, and she leaned into Matt, who, almost involuntarily, put his right arm around her.

"Is it a permanent condition?" Matt asked.

"It's too early to say," Dr. Bosch replied. "Fortunately the bullet didn't sever the spine. If it had, the paralysis would definitely be permanent. As it is, the bullet is putting pressure on the spine, and that's shut everything down. He won't be able to move his legs; he won't even be able to feel them."

"You're saying that the bullet is still in there?" Matt asked.

"Yes."

"If you took the bullet out, would that relieve the pressure on his spine?"

"I think it would, if I can get it out," Dr. Bosch said. "But the problem is the bullet is pretty deep. If I go probing round in there and don't get the bullet out, I could wind up making it even worse."

"Worse how?"

"I might sever some nerve endings that would paralyze him for the rest of his life, or even worse, I might bring on some infection that could kill him."

"But if you don't get the bullet out, the pressure is going to keep him paralyzed for good, too, isn't it?"

"Yes."

"If you try and succeed, he might regain feeling and movement. If you try and fail, he will be permanently paralyzed, and could even be killed?" Matt asked.

"Yes, that's true."

"You're right. That's not an easy choice to make."

"Only one person can make that choice, and right now he is in a deep and medicated sleep."

"Lisa is his wife. Can't she make the decision for him?"

"Yes, I suppose she could do that," Dr. Bosch said. "Mrs. Conway?"

"You said he could die during the operation?" Lisa asked hesitantly.

"I think the risk of him dying is not that that great, but yes. Mrs. Conway, I won't lie to you. If something went badly wrong, he could die."

Lisa shook her head. "Then, I'm not going to ask you to do it. For something like this, I think Hugh should decide for himself."

"Let me ask you this, Doctor," Matt said. "If you don't do anything now, will it get even harder for you to do something in the future?"

"If we wait too long, yes, it could. Scar tissue could grow around the bullet, making it much harder and much more dangerous to do anything."

"Oh!" Lisa said. "I hadn't thought of that. How long before anything like that would happen?"

"Two or three weeks," Dr. Bosch answered. "A month at the longest. Any time after a month, I would be afraid to try it."

"Thank you," Lisa said. "I'm inclined to say go ahead and try to get the bullet now, but I do want Hugh to have some say in what happens. It is his life."

"Yes, ma'am, I understand." Dr. Bosch went over to pick up his medicine bag. "You and your husband talk it over, and once you make up your mind, left me know."

"Thank you, Doctor."

With a farewell nod to all who were present, Dr. Bosch left the house, and a moment later, they heard his buggy drive away.

"Miz Conway, me 'n the other boys got some things we need to get done," Sanders said. "If they's anythin' you want done, anythin' at all, just let me know 'n I'll see that it's took care of."

"Thank you, Mr. Sanders. I appreciate that," Lisa replied in a quiet voice.

"Yes, I was in the process of cleaning the bunkhouse, so I had better go, as well," Gabe said.

Matt remained behind.

"Oh, Matt, what will I do? I can't make a decision for him," Lisa said and she went to him.

Matt put his arms around her and held her close, feeling her sobbing against his chest. He had no answer for her. The only comfort he could provide was to pull her to him. He could feel her body pressed against him and smell the scent in her hair. It was unsavory and pleasing at the same time.

"Lisa?" Hugh's voice, thin and strained, came from the bedroom.

"Oh, he's awake!" Lisa pulled away from Matt's arms and hurried into the bedroom.

Matt followed her.

"Hugh, oh, darling, you're awake!" Lisa said, stepping over to his bed.

"Was the doctor here?" Hugh asked.

"Yes."

"To see me?"

"Yes."

"Why? What happened to me? Why am I lying here like this?"

"You . . . you don't know?" Lisa asked, surprised by Hugh's question. She glanced over at Matt.

"You were shot, Hugh," Lisa said. "Do you not remember anything about it?"

Hugh shook his head. "No. The last thing I remember is riding out to check on the fence line. Listen, I can't stay in bed in the middle of the day. I've got work to do. Hand me my clothes, will you, Lisa? I'm going to get up now."

Lisa, shocked by the request, didn't respond. She just stared at him.

"Where are my clothes? I'm going to—" Hugh stopped in midsentence and got an expression on his face that turned from confusion to concern. "I can't seem to move my legs. Why can't I move my legs?"

"Hugh, don't you remember? You are paralyzed from the waist down," Lisa said.

Hugh's look of concern turned to one of dismay. "I'm paralyzed?"

"Yes, darling."

He was silent for a long time, then he looked up at Matt. "Did you say I was shot?"

"Yes."

"Who did it? Who shot me?"

"I was hoping you could tell me," Matt replied.

"The cows!"

"What cows?"

"I found several Circle Dot cows on my land. I had just started back to have Ed and the others—" Hugh paused in midsentence again. "That's when I was shot. I remember now. I felt a blow in my back. The next thing I knew Ed was talking to me. I . . . I don't have any idea how I got here."

"Mr. Sanders and the others put you in the back of the buckboard and brought you here," Lisa said.

"Hugh, are those cows still on your land?" Matt asked.

"As far as I know they are. I didn't get a chance to tell anyone else about them."

"Seeing as the Circle Dot belongs to Kennedy and O'Neil now, it might be a good idea to get them out of there," Matt suggested.

"Yes, I was thinking the same thing."

"Ed and I will take care of it."

Straight Arrow Ranch

"Wait here," Boggs said.

"What do you mean, wait here?" DuPont asked angrily. "I've never had to wait to see Kennedy or O'Neil before."

"Wait here," Boggs repeated.

DuPont seethed with anger as he waited outside the ranch office.

A moment later Boggs reappeared. "You can go in now."

DuPont glared at him, then went into the office where Kennedy and O'Neil waited.

"What was that all about?" DuPont demanded, pointing back toward the door.

"What was what about?" O'Neil asked.

"Having that no-good coyote tell me I had to wait to see you. We've been doin' business a long time 'n I ain't never had to wait before."

"Yes, well, our operation has grown considerably larger since we first started," O'Neil said. "And no doubt, Garrett and I have made many new enemies. Mr. Boggs is looking out for our safety, and it's more efficient to inform us of every visitor. Please don't take it as a personal affront."

"Yeah, well, I don't like it is all."

"I'm sure it can be somewhat troublesome, but in the long run, it shouldn't interfere with our business. Speaking of which, what is the purpose of your visit?"

The angry expression on DuPont's face fell away to be replaced by a smile. "We done it. We put some Circle Dot cows on Conway's ranch, just like you said."

"Good, very good. Now we shall be able to make the charge of cattle rustling against Conway, and if everything works out as it should, we'll be able to acquire the Spur and Latigo," O'Neil said.

"Ever since making an ally of Matt Jensen, Conway has been our biggest obstacle. I've no doubt but that once we get rid of him, the rest of the valley will fall right into our hands," Kennedy added.

"We'll handle it the same way we did with Andrews," DuPont said.

O'Neil raised his hand. "It's best that you not give us any information in advance. Do whatever you must do, then tell us afterward."

DuPont chuckled. "Yeah, I know. Some people just don't have the stomach for what needs to be done. That's why you have me."

"Indeed," O'Neil said.

DuPont glanced back toward the office door. "What I don't understand is what you need with him."

* * *

It didn't take long to find the ten Circle Dot cows and return them to Circle Dot range by pushing them through the break in the fence.

"This here ain't no natural break," Ed said, holding two wires in his hand. "If it had been a natural break, why, there wouldn't be these here two wires the same length."

"You're right, Ed. The wires were cut."

"What I don't understand is how come the wires was cut 'n all that happened was some cows got in, but there didn't no horses get out," Haverkost said.

"Because the purpose of the cut was to bring the cattle in, not steal horses," Matt explained.

"What? Why the hell would somebody do somethin' like that? I mean if rustlers done this, it don't make no sense to give you cows," LeRoy said.

"I think we'll find out soon enough," Matt said.

"I'd feel better if you would stay here for a few nights," Hugh said when Matt returned to report that the Circle Dot cattle had been found and removed. "As a matter of fact, I wish you would give up your room at the hotel and just move in with us until all this is over."

"I don't know that I should do that, seeing as I'm now the acting sheriff and I have no deputy."

"I'll be your deputy," LeRoy said.

"Yeah, make LeRoy your deputy," Jake said. "He'll be a good one."

Matt looked at the older of the two newest ranch hands. "LeRoy, do you have any experience?"

"Yes sir, I done me some deputyin' up in Buckhorn, Dakota," LeRoy said.

Matt smiled. "All right. LeRoy, raise your right hand."

LeRoy did as asked.

"Do you swear to do as good a job as you can?" Matt asked.

"Yeah." LeRoy chuckled. "Is that it?"

"It's good enough for me," Matt replied.

The others headed to the bunkhouse

"He's asleep," Lisa said a moment later, coming back into the keeping room.

Only Matt remained. "I expect that, right now, that's probably the best thing for him."

"Would you like a piece of apple pie? I baked it for Hugh, but . . . this happened," she added in a tight voice.

"Yes, that would be nice. Thank you."

Through the open door, Matt watched Lisa cutting two pieces of pie, then pouring two cups of coffee. He got up and walked into the kitchen. "You can't carry all that by yourself. Let me help." He reached for the cup, and his hand came in contact with hers.

She had a quick intake of breath, and jerked her hand back.

"Sorry," Matt said.

"No, don't be silly. You didn't do anything. It's just that—" She didn't finish her sentence.

"Lisa, are you going to be all right with me staying out here for a while?"

"Yes, of course. I . . . why shouldn't I be all right?"

"It's just this thing that has come up between us."

"Nothing can happen," she said quickly. "Nothing *must* happen."

"Nothing *will* happen. I promise you."

Lisa's eyes filmed over with tears. "I don't know what this is. I love Hugh. Oh, Matt, I love him with all my heart. I don't think I realized how much I did love him until this happened to him."

Matt took her hand in his, and she didn't fight him. "I don't know what it is, either"—he smiled at her—"but I have no doubt that we will be able to deal with it in such a way that neither of us will ever feel shame."

"Yes," Lisa said, returning his smile. "Yes, I know we can."

Chapter Thirty-four

Matt and Lisa had just finished their pie and coffee when they heard the sound of approaching horses.

"Who is that, do you suppose?" Lisa asked.

"I don't know, but I'm sure we're about to find out."

The sound of the hoofbeats stopped just outside the door.

"Conway!" a voice shouted in the night. "Conway, you cattle-rustlin' lowlife! Get out here!"

When Matt looked through the window, he saw four riders. Two of them were carrying flaming torches, which allowed him to identify them all. He had seen them most recently in court, facing the charge of lynching. Pulling his pistol, he stepped out onto the front porch.

"What do you want, Greene?"

"What . . . what are you doin' here?" Greene asked, startled by the unexpected appearance of Matt Jensen.

"I think I had better ask you the same thing," Matt said. "What are you doing here?"

"I'll tell you what we're doin' here. We just happened to be ridin' by, 'n damn if we didn't see ten

Circle Dot cows right here on this ranch. And in case
you don't know it, Mr. Kennedy 'n Mr. O'Neil own
the Circle Dot now. Them cows bein' here on this
ranch means that Conway musta stoled them. And
bein' as we're railroad detectives 'n tryin' to protect
people like Mr. Kennedy 'n Mr. O'Neil from bein'
rustled, we've come here to uphold the law."

"You just happened to be out for a ride at ten
o'clock at night?"

"Yeah, we was just out for a ride 'n we happened to
see them ten cows, like I said."

"That's very interesting because earlier today
there were ten Circle Dot cows here, so we took them
back. I thought perhaps they had just wandered
onto the property, which they could have done because the fence had clearly been cut. How is it that
you know the exact number of cows that were here,
even though they haven't been here since early this
afternoon? Do you think it might be because you and
your friends put the cows here?"

"Now why we would do somethin' like that?"
Greene asked.

"You did it so you would have a reason to lynch
Hugh Conway just like you lynched Jim Andrews and
his wife."

"They warn't really married, so she warn't really his
wife. Anyhow, what we done wasn't no actual
lynchin'. You was in the courtroom same as me, 'n
you heard what the judge said. He said there warn't
no lynchin'."

"According to the witness I talked to, you, Walter
Toone, Asa Carter, and the Mason brothers put a
rope around Jim and Mary Ella's necks, tied the

other end to a tree limb, then pushed them off a rock. If that isn't lynching, what would you call it?"

"That . . . that ain't the way it was," Greene stammered.

"Oh, I'm pretty sure that is the way it was. And now you are all here, the same bunch of you. Well, that is, all of you except for Asa Carter. He isn't here because I killed him. I also killed Shardeen, and I killed the three so-called railroad detectives who murdered Dusty and Harley Mack and burned the Pollard family's house."

"Why are you tellin' me 'bout all the people you've kilt?" Greene asked.

"I'm telling you this so you will know I'm serious when I tell you I'm about to kill all of you."

"You ought to learn to count," Moe Greene said with a confident smirk. "They's four of us 'n only one of you."

"Wrong!" a strong voice said from the darkness near the bunkhouse. "There are four of us, too, 'n none of us have our hands full carrying a torch."

The expression on Moe Greene's face turned from confidence to fear, and he looked back toward the sound of the voice. There he saw Sanders, Patterson, and Haverkost, the three of them faintly illuminated by the bubble of golden light projected by the flaming torches. All three were holding guns in their hands.

"Uh, well, if it's true that there ain't none o' them cows here now, then I reckon it could be that maybe we have made a mistake," Greene said, his voice tight with fear.

"Leave, now," Matt said as he cocked his pistol. The double metallic click was loud in the night.

"We're a-goin, we're a-goin'," Greene said, holding out his hand as if by that action he could push Matt away. "Come on, fellas. We, uh, might have made a mistake here."

The four riders turned and began to ride away.

"You might want to see how fast you can get out of gun range," Matt called out, and the four horses broke into a gallop.

Laughing, Sanders, Patterson, and Haverkost went over to join Matt, just as Lisa stepped out of the house.

"Where's Gabe?" Matt asked.

"He's back in the bunkhouse. We figured since nobody is supposed to know anything about him yet, it would be best if we kept him out of sight," Leroy said.

"Good idea," Matt agreed.

"You don't think they will be back, do you?" Lisa asked anxiously.

"Not hardly," LeRoy said with a little laugh. "I think we put the fear of the devil in 'em."

"Yeah, I think we did, too," Ed said. "But I also think it might be a good idea for one of us to stay awake all night, just to make sure they don't come back."

"Oh, would you do that, Mr. Sanders?" Lisa asked. "Thank you. I would be ever so grateful."

"Gentlemen, I think the fun is over for the night," Matt said.

"I reckon so," Ed said, then he laughed. "They sure as hell skedaddled when you told 'em to get out o' gun range."

Ed and the other two men started toward the

bunkhouse as Matt and Lisa went back into the main house.

"Good night," she said. Barely waiting long enough for his reply, and avoiding any physical contact, even if it was accidental, she hurried quickly into the bedroom where Hugh, blissfully unaware of the entire encounter, was sound asleep.

Matt, who had brought his bedroll in, lay it out on the floor and within minutes was asleep.

Rongis

The next morning, Matt rode into town, where he stopped by the newspaper office to visit with Art Walhausen.

"What you should do is ask Judge Briggs to issue an injunction," Art said.

"A what?"

"It's a court order that would prevent any of the Regulators from coming onto Hugh Conway's property."

"The same judge who let those murderers go, and who levied a postmortem tax on the Circle Dot so that Kennedy and O'Neil could steal the ranch? Is that the judge you're talking about? Art, you and I both know that Briggs isn't likely to do that, and even if he did do it, it wouldn't stop them. Briggs's court is a joke."

"I know, but in this case we aren't appealing to Briggs's court as much as we are to the court of public opinion." Art smiled. "And in the court of public opinion, *I* am the judge."

* * *

"Why should I issue such an injunction?" Judge Briggs said in reaction to Matt's request. "The purpose of the Regulators is to provide all the ranchers protection against stock rustling, and in order to do so, they must have freedom of motion. Your request is denied."

"All right," Art said with a smile as they left Briggs's office. "Now my court will be in session."

Two days later, Art's "court of public opinion" was convened by way of an article that appeared in the *Gazette*.

Regulators Make Late-Night Visit To the Spur and Latigo Ranch

WOULD-BE LYNCH MOB TURNED AWAY BY ACTING SHERIFF MATT JENSEN

Two days ago the same men who lynched Mr. and Mrs. Jim Andrews paid a visit to the Spur and Latigo Ranch. The expressed purpose of their visit was to hold Mr. Hugh Conway to account for the alleged theft of ten Circle Dot cows. But when they arrived at the ranch and made their spurious accusation, they learned that there were no such cows on the ranch.

However, while there were no cows present at the ranch when they arrived, there had been ten cows on the ranch earlier. Those cows had been discovered by Mr. Conway, who, in his attempt to turn them away from his ranch, was shot from ambuscade.

Later, even in the pain and shock of having been shot, Hugh Conway, showing the type of person he is, directed his hands to return the errant cattle to the Circle Dot range. As circumstances developed, however, the cattle weren't on the range as the result of innocent wandering, but had been put there as an act of perfidy.

Moe Greene, Walter Toone, and John and Lem Mason arrived at the ranch in the middle of the night, attempting to justify their nocturnal visit by making the claim that ten Circle Dot cows were on Spur and Latigo range. There is no doubt but that the cattle were "seeded." In other words, the cattle were put onto Mr. Conway's land for the express purpose of giving Greene and those with him the excuse to bring out the lynch ropes just as they did on their earlier visit to the Andrews home.

To the benefit of the Conway family, and for the good of all decent people everywhere, Greene and his outlaws, for there is no other way to describe them, were met by Acting Sheriff Matt Jensen, Deputy Sheriff LeRoy Patterson, and good citizens Ed Sanders and Jake Haverkost. Any idea that these evil people had of repeating the crime of lynching innocent people was thereby thwarted.

In his capacity as acting sheriff, Matt Jensen petitioned Judge John Briggs to issue an injunction that would prevent Moe Green and his associates from trespassing upon the property of innocent ranchers, but the judge refused to do so.

Judge Briggs must learn that he is a servant of all the people, not just the wealthy few who can afford to influence his decisions.

"Yes, of course I read your article," Cheatum said to Walhausen. "Everyone in town read it, and it's all anyone wants to talk about."

Art, Travis Poindexter, Ernest Dean Fawcett, and Frank Edmonston were in the Pair O' Dice, and Cheatum had come over to their table to join them.

"What I'm wonderin'," Poindexter said, "is when is the snake in the grass goin' to close your paper down?"

"He can't close it down," Ernest Dean Fawcett said.

"What do you mean, he can't close it down? He's a judge, ain't he? I reckon he can close it if he wants to," Poindexter said.

"The First Amendment of the U.S. Constitution says that Congress shall make no law abridging the freedom of the press," Art said.

"What does *abridging* mean?" Poindexter asked.

"It means I can print whatever I want, and neither Judge Briggs nor anyone else can do a thing about it."

"Damn! That's great!" Edmonston said. "I wonder when they come up with that!"

"They came up with it in 1787, when the Constitution was written," Art said.

While he was lecturing the others in the Pair O' Dice saloon on how the constitutional right of freedom of the press limited what Judge Briggs could do about the newspaper article, Matt was in the office of the very man they were discussing.

"I'm going to find out who shot Hugh Conway, and bring him or them in and put them in jail. When I do this, I will have your support, won't I, Judge?"

"You are the acting sheriff, Mr. Jensen," Judge

Briggs said. "You bring the suspect in, and if there is enough evidence to indict, we will hold a trial."

"Like the last trial?" Matt asked.

Judge Briggs shook his head. "If you are talking about the hearing that was held with regard to the alleged lynching, I'm sure you know that wasn't a trial. If you recall, there was insufficient evidence to bring about an indictment."

"Oh, yes, I remember that there wasn't even a trial," Matt said. "Believe me, I do remember."

"My hands were tied, Mr. Jensen. There are certain restrictions and impositions that put restraints upon my ability to act."

"And who puts those restrictions on you, Judge? Is it DuPont? Or is it Kennedy and O'Neil?"

"Mr. Jensen, you are bordering on contempt," Briggs said.

"I'm just bordering on contempt? Damn. I thought I had done better than *border* on contempt."

Briggs was still fuming when Matt left his office.

Chapter Thirty-five

"Hello, Matt, I was hoping you would show up," Art Walhausen said when Matt stepped into the Pair O' Dice after leaving Judge Briggs's office.

"Ah, the crusading newspaperman." With a smile, Matt joined the others and looked across the table at Lonnie Cheatum. "Lonnie, would you ask one of those pretty girls to bring me a beer?"

"Jennie Lou, a beer for my friend," the bartender called.

"When's the last time you've seen Hugh?" Ernest Dean Fawcett asked.

"Just this morning."

"How is he doing?"

"He's doing all right, considering," Matt said. "He isn't in any pain, and he's very alert. But of course, he's still paralyzed from the waist down."

"Damn, that's bad. It's a shame, too. Hugh is a fine man. One of the best men in the entire valley. How is Mrs. Conway taking it?"

"Hard, as you would expect," Matt said.

"She's a good woman," Art said. "And a beautiful woman as well."

"You'll get no argument from me," Matt said.

"Here you are, sweetie. Your beer," Jennie Lou said, putting the mug on the table before Matt.

"Thank you, Jennie Lou."

"I heard you talking about Mr. Conway. Would you please tell Mrs. Conway that all the girls here are thinking about her?"

"I'll be glad to."

"She has always been very decent to us if she happens to see us out on the street. Not every woman in town is like that."

"Oh, Matt, I nearly forgot. A letter came to the newspaper office for you," Art said after Jennie Lou walked away.

"A letter was sent to the newspaper office for me?" The expression on Matt's face denoted his surprise and curiosity as to what kind of letter would be sent to him at the newspaper officer, rather than the sheriff's office or even general delivery at the post office.

Art pulled an envelope from his pocket and slid it across the table to Matt. "Here it is. As you can see, I haven't opened it. It was addressed to you, and it would have been unethical for me to do so." Art flashed a conspiratorial grin. "Besides, I couldn't figure out how to get it open without it being discovered that it was opened."

Matt chuckled as he took the letter from Art's hand. "But you're going to hang around until I open it to see what it is, aren't you?"

"Yes, please open it now. I've been dying of curiosity."

Matt examined the envelope. "No return address. I would be willing to bet there is no signature on the letter, either." He opened the envelope and withdrew the letter.

> *Dear Mr. Jensen,*
>
> *I think you should know the bullet that has caused Mr. Conway's paralysis was meant for you. You have become quite a thorn in the sides of Kennedy and O'Neil, as well as Tyrone DuPont.*
>
> *These three men have plans for the future of Sweetwater Valley and those plans do not include you. To that end, I think I should tell you that a rather significant bonus has now been offered to anyone who can kill you. And as that offer has been made by Kennedy and O'Neil, you can be certain that it will be members of the Regulators who will attempt to carry it out.*
>
> *Please take my advice and avoid any of the Regulators, especially if you see any of them together. I'm sure that you can understand why I would rather not sign my name to this letter.*
>
> *A friend*

Matt looked up from the letter, but said nothing.

"Well now, that's what I would call a ruminating expression," Art said. "What's in the letter to make you so pensive?"

By way of answer, Matt passed the letter across the table.

Art Walhausen read the letter. "I see that whoever wrote this letter has made a special effort to remain anonymous. Do you have any idea who it might be?"

"None at all," Matt admitted.

"Well, I hope you at least take the anonymous author's advice and steer clear of the Regulators."

"I'm not going to steer clear of them. I'm going after them," Matt said. "There is no doubt in my mind but that the person who shot Hugh is a Regulator."

"I'm equally convinced," Art replied.

"Art, I'd like to get the attention of a few people. Could I persuade you to put out a special edition of the paper?"

"I would be happy to. What do you want me to say?"

"Suppose we go down to the office and compose the article together. I want the article to have some impact, and you are much better with words than I am."

When they reached the newspaper office, Art picked up a pencil and piece of paper, then he set it aside. "If I'm going to do a special edition just for this letter, I may as well set the type as we write it. What do you want to say?"

As Matt began to dictate, Art set the type, offering a few suggestions until the letter was completed. Going to the printing press, Art pulled the first proof, then lay it out on the table for both to examine.

"Is this pretty much what you wanted to say?"

Matt nodded. "Yeah, this is exactly what I wanted to say."

EXTRA EDITION
PUBLIC LETTER
From Acting Sheriff Matt Jensen

To any who would commit illegal and heinous acts under the cover of acting for the law, I hereby issue this warning.

As acting sheriff and keeper of the law in Rongis as well as the entire Sweetwater Valley, I, Matt Jensen, hereby revoke all commissions, warrants, and appointments, whether assigned as county deputies by the late Sheriff Clark, or as private detectives for the Union Pacific Railroad. All such designations are hereinafter considered null and void. In addition, I will arrest anyone who I find trespassing on the private property of valley landholders, whether those landholders be farmers or ranchers.

With immediate effect, any member of the group known as the Regulators will be arrested and jailed for impersonating an officer of the law, should they attempt to invoke the authority that I have, by this directive, stripped from them.

YOU HAVE BEEN WARNED.

"I'll do a complete print run of five hundred copies," Art said as he put the newsprint in the tray. "That will be enough to reach everyone in the valley."

"That's good, but the people I really want to reach are DuPont, Kennedy, and O'Neil."

Art smiled. "Oh, I think you can count on that."

Straight Arrow Ranch

"The question is, what are we going to do about it?" DuPont asked. He had come to the ranch to discuss the special edition of the *Gazette*, in which Matt Jensen had revoked all authority from the Regulators.

"Sean and I have discussed it." Kennedy smiled. "And I think we have come up with a solution."

"We're going to get a new sheriff," O'Neil said.

"How are you going to do that? Hold an election? What if the lousy mutt is reelected?"

"Since it was Garrett's idea, I'm going to let him explain it to you," O'Neil said.

"There's no need for a new election, as Sheriff Clark's term isn't over yet," Kennedy said.

The expression on DuPont's face showed his utter confusion over the comment. "What do you mean, his term isn't over yet? Clark is dead!"

"Exactly," Kennedy said.

DuPont shook his head. "You ain't makin' a lick of sense."

"Oh, but we are, Sheriff DuPont."

"Sheriff DuPont? Me?"

"Why shouldn't it be you? You were a policeman in St. Louis, weren't you?"

"Yeah, I was."

"Then you certainly have the experience."

"But how am I going to be the sheriff?"

"Since Sheriff Clark died before the completion of his term, that leaves Judge Briggs with the authority to appoint a new sheriff to fill the vacancy until the next election."

"Yeah, but ain't that what happened with Jensen? I mean Clark is dead 'n Jensen is sheriff on account of he was Clark's deputy."

"Yes, he is the acting sheriff at the moment, but the only reason he holds the position is because he was the deputy when Sheriff Clark died. That is a temporary position until a new sheriff is appointed to hold the office until the next election, and that's over a year from now. I think we will have no problem at all in convincing Judge Briggs to vacate Mr. Jensen's temporary position as acting sheriff and appoint you as real sheriff."

"What about Jensen?"

"Well, as you will then be the sheriff, you will have the authority to dismiss Jensen and appoint your own deputy."

"Yeah," DuPont said with a sinister smile. "Yeah, I can do that, can't I?"

"And you will appoint Mr. Boggs as your deputy," O'Neil said.

"Boggs? No, I think I'd rather have Moe Greene as my deputy."

"Oh, don't get me wrong. You can reinstate Greene and everyone else in the Regulators as deputies. But your first deputy will be Merlin Boggs. That is, if you want us to arrange for your appointment to sheriff."

"Yeah," DuPont said reluctantly. "Yeah, all right. I'll appoint Boggs as my first deputy."

"Why should I do that?" Judge Briggs said. "From all that I hear, the citizens of the town seem to be satisfied with Matt Jensen."

"What does it matter who the citizens of the town want?" Kennedy asked. "Only one person has the authority to appoint the new sheriff until the next election, and that's you. And Sean and I would be very pleased if you would do so."

"How pleased would you be?" Briggs asked with a cunning squint of his eyes.

"Oh, I would say a thousand dollars pleased."

Briggs looked over at DuPont, who was standing with O'Neil and Boggs. "Mr. DuPont, would you raise your right hand, please?"

DuPont did so.

"Say after me. I . . . what is your first name, Mr. DuPont?"

"Tyrone."

Briggs nodded. "I, Tyrone DuPont, will faithfully execute, to the best of my ability, the office of sheriff according to the laws of the Territory of Wyoming."

DuPont repeated the words.

"You are now the sheriff."

"Boggs, you are the first deputy," DuPont said. "Oh, and Judge, just so's that you know, I'm goin' to be makin' all the Regulators my deputies, too."

"As you wish." The judge's response was distracted. He was counting out the one thousand dollars he had just been given.

"You're fired, Jensen," DuPont said a few minutes later when he, Boggs, and Garrett Kennedy stepped into the sheriff's office.

"What?" Matt asked.

"You heard me. I said you're fired. I'm the new sheriff now, and seein' as Boggs is goin' to be my deputy, I don't have no need for you."

"What do you mean, you're the new sheriff?"

"I'm afraid that's true, Mr. Jensen," Kennedy said. "In accordance with the law and statutes of the Territory of Wyoming, Judge John Briggs has not only the authority but also the obligation to appoint a replacement to complete the term when the office is vacated. He has just done so. I witnessed the event and thought perhaps I should accompany Sheriff DuPont when he told you about it so you would have no reservations in turning the office and your badge over to him."

"What about him?" Matt asked, making a gesture toward the quiet man with the moustache that curved around his mouth.

"He's my new deputy." DuPont chuckled. "Oh, and all the Regulators, the ones that you said had no authority anymore? Well, they're my deputies, too. As it turns out, Jensen, you're the only one now who don't have no authority, seein' as I just fired you. So get out of m' office before I throw you in jail."

Matt took the star off his shirt and laid it on the desk.

"Ha, I bet you didn't want to do that, did you?" DuPont said in a mocking voice.

"Oh, it doesn't bother me all that much," Matt said. "I didn't really see much of a career opportunity in a job that wasn't paying me anything."

"Jensen," Boggs said, speaking for the first time.

"I'll be damned. You can speak," Matt said.

"They say you're pretty good with a gun."

"I'm good enough that I'm still here," Matt replied.

"You may not be here much longer."

"Oh? And why is that?"

"I've got a feelin' that me 'n you 's goin' to have us a little dance one o' these days."

"A dance, you say." Matt's smile was somewhat sardonic. "I think you should know I always take the lead when I dance."

Chapter Thirty-six

Spur and Latigo Ranch

As Matt was no longer the acting sheriff, he was living at the ranch full-time but was staying in the bunkhouse with Ed, Jake, LeRoy, and Gabe Short. He was in the barn sorting harness when Lisa stepped in through the door.

"Matt, Hugh wants to talk to you," Lisa said.

"Is anything wrong?"

"No. At least, I don't think so. He just said that he wanted to talk to you."

"I'll finish this for you," Gabe said. "I may not be able to throw a rope like the others, or shoe a horse, but sorting harness I can do."

"Thanks, Gabe."

Matt followed Lisa to the house but when they stepped inside, she made a motion toward the bedroom door. "He said he wanted to see you alone."

Curious, and a little concerned, Matt started toward the bedroom. Did Hugh suspect anything about Matt's relationship with Lisa? But no, what could he suspect? Absolutely nothing had happened, so there was no reason to suspect anything. However, Matt knew that Hugh was very intuitive, so it was possible that he may have sensed some libidinous though unrequited tension between Matt and Lisa.

Matt knocked lightly on the door. "Hugh?"

"Come in, Matt."

Hugh was in bed, but he was propped up by pillows so that he was in a sitting position.

"Lisa said that you wanted to see me?"

"Yes. I'm going to do it, Matt. I'm going to ask Dr. Bosch to remove the bullet. I haven't told Lisa yet because I wanted to talk with you first."

"If you want my opinion, I would say yes, go for it," Matt said.

"Yes, I was pretty sure you would agree with me. But there's something else I want to talk to you about."

Matt felt himself grow a little tense. "All right."

"Matt, when Dr. Bosch talked to me about this, he was pretty plainspoken with me about all the positives and negatives. And one of the negatives we discussed was the possibility that I could die during the procedure."

"Yes, he shared that possibility with Lisa and me, as well."

"That thought doesn't frighten me. To be honest with you, I would almost rather die than live the rest of my life as a complete burden to Lisa."

"She loves you very much, Hugh. I know for a fact that she would not look at you as a burden."

"I agree with you that she would feel like that. Still,

there is the possibility that I could die, and that's where you come in."

"What do you mean?"

"I know how you and Lisa feel about each other."

"Hugh, there's . . ."

"Please, Matt, let me finish," Hugh said, holding up his hand to stop Matt in mid-sentence. "I know that nothing has ever happened between the two of you. And I know that Lisa loves me. But I'm not blind, and I know the feelings you have for each other."

"Hugh, I—"

"If I should die during the operation," Hugh said, speaking up quickly to interrupt Matt's protest, "I want you to promise me that you will look out for Lisa. I'm not asking you to marry her. I know that you have your own life to live, but I am asking you to be there for her if she needs you."

Matt reached down, took Hugh's hand, and held it between his two hands. "Hugh, I want you to know that if something goes wrong during this surgery I will look after Lisa. I make you that solemn promise." He smiled down at his friend. "But if you die on me, I'm also going to kick you right in the ass for leaving her in her time of need."

Hugh laughed out loud. "Hell, Matt, you can do that now if you want to. One of the side effects of this paralysis is that I can't feel anything down there anyway."

Matt laughed as well.

"What are you two doing in there? Telling jokes?" Lisa called from outside the bedroom.

"Come on in, Lisa," Hugh called. "I have something to tell you."

Matt rode into town to tell Dr. Bosch that Hugh had made up his mind to have the bullet removed. He was greeted with a sign that was posted at town limits.

WARNING
All Visitors to RONGIS
MUST OBTAIN A VISITOR'S PASS!
*Failure to show pass could
result in* ARREST AND JAIL!

Matt was reading the sign when he was approached by John Mason.

"Well now, if it ain't the former sheriff. I say *former*, 'cause you ain't the sheriff no more, are you?"

"What do you want, Mason?"

"It's Deputy Mason."

"What do you want, Mason?"

The Regulator was clearly irritated by Matt's response, but he lacked the courage to challenge him. "I'm here to make sure you do what the sign says."

"Uh-huh. And where am I supposed to go to get this visitor's pass?"

"You can go down to the sheriff's office 'n see my brother. He'll give you one if you got a good reason for bein' in town."

A few minutes later Matt stepped into the sheriff's office, where he asked Lem Mason for a pass.

"What's the reason you come to town?"

"My reason for coming to town is none of your business," Matt replied. "Just give me the pass."

"Uh-uh. Accordin' to the sheriff, anyone that comes to town has to have a reason."

"I came to get a beer."

"Well now, that warn't so hard, was it?" Lem asked as he signed his name to a printed sheet of paper, then handed it to Matt.

— PASS —
(MUST BE RENEWED EACH DAY)
~ Deputy Lem Mason

Matt went directly from the sheriff's office to Dr. Bosch's office. "Doc, Hugh Conway says he wants you to go after that bullet."

Dr. Bosch nodded. "I thought he might decide to have me do it. I'm glad he came to that decision. When does he want me to do it?"

"As soon as you can."

"All right. I have a few appointments this afternoon, but I'll come out first thing tomorrow morning," Dr. Bosch said.

From the doctor's office, Matt went to the Pair O' Dice to have a beer. When he pushed through the swinging doors, he was surprised by the paucity of customers. He had never been in the saloon when there were fewer than thirty people inside. Right now there were only seven, and five of the seven worked at the saloon.

"Hello, Matt." Unlike the normal gregarious welcome, Cheatum's greeting was quite subdued.

"What's happened? Where are all your customers?"

"DuPont is what happened to them. His deputies patrol the streets and anyone seen leaving either of the saloons is subject to being arrested and fined for public drunkenness."

"Public drunkenness isn't a crime unless it also becomes a public nuisance," Matt said, remembering the city ordinances from his brief time as a law official.

"Oh, that isn't the half of it. They've arrested 'n fined twenty or more that I know of, and not a one of them was actually drunk. Plus this visitor's pass thing is cutting into my business as well. The girls?" He made a motion toward Jennie Lou and the other three girls. "There's not enough going on to keep all of them busy, but I don't have the heart to just send them on their way."

"Buy a drink for all four of them," Matt said, putting the money on the bar.

"I'll tell you this, Matt," Art Walhausen said a few minutes later when Matt visited the newspaper office. "There's not a businessman in town who doesn't miss Sheriff Clark, for all that he was a weak sister. They'd rather have somebody who does nothing than an overbearing fool like DuPont and his draconian concept of law enforcement."

"I don't understand what DuPont hopes to gain by all this. Lonnie told me DuPont was fining people for drunkenness, but surely that doesn't make enough money for it to be very worthwhile," Matt said.

"Oh, he's not doing that for money. He's doing it to kill the town," Walhausen said.

"What? Why would DuPont want the town killed?"

"He's doing it for Kennedy and O'Neil," Walhausen said. "The idea is, once the town dies, there will be little to hold the other ranchers and farmers in the valley, and they'll be forced to sell out."

"As far-fetched as that sounds, your guess is probably correct."

"It isn't just a guess. Luke McCoy is one of DuPont's Regulators. That is, until he quit. Before he left, he stopped by to see me and told me that this is Kennedy and O'Neil's plan."

"You say McCoy left?" Matt asked.

"Yes, he said he couldn't go along with what the Regulators are doing. The good thing is that Kennedy and O'Neil's private army is attritting. You've killed five of them, McCoy left them, and before McCoy it was Isaac Newton. Oh, by the way, McCoy told me where Newton is."

"Where is he?" Matt wanted to know.

"You know Fancy, the pretty little colored girl over at the Wild Hog?"

Walhausen nodded.

"Apparently she is putting him up, somewhere," Matt said.

"I hope DuPont doesn't get wind of it."

"Yes, you and I share that same hope."

When Matt stepped into the Wild Hog, he saw that it was nearly as empty as the Pair O' Dice had been. From his time as acting sheriff, he knew the bar girls who worked here, and he saw Belle sitting with the only two customers in the place. Fancy and Candy were standing together at the bar, and both looked toward Matt when he came in.

When Candy started toward him, Matt held up his hand. "Candy, get a drink from Mr. Kendig. Buster?" he called to the bartender. "Give the lady a drink. I'll settle. But for now, I would like to spend some time with Fancy."

"You sure you want me, honey?" Fancy asked, surprised by the request.

"Looks like business is way down in here," Matt said. "I imagine you haven't had too many customers lately."

"No sir, my, uh . . . special customers don't seem to make it in much, anymore."

Matt smiled at her. "Then you won't mind spending some time with me, will you?"

"No sir, not at all."

Matt paid for Candy's drink, Fancy's drink, and his own, which he took to a table as far away from the other customers as he could get. "Fancy, I'll get right to the point. I need to talk to Isaac, and I think you know where he is."

"What do you want Isaac for?" she asked defensively.

Matt held up his hand to put her fear at ease. "I need his help. Also, I want to help him. I know you don't want DuPont to find him."

"I . . . I don't know," Fancy said hesitantly.

"Look. Let's do it this way. You don't have to tell me where he is now. All I want you to do is go see him. Tell him I would like to visit with him, and if he is willing to meet me, to come to the Spur and Latigo Ranch. He'll be safe there."

"There ain't no sense in puttin' this off any longer, Jensen." The hissing voice could only belong to one person.

When Matt looked toward the door he saw a man with a black moustache that curled down around his mouth.

Just the suggestion of a grin showed on Boggs's face, and it was diabolical. "Kennedy 'n O'Neil hired me to do a job for 'em, so I figure it's time I earned my pay."

"You were hired to kill me?"

"Yeah, I was," Boggs said, the grin widening just a bit. "Me 'n you 's about to have that dance I told you about."

"Are we? Well, you might remember that I told you I always take the lead."

Without another word, Boggs went for his gun. He was incredibly fast, as fast as anyone Matt had ever faced.

The two pistols discharged almost simultaneously, but Boggs had sacrificed accuracy for speed, and even as his bullet fried the air less than an inch away from Matt's ear, the bullet from Matt's gun plunged into Boggs's chest.

Boggs looked at Matt with an almost whimsical smile. "Damn. I thought . . . I really thought . . ." His sentence ended with a cough, then he fell on his back. The pistol still dangled from his hand by the finger hooked through the trigger guard.

"Jensen, I expect you'd better leave now, while you can," Buster warned. "Soon as word of this gets out, DuPont will be coming after you, and he won't be coming alone."

"Come with me," Fancy said.

Matt shook his head. "No, I'm not going to put you in danger."

"You want to see Isaac? Come with me."

Fancy led Matt to a little cabin on the north side of the Sweetwater River. Made of adobe bricks, the cabin blended in with the surrounding rock outcroppings. One could pass within a hundred yards and never notice it.

"How did you find this place?" Matt asked.

"It was my pa's. Wait here. I'll go see Isaac."

A moment later she and Isaac stepped out of the cabin, and Isaac motioned for him to come ahead.

"Gentlemen," Matt said to the other residents of the bunkhouse about an hour later. "This is Isaac Newton. He'll be staying here with us for a little while."

"Glad to have you with us, Isaac," Ed said, extending his hand. He indicated the other two men who were riding for the Spur and Latigo brand. "This is Jake Haverkost and LeRoy Patterson."

"And this is the man I told you about." Matt introduced Gabe Short.

"You told him about me?" Gabe asked, curious as to what that was about. "Is he a cowboy?"

"No," Matt said with a smile. "This is the man who is going to help you get the title back to your ranch. He's a lawyer."

Chapter Thirty-seven

The next morning Matt, Lisa, and Ernest Dean Fawcett sat in the keeping room of the Conway house, drinking coffee as they waited nervously for the results of Dr. Bosch's attempt to remove the bullet from Hugh's back. Ernest Dean was there because his wife, Anne, had done some nursing and was assisting the doctor.

They had just started their second cup of coffee when Dr. Bosch came out of the bedroom. Everyone tried to read his face, which was impassive.

"I have something I want to show you," he said, the expression on his face not changing. Then, with a huge smile, he held out his hand and opened it. "Here's the bullet!" he said happily. "I got it out with no additional damage."

"Is he going to be all right? Will he be able to walk again?" Lisa asked anxiously.

"I would say he'll be walking again within a week," Dr. Bosch said, his smile growing even broader.

"Oh, Dr. Bosch, thank you. Thank you so much." Impulsively, Lisa threw her arms around his neck. "Can I see him?"

"He's still very groggy from the laudanum, but I think that by the time the nurse has finished cleaning him up that he'll be able to talk to you. Oh, and, Mr. Fawcett, I want to thank you so much for bringing her here to help. The assistance she provided was invaluable."

Cheyenne, Wyoming Territory

It was just under two weeks since Doctor Bosch removed the bullet from Hugh, and while he could walk on his own, he welcomed the assistance that Matt and Isaac provided in helping him step down from the train. Hailing a cab, Hugh gave the driver the address. "Take us to 200 West Twenty-fourth Street, would you please, driver?"

"Ah, you're here to visit the new capitol building, are you? Well, sir, it's a beauty. Bet there ain't a capitol buildin' that's no purtier anywhere in the whole country."

Once inside the impressive-looking capitol building, they went to the governor's office.

"My name is Hugh Conway, and I would like to speak with Governor Warren, please."

The secretary examined his appointment book, then shook his head. "I'm sorry, sir, but I don't see your name listed here."

"Please tell the governor that Captain Conway would like an audience," Hugh said.

"Captain Conway?"

"I'm the one who recommended the governor for his Medal of Honor," Hugh said.

The appointments secretary smiled. "Oh, my. Yes,

I'm certain the governor will want to see you. He's quite proud of that medal."

"As well he should be," Hugh said. "I still remember the citation that I wrote. 'Corporal Warren volunteered in response to a call, and took part in the movement that was made upon the enemy's works under a heavy fire therefrom in advance of the general assault.' I was Adjutant of the 49th Massachusetts Infantry."

"I will tell him Mr. Conway. Uh, are both of you wanting to see him?"

"Both of us? There are three of us."

"Uh, yes, indeed, three, but I wasn't aware that you meant to include the colored man."

"Mr. Newton is precisely the reason we want to see the governor."

"Yes, sir."

"Hugh Conway!" Governor Warren said a moment later, walking around his desk to greet him. "How good to see you! Are you still on the concert tour?"

"No, sir, I'm a rancher now, here in Wyoming."

Governor Warren nodded. "Well, the music world will miss you, but many of our most outstanding citizens are ranchers."

Governor Warren looked at the others. "You and your friends have a seat and tell me what I can do for you."

"Francis, this young man is Isaac Newton. He is a . . ."

"Lawyer," Governor Warren said before Hugh could finish his comment. "Yes, I have heard of you, Mr. Newton. You represented that colored officer, didn't you?"

"Lieutenant Henry Flipper. Yes, sir, I did defend him, but not very well, I'm afraid."

"I was told that you handled the case brilliantly. The finding was a miscarriage of justice." Governor Warren looked back toward Hugh. "Your visit has to do with Mr. Newton being a lawyer?"

"It does, but only in that he is representing us. Isaac, you have the floor."

"Governor, I intend to introduce a brief for *fieri facias* on a case of *scandalum magnatum* against Judge John Briggs of the Sweetwater District Court."

Governor Warren chuckled. "I'm not trained in the law, Mr. Newton. I'm afraid you're going to have to repeat that in English."

"I'm sorry. What I mean to say is that on behalf of the people of Sweetwater County in general and Mr. Gabe Short in particular, I am petitioning for you to rule upon the malfeasance in office of Judge John Briggs. We are asking you to vacate his office as well as all of his rulings, orders of the court, and appointments he may have made."

"And why Gabe Short in particular?"

"Let me answer that, Isaac," Hugh said. "Francis, this man Briggs has no right to call himself a judge. He virtually stole a ranch from Mr. Short by assessing a tax without making public the assessment so that Gabe had no opportunity to make the payment. In private, Briggs told two other men, Garrett Kennedy and Sean O'Neil, about that assessment so they could pay the taxes and take over the ranch."

Governor Warren nodded in understanding.

"He also refused to prosecute four men for murder when they lynched a man and his wife," Isaac added.

"You would be talking about Jim Andrews and his wife? I read of it in the paper. How certain are you of the guilt of the four men who were alleged to be there?"

"I am absolutely certain."

"May I ask why you are so certain?"

"I was an eyewitness to the lynching," Isaac said resolutely.

Governor Warren nodded. "I would say that is pretty certain. Have you prepared the paper you want signed?"

"Yes sir, I have the *Effectus Ordinis* ready for your signature."

"That would be an executive order?"

"Yes, sir," Isaac said, laying the document on the desk.

"Well," Hugh said a couple of hours later after they were on the train and well underway for the return trip. "Isaac, you now have a full pardon from the governor for any laws you may have broken, as well as a writ of removal for Mr. Briggs. And you, Matt, are a specially appointed territorial marshal with jurisdiction to serve the writ on Briggs and to remove DuPont from the office of sheriff. I would say this was a good trip."

"Yes, sir, but it's all thanks to you," Isaac was quick to point out. "We wouldn't have even been able to see the governor if you hadn't been with us."

"Nonsense. You made the argument for us. Speaking of which, let me see that executive order again," Hugh said. "And if you don't mind, I'll just read it aloud."

Clearing his throat, Hugh began to read in an affected "official" voice. "This *Effectus Ordinis* is in result of extensive findings of fact and conclusions of law as to numerous acts of judicial misconduct of Judge John Briggs for failing to diligently and competently discharge the administrative responsibilities incumbent upon him as a judicial officer. It has been determined that Briggs did improperly dismiss those who have committed criminal actions, and has without cause transferred ownership of property.

"Therefore I, Frances Warren, Governor of the Territory of Wyoming by appointment of Chester A. Arthur, President of the United States, and acting as Commissioner of Retirement, Removal, and Discipline do hereby order that John Briggs be removed from the office of Judge of the Sweetwater Country Judicial Circuit of the Territory of Wyoming.

"I hereto affix my hand and seal."

Hugh looked up from the reading. "And it's signed, Frances E. Warren, Governor." He handed the document to Matt. "It is up to you, Territorial Marshal Matt Jensen, to send Mr. Briggs packing."

"And DuPont," Isaac said. "I personally will be particularly happy to see him leave."

Two days later Matt, Ed Sanders, LeRoy Patterson, Isaac Newton, and Gabe Short rode out to the Circle Dot Ranch. Two men, Chris Dumey and Marvin Usher, riders for the Straight Arrow, were staying in the bunkhouse rather than the main house. They came out to meet Matt and the others as they rode up.

"You folks is trespassin', lessen you're comin' to visit someone. There ain't nobody here to visit but me 'n Marvin, 'n I don't think you're here to visit us."

"Which one of you is in charge?" Matt asked.

"I'm the one that's doin' the talkin'."

"His name is Dumey," Sanders said.

"Mr. Dumey, are there any Straight Arrow cattle on this ranch?" Matt asked.

"I reckon there is, seein' as ever' cow on this land belongs to Mr. Kennedy 'n Mr. O'Neil now."

Matt continued. "Are there any cattle here with the Straight Arrow brand?"

"Prob'ly a few, but not many. Why are you askin'?"

"I want you and . . ." Matt looked at Sanders.

"Usher," Ed said, naming the second man.

"I want you and Usher to gather up whatever is yours, then leave."

"What do you mean, leave?" Dumey asked. "It was Mr. O'Neil his ownself that told us to come over here 'n keep anyone else off their land."

"This isn't their land."

"How is that?"

Matt looked at Isaac. "Mr. Newton, would you explain the situation, please?"

"The adjudication that awarded this ranch to Kennedy and O'Neil was deemed to be without merit and has been vacated. Ownership has thus devolved to Mr. Gabe Short. That would be this man." Isaac pointed to Gabe.

"I don't have no idea what it is that you just said," Dumey said with a look of total confusion on his face.

"He said the ranch belongs to me." Gabe smiled. "I imagine I'll be looking for riders in case you two are interested."

"I know you two boys. You're good men," Sanders said. "I'll vouch for you to Mr. Short."

"Why would we be interested in leavin' the Straight Arrow?" Usher asked.

"Because before this thing plays out, you and every other man that's working for Kennedy and O'Neil will more than likely be looking for work," Matt said.

Leaving Sanders behind to show Gabe around his ranch, Matt, LeRoy, and Isaac rode into town, stopping at the courthouse. They went inside and stepped into Briggs's office before being invited.

"Here, what is this?" Briggs asked, obviously irritated by the intrusion.

"Briggs," Matt started.

"How dare you address me so?" Briggs said angrily. "You will show this office proper respect or I'll hold you in contempt!"

"Briggs, do you remember in that farce of a hearing of the four men who murdered Jim and Mary Ella, how you wouldn't let me speak because you said it was hearsay? Well, this man is the eyewitness I was talking about. Tell him, Isaac."

"I personally saw Moe Greene, Walter Toone, Asa Carter, and the Mason brothers lynch Mr. and Mrs. Andrews," Isaac said.

"Is that so? Well what do you expect me to do about it now?" Briggs blustered.

"We don't expect you to do anything about it," Matt said. "Even if you wanted to do something about it, you couldn't, because you no longer have the authority." He removed a letter from his pocket and showed it to Briggs. "This is my commission from the governor as a territorial marshal. And you, Briggs, are no longer a judge. You have been removed from office, and I am here to see that you comply with the governor's order. Read it to him, Isaac."

As Isaac read the writ, Matt watched Briggs as the expression on his face changed indignation, to confusion, to acceptance, and finally, despair.

"Am I under arrest?" Briggs asked quietly.

"Not as yet. But it might be better for you if you would leave the area," Matt said.

DuPont was in the sheriff's office playing a game of three-handed poker with the Mason brothers when Matt, Isaac, and LeRoy stepped inside.

"You got some nerve, comin' in here like this after killin' Boggs like you done," DuPont said. "I ought to arrest you for murder."

"Boggs drew first," Matt said. "Anyway, you don't have the authority to arrest anyone. You are no longer the sheriff. Get out."

"Who are you to tell me to get out of my own office?" DuPont asked angrily.

"I am a territorial marshal. Do you want to see my appointment?"

"Briggs appointed you?"

"No, Briggs doesn't have the authority to appoint anyone. He's no longer a judge."

"What? What is going on here?" DuPont's question was an angry shout.

"A new order has come to Sweetwater Valley, and you don't fit in any more," Matt said easily. "Now, get out of here like I said.

"Newton, you are with them?" DuPont asked.

"I am."

"What a traitorous piece of dirt you turned out to be."

"No, DuPont. My treason was to society and the law

when I was with you. Now I have put that treason behind me."

"What if I don't get out?" DuPont challenged.

Matt smiled confidently. "If you don't get out, I'll kill you." He looked at the Mason brothers, who were following the conversation with shocked expressions on their faces. "And I'll kill these two as well," he added.

"Tyrone, I'm gettin' out of here, now," John Mason said, standing quickly.

"Me too," Lem said.

"I don't intend to let him run me out like this," DuPont declared.

"Draw or leave, it's your choice," Matt said.

After a long moment, DuPont stood. "I'm leavin', but this ain't over," he said with as much defiance as he could muster.

"Leave the badge," Matt demanded.

With an angry sigh that was almost a snarl, DuPont took off his badge, slammed it down on the desk, then left.

"Did he seem mad to you?" Matt asked.

LeRoy laughed.

Chapter Thirty-eight

From the *Red Desert Gazette:*

New Judge to be Appointed

In a move that is unprecedented in the history of the Territory of Wyoming, a sitting judge has been removed from his office by the governor of the territory. Citing improper behavior and malfeasance, Governor Warren vacated not only Briggs's office, but also all recent rulings and injunctions.

This means that:

1) The case of the lynching of Mr. and Mrs. Andrews may be reopened.

2) The appointments of Tyrone DuPont and his minions as sheriff and deputy sheriffs are revoked.

3) The tax judgment against the Circle Dot Ranch is hereby vacated. The tax money paid by Messrs. Kennedy and O'Neil will be

returned to them and ownership of the ranch awarded to Gabe Short, who is the legitimate heir.

It is the absolute belief of the publisher of this newspaper that these rulings of the governor, set into motion by the actions of Matt Jensen, Hugh Conway, and Isaac Newton, cannot help but improve the quality of life in Rongis, and in the entire Sweetwater Valley.

Matt and Isaac were out at the Spur and Latigo Ranch making plans with Hugh and Ed to take the horses to Bitter Creek.

"There will be a buyer there," Hugh said. "And though we could probably get more for them if we sold them in San Francisco, the cost of shipping would cut deeply into the difference, so I think I'll sell them to the buyer at Bitter Creek."

"I think that's probably a pretty good deal. You'll get your money faster and you won't have to deal with the problem of shipping them," Matt agreed.

"Here comes a couple of riders," Ed said.

"It looks like Colleen O'Neil and Cooter Gregory," Hugh said. "I wonder what they want."

"You're a little off your range, ain't you, Cooter?" Ed asked when the riders approached.

"Mr. O'Neil 'n Mr. Kennedy are both dead," Cooter said.

"What?" Matt asked, surprised by the announcement.

"It's true," Colleen said in a choked voice. "Papa and Mr. Kennedy are both dead."

"DuPont killed them," Cooter said. "DuPont was the one who actually shot them, but Moe Greene was there, too. I saw them, but they didn't see me. And I overheard the two of them talking, Mr. Jensen. DuPont said you're next."

"What about the other cowboys who work on the Straight Arrow?" Matt asked.

"Not all of them know what happened yet. I thought the best thing to do would be to get Colleen away before DuPont or any of his men got to her. I told Rodney Gibson and Murry Boston about what happened, and they said they would clear the others out of there."

"Where are you headed now, Cooter?" Hugh asked.

"I don't know. I haven't thought that far ahead. All I could think of was getting Collen out of there."

"You and Miss O'Neil can stay here until we get this all sorted out."

"Thank you," Colleen said.

"There's only way we're going to get this sorted out, and that's to get rid of DuPont and the men who ride with him," Matt said.

"You know what I think?" Hugh said. "I think maybe I should get Ernest Dean, Frank, Travis, Bob, and—"

"No," Matt said, holding up his hand. "I'm the one they're after, Hugh. There's no need in getting anyone else involved."

"There are five of them, Matt. You can't go up against all five of them by yourself," Hugh protested.

"Yeah, I can. Cooter, are they still at the ranch?"

"No, sir. They left just before I did."

"More than likely they're at Purgatory Pass," Isaac

said. "That was the headquarters before they all moved into town, and since you ran them out, I'm pretty sure that's where they've gone back to."

"Then Purgatory Pass is where I'm going," Matt said.

"I'll go with you."

"Isaac, have you ever killed a man?" Matt asked.

"No, but I'm willing to do it if it becomes necessary."

"You don't need to start here."

"Matt, you know Moe Greene, Walter Toone, and the Mason Brothers murdered Mr. and Mrs. Andrews, and it was DuPont who gave the order. My only real friend in the group was Luke McCoy, and he left. As far as I'm concerned the rest of them deserve to die. As I said, I'm willing to do it."

"That may be so, but I am not only willing to kill them, I can do so quite efficiently. And I am even more efficient if I don't have to worry about anyone else."

"All right. But there must be some way I can help."

"Tell me as much as you know about Purgatory Pass."

The approach to Purgatory Pass could be easily monitored from a little precipice called Devil's Point, and though it was Lem Mason's time to be standing guard, John had come up to keep his brother company.

"I wonder what's goin' to happen to the ranch now that O'Neil 'n Kennedy is both of 'em dead?" he asked.

"DuPont said it all belongs to us now," Lem said.

"Yeah, I reckon that's a good thing, all right,"

John said. "But I don't particular want to be a-doin' any cowboyin'."

"Accordin' to what DuPont said, there ain't goin' to be that much cowboyin' to it. Turns out he'd been plannin' on killin' Kennedy 'n O'Neil all along. He's been in contact with a feller who'll take eight thousand head from us for twenty-five dollars a head, 'n he won't be askin' no questions 'bout where the cows come from. All we have to do is move 'em to Green River."

"How much money is that?"

"That's two hunnert thousand dollars. Forty thousand dollars apiece."

"Damn, that's a lot of money. But they's more 'n eight thousand cows here. There's at least ten thousand. How come we don't take all of 'em?"

"We're goin' to have to push the cows almost two hundred miles, 'n there's only five of us left to do it. Eight thousand head is about all we can handle. And I don't know 'bout any of the others, but I don't think me 'n you should plan on comin' back here after we get the money. I think the best thing would be maybe go to Denver or San Francisco or some such place. Before we can do all this, though, DuPont says the first thing is, we're going to have to kill Matt Jensen."

"What for? I mean if we're goin' to get out of here, ain't no need for us to see him no more."

"Think about it, Lem. Do you really think Jensen would just let us go? No, sir, he'll come lookin' for us. And if he does that he could just real easy pick us off one at time. It'd be a lot easier to kill 'im iffen we're all together."

"Yeah, I see what you mean. I wonder where the blankethead is now?"

"I don't know what blankethead you're talking about," Matt said. "But I'm right here."

Both brothers gasped in surprise then turned to see Matt Jensen standing behind them.

"How the hell did you get here? We been watchin' the pass the whole time!" Lem said.

"Apparently you weren't watching closely enough," Matt said. "How about you two men leading me down to DuPont and the others? I'm putting you all under arrest for killing Kennedy and O'Neil."

"It wasn't us that done that," John said. "It was DuPont that kilt 'em."

"All right. I'll arrest DuPont for killing Kennedy and O'Neil, and the rest of you for killing Jim and Mary Ella Andrews. Now, lead the way."

"Hey, look!" Moe Greene said. "There's the Masons comin' down from the point, 'n both of 'em has their hands up."

"What for do they have their hands up?" Toone asked.

Greene, Toone, and DuPont had been standing just outside DuPont's cabin.

"On account of Jensen's behind 'em!" DuPont shouted. "Inside, quick!"

The three men hurried into the cabin and slammed the door behind them.

"What about John and Lem?" Toone asked.

"To hell with them," DuPont replied. "If they had been lookin' out like they was supposed to, Jensen woulda never got in here."

"But as long as he's got 'em out there, he can force

us out," Toone suggested. "I mean he could say he'll kill 'em if we don't—"

That was as far Toone got before DuPont picked up a rifle and fired through the window, not at Matt, but at Lem Mason.

"Uhh!" Lem called in shock and pain as he fell.

"Get down!" Matt shouted at John Mason, who stood there for a moment looking on in disbelief.

"He won't be using 'em now, will he?" DuPont said as he fired again, and John went down.

"What are you going to do now, Jensen?" DuPont called. "They's three of us 'n only one of you. 'N we're inside 'n you ain't got no way of forcin' us out."

"Jensen." John's voice was weak and strained with pain. "Jensen, the back of the cabin."

"What?"

"There ain't no windows in the back of the cabin . . . for 'em to see you comin'. The bar is broke on the door . . . back there . . . so it can't be locked. Push on it . . . you can get inside easy."

"Why should I believe you?"

"On account of them sons of bitches . . . kilt Lem . . . 'n . . . me," John said with one final expulsion of breath.

Staying low on the ground, Matt slithered away. Reaching a point where he was concealed by rocks, he started toward the cabin.

"Jensen! Jensen, you still out there?" DuPont called. "Jensen, there ain't no way for you to get out of here. If you start back toward the pass, we'll have a clear shot."

When he reached the end of the line of rocks, he

had about a twenty-five-yard dash to the corner of the cabin. As he examined it, he saw he would be exposed for the entire twenty-five yards.

"Jensen, where are you?" DuPont shouted.

"I'm right here!" Matt shouted, and he fired several shots toward the window.

The shots had the effect he wanted in that they caused DuPont, Greene, and Toone to drop down from the window, giving Matt a few seconds to dash across the open area until he got to the side of the cabin. There, he backed up against the adobe walls, where he stood for a moment as he reloaded his pistol.

He heard some shots being fired from the window and saw dirt being lifted from the end of the rocks where he had been but a moment earlier.

With his pistol reloaded, Matt moved around to the back of the cabin. It was just as John had told him. There was a door but no windows.

Raising the pistol, he kicked the door open then dashed inside. "Drop your guns!" he shouted.

All three spun around and fired at him. Matt returned fire, shooting three times. Three shots was all it took.

One month later

Hugh and Lisa, Isaac and Fancy, and Art Walhausen were having a farewell dinner for Matt, who would be leaving Rongis the next morning.

"Two weddings in one week," Art said. "Cooter and Colleen are now Mr. and Mrs. Gregory and"—he held his arm out—"sharing our table tonight, Mr. and Mrs. Newton."

"Congratulations to you," Matt said, lifting his glass toward Isaac and Fancy.

"And Isaac, a special thank-you for all that you have done for us," Hugh added.

"I should thank you for allowing me the opportunity," Isaac replied.

"And Matt, my special thanks to you," Hugh added. "There have been quite a few changes since you came here and all of them for the better. I was able to get my horses to market, Frank, Travis, Bob, Ernest Dean, and Gabe got their cattle to market. And who would have ever thought that Straight Arrow would invite the smaller ranchers to join their herds with them in the drive to Bitter Creek?"

"Colleen feels obligated to make up for all the trouble her father and Kennedy caused the area ranchers," Lisa said. "She's such a sweet girl. I always believed that she was nothing like her father."

"Young Dunaway got the ranch back that had belonged to his father, but it's too bad some of the people who lost their ranches earlier aren't here to take advantage of all the changes," Art said.

"Oh, the lawyer—as we have every confidence he will soon be restored to the bar—who now represents the Union of Landowners of Sweetwater Valley is taking care of that, aren't you, Isaac?" Hugh said.

"Yes, sir, as soon as the Board of Directors of the bank gets a replacement for Bob Foley so the mortgages can be renegotiated," Isaac said. "Miss O'Neil, uh, I mean Mrs. Gregory, said she will work with the bank and the original landowners."

"It's a shame," Lisa said, and everyone looked at her, puzzled as to why she would make such a remark.

"What?" Hugh asked. "What do you mean, it's a shame?"

"It's a shame that Jim and Mary Ella didn't live to see all this."

"Oh, yes, I agree with you. It is a shame."

"May I suggest a toast to them?" Art lifted his glass. "To Jim and Mary Ella. They will be missed."

"Very much so," Lisa said as they all lifted their glasses.

Matt headed south the next morning with no particular place to go and no hurry to get there. He heard a distant roll of thunder from a bank of clouds that had gathered over the Wind River Range. He was pretty sure that the mountains would draw the moisture from the clouds so that the rain wouldn't get to him, but he took out his poncho and lay it across the saddle in front of him just in case.

Keep reading for a special excerpt.

*The bestselling Johnstones kick off their blazing
new western series with a real bang—a fatal,
fateful shoot-out that sends a man named
Buck Trammel on the ride of his life . . .*

NORTH OF LARAMIE
A Buck Trammel Western

Once upon a time in the Old West, Buck Trammel
was a Pinkerton agent with a promising future.
But after a tragic incident in a case gone wrong,
he struck out for the wide-open spaces of
Wichita, Kansas. Working as a bouncer at
The Gilded Lilly Saloon, he hopes to stay out of
trouble. But soon enough, his gun skills are put to
the test. The Bowman gang shows up, turning a
friendly card game with a Wyoming cattleman
into a killer-take-all shooting match. Buck saves the
cattle baron's life but at the cost of Bowman's two
sons. That's when Deputy Wyatt Earp arrives.
He warns Buck that he'd better get out of town,
pronto, and take the cattle baron with him. The rest
is history—if he lives long enough to tell it . . .

This is the story of Buck Trammel. Hunted by
outlaws. Fighting for justice. Marked for death.
This is how legends are born . . .

Look for NORTH OF LARAMIE, *on sale now.*

Chapter One

"Hagen!" one of the Bowman boys yelled. "You are a drunk, a cheat, and a liar!"

From his perch in the lookout chair, Buck Trammel watched the unfolding argument between the gambler Adam Hagen and two boys from the Bowman Ranch. All of the men were still seated around the poker table, which Trammel took as a good sign. A man on his backside was often less likely to cause trouble, at least without some warning. And since all of them had checked their guns with the barman, a fistfight was the worst he could expect. Given his size, Trammel found those much easier to break up than gunfights.

Experience had taught Trammel that he was better off staying in the lookout chair and allowing the matter to unfold on its own. He looked out at the rest of the room just to make sure none of the other patrons of The Gilded Lilly saloon were preparing to take sides in the argument. A glare from him usually discouraged such decisions. The double-barreled shotgun lying across his lap helped, too. Trammel's size and reputation for violence were usually enough to keep amateurs and brawlers at bay, but the sight of a coach gun never hurt the prospects for peace.

The drunken Hagen held his cards as he laughed at William Bowman's growing rage.

The cowhand only grew that much angrier. "I called you a cheat and a liar and all you can do is giggle like an idiot?"

"No," Hagen slurred. "I giggle because I'm dumb enough to gamble with an idiot." He slapped his hands at the cards laid out in front of him. Aces and eights. A handful of nothing. "I laugh because it's the first hand I've won in an hour. I laugh because I bluffed you into building up the pot before you folded. I didn't cheat you, Billy Boy. I didn't have to. You cheated yourself by losing your nerve."

Both Bowman boys stood at the same time as the other players scrambled away from the table. Armed or not, Trammel knew every member of the Bowman clan was a brawler and not to be trifled with, especially after being called stupid.

"Get up, you drunken sot," Tyler Bowman said. "Get on your feet and repeat what you just said to Billy and me."

The sound of chair legs scraping against wood broke the silence as gamblers and drinkers moved out of the way. Some stood on chairs to get a better look at the action.

A nervous look from Lilly, the owner of the Gilded Lilly, told Trammel what he had to do. He left the shotgun in the slot on the lookout chair as he quietly climbed down. No one was paying attention to him anyway. They were waiting to see what Hagen and the Bowman boys did next.

Hagen swayed in his chair as he pulled the pile of cash toward him, but made no effort to stand.

Trammel, a full head taller than any man standing and twice as wide, eased his way through the customers craning their necks to see what would happen. It had been too quiet for too long in Wichita—nearly three days since the last killing—and the patrons were anxious for a fight.

Will Bowman shoved aside the chair he had been sitting in. "Damn you, Hagen. We're calling you out. Are you going to be a man and stand on your own, or am I going to have to rip you out of that chair?"

Trammel pushed his way through the crowd and came out behind the Bowman boys. "That's enough. You've all made your point. The game's over. Collect your guns and head on home."

Both of them turned and had to look up to face him. He knew they didn't like that. No one in the Bowman clan liked looking up at anyone. The family had enjoyed a free hand in Wichita for as long as anyone could remember, certainly long before Trammel had come to town a year before.

But Miss Lilly hadn't hired him as the bouncer at The Gilded Lilly to be popular. She had hired him to keep the peace in her place, and that's what he planned to do.

Tyler, the younger of the two, took a step toward Trammel. "This here is a private matter, boy. Best if you just climb back up in your perch and let us be."

Trammel looked at the chair that had been thrown aside. "Your private matter's hard on our furniture and I can't have that. Game's over anyway. Take whatever money you've got left, collect your guns, and try your luck somewhere else."

But Will Bowman hadn't budged. He continued to glower down at Hagen. "Damn you, I said get up."

Hagen waved him off with a boozy hand as though he were a fly. "Mr. Trammel, I would appreciate it if you would remove these men at your earliest convenience. They are interfering with the effects of my whiskey, which I'm afraid may soon cause me to become sober."

Tyler Bowman remained between Trammel and the table. "What's it going to be, big man? You taking orders from a drunk, now?"

"I only take orders from her." Trammel nodded at Lilly, who'd been anxiously watching things from the bar at the left side of the room. "She doesn't want any trouble in here. She wants you gone, so out you go." He looked down at Tyler. "And that means all of you. Hagen included."

"We'll kill him the second we hit the street." Tyler had said it like it was supposed to be an insult to Trammel. "We'll kill him right in front of you."

"What happens outside is between you and the town sheriff." Trammel took one step closer to Tyler, making him crane his neck even more to try to maintain eye contact. "And I'm getting damned tired of repeating myself, *boy*. Everyone leaves. Right now."

"We ain't going anywhere 'til this is done." Will Bowman reached for something tucked in the back of his britches.

Trammel shoved Tyler out of the way, sending him crashing into the poker table behind him, before grabbing Will's wrist just as it came around to the small of his back.

Will tried to break free from the bigger man's grip,

but Trammel pulled up hard on his wrist until he heard the unmistakable sound of cartilage popping.

Trammel ignored Bowman's screams as he searched for what he had been grabbing for. He found a knife handle sticking out of the back of Bowman's britches. He pulled the blade free and threw it aside. He hated knives.

Still holding on to the broken arm, Trammel grabbed the screaming Bowman by the back of his shirt collar and steered him toward the door. "Out you go, boy. Best head over to Doc Freeman's. Get that arm tended to."

But Trammel stumbled when a glass bottle shattered across the back of his head.

Everything slowed. Sight and sound blurred and, for a fraction of a second, Trammel couldn't feel anything at all. Not pain. Not surprise. Not even anger.

All he could feel was rage.

He yanked Will Bowman off his feet and threw him aside as he turned around to face his assailant. Tyler. The younger man was scrambling for another whiskey bottle at another table, but Trammel launched a roundhouse right that caught Tyler square in the jaw.

From his slowed perspective, Trammel could see the jaw was as broken as the dam that had once held back his temper.

Bowman was falling, but not before a left hook from Trammel connected with Tyler's temple. The cattleman landed in a crooked heap on the floor between two card tables as men scrambled to get out of the way.

Somewhere in his mind, he could hear Lilly calling

his name as he picked up a chair and brought it down hard on the fallen Bowman's back. The chair splintered into pieces. A leg landed nearby.

Trammel picked up the leg and dropped to his knees, straddling the prone man. He brought the chair leg over his head like a club, intending on bringing it down on Tyler again and again until Lilly's kind face filled his vision. The same face that graced the sign that hung over the front door, though this one bore more lines and was not as soft.

"No, Buck!" He felt her hands on his shoulders. "That's enough. Stop, please!"

Trammel let the chair leg fall behind him as his senses returned and time began to become normal. He remembered the other Bowman boy. William.

Trammel rocked back and got to his feet in one motion, remembering he had thrown him aside right after Tyler had hit him with the bottle.

Some of the patrons had gathered around the place where Will had landed, trading glances amongst themselves. They knew what Trammel could see just by looking at Bowman's neck. The twisted, unnatural angle against a broken chair only meant one thing.

"He's dead," one of the customers said. "His neck broke when he hit the chair."

"Did you see how he flew?" another said. "Hell, I only ever saw a man fly like that when he was bucked off a horse."

A cry from Lilly made Trammel look down. Her delicate fingers were pressed against Tyler's neck, as if the Bowman boy's vacant stare wasn't proof enough for her. "He's dead, too, Buck. You've killed both of them."

"And with his bare hands, too," said someone in

the saloon. "Not a hog leg or a blade on him. Killed 'em both by touch alone. Lord have mercy."

Trammel looked up when he heard the sound of clapping. It was coming from the poker table. It was Adam Hagen applauding him from behind his pile of money. "Bravo, Mr. Trammel. The citizens of Wichita salute you for the public service you've done here tonight, for the world is a far better place with two fewer Bowman boys slithering around in it."

Trammel's knuckles popped as he felt his fists ball up. Two dead men was nothing to clap about, even if it was two Bowman boys. "Someone get him out of here."

Hagen tried to sit upright in his chair. "But I live here, sir, and my luck has changed for the better." He gestured grandly at the empty chairs at the table. "Anyone care to play? We appear to have two vacancies at the moment."

Trammel started for him, but Lilly scrambled to block his way. "Someone get him up to his room before Buck kills him, too."

Three customers pulled Hagen to his feet, but not before the drunkard stuffed his winnings into his pockets. Gold and greenbacks bulged from the pockets of his coat and pants and vest.

Two men threw his arms over their shoulders as another cleared a path for them to the stairs and the rooms above. "Such service!" Hagen laughed. "Will one of you be so kind as to draw me a bath, as well?"

The man who had his right arm said, "The only thing you'll be drawing is blood if you don't keep that damned drunken mouth of yours shut."

Trammel's rage ebbed once more as he watched the men take Hagen upstairs and he realized Lilly was still holding on to him. He placed his large hands on her slender shoulders and gently eased her away. "I'm okay now, Lilly. I promise."

Lilly didn't take her eyes off him as she yelled, "Show's over, boys. Sorry for the trouble. Drinks are on the house, courtesy of your Aunt Lilly."

The patrons cheered and quickly went back to their respective games, the trouble and the dead men on the floor seemingly forgotten by everyone except Trammel and Lilly.

"You're hurt, Buck." Lilly popped up on her toes to reach the wound on his head. "You're bleeding."

Trammel had nearly forgotten about the whiskey bottle that Tyler had broken over his head. He felt at the back of his head and found a shard of glass just behind his ear. He winced as he pulled it out and let it drop to the floor. He flicked other bits of glass from the wound, too, some of them falling down his collar. "It's not the first time someone's busted a bottle over my head. Doubt it'll be the last."

Lilly stepped away from him and looked at destruction all around her. "This is bad, Buck."

"No, it isn't. I'll live." He checked his hand and was surprised there wasn't more blood. "I've been through worse."

"I don't just mean you. I mean the Bowman boys. Their people won't take kindly to you killing two of their kin, even if they had it coming."

Trammel looked down at the men on the floor. The two men he had just killed. He waited to feel something. He waited to feel anything at all. All he felt was tired. "Like I said. I've been through worse."